THE THINGS THAT COME

Dan Ackerman

Supposed Crimes LLC • Matthews, North Carolina

This book is a work of fiction. Names, characters, places, and incidents are products of the author's imagination or are used fictitiously. Any resemblance to actual events or locales or persons, living or dead, is entirely coincidental.

Published in the United States.

ISBN: 978-1-944591-56-4

www.supposedcrimes.com

This book is typeset in Goudy Old Style.

For David

5/11/15

DAVID WAS shaking. He wished he wasn't but no matter how many deep breaths he took, no matter how many times he closed his eyes and thought of somewhere nice, he couldn't keep his hands from trembling. He wished he'd had more to drink, but he had needed to drive himself here. He appreciated the irony in disparaging drunk driving and still planning on doing what he had come here for.

He hesitated in front of a dingy door with pollen caked along the seams. The pollen counts had been astronomical that spring. He didn't know if he should knock. With one hand, he tightened his grip on the strap of his backpack and with the other, reached out, rapping on the door.

From within the room, a woman called for him to come in. Her voice did not sound as he had expected, but he didn't know what he had expected. He hadn't expected her to sound so young, that was certain.

He entered and saw her on the other side of the room, short and dark-skinned, with coiled hair that was clipped close on the sides, but left longer on the top and back, a Mohawk held up by the texture of her hair alone. Or so he assumed; his knowledge of black people's hair was not perfect. He stared at her for a moment, then set his backpack down by his feet as she turned around.

"Don't," he said.

She paused before she had finished turning.

"Don't turn around," he clarified, "Don't look at me." He had his hood up still, but it didn't matter, he didn't want to see her face.

"You don't have to be shy," she said, still facing towards the opposite wall. She had her phone in her hand.

"Sit on the bed."

She sat. "Have you got the money?" she asked, "Before you go ahead and tell me to do anything else."

He reached into his pocket and tossed the cash on to the bed. Exactly the amount they had agreed on through the Craigslist ad. Not that it mattered.

She picked up the money, counted it and slipped it into the back of her phone case. "Do you want to tell me your name?"

"No."

He unzipped the backpack, praying that she wouldn't turn around. He rummaged through until he found what he needed, all the way at the bottom, of course. Seeing her face would make it so much harder to do what he had to do. And he had to do it, no matter how much parts of him screamed not to, he needed to do this before everything came unraveled.

I want to do this, he reminded himself.

It wasn't true, but it would have made things easier.

He tossed a bag made of black fabric onto the bed, a hood he had clumsily put together out of a pillowcase and hot glue.

"Put it over your head," he said.

She picked up the hood, then set it aside. "You didn't say anything about this sort of stuff. I'm going to turn around."

"Don't," he warned, scrambling to shove some of the things he had brought back into his bag.

She stood, her hands raised slightly to show that she was harmless, and turned to face him. She looked at him, then at the things that he had not managed to shove back into his bag. Some of the things could be passed off as harmless but kinky, but the knife, the plastic sheet, those were unmistakably tools of his task.

"You gonna kill me?" she asked, looking at the knife he gripped.

He had not yet taken it out of his sheath. He stared down at it. "Yes."

She had no chance, not really, she must have known that. She was short and not exactly thin, but smaller than the average woman, and he was over six feet tall. He did not know if he could do it, not now that he had seen her. But, he felt, he had to. She would rat him out, call the cops, for sure.

"Let me see you," she said.

He wished she would stop talking; her voice was not what he had expected, it was soft and kind, it was a voice that made him think of a friend. "No."

"You wanna kill me but you can't look me in the eye?" she demanded.

He couldn't.

"Then I wanna show you something." She turned her phone to face him. He did not want to look, but he did anyway, glancing for just a moment, then staring at the chubby-cheeked baby. "That's my baby. He's gonna be six months old soon."

"Stop!"

"So you wanna kill me, but I've got a baby at home, he needs me. His name's Noah."

He clamped his hands over his ears. It was a wash, from the moment she had turned around, he had known he wouldn't be able to do it, but now he didn't know what else to do. She could not go free; she would tell the police.

"All you've gotta do is move, I'll walk right through that door like I was never here."

"No!" he said.

He began to pace. Things had gone wrong and they would come back. Or worse, he would be caught, he would go back and he couldn't, he couldn't go back. His chest tightened and he was torn between the need to flee and obligation to stay and kill this woman.

He grabbed his hood, gripping his hair and wanting to rip it out. Panic rose in him, a dozen times worse than it had ever been before, and settled in his chest and gut, making his throat ache and eyes burn. He needed this feeling to go away, this fear and weakness.

At first, it began as a tap, rapping his knuckles against the hard bones in his chest, but that was not enough, and he struck himself harder.

"Hey," the woman said, "Listen, hey, we can get you help, alright? Nothing's happened yet, there's still time."

He shook his head and hit himself again, the pain dislodging some of the panic.

She grabbed him by the arm, not strong enough to stop him, but her touch enough to shock him. "You're okay."

She looked directly up at him, her jet-black eyes meeting his. Her face changed after a moment.

He pulled back.

"I know you," she said.

He shook his head. If she knew him, she had to die, he couldn't let her go knowing his face as well as his name. Coming back here had been a mistake. This was not home; it never would be.

"Let me get a look at you." She touched his arm again.

He stepped back, not wanting to look at her face again, not wanting to know why she looked familiar.

"My name's Zhané. Tell me who you are."

Zhané, he thought, recalling suddenly a girl he had known, not just known, but loved, having to say a hundred times 'It's pronounced jah-nay' to every teacher, to every substitute, to every new person she met. He pressed the heels of his palms against his eyes so hard it hurt and he saw spots. He should not have come back.

He had backed up as far as he could go, hitting the wall with his back. He slid down the wall to his knees, not near the door. She could flee if she wanted now, to get the cops, to go home to her baby.

The woman crouched beside him and pushed the hood back from his face. He could feel her eyes on him. "David," she pronounced. "David Craft, what in God's name are you doing?"

"I don't know."

"Are you a goddamn serial killer?" she asked, somewhere between incredulous and amused.

"I don't know." Technically, he was not yet a serial killer. He would need to kill three people at least to be considered a serial killer. Right now, he was just a murderer.

"What are you high on?" she asked.

He wanted to laugh. "Nothing." He wished he was on something, he wished there was something to explain what he saw and what he did.

She took the knife out of his hand and set it as far away as she could reach. If he really wanted it, he would be able to grab it. She sat cross-legged beside him and asked, "Where the hell have you been?"

He blinked, not sure how to answer. He had been away from Milwater for years now; four, if he remembered right.

"You know we all thought you were dead!" she said. "After Nicki and Becca, we thought, you know, whatever it was got you too."

"No, not dead."

"Yeah, we heard you moved, you know, someone saw your parents up in, uh...where did you go?"

"Vermont," he said, "We moved to Vermont. Kathy Burges' parents saw mine at a...with the vegetables. And like...A, a farmer's market."

She nodded. "But you never called or wrote or anything. Not even a goodbye text. I mean, I know we broke up but still!"

"They took my phone away."

"Who?"

"I went to a place," he said, "To get better."

She tilted her head. "Did you go to rehab?"

Drug addiction or heavy drinking would have neatly and easily explained the tailspin he had entered following their junior year. "No. For...you know, fucking psychos and whatever. Uh, an inpatient place." He rubbed his eyes again. "A couple years. No phones, though. No radios. No TV."

"That's gotta be illegal."

"No, they, uh, I...was hearing things on them," he said. "I got them back when everything calmed down."

"What are you doing back here, then? Are your parents with you?"

"No."

She gave him a long hard look. "Were you really going to kill me?"

"I have to," he said.

"You *have to?*" she asked, an eyebrow raised.

"I mean...if I don't," he hesitated. He didn't know how to explain this. "There's these things. Bad things. If I don't, they'll come back."

"Uh...David, did you get cleared to leave that place?" she asked.

"They didn't come until after I left."

"Do you have meds you're supposed to be taking?"

He reached into the inner pocket of his hoodie and showed her the bottle of pills, displaying the little white label that he had faithfully followed every day since he'd been released. "I do take them."

"And you still see things?" she asked, sounding understandably concerned.

He nodded. It was a common misconception that antipsychotics would magically get rid of all hallucinations and he didn't usually take the time out of his day to explain that to people. It was easier to let him think he didn't hallucinate instead of letting him know that yeah, he did, sometimes, but not in a bad way.

She made a face, then sighed. "Where are you staying?"

"The Pine Lodge."

"Eugh, you know they've got roaches."

He nodded. He had seen them, the same as he'd seen the stains on the carpet and the mold in the sink.

She scratched at her neck for a moment, then clicked her nails together, the acrylic tapping pleasantly. "The things you're seeing..." she began, then shook her head. "David, square with me, alright? Can you do that?"

He shrugged. He didn't know how much he would tell her.

"How long have you been in town?"

"A week. Ish."

"You swear?"

"Sure, why?"

"Cause Kevin Duran is missing. Bobby's little brother."

He nodded. He remembered seeing the child at football games with Bobby's parents and sister. "No, uh, no body?"

"No, but...well, they found Mara Copeland face down in the reservoir two months ago."

He leaned his head back against the wall, overwhelmed. Nicki and Becca had died eight weeks apart his junior year, right at the end. Becca had been found a few weeks before she was set to graduate. No one had been caught but no one else had died after the Crafts had uprooted themselves and hightailed it to Vermont.

His parents had never directly accused him of anything, of course, and they hadn't needed to explain themselves much when they had brought him to Mansfield Behavioral Health Center. He'd been hearing things, hurting himself, and spending days away from home, not to mention drinking to try to deal with it. His parents had said, quietly and calmly, that he needed time to deal with deaths of his friends since he was having such a hard time with it.

"Did you...shit, David, we spent all summer trying to figure out who did that to Becca and Nicki," she said, "And no one ever figured it out."

With a half-smile, he asked, "No? Everyone seemed to think it was me."

"No," she reminded, "Half the town thought it was one of the truckers that stop at Suzy's Diner and at least a quarter thought it was Dirty Bob."

He really smiled at that.

"Besides, there was no evidence, it was all circumstantial," she said. "Where were you, though, on those nights when no one could find you?"

"Blowing Paul LaRosa," he admitted.

It had felt like a big secret in high school, especially when he'd had staunchly Republican parents. Paul had also made it perfectly clear that if David had ever told about their time together, not only would Paul deny it, he would get all his soccer pals to help him make a point. Their affair had been brief, only a few weeks in August, but it had been at the height of his behavioral problems, as his mother had liked to call them.

Zhané laughed, covering her mouth as an apology. "Gross, David, he's such a douche!"

He shrugged. "I guess I couldn't find any other dicks to suck."

"Alex Thomas came out senior year."

"Well, shit," he said, "I always thought he was cute."

"Paul LaRosa sleeps with exclusively Asian escorts that he goes to Hartford to bang," she informed him after a minute of silence.

"Boys?"

She nodded. "He's living with Jen, uh...not Jen Copeland, the other one."

"Marsh?"

"I think so." Zhané reached out and put a hand on his knee, which he could not believe. "You're not going to kill me, are you?" She asked it like she already knew the answer.

"No."

"I'm not gonna tell the cops, either, you know."

"Thanks."

"Are you...you're not gonna go after anyone else, are you?"

He shook his head. The things would come and they would be terrible, but he would not kill anyone that night.

"Do you have a phone now, though?"

He nodded.

She held out her phone to him. "Give me your number, alright? I'll give you a call in the morning."

"Why?"

"I want to show you something."

"Uh, okay." He added his number to her phone and handed it back to her.

A moment later his phone dinged. "That's me." She checked the time then said, "I'm gonna go."

"Bye."

She stood and took his knife with her, which made him smile.

He sat on the floor for about fifteen minutes, trying to wrap his head around what had happened. Eventually, he made himself stand and put his backpack back together. He left, getting into his car and returning to Pine Lodge, where the pillow smelled like a basement.

He looked at the clock, which read 11:23 in large, green numbers. Maybe he would have time to sleep for a few hours before they realized he had not done as they'd demanded. He wondered, not for the first time, if he needed his meds adjusted.

He dropped off to sleep and woke several hours later because of the pain in his eyes. When he rubbed them, he realized he hadn't taken his contacts out. He made himself get up and struggled to get his contacts out with sleep-heavy hands. The one in his left eye had gotten stuck under his eyelid and he had to work at it until he was able to pluck it out.

He squirted saline into the case, twisted on the lids and wondered where his glasses were. He turned to leave the bathroom and found something sitting on his bed. It was just a shape, a form almost indistinguishable in the darkness of his room. He froze, staring at the thing, wanting to blink to see if it would go away.

From beside him, another form grabbed his arm, its hand feeling not like a hand but a fleshy, flat tentacle. It pulled him towards the bed and the other form reached out to him, standing as it did so.

They would not say anything. They did not speak, not when he obeyed or when he failed. Sometimes the radios would hiss or his phone would take a call, but they did not speak. He wanted to think they didn't have mouths.

"Please don't," he said but they only tightened their grips on him.

His phone rang, answered itself and went to speakerphone. Words crackled through, stuttering and faint. "Must pay...owed..." he heard.

"No, no, don't," he begged, but they dragged him over to the bed anyway, one on each side, their strange arms wrapping around his up to the shoulder. A third thing stepped forward from the end of the bed.

The first time he had refused them, they had taken a portion of his liver; that had been about six months ago. The time after that he was reasonably certain they had taken his wisdom teeth. He wasn't sure if they needed his body parts or if they did it just to fuck with him.

The thing at the foot of the bed snipped open one leg of his jeans, all the way up to the thigh. He could not see what it was doing, but he knew that it hurt immensely. When he began to scream, something was shoved into his mouth to muffle the sound.

He blacked out after about ten minutes and woke to pale light streaming through the crooked blinds of the motel window. He sat up, looking down at his thigh to find that they had taken a strip of skin about six inches wide and eight long.

"What the fuck," he groaned.

He stood and his jeans flapped against the wound, making it burn as though he'd drizzled salt water over it. He hissed and carefully peeled back the fabric, then ripped the rest of the pant leg off. Each jostle sent jolts of pain through him.

He finally limped his way to the bathroom, snagging his toiletry bag along the way. He sat on the toilet seat and rummaged through his bag for peroxide and gauze. These supplies were kept not in case horrible figures came to harvest his skin, but in case the need to harm himself became impossible to ignore.

He soaked a wad of tissues with peroxide and, gritting his teeth, cleaned the wound, then tapped a rectangle of gauze over it. He should go to the hospital, or at least, one of the urgent care centers, but right now he couldn't handle that. He worked to get the rest of his jeans off, went to his phone to google how to care for this type of wound and found it dead.

He swore, looked around for his charger and plugged it in. It was just after five in the morning. He swallowed more Advil than he probably should have taken in one dose and washed it down with a handful of water from the sink.

After that, he returned to bed, slightly woozy and wondering if maybe he would go into shock and die.

It would be easier to be dead.

5/12/15

DAVID WOKE to the sound of someone pounding on his door. At first disoriented by the unfamiliar surroundings, he slowly recalled where he was and what had happened. He looked at his phone to see that he had several missed calls from a number he didn't recognize, as well as a few texts. He made himself stand and went to the door.

Zhané stood there with a child on her hip, a bright-eyed little thing with a curly halo of hair around his head. "I called you."

"I, uh, I slept through it."

She looked him up and down. "What happened?"

He shook his head.

"David, what happened to your leg?"

"Uh...these things, they came."

"And hurt you?" she asked.

He nodded, wishing he could lay back down.

"You gonna let me in?"

He stepped aside, then shambled back to the bed. She closed the door behind herself. He spied his glasses tossed on top of his duffle bag and grabbed them, putting them on and bringing the world into focus.

"Can I take a look at that?"

"Are you a doctor?" he asked.

"I've got an associate's and I passed the exam for being an RN," she told him, not without a little superiority in her tone.

He looked up. "Really?"

"Yes."

He frowned.

"I know, so what am I doing tarnishing my virtue with strange men in motel rooms?"

"I guess." He shrugged. "Not, you know, that I care? Not to be rude."

"Let me take a look, really," she said, glancing at his leg.

"I guess."

She set her baby on the bed next to him and peeled back the gauze. "David! What the hell!"

He could tell by the look on her face that she had expected the straight, horizontal cuts produced by razor blades. Those she would have found on his arms. He noted that the wound had wept a lot since he had applied the gauze.

"Did you do this to yourself?"

"No!"

"Come on, you're telling me someone came and *took your skin?*" she asked, clearly hoping the incredulity in her voice would make him realize the insanity of his lie.

"Yes." He glanced at her baby, which had squirmed his way close to the edge of the bed. He reached over and returned him closer to the center, though the child did not seem pleased, giving him a look of concern.

"David, seriously."

"Zhané, seriously," he returned, "Maybe I'm batshit, but what I remember is that something else did this to me."

"The things that want you to kill people."

He nodded.

She stood, reached for her child, and shook her head at him. "Maybe you should go back to that place, or somewhere like it."

He shrugged. He did not want to go back and he wasn't sure that those things wouldn't follow him there. He returned the gauze to where it had been. "You said you wanted to show me something."

She shook her head.

"So why'd you come here?" he asked.

She adjusted the baby on her hip and sighed. "You need to get help."

"You came to tell me that?"

"David, have you killed people?" she asked. "Tell me, honestly."

"One person," he admitted, not sure why he would tell her. They had been friends, good friends, for a long time when he had lived in Milwater.

Before he could say anything else, she held up her hand. "Don't."

After losing part of his liver, some of his teeth, and all his fingernails, he had not been able to disobey any longer. Besides, he had always been a creep, a loser who liked to look at crime scene photos and read about serial killers. This had been his fate, he imagined.

She turned to walk out the door, then stopped and turned back to look at him. "Who?"

"Uh," he said. "This guy. He, uh, lived next to me. Hit his dog. A lot. I heard it crying all the time. All the time."

"So you killed him."

"I get these phone calls. Three days before they come. They ask for...uh...harvest, a harvest. Say that I owe it," he said, knowing exactly how insane he sounded. "So, I killed him and they took him." *And they didn't take anything from me.*

"And then you decided you were gonna start murdering sex workers?" she asked.

"I don't know, I didn't know what else to do." His first victim had been convenient and born of a long-standing hatred, but he hadn't stumbled across anyone else who he wouldn't feel bad about killing.

In retrospect, choosing to kill a sex worker had been in poor taste, to the extreme.

She frowned at him.

"Every eight weeks," he said, "They call. At first, I thought I was just hearing bad things again. Until they showed up. They came to my apartment, Zhané."

"How do you know they need you to kill a person?" she asked.

"Because I tried buying them off with, you know, meat and stuff. It didn't work." *Must be human, must be fresh,* he thought to himself.

"So you're telling me that in two months, you're either gonna kill someone or they're gonna come take a piece of you?" she asked.

He nodded.

"Why don't they just kill you?"

"I don't know."

She shook her head and again looked like she was going to leave, but she stayed. "You know you're crazy."

He nodded.

"Why'd you come back here?" she asked, "Did you mean to kill someone local?"

"No." He shook his head and pressed his fingertips to the bones in his chest. "Bad timing. I got a call a couple of days after I came into town."

"So why are you *here*, though?" she asked, "Why'd you come back?"

"You already think I'm crazy, right?"

"That's for fucking sure," she said, sending a guilty glance towards the baby.

"Becca and Nicki were two months apart," he said, "And...two months after them, Jim Roberts went missing."

"And *you* found him," she accused.

"That's, uh...Zhané, I didn't kill those girls." *I didn't kill our friends.* "I really...and if I did, then I don't remember it. And I remember last night, I remember the first guy," he said, "But two months. Two months between them, two months between these calls..."

"But?"

"But they didn't get Jim," he said. "Because of me. I owe them. Or, they think I do."

She came to sit beside him, her baby gnawing on a fistful of her tank top. "That's insane."

"Zhané, I mean, I was weird, but I never wanted to hurt anyone. I heard things, bad things, but...not like this."

She leaned forward, giving her baby a kiss on the top of the head.

"And I take my meds and it helps with hearing other things. The regular things. And...I was kind of doing okay. Almost human," he said. "But then I get out, I get settled and into my own place...and two months later..."

"So what," she said. "You caught...some kind of, I don't know, murder hallucination? Or like...a fucked-up poltergeist?"

He thought for a moment. "I looked into poltergeists since they haunt a person more than they haunt a place. But, um, they're more about scratching and throwing stuff than driving people to murder and harvesting body parts. As far as I've turned up."

"Aliens?" she asked.

"I don't know," he said, "And I mean, I've spent months reading about this, or trying to, but there's not a specific spirit, demon, alien or other paranormal entity that I've found that drives people to kill under pain of having their renewable or non-essential body parts harvested."

She squinted at him. "I kind of forgot you were such a dork."

"Really?" he asked. He had never forgotten, even for a second, that he was a loser.

She nodded. "I really can't believe you're gonna talk me into believing this."

"I can't talk you into anything," he said, "Never could."

"You talked me into trying sushi," she reminded.

He looked down at his hands. He yawned.

"You're gonna need to rest," she said, glancing at his leg. "No matter how that happened, it's not good."

He nodded. He should probably also eat. He had been too worked up to eat much for the days leading up to his attempted murder. Or planned, he should say, he hadn't really attempted to kill her, just planned to do it.

"Hey," he said.

"What?"

"I'm sorry. Really. It was a fucked-up thing to think about doing."

"Well, you're right about that. Never figured you for this kind of misogynist shit," she said.

He sighed, wanting to argue but knowing that she was right. "I won't do it again?" he offered.

She snorted. "Goddamn better not," she warned. She glanced up at him. "You get some sleep." She gave him a pat on the leg, the good one. "I'll check in on you. You better answer me this time."

"I will."

She left, giving him a little wave, and closing the door behind her. Once she left, he wondered why, knowing that he had planned to kill her, she had brought her baby with her to see him.

He pushed himself into the center of the bed and set his glasses on the pillow beside him. He took about ten more Advil, dry swallowing each of them, which made him want to gag; when he woke up this time, he would definitely need to eat something. And shower, he would need to shower.

After about five minutes, he needed to push himself up, arranging the pillows so that the bottoms of his feet were not so close to the edge of the bed. He was, lying perfectly flat, about an inch longer than a twin or full-sized bed, but normally he could curl up. It had been a long-standing dream of his to sleep on a California king mattress, the longest of all mattresses.

His last thoughts were of how much a mattress that size would cost and how long he would need to work to afford it. He didn't even need a bedframe; he would just put the mattress on the floor.

At about three in the afternoon, he received a series of texts that roused him. He put on his glasses and pushed himself up. There was one from about eleven that told him not to get his leg wet and now one asking him how he was feeling.

He responded honestly, telling her he felt like shit.

She asked him to meet her at Tommy's, which was the nice diner in town, the one at which residents and not truckers would eat.

He agreed and pulled himself out of bed, feeling sick to his stomach and ready to die. He wrapped his leg in a plastic bag and taped it shut to keep out the water, his gut churning at the idea of hot water against that open wound.

He washed, didn't bother to shave, and gingerly pulled on the loosest pair of pants he could find, which were gym shorts he didn't normally wear in public. He knew he probably looked like a mess, with his ratty t-shirt and his dark hair still wet, but if he didn't move now, he might not make it to the diner. The whole time he drove he had the feeling he was going to pass out.

When he arrived at the diner, he didn't see Zhané, so he took the first booth he could find and waited for a waitress to approach. A woman in her thirties, he guessed, brought him a menu and asked if he wanted coffee.

He did not, he hated coffee, but he felt that he needed it, so he said yes.

Zhané, baby in tow, arrived a few minutes later and came to sit with him. "You look hungover."

"Well, I'm not."

The baby smacked his chubby little hands against the table, reaching for the cutlery roll on the table. Zhané moved it out of his reach and asked, "Did you order yet?"

"No, just coffee."

"How's the leg?"

"Not amazing," he said, trying not to sound ungrateful.

She clicked her nails on the table for a minute. "You want some painkillers?"

"Yes," he said immediately, then realized she might have just been offering him more over-the-counter stuff.

"I've got something at home that might help, you'll have to come grab them," she said.

He didn't believe that she had offered to let him anywhere near her home.

Their waitress returned and they ordered. While they waited, he said, "You did say you had something to show me, though."

From within her bag, she produced a handful of pictures and, keeping them out the baby's reach, pushed them towards him.

He struggled to pick them up for a second, but when he had he brought them closer, flipping through them, not sure what he was supposed to be looking at. They were crime scene photos of places he recognized around town, none of them with the bodies in the pictures.

She took out a manila envelope and handed that to him as well. He pulled out the papers and skimmed them, finding photocopied autopsy reports inside.

"How did you get these?"

She shrugged. "The coroner and I came to an agreement."

"Why? What do you want with this stuff?"

"They never found who did Becca and Nicki," she said, "And now there's a kid missing."

It had been years since the summer they had spent skulking around crime scenes and poking into police affairs. They had turned up some family secrets and pissed off the cops, but they had not done anything to find their friends' killer.

He reread the report. "They're all missing parts."

She nodded. "Just like you."

"But the things, they don't tell me to take anything..." he said, staring at the reports for a moment more. On the occasion he had provided a body, he had not stayed to see what they did to it. He had fled as soon as they had appeared and they had let him flee, on that occasion only. The other times they had restrained him.

He set his glasses on the table and rubbed his eyes. When their food arrived, he set all the documents on the seat beside him and returned his glasses to his face. Eating so soon after reading that

Nicki's lungs had been missing felt wrong, but he was hungry.

"So you didn't like nursing?" he asked.

She smiled. "Not really. What about you? What do you do?"

"Three years inpatient."

"Jesus, that's a long time," she said. "You, uh, I mean...were you doing stuff like this?"

"Cutting off pieces of my skin?" he asked, "No. But I was underage when my parents had me committed so I needed to do this evaluation process to get out. And, uh, well, I don't have any proof or anything, I think my parents may have been paying off the staff so I wouldn't be able to pass the eval."

"Really?"

"And I didn't do this to my leg."

She didn't argue but didn't look convinced.

"Listen, I mean, do you believe me or not about this? About the things that come?"

"I think something weird is going on, David, but that's all I can say right now. I don't know if your visitors are real but I know that people are getting hurt."

He looked down at his plate. That was enough, he figured.

"So how'd you get out?"

He shrugged. "I called out my mom. She denied it and told me that even if I did get out, I wouldn't be able to stay with them. Considering my lifestyle, she said. I said I didn't care, that I didn't want to stay with them. So after that, I don't know, I guess they figured they could wash their hands of me."

"Lifestyle?"

"Casual same-sex encounters," he said, "When I could get away with it. No fraternizing, all that."

"Jesus," she muttered.

"I know, its twenty-fifteen, you'd think they'd get over it," he said with a shrug.

The baby reached onto his mother's plate and grabbed a soggy piece of pancake, shoving his entire fist into his face. She sighed and wiped his face.

"Where'd you get a baby anyway?" he asked.

She made a face. "My uterus."

"No, I mean, who knocked you up?"

She shrugged. "Does it matter?"

"So, like, there's...uh, not a dad in the picture, I mean?"

"Nope." She tapped her nails on the table. "Didn't know it was your business," she said after a moment, a clipped tone to her voice.

"It's not. I was just asking, though, like…I don't know, did I come off like a douche?" Sometimes people took things he said in a way he didn't mean them; he knew there was something about the way he talked, something to his tone or his cadence that made people think he meant to sound like a dick, instead of sounding like one by accident.

"It's just not any of your business," she said.

The baby shoved another handful of pancake into his mouth and David couldn't help but smile.

"No, it's not, sorry," he said.

"Whatever."

"Is he supposed to eat pancakes?" he asked.

"What? Yeah, he's fine. He's started solids." She wiped his face again. "You're gonna be all sticky, little man. All sticky."

He picked up a piece of toast and took a bite. He picked up the pictures he had set to the side and asked, "What am I supposed to be seeing here?"

"I don't know. There's just…something bothering me about this. All of it. I need fresh eyes," she said. "Take them with you, look them over."

"Sure," he said, no reason to argue.

She looked at her phone, pressing the middle button so that the time showed. "Anyway, I've got some errands to finish up," she said, taking out her wallet. "Check in tomorrow?"

"Sure." He reached for his wallet.

"No, I've got it." She set a few bills on the table. She dipped a napkin in his glass of water and used it to wipe down her child.

He knew he should argue, or at least ask if she was sure, but his finances were strained, so he said, "Thanks."

"No problem. I'll see you, okay? Text me if you think of something."

He nodded.

She left, her baby on her hip and her bag on her shoulder.

The waitress came over to pick up the bill and told him, "You look familiar."

"I, uh, I used to live around here."

She gave him a look like she was trying to place his face. "You know she's a hooker," she said, a mix of warning and accusation in her voice.

He didn't know what to say and realized after second that he was grimacing.

The waitress gave him another look and then walked away with what she had come for.

He gathered up the documents Zhané had given him and left, setting them in the passenger seat. He pulled into the grocery store and skulked around, his hands in his pockets as he searched for things that could be made in a microwave. Pine Lodge had roaches but it also had a microwave.

He also went to the pharmacy aisle and looked at every bottle of painkillers they had. He finally picked one and went up to the register, where a girl his age checked him out, glancing at him out of the corner of her eye the whole time.

When he handed over his card to pay, she looked at it for longer than necessary and he guessed she was checking his name. She returned it without asking anything but seemed more uncomfortable than she had before.

Once back in his room, he fell asleep with his glasses on his chest and the local news playing.

5/13/15

IN THE morning, after he washed, he sat on the end of the bed with his phone in his hand. Zhané had not yet contacted him and he felt it untoward to get in touch with her. He glanced up when something a news anchor said caught his attention.

They had found the body of Kevin Duran, a sophomore who had been missing for a few days. He had been found behind an abandoned gas station, one that had been out of use since the early eighties.

David recognized the person who had found him, a teacher at one of the elementary schools in town, though not the one he had gone to. She had been walking her dog on the exact same walk she took every day after school.

He looked down at his phone, hesitated, then sent a message, asking 'did u see the news' and waited for a response. He searched around for the bags of groceries he had bought yesterday and limped over to them, rummaging through for a granola bar.

As he ate and waited for Zhané to text him back, he wondered for the thousandth time why these things didn't just kill him. They wanted bodies but not to make them, though they seemed to have no problem taking pieces. Maybe they were like the doctors who had bought cadavers from body snatchers; hungry for specimens but not wanting to get their hands too dirty.

His phone buzzed and it was not a text, but a call. He answered, "Mom?"

"We went by your apartment."

"Oh."

"Where are you?"

"I, uh, went on a. For a drive, you know. A trip." He had not expected his parents to stop by anytime soon.

"The landlord says you didn't renew your lease."

He sighed. "It's month-to-month, I don't have to renew if I don't want to," he said, "I figured maybe I'd find somewhere nicer."

"Where?"

"I'm, uh, I'm in Connecticut," he confessed.

"David!"

"Mom, it's not a big deal, alright? Besides, it's not, like, you know, it doesn't matter how far away I am. We don't visit."

"We visit you."

"No, you check in on me. Visits involve coming for dinner or staying to talk, not just seeing if I've filled my prescription and checking the fridge for heads."

His phone made a sound and he looked down to see that Zhané was trying to call him.

"Anyways, I've got to go," he said and hung up without a goodbye, switching over to Zhané's call. "Hey."

"Hey, I saw the news. About the boy, right?"

"Yeah."

"Did you look at everything?" she asked.

"Uh," he said, thinking about lying. "No, I'm sorry. I kind of passed out."

"How's the leg?"

"Oozing."

"Puss?"

"No, uh, the other stuff. Weepy, I guess is the word."

"I still think you should go to a doctor."

He diverted, saying, "So are you gonna get this kid's autopsy report, too?"

"I'm gonna try."

"I didn't know coroners were this easy to bribe," he said.

"Bribe?" she said with a laugh in her voice. "Try blackmail."

He grinned.

"Look over those papers."

"I will."

"Anyways, I gotta go, my shift is starting."

"Shift?" he asked, not aware that her line of work called for shifts.

"Yeah, at this animal shelter, I volunteer to walk the dogs and pet the kitties," she explained, "You know."

She had, as long as he'd known her, said that her ideal job would be hanging out with animals and he was glad to know she'd found a way to make that happen, in a roundabout way. "Have fun," he said.

"Bye."

He tossed his phone on the bed and brought over the documents she had given him. He looked at the crime scene photos again. Nothing stood out, no matter how long he looked at them, so he turned his attention to the reports. Each body was missing something, but something essential, like the lungs or heart or, in the case of Mara Copeland, her entire spinal cord. He wondered if something had been taken from the Duran boy.

He glanced down at the bandage on his thigh. From the bodies, they took things people could not live without, but they hadn't killed him to get one of the essential organs they were after. From him, they had only taken bits.

He set aside the reports and picked up his phone again, googling alien abductions. Again. Aliens were the only thing he could think of that manipulated technology and took organs and the like from people, but he had not come across any aliens that looked like the things that came for him. There were grays and goblin-like monsters, and the cartoonish little green men, but no beings made of indistinguishable dark shapes.

Maybe, he reflected, the problem was that the lights had never been on. Or that he had been attempting to flee or struggling to be released.

He got up and went to his duffle bag, rooting around for the notebook he had started when he had begun to suspect what happened to him and what had happened that summer could be related.

On the first page, headed '2011', were the dates that Becca and Nicki had been found and the date that he had found Jim. On the next page were the dates that he had gotten calls and the dates he had gotten visits. Eight weeks exactly between calls, three days between the calls and the visits.

He took the pen from the spiral binding and copied down the things that had been taken from each body, then started a third page that said '2015' and wrote the names of Mara Copeland and Kevin Duran.

He pulled up the calendar on his phone and gave up before he figured out the exact date he would have to expect his next phone call, but it would be sometime in July. At least, he thought with no real enthusiasm, he knew he would not have to do this on his birthday; on June fifteenth, he would be free to get his first legal drink, instead of debating between murder and mutilation.

Zhané seemed to think something could be done about this, and in the summer of 2011, he had thought that, too, but that was when they had thought it was some perv killing girls.

He turned the page again and jotted down all the types of go-bump-in-the-night creatures he could think of that might be responsible, though he didn't really believe any of these monsters were the right kind of monster. At the bottom of his list he added, 'or something else idfk' and added some question marks. Beneath that he drew a very rudimentary sketch of the things that had come, which given that they were nothing more than dark and humanoid shapes to him, came out fairly accurate.

He dropped the pen on the page and took off his glasses and, like an idiot, dropped them onto his lap, then gasped in pain, momentarily seizing up, unable to breathe or think. After that, he gobbled a handful of pills and wondered how hard it would be to find a drug dealer. He reread the label on the bottle, wondering if his liver could handle this.

He microwaved a shelf-stable meal that tasted significantly better than he had hoped for and then lay down, his glasses next to his phone. He didn't sleep but didn't feel very awake either; he was not quite content to lie and do nothing, but he had nothing else to do. He did not have friends anymore and did not want to talk to his family, which was to say, his parents. He did not have any siblings or close cousins.

He was entirely alone in this world, or at least it felt that way.

You reap what you sow, his father always said that. David had sown nothing. The closest human contact he'd had was with the orderlies he'd screwed around with, a few patients and with his psychiatrist. Though, as his time at Mansfield Behavioral Health Center had stretched from months to years, he had begun to assume that his therapist must have graduated with a shitty GPA to work in such a place. Sure, he'd gotten David on meds that worked and talked out a couple things with him, but all in all, David did not feel that he had reaped the benefits of going to counseling.

It wasn't that he thought therapy was a crock. He had respect for people who could do it well, but Mansfield Behavioral Health Center had been a small place tucked away in a rural town. Some of the patients had been frequent fliers, coming in and out with their nervous breakdowns and substance abuse; others had been harmless and sweet, but unable to care for themselves. He had met a handful of attempted suicides who wanted nothing more than to be at peace, he'd made friends with a lifer named Harley whose sister had left her there once she'd gotten married.

It had been Harley who'd pushed him to get out, Harley who had squeezed his hand and said, "Don't let them make you useless, David."

"I'm not useless," he'd said, offended.

"No, but you will be if you spend much more time in here. And if you can't take care of yourself when you get out, you'll find yourself right back here," she'd said. "I'm fifty-four and I had five months on my own."

"What happened?"

"Oh, David, it was *wonderful*," she said, "And terrifying. Suddenly, everything that had been done for me I had to do on my own. No one showed me how, no one checked in until I had to go crawling back home at *thirty-six*."

He had thought of the weekly laundry collections, the food he'd never had to cook served on plastic trays, he thought of the janitors that kept things neat for him. And he'd thought of the bedtimes and snack limits, the rules about how patients could spend their time together, the need for chaperones.

"Children," he'd said to her, a moment of clarity coming over him. "We'll always be children."

"Because it's easier to pay someone to do it than to teach," she'd confirmed. "Get out while you can, okay? You're a healthy young man, David, you should have a life."

Freedom hadn't worked out so well for him, though. He'd killed someone. He'd killed a human garbage heap, but still, he shouldn't have done it. And he should have felt worse about it. He would not do it again, that much he knew; he didn't have it in him to be some vigilante who struck down abusers and rapists, nor could he ever take the life of someone like Zhané.

What a rotten situation to be in, he thought again. He did not want to live like this any longer. Maybe he could kill himself. Maybe he could turn himself in and go to jail. The things had not come for him at Mansfield, maybe they wouldn't come for him in prison.

He didn't know what to do, but he did know that lying here on this musty bed was not the answer. He put on his glasses, made himself get up and shoved his phone and keys in his pocket. He did not bother with his wallet, as he had nothing in it.

Once outside, he looked around, not knowing where to go. Pine Lodge was on the outskirts of town, one of four motels that lingered near the edges of Milwater. There was a nicer place off the main strip where real, human visitors could stay.

He was near the reservoir. It should have been walking distance, but not with his leg the way it was. Instead, he drove down, parking under a tree. No one was out fishing, not in the middle of the afternoon, though he saw the signs of careless fishermen: tangled knots of line, broken bobbers, and lead weights that had been dropped and never picked up.

He sat on a bench, one of two that had been made by some Eagle Scout years ago. It was in the high sixties, not as warm as it had been yesterday or the day before. The weather had been strange lately, not in a spooky way, but in a way that said there was something wrong with the earth's weather patterns.

Someone walked by with a dog and he thought of the poor little thing whose owner he'd killed. The dog had weighed about ten pounds and he had spent nights listening to it yelp and cry, beaten for barking to go out and beaten again for having accidents when it hadn't been taken out. The dog had belonged to the man's 'whore of an ex'.

After he'd killed the man, David had wanted to keep the dog, but that would have been much too suspect. Instead, he'd left the door open and brought the dog to a local park, trying to make it look like it had wandered away. He'd done his best to stage the murder as a botched robbery.

The cops had talked to him briefly, but he had never really been on their list of suspects. The man had possessed a list of enemies and debts a mile long.

Looking out over the reservoir, David again thought that he should feel worse about killing that man. Cosmically, he thought, either it didn't matter because the man had been scum, or, if there was a Heaven and a God, David would get his eventual punishment for the crime.

Mara Copeland had died here, he thought. Drowned, the report had said and last seen on a date with long-time boyfriend Joe Lake. But he had returned home and stayed there with his mother for the rest of the night. Somewhere between City Pizza and the home to which she had never returned, Mara had been waylaid and murdered. She had not made or received any calls, either, between her date and her death.

He had to think who was dumb enough to kill two people in the town where they lived. He didn't imagine anyone would come to Milwater to kill someone, since the cities were, obviously, more abundantly populated with people who wouldn't be missed. So it had to be a local and one who wasn't thinking straight.

Zhané would know better who fit that description. There was not a lot to go on, all things considered. He did not know of anyone who could buy into this idea.

A thought came to him and he texted Zhané, 'is Jim Roberts still in a coma' and set his phone on his good leg to wait for an answer. Six minutes later she told him he was. He limped back to his car, returned to Pine Lodge for his wallet, and drove to the nursing home Zhané had said Jim would be at. He'd showed no signs of waking, needed no serious medical care and so had been sent to an old folks' home, despite having the relatively tender age of forty-nine.

When he entered the home and approached the reception window, the woman there gave him a once over and asked, "Can I help you?"

"I wanted to visit Jim Roberts?"

She raised her eyebrow. "Are you a relative?"

"No, I, uh," he said, not really sure what to say. He hadn't thought she would ask. "I'm David Craft, I, um, I was out of town for a few years, but I wanted to pay my respects."

"David Craft," she said, "Why does that sound familiar?"

"I found him."

She looked him over again. He was a little more put together than he had been yesterday, in jeans instead of gym shorts and with his hair relatively tamed. It fell into his eyes a little, but haircuts had not been a priority lately.

"I...I just want to pay my respects," he said again.

"I'll give his brother a call, see if he'll okay it," she said.

He had not thought it would be so difficult, especially because as a child he had visited his grandfather here with no difficulties at all, his whole family walking in with just a wave to the nurse. Maybe because they had been a family unit or familiar faces and he was just some twenty-year-old guy.

"I can't get a hold of him," she told him said after a minute. "He's probably at work. Why don't you try again some other time?"

He nodded. "Thanks, then."

He returned to his car and sat there for a while. He had nothing else to do; he thought about going to the library to find a book or movie but couldn't even do that. He was not a resident of the town or of Connecticut anymore. His options exhausted, he returned to the motel, scribbled down the musings he'd had about the crimes throughout the day, and watched TV.

Around nine, he fell asleep, having at least the wherewithal to turn off the television beforehand.

On the morning of the fourteenth, he awoke to knocking on the door and he pulled himself out of bed, rubbing his eyes and finding not Zhané, as he had expected, or even the motel manager, but two uniformed police officers.

"David Craft?"

His first instinct was to lie, but instead, he said, "Yeah."

"You used to live in town, right? Forty-three Fox Run Road?"

He nodded automatically. Seventeen years in that house until it had come to an end one weekend with no warning. He hadn't even been asked to pack his things, they had done it for him.

"We'd like you to come down to the station with us."

He licked his lips. "For what? Am I under arrest?"

"We've got some questions about the people who've been murdered," the officer said.

"I'm sorry, what did you say your name was?" he asked, knowing well that they had not given their names.

"I'm Officer Bryant, this is Officer Monroe." The male officer gestured to the woman at his side.

"Am I under arrest?" he asked again, doing his best to commit their names to memory, repeating them over and over.

"Listen, I'm sure you saw on the news about the Duran boy," Bryant said, "The last time we had something like this happen, you were questioned and we just want to clear some things up. Maybe go over some stuff about the night you found Jim Roberts. It's not a big deal, it'll be quick."

He almost laughed. He knew well enough that they would

leave him to sweat in some room for hours, as they had the first time.

"Just, you know, I'm sure it's nothing," Bryant said.

"No."

"And there's the matter of the blood," he said, his tone souring a little. "The manager here says when someone came to change the sheets, they had blood on them."

"And?"

"Well, with two people dead and you involved in the last crime," Bryant said, letting the implication sit in the air for a moment before adding, "I'm sure we'll clear it all up when you come down."

"It's my blood."

"Yours?"

David nodded. "I know they've got all my stuff on file, the stuff they took last time. Run one of those tests if you're worried."

"Listen, son, how about you come down with us," Bryant urged, "We'll get everything sorted out."

"Am I under arrest?" he asked again, this time not asking Bryant but turning to look at the other officer. Monroe.

She looked bored and irritated, but not with David. She was a little older than David himself, but he didn't recognize her, which made him think she was from out of town, or new to Milwater, at least. Bryant was significantly older than her, late thirties or early forties. David wasn't sure, but he could have guessed how their work dynamic was.

"No," she answered.

"Thanks," he said.

Bryant's face twisted for a moment and, even being a white man, David could not help feeling worried. Stories of cops murdering people had been national news recently.

"Since I'm not under arrest, I'm, uh, I'm gonna close the door," he said.

If they'd had anything to tie him to the crimes, he'd have been under arrest. After the 2011 murders, he'd been questioned and fingerprinted, even swabbed for DNA. It hadn't turned up anything then and it wouldn't turn up anything now. He hadn't been involved.

He shouldn't have gone to see Jim Roberts, he concluded. It had been suspicious. Revisiting the crime, wasn't that what it was called?

He backed up and shut the door on them, giving Monroe an apologetic smile. Maybe she was playing him or maybe she thought this was stupid, but he held nothing against her.

He sent Zhané a message asking her to call if she had the chance, not knowing what else to do. He needed to talk to someone and he couldn't very well call his parents. Along with sleeping with men, being questioned by the police was another thing they didn't approve of. They didn't approve of hallucinating either, but at least they couldn't call it a lifestyle choice. It didn't matter in the end, he knew. No matter what he did, they wouldn't have liked it. They hadn't liked it when he'd dated Zhané, they hadn't liked it when he'd mentioned going to college for teaching, they hadn't liked it when he'd played soccer or when he had stopped playing soccer.

They didn't like anything, not themselves and not each other.

David sat on the edge of the bed, staring at his phone, wishing she would call, but more than anything wishing that his parents had never dragged him away to Vermont. His behaviors that summer had been erratic and unsafe, but he had never done anything to his parents. He hadn't hurt anyone but himself.

Well, himself and Zhané, who had been his girlfriend for more than a year at that point and his friend since childhood. When he had acted the way he had, he'd scared her, but he'd scared himself too.

At the end of sophomore year, he'd started having the occasional hallucination or paranoid delusion, nothing too serious, but not something he wanted to tell anyone. Zhané and a few friends had known something wasn't right, but he had not told his parents. After Nicki and Becca had been killed, things had officially crossed over into bad, and, at their height, Zhané had given him an ultimatum: he needed to take care of himself and get help or she would end this relationship.

He had told her to go fuck herself and that he was glad she was going to dump him. He'd stormed off and found Jim Roberts after that. August second. He remembered it because August fifth would have marked a year and a half for them.

Between breaking up and his departure, they'd reconciled somewhat and even agreed that things were not totally unsalvageable, given that he did get his mental health sorted.

His phone began to ring and he answered with a nearly teary, "Hey."

"Hey, what's up? What did you need?" she asked, sounding

worried.

He cleared his throat. "The cops came."

"Did you get arrested?"

"No."

"Shit, you didn't go with them, did you?"

"No."

She let out a breath. "Alright, good. What did they want?"

"They had questions," he said, then added, "I tried to visit Jim Roberts." And, he thought, he had been seen at the reservoir, another crime scene.

"Okay."

Suddenly he felt stupid for having needed to talk to someone. Nothing had happened. "I just, I got spooked, I guess. I'm sorry."

"That's fine. I'm gonna come over."

"You don't have to."

"Shut up, David," she said and hung up.

He ran his hand through his hair, not sure how to feel. He peeked out the window to see an unmarked police car tucked off to the side. Or, at least, he thought it was one. He looked again, unsure, wishing he could trust himself more fully.

He tried to tidy up before she arrived, but she still glanced around with distaste when she stepped inside.

"There's an unmarked over there," she told him, nodding her head towards it.

He nodded, glad that she had thought the same thing as him.

"They might come over."

"Why?"

"Try to bust you for soliciting," she said.

"Where's the baby?" he asked.

"Oh, my mom wanted to bring him to some playgroup," she said, "Some, I don't know, something at her church. She thinks he needs to spend more time around other kids."

He nodded. "How are your parents?"

"The same."

He nodded again. He handed her the notebook he'd been filling. "Just, you know, some thoughts."

She began to read and then said, "Jesus, David, don't you smell that? What is that, mold?"

"I think so."

"Ugh. How long are you gonna stay here for?"

He shrugged.

"I mean, are you back for good? Do you want to stay in Milwater?"

"Kind of. It's not like I wanted to leave in the first place."

"True," she said, "Alright, I can't stay here. Do you want to come back to my place?"

"Really?"

"Yeah, really," she said and her phone buzzed. She glanced at it and then hissed, "Oh, you fucking bitch."

"What?"

"My babysitter canceled. Look at this shit," she said, showing him the text. "My mom says I have to be *careful* who I work for. Fuck!"

He looked at his feet, thinking. He knew what he wanted to say but didn't know how it would go over with her. "I. I don't have plans. If you don't have a...uh, a second...a backup."

She looked up.

"I know it's weird."

"Do you know anything about babies?"

"I changed a diaper once."

She shook her head, scrolling through something on her phone, then declared, "Yeah, you know, what? Sure. I'm done with these fucking teenagers. *My mom said.* Let's go."

He followed her out the door and she gave him her address.

David pulled up to Zhané's house, a Cape Cod with a modest sized yard and an attached garage. He had been here before, driven by it a thousand times, and he tried to remember why it looked so familiar.

As they approached, he asked, "Isn't this your grandmother's house?"

"Yeah. Well, technically it's my house, now."

"What?"

"Yeah, she signed it over to me when she went to the nursing home," Zhané said.

"Really?"

She nodded. "Uncle Reggie was *pissed*, too, he thought it was gonna be his for sure. But she wanted Noah to have a home. Her first great-grandbaby and all. She loves the shit out of that kid."

He smiled. He'd met her grandmother a handful of times and wasn't surprised that she'd given Zhané her house; she'd made it clear who her favorites were. He followed her inside and sat on the couch when she gestured to it, running his fingers over the spiral binding of his notebook. He had brought the notebook and documents with him.

"You want something to drink?"

"Water?"

"Sure thing."

As she got him a glass of water, a tortoiseshell cat jumped up beside him. "Is that Figaro?"

"Yes."

He reached out his hand to the cat, who brushed against him, then walked straight across his lap to get settled onto the arm on the other side. He grunted and bit his lip hard to keep from crying out, but when she returned with a glass of water, she frowned and asked, "Are you crying?"

"The cat stepped on my leg," he whispered.

"Oh, that reminds me," she said and returned with a little prescription bottle. "These should help."

He took one immediately, washing it down with a lot of water. "Do you have a map of town?"

"I can find one. Why?"

"We should look at all the dump sites," he said, "And the places they were last seen alive. See if there's a pattern or something."

She sat beside him and reached over to the coffee table to turn on her laptop. While she waited for it to boot, she glanced at him and asked, "Listen, you find a map, I'm gonna, uh, make a list of numbers and stuff like that. For the baby."

"Thanks."

She reached over and took his notebook, going to the last page and jotting down the doctor's number, as well as her mother's, then filling the rest of the page with instructions. How to make a bottle, where everything was, what he liked, what he could and couldn't eat.

He eventually ended up asking, "Do you mind if I put Google Earth on here?"

"Is it free?"

"Yeah."

"Go ahead."

Once it had downloaded, he flipped through the files and added pushpins to the dump sites and to the victims' last known locations. Zhané watched over his shoulder.

"I'm sure the cops already did this," he said and it felt like an apology.

"Yeah, cops don't know shit, though," she said, "They're grasping at straws if they're going after you."

He nodded. "Hey, can I ask you something?"

"What?"

"About that guy, the one I killed."

"What about him?"

"I mean...you know, um, we used to be close. Is that, is me doing that, does it mean we can't be friends?" he asked.

She made a face like she didn't know what to say. "Um, shit, David, that's kind of sudden. You just got back into town and a lot has changed. Four years is a long time to think we can just...pick up."

"No, like, uh, are we friends, still?" he asked. "I didn't mean like boyfriend-girlfriend stuff."

"Oh. Then, yeah, we're friends. I mean...I guess I don't really approve of you killing people, but I think there are some circumstances going on here."

He smiled. "Good, I'm glad," he said, "Cause, you know, I really missed you."

"I missed you too." She reached out to pat his knee, then pulled her hand back, saying, "I don't want to touch your, uh, missing skin? By accident."

He nodded.

The door opened without warning and he flinched. It took him a moment to recognize the woman who had entered as Zhané's mother, whose name was Amanda, though he had always called her Mrs. Smith.

"Oh, don't you tell me," was the first thing she said, her eyes on David.

"Don't tell you what?" Zhané asked, getting up and taking the baby from her mother.

"Don't tell me you are bringing this sort of stuff into your home," she said, "It's bad enough you do it in the first place!"

"Mom," Zhané said, her nose wrinkled, "It's just David."

"And *who* is David?"

"That's David," Zhané said, pointing, "David Craft. From high school."

"David Craft?" her mother asked.

"Yeah, he came back to town."

"Not that boy you dated. The one who had all those issues."

"Mom, he's *right there*," she said.

"I know where he is." Looking him over, Amanda said, "And what have you been up to?"

He didn't know what to say and looked at Zhané for help. He had never felt comfortable around her family; they asked questions, to-the-point questions, and they looked you in the eye when they did it. In the Craft family, questions were whispered to other family members behind backs. "Um, just, missed Milwater, you know? Figured I'd see how things are around here."

"How things are around here?" she asked, "People getting killed. Might as well move to the city."

He gave a nervous smile.

"Thanks for taking Noah, anyways," Zhané said.

"Your brother has been trying to get a hold of you," Amanda said.

"I know."

"Are you going to get back to him?"

"I don't want to go to his barbecue," she said.

"Why not?"

"Because he always gives me shit, Mom, you know that."

Her mother rolled her eyes. "You're gonna come, you let him know. And someone's got to pick Nana up from the home."

"Fine," she said.

Once her mother had left, David asked, "Your parents know what you do?"

"Yeah. My fucking brother ratted me out."

"How did he find out?"

She snorted. "Cause 'one of his friends' saw my listing," she said.

He shook his head. "What time do you have to go?"

"Eight."

He looked at his phone. He had hours to wait.

She came to sit beside him, and the baby ogled David for a moment. He waved. The baby continued to stare. "Are you sure you can do this?" she asked.

"Sure. I mean, not to sound like an asshole, but how hard can it be? Being a parent is...non-stop menial tasks, not a single skill-based activity."

She frowned.

"Right?"

"No, you're right," she said. "Here, actually, take him for a second. If he's not dead by the time I get back from the bathroom, you're hired."

She passed the baby over to him and he set the child's rear on the thigh of his good leg. "Hi," he said, not able to stop smiling. "I'm David."

The baby said nothing.

"And you're Noah." He had wanted to hold this baby since the first time he'd seen him, but it had seemed inappropriate to ask. "That's a good name, Noah, I always liked it."

Noah leaned forward a little, grabbing on to David's shirt, then leaned forward more, trying to shove the fabric into his mouth. David pulled his shirt back and replaced it with a toy he found on the coffee table.

"Here, take this, I'm not sure this shirt is clean," he said. He had, for the past few days, lost track of his life. The shirt had smelled okay that morning. Not great, but okay.

Noah mouthed the toy for a few minutes, then threw it. David feigned shock, saying "Oh, you threw it! I can't believe you. So rude."

The baby laughed and David imagined that this was going to go well.

When Zhané returned, he said, "Look, he's alive."

"I can see that. You want to give him back?"

"No, I'm okay."

"I'm going to eat. You want something?"

"Please."

She went to the kitchen, returned a minute later, and said, "Here, if you're planning on staying in town, you're going to need a job, aren't you?" She handed him the local paper. "Greene's IGA was hiring last time I checked and they let idiots work there."

He set the paper on the table and, holding Noah with one arm, leaned forward a little and searched for the classifieds. He saw the one she had mentioned, as well as a few others. Maybe, between now and eight, he would make the rounds and ask for applications.

She called him to the kitchen and he went, baby on his hip; he would have been able to forget the strangeness of his life were it not for the pain in his leg. As he ate, he ran his idea by her and she approved.

That afternoon, he stopped at half a dozen places, asking for applications. His last stop was the IGA and he asked the first staff he saw, a young man about his age with brown skin and neatly parted hair, "Hey, um, are you guys hiring? I mean, I saw in the..., uh."

David gestured in a way he hoped indicated a newspaper.

The kid stopped sweeping and evaluated his gesture. "The newspaper?"

"Yeah."

"Yeah, we're hiring."

David did not recognize him but thought they would have been in high school at the same time. "Can I ask you for an application, or...should I ask someone else?"

He pointed. "If you go back, you'll see a sign for the office."

David nodded. "Thanks."

He'd said it with his best smile. He wasn't able to place him but knew he would have remembered him if they had gone to school together, given how, as he walked back to find the office, he hoped that he would be able to see him on the way out.

He found the office door, knocked, and was told to enter.

A man in his thirties, white and slightly paunchy, sat at a desk. He asked, "Hey, what can I do ya for?"

"I saw you're hiring."

"Sure thing, what's your name?"

"David. Craft."

"You look familiar."

"I used to live here. We moved to Vermont for a while, uh, but I decided to come back."

"Oh yeah?"

He nodded.

The man said, "I'm Johnny, let me see if I can find you an application." He searched through a few drawers and finally pulled out a sheet of paper. "You can go on and fill it out, drop it off as soon as you can."

"Yeah, I will. Thanks."

Johnny nodded.

David stood for a moment, then gave an awkward wave and left the man's office, closing the door behind him.

He did not pass the young man on the way out and felt disappointed.

He returned to Pine Lodge, filled out all the applications and napped for an hour or so. He returned to Zhané's house at just before seven-thirty, as she had requested.

"How'd it go?" she asked.

"I got a couple."

"Alright, well, Noah's asleep, he'll probably wake up in a few hours to eat. Once he eats, he'll go right back to sleep and be fine through the night. You can watch TV or whatever, I've got Netflix. I should be home, um, around one, I think. If I'm not home by two and you don't hear from me, give me a call. If I don't answer, call the cops, I wrote down the places I'm going."

"Oh."

"Thanks," she said.

"Be careful."

She laughed. "You're funny." As she left, he heard her say, "Tries to fucking kill me and tells me to be careful."

Once she had gone, he sat on the couch and spent the better part of half an hour figuring out her TV and remotes. Eventually, he got Netflix working and dozed through two hours of anime before he heard the baby start to cry.

Bouncing the child on his hip, he triple-checked the directions for heating up a bottle from the fridge. He looked at the date scribbled on the bottle and wondered if it was breast milk. He checked a few cupboards and did not see any tins of formula.

Noah fussed as the bottle heated up and David googled 'is sleeping a lot normal after being injured'. He found no conclusive answer but did find a forum about sleeping a lot after surgery.

Once the bottle warmed, he took Noah to the couch and got the warm-fuzzies as he fed the baby. It brought back old dreams he'd had; the idea of being a father had always appealed to him. Seeing babies and children had always lit up something inside of him, something that made him smile like an idiot. He'd never had any brothers or sisters and his cousins were all his age, so he'd never gotten the chance to be around any little kids. He'd always been jealous of classmates showing off pictures of their baby cousins or nieces and nephews.

Noah fell back asleep after about fifteen minutes, though David lingered in returning him to his crib.

Since Mansfield, he had not thought about having children or anything like that. And now, almost twenty-one, with no secondary school and inhuman visitors, he did not think it was an option for him now, either, no matter how badly he wanted it.

He put Noah back to bed and lay down on the couch, overwhelmed by a despair that had come on suddenly. Until then, it had not struck him how much his life had been set back by his time away. He hadn't been able to get back together with Zhané or to find anyone else to date; there had been no chance to go to senior prom, he hadn't even been asked if he was thinking about college.

His parents, he realized, had planned to leave him in Mansfield for his entire life.

The tears snuck up on him and before he knew it, he was

crying, bent over himself with his face buried in a crochet blanket that must have been made by Zhané's grandmother. He wanted his life back and there was nothing he could do to get it, not if every other month something was going to come and snip off one of his body parts until he was used up.

He cried himself out and lay down on his side, watching the door and waiting for Zhané to come home.

Just after one, she walked in and turned on the light. "You awake?" she asked.

"Yeah."

"Everything go okay?"

"Yeah, he's asleep."

"You okay?"

"No."

"What's wrong?" she asked, putting her bag down and tapping his shins.

He sat up and rubbed his face. "I don't know. I just...this isn't what life is supposed to be like, I want it to be back to normal."

"I know what you mean," she said. "Well, kind of. I really hated being a nurse."

"It sounds like a shitty job."

"I wasn't cut out for it," she said, "I can admit that. Besides, I make good money now and I have time to volunteer during the day. Plus, I get to stay home with my baby and that's great, cause I went to a couple daycares and those people give me the creeps."

He snorted.

"I don't get it, though. I hear people bitch all the time about their shitty boyfriends or bad hookups or how they're always a booty call. Like what I do is somehow worse than letting the same guy you don't even like lazily plow you for two years before he dumps you for someone else? I paid off my loans."

He rubbed the back of his neck.

She rubbed his arm. "If you want things to be normal, you gotta make it normal. You'll get there."

"With monsters stealing my organs?"

"We'll figure it out. You've got two months, right?" she asked.

"Give or take."

They sat together quietly for a moment and she said, "Hey."

"Yeah?"

"You promise not to murder anyone else?"

"Yes."

"So, do you want to move into my in-law apartment? Above the garage?" she asked.

"You have an in-law?"

"Uncle Reggie lived in it so he could help out Nana," she explained.

"You mean it?"

"Sure."

"I don't have money."

"And I don't have a babysitter," she said. "All these prissy little teenagers," she muttered. "And you can mow the lawn."

"Zhané, are you really sure?"

"I'll hit you up for utilities once you have a job."

He started to well up again and put his arms around her. "Thank you. I don't want to live in the roach motel anymore."

She gave him a squeeze.

"And I like your baby."

"I like him, too. You should get some sleep. Take the couch."

"Thanks."

"Night." She patted his back and stood up.

He stared up at the ceiling for most of the night, alternating between hope and despair.

5/18/15

DAVID GOT a call back from Greene's IGA over the weekend, after he had packed up his few belongings and moved them into Zhané's mostly empty in-law. He went in to fill out his tax information, get a shirt and was told to come back at six Monday morning. He could wear jeans as long as they didn't have rips. The part-time job stocking and cleaning paid minimum wage, but it was better than nothing. He'd be able to pay his bills without worrying if he'd finally tap out his savings, at least.

When he arrived at the store, he wandered around until he found a door that was unlocked and found the manager farting around at one of the registers.

"Oh, hey there," Johnny greeted him.

David did not know how he could be so enthusiastic this early. Dead on the inside, he assumed. "Hi. Morning."

"Alright, come on back, we'll get you set up," he said.

He followed Johnny back to where the young man he had seen on the first day was standing in front of a shelf of cans, taking things down.

"Brian did that last night," Johnny said to him.

"Brian put the corn where the peas go," the young man answered in a nearly robotic voice.

To David, the manager said, "Well, this is Akmed, he'll show you around." He gave David a pat on the back and walked away.

Once he had gone, the young man looked up. "It's Ahmed."

"Hm?"

"My name, it's Ahmed."

"I'm David."

"Can you help me move all these cans?"

David nodded and moved closer, finding that Ahmed smelled pleasantly soapy and little like fresh laundry.

Ahmed said, "I think he does it on purpose."

"Hm?"

"Says my name wrong."

"Oh." After Ahmed said nothing else, he asked, "Are you from around here?"

"Yes," Ahmed replied, his answer clipped.

"No, uh, cause...I didn't...I used to live here. I don't remember you from high school or anything, though," he babbled, feeling like an asshole.

"I went to a Catholic school in the next town over."

"Oh," he said. "Alright."

Once they had moved all the misplaced corn, they had to then move the pea cans into the empty space. When that was finished, he followed Ahmed around, waiting for him to explain each of the tasks they were to complete; Ahmed gave him three or four warnings that came with everything they did, usually concerning questions that customers would ask most often.

Every so often, he caught Ahmed looking at him and he was sure that Ahmed had caught him looking back. Ahmed was average height, about five-ten, which still put him at half a foot shorter than David.

At one point, he squinted up at David. "You're awfully tall, though."

"Sorry?" David said.

"No, just, you're replacing Jason and he was like...five-four."

"Oh."

"You live here? I don't think I've ever seen you come in before."

"I, uh. Just moved back."

"Away at school?"

David shook his head. "No, I, uh, just high school for me. You?"

"I'm doing my gen eds at NVCC cause I couldn't figure out what I want to major in," he shared, "Or, I couldn't figure out a major my parents liked."

David nodded.

"Anyways, people will be here soon. I guess, I don't know, just stick close for now. You'll get the hang of it."

He could have thought of a hundred worse ways to earn money than following Ahmed around. He gave another of his best smiles and Ahmed smiled back, but quickly, looking away after a second. He turned and started to walk towards the front of the store and David couldn't help but feel giddy.

It was stupid, just a little crush, but it was nice. Crushes were normal, working was normal.

Until one, when his shift ended, David watched Ahmed field questions about the produce, take imaginary trips to 'the back' to check for things they didn't have and returned abandoned items to where they belonged. They wrangled carts, cleaned up messes and David learned how to use the price gun, which he found rewarding.

At one, Ahmed looked at his watch, which had a deep orange leather band, and said, "Alright, we're done."

"You wear a watch?"

With a crooked smile, Ahmed said, "No, it's just drawn on."

David grinned. "Are you, uh, are you on...not tomorrow. The next one. Wednesday?"

"Yeah, we work the same shifts. I think. Unless Johnny wants to switch things around, but me and Jason always worked the same shifts unless we had to trade or something."

"Alright, great."

David left the store with butterflies about coming back on Wednesday, when he would work the closing shift, one to nine, then opening again on Friday. He also had been told he'd get a shift every other weekend, which meant he would get between twenty-two and twenty-nine hours a week, depending on if he got one of the shorter Sunday shifts.

That Wednesday, as they left after closing, David said, "Hey, hang on."

"Hm?"

"Do you want to give me your number? You know, in case something comes up or whatever?" he asked.

"I guess," Ahmed said after a moment. They exchanged numbers and before they parted ways, Ahmed said, "Uh, not that anyone makes phone calls, but texting is better."

"Really?"

"Yeah, my phone and my hearing aid don't always get along."

Without meaning to, David looked at his ear, noticing the hearing aid he hadn't before. "Oh."

"You didn't notice?"

"No."

"Wow, I figured you were being polite, not that you were blind," Ahmed said, not mean but teasing.

David smiled. He answered in a voice that was supposed to sound flirty, "No, I can see fine."

Ahmed let out a small laugh. "Anyways, see you Friday."

David nodded and watched him walk for a second before he headed to his own car. When he got home, he stopped into Zhané's kitchen and said, "Hey."

She gave him a wave. "What's up?"

He shrugged.

"Do you want to hang out?" she asked, clearly already knowing he would say yes. He didn't yet have a TV or really anything more than a futon in his apartment. When his first paycheck went through, he would start to add furnishings, but until then, he would hang out with Zhané and Noah during his free time.

She pointed to a manila folder on the table. "Kevin Duran's autopsy."

He sat at the table and picked it up, not really wanting to read it. His intestine, large and small, and all of his teeth had been extracted. He found his notebook and found that Zhané had already added the new details to their notes.

"What could they want with all this?" he asked, "I mean, they're hodgepodge body parts."

"Food?"

"Teeth aren't food," he pointed out.

"I want to go to the gas station."

"Aw, come on, the cops already tried to question me once."

"The last time you found Jim really close to where they found Becca."

He asked, "Do you think it's the same killer as last time?"

"I don't know, maybe."

"So why would they be, uh, dormant for all these years?"

She said, "I've actually been thinking about that. You were somewhere they couldn't get to you right, in that institution or whatever? So they waited for you to get out."

He nodded.

"So what if this guy was somewhere, too? What if he ended up in prison for something unrelated?"

"That is what they say on all the crime shows," he said, "So I'm sure the cops are looking into that."

"David, don't you see? They *did* look into it. They looked into you."

"But I...I didn't go with them." With no reason to think she would know the answer, he asked, "Are they gonna come looking for me again?"

"I think so. They're not really broad thinkers around here."

He sighed. "But, here's the thing, if I'm getting calls *and* these other people are going missing, that means there's two, uh, sets of these things, right?"

"You don't think it would be one set running both operations?"

He shook his head. "No, I don't think so, they're...they follow a schedule and the Duran kid doesn't line up with my schedule. Does he?"

He pulled over the autopsy file and looked at the date of death for Kevin Duran; he had been found on the morning of the thirteenth, two days after he had planned to kill Zhané, but he had died, according to the report, sometime between the night of the eleventh and the morning of the twelfth.

He added that to the notebook and wrote underneath 'same schedule???'.

"It lines up?" Zhané asked, reading over his shoulder.

"Looks like it."

"I'd rather deal with one group. How many are there?"

"Three. It's always three of them. I mean, I don't know if they have, you know, behind-the-scenes partners," he said.

"Me neither."

He stared at the notebook, at the files she had collected. "Do you really think the cops are looking into me?"

"Seems likely."

He frowned. That idea did not sit well with him, but it made sense. The cops had come to see him before, but now, he worried, he would see them at every turn. He gathered up the papers and notebook into a neat pile.

Zhané asked, "Are you working tomorrow?"

"No."

"I want to go to the gas station."

"Um." The idea didn't appeal to him in anyway.

"And I think check out the library, see if maybe...like if these go back further than just that summer."

"Don't you think someone would have noticed? If every two months someone died? It's not a big town."

"Yeah," she said, "If people were smart, but we live in a country where rapists can sue for custody and cops can get away with murder. People aren't smart, they don't look at things. Besides, maybe someone *did* notice but they were, you know, like us."

"Like us?"

"A hooker and a whack job. People no one listens to."

He would have protested being called a whack job, but she had referred to herself just as disparagingly. He realized after a moment, "We have to go talk to Dirty Bob."

"Dirty Bob died."

"What!"

"Yeah, he got run over by a garbage truck. He was passed out and they went to pick up the dumpster he was sleeping next to."

"Oh no," he said, feeling genuinely sad. Dirty Bob had been a town fixture.

"Who we should really talk to is, uh, the trailer lady at the end of Montgomery Circle," she said. "What's her name?"

"Mrs. Grady?"

"I think so. Anyways, she watches everything."

The frazzled and bug-eyed woman who lived in the mobile home at the end of Montgomery Circle had long been a judgmental watcher of the people of Milwater. She had been there to protest a gay couple going to prom and she had been there to complain about the ex-cons who worked at the bottle return; she had told anyone who listened about how the element was ruining the local beach and how Puerto Ricans from Waterbury came to deal drugs at the park.

"I don't want to talk to her, she gives me the creeps," he said.

"I'm not going alone. Do you want to watch TV or something?"

He nodded and followed her out to the living room.

The following morning, she let herself into his apartment and asked, "Hey, you up?"

He rolled over and then winced, having rolled onto his bad leg.

The shock of pain woke him up completely, so he sat up and said, "Yes."

"Good, get up," she said and as she left, added, "We're gonna go to the gas station."

He sighed. He didn't know what she thought she would find at the gas station but he understood that she felt the need to do something. Becca and Nicki had been her friends, too, and she must have felt their loss more keenly than he had in the past years. Not because she had loved them more but because he had left; the whole situation had been surgically cut out of his life, leaving a huge numb spot.

He'd had no one to talk to about it after moving and no one had known the girls where he'd gone. But Zhané had been left behind, she'd had to finish high school with two friends dead and a third whisked away.

He showered and went to her kitchen to eat. She handed him the baby as soon as he walked in because the kettle on her stove had started to scream. "Hold him for a second."

He obliged, managing to put two slices of bread into the toaster with one hand.

"You can watch him tonight, right?"

"Sure."

Noah looked up at him, then reached out to try and grab the knife David had gotten to spread peanut butter on his toast.

"Hey, watch it," David said, moving the knife out of the child's reach.

"Put him in the chair," she advised.

He set the knife down and put him in the high chair. He alternated between eating his toast and spooning mouthfuls of rice cereal into the baby's mouth, though Noah spat most of his food back onto his own face. After a few minutes, there was a lot of cereal on Noah's face and David said, "Can I have a napkin?"

Zhané looked up, took the tiny spoon from him and scooped up the food Noah had spit out, putting it back into his mouth.

"You can do that?" he asked.

"If I threw away all the food he spits back out I'd go broke," she said.

"Oh."

They ate and the baby needed a change before they could go, but they arrived at the abandoned gas station by mid-morning. It was supposed to be nice today, in the high sixties or so, a standard spring day and as they stood in the dirt patch behind the gas station, the urge to go for a long walk overcame David. Maybe when his leg was more fully healed he would go. Maybe he would invite Ahmed to go with him.

"Faggot," accused the voice of his mother, perfectly clear and near to him.

He looked around, concerned for a moment, then frowned. "Shut up."

"I didn't say anything," Zhané said.

"No, not...I heard something."

She gave him a hard look for a moment, then said, "Alright, whatever."

"It's not like it was before," he said, feeling the need to explain. The last time she had been around him, he'd been hearing not just voices that liked to call him names but cries from the girls who had died. It had been more than that, it had been screaming and scratching, he had heard footsteps. He had been convinced that they were haunting him, demanding they catch their killer.

Stress, he had been told by his therapist, and grief had caused the shift in tone and severity. A simple, straightforward answer to which he had responded, "No shit."

"It happens a lot less," he told her, "And it's just...little things now. It's not like it was."

"I believe you," she said, which made him feel better because he did not always believe himself.

With Noah not on her hip, but in a baby sling, she paced the perimeter of the dirt back lot, staring at the ground.

"What are we looking for?" he asked, staring at the dirt. He took a few steps closer to the back of the building, where the body had been propped up.

"Anything."

"I don't know that they leave things behind. I don't even know how they get here," he said, staring a rumpled patch of weeds. He had no way of knowing that this was where Kevin had been placed, but he felt it. He peered through the broken, grit-crusted window. "Hey."

"What?"

"Come here," he said.

She approached and he pointed out a thin, grayish drip on the window. It looked the way that blood would have if someone had cut themselves on the window, just the wrong color. She squinted at it, then took out her phone and took a picture.

"Can you go get me a rag out of the diaper bag?" she said.

He nodded and went, but when he returned and handed it to her, she did not use it to wipe up drool, but to snap off the piece of glass that had the drip on it. She wrapped it carefully then handed it to him.

"What am I supposed to do with this?" he asked.

She shrugged. "It's evidence."

He didn't argue. They were doing their best. He placed it in his back pocket and hoped he would remember to take it out before he sat down.

"I'm going to look into arrest records," she announced.

"Oh?"

"See if anyone went to jail four years ago and then got out recently. I figure it's worth a shot."

"I should get a library card," he said and she looked at him sideways. "You said you wanted to go a look at old papers, right, see if it's happened before?"

She nodded.

"I still think...I think this has got to be something newer. We would have heard, there would be more people talking about it. News travels in a town like this."

"Tell me about it," she said, looking past him at the police vehicle that had driven up to park beside hers.

David glanced around. The gas station was on a quiet road with nothing much else around; about five miles south, there were some houses and if you took a left turn half a mile up you could get to a baseball field. "How?" he asked.

"Someone must have driven by," she said with a shrug.

A cop got out and David's stomach sank to see it was Bryant. He didn't know how many cops there were in town, but there had to be about a dozen, not including higher-ups. He did not know why it had to be Bryant.

"Hey there," Bryant said.

"Hi," David returned.

Zhané said nothing but put her arm around Noah.

"Got a call that some people were out here, poking around," he said, "Figure that's you two."

"Figure," David said.

"Can I ask what you're doing around here?"

David had already come up with a lie; he'd started thinking as soon as he'd seen the car pull up. He was good at coming up with lies and good at sticking to them. It had pissed his parents off to no end. "Just came to spend some time together."

"At a crime scene?"

"It wasn't always a crime scene, you know," David said, "It, uh, we used to come out here in high school and stuff to, you know, fool around."

The most important part of lying was making it a little bit true. He and Zhané had come here to fool around; neither of their parents had allowed them to have the other over alone.

"And, what, romance was in the air?"

David shrugged. "I just got back into town, I don't know, figured I'd see where things went," he said, giving Zhané a glance that was half-embarrassed, half-amorous.

Bryant looked at her, too. "You two used to poke around other crime scenes, too."

David shrugged again. "I guess. They were our friends, though, sometimes...you know, you want to see. It doesn't feel real."

Bryant frowned. "Funeral isn't real enough for you?"

David asked, "Did a lot of your friends die during high school?"

The officer did not know how to respond to that. Most people's friends did not die, not until they were older, and usually they were not victims of the same killer within a few months of each other.

"Anyways, we didn't think it would be a big deal," David said, "But we'll go if this is still active or whatever."

He put a hand on Zhané's arm and walked her away before Bryant could say anything else. As she buckled Noah into his car seat, Bryant approached them again.

"If I were you, I'd be careful," he said to David.

I am careful, David thought. "Careful doing what?"

"You're gonna get caught. Whatever you're doing."

David raised his eyebrows. "Didn't think tryna get laid was such a crime around here."

It was a coarse thing to say, the kind of thing to which most people didn't know how to respond. Bryant didn't, at least not right away, so David got into the car while he was speechless and Zhané started to drive, glancing back in her mirror, taking the first turn she came to and then the next.

Eventually, they ended up on a residential street, pulled over to the curb. "Asshole," she accused, breaking the silence.

"Me?"

She snorted. "Yeah, you. You're gonna get me in trouble, dragging me around."

He laughed. "So no more crime scenes and no more visiting Jim Roberts."

"And maybe looking up stuff at the library won't go over well," she said, "At least not right now."

He nodded. The boy's body had only been found recently; the town needed time to cool off. The police were probably out of their minds with this; two dead bodies and no real suspects. People would start to get restless and angry, and they would get scared. And scared people never did anything good.

"Hey," he said.

"What?"

"Can we go to a thrift store while we're out? I need something to put all my clothes in," he said.

"Sure, why not?"

He didn't find a dresser at the thrift store, but he did find a side table, some plates, and a few pots and pans. The cashier advised him to check back next week and he said he would.

Friday, at work, at eleven-thirty Ahmed paused in the middle of what they were doing, which was putting together cling-wrapped packs of fruit in the stock room and looked at his watch. Seeming uncomfortable, he looked at David and said, "Hey, uh, I leave at eleven-thirty on Fridays. Are you good finishing this?"

"I don't know if I can handle it," David teased.

"Uh, it's just, I don't want to be late for Jumu'ah," he said, seeming to think David was serious.

"For what?"

"Friday Prayer," he clarified.

"No, it's fine, go," David said, "I was just teasing." He felt bad that he'd made him worry.

"You sure?"

"Yeah, it's fine, go ahead." David gave him a smile that he hoped would ease his discomfort.

Ahmed gave him a quick smile in return and left.

A few minutes later, Johnny said to him, "He doesn't really have to go, you know. If you need him to finish something."

David looked up, a pear in his hand. "I mean, but it's church. I'm not gonna tell someone they can't go to church."

"I already gotta let him take breaks for that praying shit," Johnny huffed.

"Uh. He does it real quick, though."

"He better."

David smiled nervously and placed a pear with three others in a tray. He tore a piece of cling wrap and sealed it.

He had not yet found it in him to go back to church; it wasn't that he didn't believe in God or that he no longer considered himself Catholic, but he'd been asked to pray to keep marriage sacred or to prevent the legality of abortion too many times. Jesus, David believed, would have cared much more about feeding the hungry and housing the homeless than abortion and gay marriage.

He wrapped another set of pears and reflected that it was difficult to feel a part of a church with such old-fashioned views on birth control and things like that.

Without Ahmed, the job seemed lonelier, though David felt that it would have been better if Johnny had not been in the back too, pacing around with a clipboard and looking at boxes and bags. Considering that he didn't seem fond of Ahmed, David wondered what Johnny's thoughts on LGBT people were.

Not favorable, he decided, though it wasn't necessarily a fair assumption make. A person could be racist without being homophobic.

At one, he left and found he couldn't wait for Monday.

5/27/15

DAVID WAITED for Ahmed so they could walk out together. It didn't feel intrusive, as the parking lot could be creepy at night, or worse, there was the likelihood that a straggling customer would be there, asking if they were still open, if they could just grab something quick.

"So you're going to leave early this Friday, too?" David asked.

"Um, yeah. Sometimes if it's busy, he'll call in someone to cover, but, uh, you know, it's kind of important," Ahmed said, then added, "To me."

"No, I get it."

"But I'll see you." He started to split off towards his car.

"Hey," David said.

Ahmed paused. "What?"

"Um. Do you want to hang out sometime?"

Ahmed tensed up and David wondered if he had read things wrong. "I'm not allowed to date," he said finally.

"Oh."

"Especially not a guy."

"It...you know, it doesn't have to be a date, we can just hang out," David said, "Like, totally no pressure or anything. I just. I don't know."

Ahmed sighed.

"Am I out of line here?" David asked, his stomach uneasy and his heart pattering. "I kind of, I don't know, got a, uh, you know, a feeling."

"Good Muslim boys are not allowed to be gay." Ahmed added, "At least, not according to my parents."

"Well, good Catholic boys aren't supposed to be bisexual," David told him with half a smile. "But, really, we can *just* hang out. If you want." He didn't care what they did, he just wanted to be around Ahmed.

"I don't know."

"Um, well, if you ever want to, text me."

"Yeah," Ahmed said, "I've got to go."

David nodded and stepped towards his car. "Bye."

Ahmed did not return the farewell, just walked away and got into his car without looking back. He drove away and David sat in his car. Things had not gone the way he'd expected; he hadn't stopped to consider what factors could be present in Ahmed's life.

He returned home and looked at the list of potential killers Zhané had found. Bill Clearwater had gone away for domestic abuse, Janet Mills had gone away for possession, and James Declan for robbery. They had all gotten out and returned to Milwater within the last six months.

"You think they'll just confess?" he asked her, handing the notebook back.

"I think they might talk to you about it. If you talk to them."

"Maybe." He shrugged.

"You look sad."

"Ahmed's not allowed to date."

"Who?"

"The boy at work."

"Oh, right. Well, there's other boys. Or girls."

"Yeah, just, I don't know, I like him," he said, feeling stupid. Of course, he liked him, he had asked him out.

"Maybe he was just nervous, he might come around. My cousin Shanae wasn't allowed to date but that didn't stop her."

He let out a sigh. "Want to binge watch *Supernatural* with me?"

She smiled. "Sure."

He went to bed around midnight, wishing he had something hold onto. Not something, specifically he wished he had his stuffed rabbit, Benjamin.

When he woke Thursday morning and checked his phone, he found a text from Ahmed which had been sent at about three in the morning.

It read, 'Hope I wasn't too weird I don't want things to be awkward at work'.

David put on his glasses and propped himself up. He wasn't sure what to say back so he stared at his phone, thinking. Finally, he typed 'sry just saw this. we're fine I didnt mean to make u uncomfortable. i wanna keep being friends no matter what'. He didn't know if saying friends was too forward. They had only worked together for a week and a half. 'Friends no matter what' seemed too forceful so he amended it to 'friends even if that's all.

He hit send and set his phone down on his chest, not wanting to just stare at it until he got a text back. He looked up at the ceiling, praying. After several minutes, his phone buzzed and he looked at it.

Ahmed had replied 'ok good im glad' and then a moment later followed up with a smiley face, a colon and a parenthesis, not an emoji.

David returned the smiley face, feeling pleased. It would be too much to offer to hang out again, but maybe if he could think of something non-threatening, a group activity or something public, Ahmed would accept the invite.

He wondered if it was wrong of him to want to spend time with someone who had said they couldn't date, if he was putting his own agenda over Ahmed's needs. It wasn't that he hoped spending time together would change his mind about dating, it was that he wanted to spend time with him.

And, he thought, Ahmed had not told him off. He had not said he wasn't gay or that David was out of line. Tomorrow they would see each other and David would really be able to tell if things had gone sideways.

As they ate breakfast, Zhané looked at her phone, then looked at him and asked, "Do you want to come to my brother's barbecue?"

"Uh."

"It's on Sunday."

"Do you want me to go?" he asked, not sure why she had invited him and having no real desire to go.

"Yes."

He heard a knock at the door and started to get up, then asked, "Did you hear that?"

"What?"

"The door?"

"No."

He nodded and didn't go to answer it; another knock didn't come. "Does your family really give you a hard time?"

"Of course, they do. They worked their asses off to get what they had, to be middle class and suburban and what do I do to pay them back?" she asked and then proceeded to put up a finger for each offense, "Become a sex worker. Get pregnant at nineteen. Keep the baby as a single mother *and* continue working as a prostitute instead of sticking with nursing."

"I...man, I don't know, it seems like it's really working out for you, though," he said.

"It seems that way because it *is* that way. This works for me. Maybe it won't always but for right now, I'm pretty pleased. And it's not like I've got some pimp who knocks me around and makes me do things, I work for myself."

He reached over to the high chair to take Noah's hand and give it a little squeeze. "Besides, this is a good baby. When's his birthday, anyway?"

"November fifteenth," she said.

He put an event in his phone. "Is that the term you prefer? Sex worker?" he asked.

"Yes. I want to go talk to Janet Mills today," she said.

"You think it's her?"

"Hmm, I think...I mean, I have this suspicion that they, uh, these things, if they're real, I think they get people to do their dirty work, right?"

"Yeah."

"And I think they get people who...don't take this the wrong way, but people that no one will believe," she said, "There's you and your thing."

"Schizophrenia," he supplied.

"Yeah. And if a druggie shows up with a missing kidney and says that formless black monsters took it...well, she just had a bad trip, didn't she?"

"That makes sense," he agreed, not liking that his word had been deemed so unreliable but understanding why. "Do you believe me?"

She tapped her nails against her glass for a second, then explained, "It's not that I think you're lying or making things up.

It's that all of this is...you know, it's crazy. It's outside my realm of experience. I want to believe you."

He whistled the *X-Files* theme.

She gave his arm a little smack. "I don't think this is just you hallucinating or anything, though."

"Thanks."

Following breakfast, they went to visit Janet Mills, who lived in the shitty part of town. Zhané parked the car and nodded towards the house. "Go ahead."

"What?"

"She might be all drugged up, I'm not bringing Noah over there. Go talk to her."

He sighed and got out of the car, approaching the small, dingy house. The lawn needed to be mowed and several dead animals lying on the walkway up told him there was a cat here somewhere.

He knocked on the door and got no answer, so he waited a minute and then knocked again. There was no car in the driveway, but that didn't mean no one was home. He thought he heard movement within but he wasn't sure that it was real.

He knocked one more time. "Hey, is anyone home?" He thought he heard movement again, so he called, "I, uh, I want to talk to you. About the things. The visitors."

He heard the patterning of nails on tile and then barking. He peered in the window and saw a tiny dog.

David went back to the car, tapping on Zhané's window. She rolled it down and asked, "What?"

"You have a burner phone, right? For the sex stuff?"

"Yes."

"Write down the number, I'm gonna leave it."

She made a face but searched her car for a pen and a piece of paper, then wrote down the number and gave it to him.

"Pen?"

She handed it over.

Above her number, he wrote, 'Janet, The things visit me too. The harvesters. Call me.' He put the note on her door; either Janet would know what he meant and call or she would think he was nuts and throw it away.

He returned to the car and asked, "Are you gonna make me do this at the other two houses?"

"Not today. I've got a feeling about this one," she said, beginning to drive.

She brought him to the library and he said, "I thought you decided to skip this part?"

"Yeah, didn't you want to get a library card?"

"Oh, right, yeah," he said.

At the library, Zhané told him to go in, that she had to make a call, so he took Noah from his car seat and carried him inside. Several people looked at him when he walked in and the person at the front desk, a guy in his late twenties, frowned at him. David didn't think he meant to frown because once David stood before him, he pleasantly asked, "Hi, can I help you?"

"I, um, wanted to get a library card."

"Sure, what's this little guy's name?"

"No, for me," David clarified, "I just got back into town."

"Oh, alright, sure, I just need to see your driver's license."

"Oh." David hadn't thought this through. He took out his wallet and checked his license, not sure what address it gave on it. "I, um, I'll come back, I guess, I have to change my license."

The man behind the front desk nodded. "Sure, no problem."

David turned and left, feeling stupid; he should have known this. He went back outside and waited for Zhané to finish her phone call. When he told her the situation, she said, "Well, I'm not taking you to the DMV. That place is a hellscape."

He cracked a smile.

She took him home, where he spent the rest of the afternoon playing with Noah and reading him books. Once or twice, he looked up to find Zhané looking at them, her arms crossed and the look on her face somewhere between wistful and annoyed.

"What?" he asked finally.

"Nah, just figures you'd show up once he's sleeping through the night and not screaming all the time," she said. "Could have used someone else around for that ear infection, though."

The strange wish that he had been around for those times as well hit David unexpectedly. It had been easy to settle into this life, to be comfortable with his old friend, to be comfortable in her home and with her child as though he hadn't lost four years. He did not know what he would do when that next call came, or when the call after that one came.

5/29/15

THE IGA had been open for about an hour when David had to seek out Ahmed to ask, "Hey, uh, who here is Mexican?"

"What?" Ahmed asked, his brow furrowed as he looked up from the spill he mopped.

"This lady, uh, she made me carry her groceries to her car and was all pissed that some Mexican guy was rude to her? But I don't think anyone Mexican even *works* here."

"Oh," Ahmed said with a large exhale, all through his nose. "Me. That's me. If you ever get a complaint about someone who's, basically, you know, not white, that's me."

Feeling like he was staring, David forced himself to blink, not sure what to say to that. He tried to think of something comforting but he had nothing. "I'm sorry people do that to you," he said.

Ahmed said, mostly to himself and not sounding convincing, "Well, it's better than being called a terrorist."

"Jesus," David breathed. "That's really fucked up, I'm sorry."

The other man gave a shrug and returned to mopping.

David hesitated in the aisle for a few seconds, wanting to make this right or to comfort him somehow, but he didn't know what to do or what his place was in the situation.

For the rest of the shift, he thought about what to do, until

Ahmed found him at slightly before eleven-thirty to say, "I'm leaving, unless you need me to stay."

David set down the case of yogurt he'd been about to take out onto the floor. "Ahmed, you don't have to check in. I won't ever ask you to be late for, uh...your services." He couldn't remember the name of the prayer service.

"Oh. Thanks."

"And, um, if you ever want me to say something to someone. You know, if they're being assholes and you don't feel comfortable. You know, like, um, with your name and stuff?" he offered. Being white, he had the privilege of being able to call out other white people more easily.

"Oh."

"Just let me know."

Ahmed nodded. "Thanks." He looked at his watch. "Bye."

"Bye," David said and returned to bringing the yogurt out to the refrigerated section.

When he returned home from work, Zhané asked if he wanted to go see a movie, as her mother had taken Noah again. He agreed immediately, then asked, "Hey, can I—"

"Invite Ahmed?" she asked.

He nodded.

"Sure."

He grinned, took out his phone and typed 'My friend and I are going to see fury road later do u want to come?'. It was perfect, he thought, since three people would not be a date.

Minutes later he received the response 'I'm supposed to hang out with my cousin so he'd come with me'.

Peering over at his phone, Zhané snorted and he stepped away, holding his phone up higher so she couldn't read it. 'That's fine. the movie starts at 425' he wrote back, butterflies in his stomach.

He fought the urge to follow up with something cute, but he couldn't keep the smile off his face. Zhané shook her head at him and said, "You're a dork."

"I'm not, I'm just excited."

"Alright, not to be a bitch, but what are you gonna do if he's not into you?" she asked. "Like, he said he doesn't date."

"It's not a date."

"Then what's that look on your face for?"

He sighed. "It's a crush. If we're just going to be friends then I'll get over it."

"Just like that?"

"Just like that," he said.

She made a face but didn't say anything.

He knew that she wasn't wrong. He was treading on dangerous ground, trying to hang out with a guy he liked but who had no intention of taking things further. It could go disastrously, but David could also imagine two decent outcomes: he really would get over his crush, allowing them to be nothing more than friends, or maybe Ahmed would give dating a chance and not face any severe repercussions from his family. David's parents, as Catholic and Republican as they were, had never supported him and they had certainly tried to convince him his sexuality was a phase, something to be ignored, but they hadn't ever done much other than that. He had not been sent to a conversion camp or abused.

"Alright, well, let's go get some snacks." She shouldered her bag and fished out her keys.

At four-seventeen, David had checked his phone six times since entering the theater until Zhané elbowed him in the side. "I'm assuming that's them," she said.

He looked up, saw Ahmed with another person and waved. The two went to the ticket line and then came over to stand next to David. Gesturing to the teenager next to him, Ahmed said, "This is my cousin Omar."

David waved. "Hi, I'm David."

"Hi," Omar said.

"This is Zhané," David said.

"Did you get your tickets already?" Ahmed asked.

"Yeah, yeah, we're all set," he said

In the theater, Omar sat the furthest in, followed by Ahmed and David next to each other, with Zhané on the end. David wanted to say something but was unable to settle on one thing. Finally, he asked, "Have you seen the other Mad Max movies?"

"Uh, I think one of them," he said, "It was on TV a lot?"

David nodded. "This one is supposed to be really...um." He glanced at Zhané but she wasn't paying attention. "Uh. People liked it?"

"Yeah, I heard it was good, too."

A few quiet minutes later, the lights went down and the previews started. About ten minutes into the actual movie, Zhané handed him the bag of Swedish Fish she'd smuggled in for him. He ate a few, then offered some to Ahmed, leaning in a little closer to whisper, "You want some?"

"What are they?"

"Swedish Fish."

"Uh. Can I see the bag?"

"Why?"

"I have to check the ingredients," Ahmed explained.

From beside him, Omar whispered, "Swedish Fish are okay."

David thought that checking the ingredients on everything would be a pain in the ass but kept that to himself. He also thought that he'd like to reach over and hold Ahmed's hand, but he didn't. He did continue to offer him candies throughout the movie.

When the movie finished, they stood together in the parking lot for a while, the four of them around Zhané's car, with Omar and Zhané totally absorbed in their conversation about the look of the movie, raving about the colors, the costumes, the makeup effects. Zhané had always wanted to pursue art and film as a career, though her parents had always reminded her that it was impractical and that she wasn't talented enough. Omar, it seemed, faced a similar dilemma currently.

"He is really good," Ahmed confided to David as the two of them stood to the side, watching the others talk.

David looked at his feet. He'd never had any talent to pursue; he'd been decent at soccer and swimming but had never had any delusions of grandeur about being a competitive athlete. His grades had been average and his interests had been nothing more than interests, except for his fascination with true crime, but knowing too much about the Manson murders was not something to put on a resume. Nothing had ever motivated him or galvanized him towards a career path.

"What about you?" David asked.

"Hmm?"

"What are you good at?"

Ahmed shrugged. "Nothing, really. I mean, nothing you make a career out of, really."

"That's not just nothing, then, what is it?"

"I, uh, I like to write," he said, sounding embarrassed.

"Really?" David asked. He would have never guessed. "What do you write?"

Ahmed shrugged. "Short stories, mostly."

"That's really cool," David said. "What kind of stuff do you write about?"

Ahmed shrugged again. "I don't know, just stuff."

David didn't press the issue.

Ahmed's phone began to ring and he sighed. He answered and David did not understand a word he said, but he would have bet real money that he was talking to his mother based on the tone and nothing else. The conversation lasted about five minutes and at the end, Ahmed turned to look at his cousin.

Before Ahmed could speak, Omar said, "Dude, your parents are *so* strict."

"Oh, gee, I never noticed," Ahmed said.

"Your parents aren't?" Zhané asked.

"Our moms are sisters but his mom is older. Like a lot, right? Like, fifteen years?" Omar said, "So my mom grew up here and Auntie Safia was already a teenager when they came over."

"That's a big gap," David agreed.

"Oh, well, there's other kids in between," Omar said.

"My mom's the oldest," Ahmed said.

"And my mom's the baby," Omar added.

David nodded.

"Anyway." Ahmed let out a breath. "I've got to go before she files a missing person report. I'll see you at work."

Instead of saying goodbye like he should have, David said, "I'm glad you could come. It was fun."

Ahmed's mouth hung open for a second, his eyes meeting David's before he looked away. He jangled his keys. "Yeah. Me, too." He glanced at his cousin, then told the empty space between David and Zhané, "Thanks for the invite."

As Ahmed and Omar walked away, David heard Omar ask, "Is he gay?" but did not hear the answer Ahmed gave if he gave one at all.

After hearing that, he turned to Zhané and asked, "Am I gay?"

"I don't know, are you?"

"No, I mean, like, do I come off as gay?"

"I don't know. Sometimes. Why?"

"Just, I don't know, how do I come off as bisexual?"

She snorted. "Do you want people to know?"

He thought for a minute, not sure how to answer, but eventually settled on, "I don't want people to think I'm something I'm not. And I'm not gay but I'm not straight either. You know?"

"Sure."

"Is that weird?"

"It's definitely the least weird thing about you."

He smiled.

She reached over and gave his back a rub. "Come on, let's get home, I think Mom will be dropping off Noah soon."

When Zhané's mother dropped off the baby, she gave David a look and asked, "You're here again?"

He glanced at Zhané. His first instinct had been to say that he lived there, but he didn't know how much she wanted her family to know.

"Mom," Zhané scolded. "Am I not allowed to have friends?"

"You know, it would break your Nana's heart to know you're doing this."

"Having friends?"

"You know what I meant."

"Well, she's never said anything about it."

Amanda paused and looked at her daughter. "You didn't tell her, did you? You trying to give her a heart attack?"

"She doesn't care."

"Zhané!"

"What? Nana might be old, but she isn't some uptight prude like you make her out to be."

Amanda looked at David again and he pretended he didn't notice, instead nibbling on Noah's fingers and babbling to him. The baby gurgled happily and David could almost convince himself that his ex-girlfriend's mother wasn't staring him down.

"Did you need anything else?" Zhané asked her mother.

"You better be there tomorrow."

"I know. Bye."

"I'm not messing around, your brother—"

"I said I'd be there," Zhané said.

Once Amanda had left, David looked at his friend and said, "She's really displeased about all this."

"It's not her life."

"I know. Do you really want me to come to that thing? Your brother's party or whatever?"

"I just don't want to have to be there alone. It's like...they all treat me like I did something horrible, like I'm smoking crack in back alleys and leaving my baby home alone for hours. You know, they make these assumptions and then they don't want to hear it when I say it's not like that."

"I understand," he said and felt the need to clarify, "Not about being a sex worker or anything, but like...my parents know I'm bi and they still...they think everything with a guy is automatically a hook-up and that someday I'll grow out of it and just marry a girl."

"Did you have a boyfriend?"

He shook his head. "Not really. Like...I knew it couldn't ever be anything serious cause I was a patient and he was an orderly and, you know, older than me. Not like, you know, *a lot* older, but about ten years. Louis."

"So what happened?"

"We got caught," David said with a shrug. "My parents wanted to press charges, made him seem like a rapist, but...I don't know, I really liked him. He was sweet. But anyways, he got fired and my parents said they'd press charges if he kept in contact."

"Shit."

"So after that I, I don't know, I kind of slept around to piss them off," he said, "Which wasn't that bad, it was...easy. You know, it didn't matter, I didn't have to worry if I'd get someone in trouble or if it would ever get serious. Sometimes it's easier to not give a shit."

"See, you should come and tell my family this, they'll finally have someone else to give shit to," she said with half-smile, though he could tell by her face that she felt bad for him.

He felt bad for himself, too, a little bit. It didn't do any good to wallow in self-pity but considering the details of his life for the last half-decade, he felt entitled to a little wallowing.

She glanced at his arms, which today were bare, showing the scars that lined his arms. He waited for her to ask, but she didn't.

Instead, she said, "This family shit, the way they act, it's the only part of my life that sucks, but it's also the only part I can't do anything about."

He nodded.

She took Noah from him and gave the baby a kiss. "Don't worry, Mommy won't ever treat you like that."

Without warning, David felt the need to lay down. "I'm gonna go take a nap or whatever."

"Are you gonna eat?"

"Don't wait for me, I'll figure out something on my own."

"You sure?"

"Yeah, thanks, I was just up early, you know?"

She nodded.

He returned to his apartment and crawled into bed, consumed

by the need to sleep and the desire to never wake up; he never ate dinner, instead sleeping straight through until morning.

WHEN ZHANÉ woke him in the morning, he was ravenous and ate several bowls of cereal while she gave him the rundown of what to expect for the day. When he reached for the cereal to pour a third bowl, she stopped what she was saying to ask, "Are you serious?"

"What?"

"You already had two."

"I didn't have dinner."

"Well, there's gonna be food there."

"Oh." He returned the box of cereal to the cabinet. "Is your family going to think we're dating?"

"I don't care."

He reached over and gave Noah's foot, bare and pudgy, a little squeeze. "Is there an occasion? Or is this a just-for-fun barbecue?"

"I don't know," she said and he got the feeling he shouldn't ask any more questions, so he played around on his phone. He could not believe that it was almost June or that he would be twenty-one in a few weeks.

Noah burbled something and David looked over at him. He reached over and offered his finger to the baby, who grabbed it, smearing David with baby food. "Can I help you?" he asked.

Noah babbled.

"Oh, what? I can't believe it," he said.

Zhané looked up from her phone to watch them. She gave the

baby a pat on the head and said, "I know, you made a friend." To David, she said, "My brother's gonna be pissed."

"Why?"

"Oh, Noah's terrified of him," she said, "Cries every time he comes anywhere near him."

"Really?" David couldn't see that. Noah seemed to be an agreeable baby, not particularly fussy or needy. "Are you afraid of your uncle?"

"He's too loud," she said, "Like he has no control over the volume of his voice."

David thought back. Her brother was five years older than her, already out of school and away at college by the time he and Zhané had dated. They'd only really interacted a few dozen times over the years and David's stomach sank when he asked, "He's gonna ask me to dance, isn't he?"

Zhané frowned for a second, then the realization came over her and she cried, "Oh, shit! You're right, I bet he is."

It had been sophomore year and Zhané and Becca had persuaded him to do the talent show with them, thinking that having a gangly boy doing the Single Ladies dance along with them would be particularly hilarious. During their practices, they'd learned that David had the uncanny ability to memorize and flawlessly execute any dance for which there was a music video. Left to his own devices, he was a hopeless dancer; he could not freestyle or pick up a beat, but if he studied a choreographed dance for long enough, he could imitate it perfectly.

Nicki, who had not wanted anything to do with the dance, had watched, laughing until she'd almost had an asthma attack.

"You learn any new dances?" she asked.

He shrugged, not wanting to admit that memorizing dances had become a hobby of his while he'd been away. There had been nothing else to do, especially considering the restrictions on his access to technology, but he had found DVDs and VHSs of old music videos.

"I can do the Thriller dance like a motherfucker," he admitted, getting the laugh he'd hoped for out of her.

At the sound of his mother's laugh, Noah giggled triumphantly, kicking his feet. David felt his heart melt a little bit and almost let the tears spill down his cheeks. He had not grown used to these frequent and intense emotional bursts, but they were better than the first few years of anger and confusion, followed by several more of hazy numbness.

David reached over and gave the baby a pat on the head. He was, for now, intensely happy, but also terrified to think of what would happen the next time those things called him. He tried not to think about it, taking Noah out of the high chair and saying, "Come on, little man, let's get you cleaned up. You got a messy face. You got some in your hair, how'd you do that?"

Noah babbled back to him as David washed his face and got the food out of his hair. He wondered again what his life would have been if his parents had not taken him away to Vermont, but he knew that there would likely be no Noah. If felt presumptuous to think that his presence had that much influence over Zhané's life; maybe they would have stayed broken up, or broken up again, and maybe Noah was one of those predestined things, a little life that would have happened no matter what.

Not that it mattered now. David gave the baby a kiss.

"Sap," Zhané accused.

He shrugged.

"I knew you were, under all that spooky shit."

He gave a small smile. People had always assumed that David was cold on the inside, twisted up and rotten, just because he could detail the crimes of Dahmer and Gacy the way most guys rattled off stats from their favorite teams. And maybe he was a little rotten and twisted, given that even now he could not look away from gore, that he wondered what it would be like to touch a corpse or feel the warmth of another person's guts.

When he had killed the man in 8F, it hadn't been like that. It had not been fascinating or thrilling, it had been nerve-wracking, and he had fled the scene as soon as the things had come and descended on the corpse. The crime itself had been too simple, nothing more than a few blows to the head and then waiting, waiting for his breathing to stop, for his heart to still and waiting, most of all, for the things. 8F hadn't received a lot of visitors, ever, and David had sat in the apartment, waiting for the things to arrive. It had taken hours for them to show and those hours had been jumpy, leaving David flinching every time someone walked by.

No, David decided, he was not cut out for murder in real life, no matter how much the crimes of others interested him. No more, he decided, no more killing, no more even planning to kill someone. He hoped he could stick by that choice, but he worried that these things, their visits and demands, would drive him to kill, either someone else or himself, to escape having his own pieces stolen from him.

"Hey," Zhané said, snapping him out of his murderous contemplations.

"What?"

"What's wrong?"

"Nothing."

She frowned. "You sure?"

"Yeah, I was just thinking," he said. Thinking about whether or not he would capitulate again, whether or not he would be driven to suicide. He pushed that aside. He would deal with things as they came, as there was nothing else he could do. "What time are we supposed to be there?"

"One."

"Ugh," he said. Hours of waiting.

He waited with Noah, playing with the baby and napping with him as well, unintentionally falling asleep halfway through a children's show with the baby on his chest. Zhané woke him up at twelve and they drove to her brother's house, which was not in Milwater. They stopped to pick up her grandmother before they left town.

David didn't know what her brother did, but he was surprised when he saw the house. It was large, with a lush, landscaped yard. He glanced at Zhané, who had a sour look on her face. Her grandmother gave her a pat on the arm.

They did not go through the house, but walked around back, following a stone walkway that brought them to a fenced-in backyard full of people. Zhané's parents he recognized right away and heard her brother before he saw him.

"Nana!" the older man cried.

Tall, but not as tall as David, with an athletic build, Zhané's brother swooped down to hug his grandmother, and then his sister, at which point the baby started to fuss, his face scrunching up.

"Aw, little guy, what's wrong?" her brother asked, almost shouting.

"Malik, you're too loud," Zhané scolded, stepping back as he reached out a hand towards the already spooked child.

The grandmother walked away, going over to greet the rest of her family.

Malik turned his eyes from Noah to David. "I didn't know you were bringing someone," he said.

"It's just David," she said.

"Who?"

"From high school," she said.

David shook Malik's hand when it was offered, not particularly wanting to do so. He felt the other man's eyes on his arm, staring at the scars, then darting away.

"From high school?" Malik asked, studying David's face.

He nodded.

"David, uh…"

"Craft," David offered.

"Yeah," Malik said with a smile, looking pleased. "I remember you. What happened to you? You up and left. Broke her poor little heart," he teased, giving Zhané a glance.

She rolled her eyes.

"I was institutionalized," David said, not wanting to admit it but he had given up on finding a better lie. And, he told himself, it was nothing to lie about.

"What, like prison?" Malik asked, his eyebrows shooting up.

David almost said yes. It would be easier, and funnier, to let them think he had gone to jail. "No," he said and decided not to elaborate. If Malik wanted, he could google what institutionalized meant.

They stood for a moment in uncomfortable silence until David said, "Nice yard."

"Thanks."

He wanted to know what Malik did for a job to be able to afford this. Someone called their host away and David surveyed the yard again, then leaned in to ask Zhané, "Why are there so many white people?"

"Oh, that's his girlfriend's family."

He looked around, eying the white people. "Which one?"

"No, she's mixed," she said. She pointed with her eyes towards a tall, thin woman with light brown skin who looked to be around Malik's age. "Mom's a lawyer, dad's an orthodontist and she's a fucking princess."

"Ah," David said.

"How's your brother afford this house?"

"Oh, he's a software developer," she said.

"Really?"

She shrugged. "Yeah, I thought he'd be a burnt-out car salesman or something. I fucking hate him."

"Zhané, are you just going to hide in the corner or what?" her mother called over. "Bring that grandbaby over here."

Zhané sighed and went; David trailed behind her, eying Malik's girlfriend, who was absolutely picture perfect, with her full lips and wide nose, with her doe eyes and beautiful mass of curls. When she laughed, it sounded like music.

Amanda took Noah, cooing over him.

"Is she a model?" David asked.

"Working on becoming an OB-GYN," Zhané answered.

"What's that nasty tone for?" her father asked. "Daysha's a smart girl, she works hard."

"I never said she didn't," Zhané said. She walked away towards a long table laid out with snacks. She didn't warn David that she was leaving, so he stood awkwardly beside her father, whose name he couldn't recall.

"How do you know my daughter?" her father asked.

"Um. We went to high school together. I took her to junior prom?" He was surprised how easily her family had forgotten him; he wondered if his family remembered Zhané.

The other man still looked at him, not remembering.

"My name's David."

"Oh, the one she dumped."

"That's me."

"Cause you were hearing voices and all that," he elaborated.

"Yup."

Her father asked, "So what are you doing now?"

"Working," David said.

"They're *friends*," Zhané's mother told her husband.

"Friends," her father repeated.

"Yeah, that's the plan." David did not like the tone either of them had. He wished Zhané would come back.

"You know, she's got her head mixed up about stuff right now," her father lectured, "But she's a good girl. She's a mother."

"Okay."

"So she has a *baby*, she doesn't need someone coming around—"

"Hey, listen," David interrupted.

"Someone who hears voices and all that," her father continued over him.

"Hey!" David protested, not liking that at all. The statement slid through every inch of armor he'd ever gathered. "The fact that I have schizophrenia *doesn't* mean that I'd be a bad boyfriend."

Zhané came back with a paper plate full of snacks. "What?" she asked, glancing at her father.

"Nothing," her parents chorused.

Zhané looked at him and he shrugged. He would let her know later, maybe. He took out his phone when he felt it buzz. A text from Ahmed. Butterflies bloomed in his stomach. Only one word, 'sup'. He replied, 'nothing at a thing why?' and wondered if he had been too vague.

A few minutes later he got another text that said, 'Just bored'.

Bored and thinking of me, David thought elatedly. He did not know what to say; everything seemed either too flirty or standoffish. 'had fun the other night' he decided on.

"Who are you texting?" asked a raspy voice accompanied by the smell of cigarettes.

He looked down to see Zhané's grandmother standing by him. She did not have a cigarette in hand but must have just finished one, absolutely reeking in the most comforting way. Smoking reminded David of Sundays after church at his grandfather's house, who had smoked literally until the day he had died, a fresh butt in the ashtray.

"A guy," he said.

"Mom, I wish you wouldn't smoke," Zhané's mother complained.

"I wish a lot of things, Mandy," said the grandmother. To David, she asked, "What guy?"

"From work."

"I hear you're living in Reggie's old room."

He nodded. "Working on making it livable."

"He was so mad." She looked across the party at a middle-aged man.

"Mom," Amanda scolded.

To David, she said, "I'm gonna go have a seat over in the shade. Why don't you bring that baby over to me?"

He looked at Zhané's mother and she handed the child over to him, not looking pleased. As they walked away, he heard Amanda warn her daughter, "You better watch him around Noah. You don't know what he's capable of."

"Mom!" Zhané snapped. David could imagine the look she'd be giving her mother.

The old woman settled herself into a lawn chair and he placed

Noah on her lap, sitting beside her. "About Zhané."

"What about her?" he asked, starting to feel queasy.

"I'm glad you came back," she said, "She's been awful lonely."

"We're just friends."

"I didn't think you'd be texting some boy if you were more than friends. But you and her, you go way back."

"Do you remember me?" he asked. He remembered her. He remembered most of Zhané's family, but sight if not by name. He'd been around for birthday parties and cookouts; they'd played in the sprinkler in her parents' front yard.

She gave him a look. "I'm not that old."

"No, I mean...everyone else, her parents act like they don't know who I am, but we were friends for *years*."

"Well, all you white boys *do* look the same." She cackled.

He gave a small smile.

"No, David, you...you got forgot on purpose," she told him. "You're nothing but a bad memory for them. That was a bad time for this town and you ended up right in the middle of it. And now it's happening again, isn't it?"

A thought came to him, a wonderful thought that meant maybe they wouldn't have to visit a racist old woman in her stinking trailer. "Have you lived here all your life?"

"No, just since the seventies."

Long enough, he thought. "Do you remember if things like this happen a lot?"

"Like what?"

"People going missing, getting killed?"

"No. That summer, what was it? Twenty eleven? When they found that first body it was the first murder we'd had in twenty years."

"Really?"

"Sure, the last one was when Bobby Jenkins left his baby in the car on purpose," she recalled. "Why?"

He shrugged. "Because it's happening again."

"You think we got some kind of serial killer loose in town?"

"I don't know. It's weird, though, isn't it?"

"It's not normal, that's for sure," she agreed. "I see that man, Jim, sometimes, I go check on him. No one visits much. All he's got is a brother."

His phone buzzed, making him jump. He had forgotten that he'd been texting anyone. He glanced down; Ahmed had taken a long time to text him back and his answer had been short, just 'yeah'.

"What's that look?" the old woman asked.

He shook his head. "Just. I don't know."

"What?"

"He's not allowed to date," he confessed. "And I don't want to be pushy or, I don't know, make him go against what he believes."

"What does he believe?"

David thought, then answered, "I don't know."

As a Catholic, he knew that what the Church said and what he believed were different. He had not asked if Ahmed believed that he shouldn't be gay or if his parents were the only ones who thought that.

She suggested, "Maybe you should ask."

"It feels nosy."

She shook her head. "It's better to ask now."

"Probably," he admitted, looking down at his phone. He couldn't do it through text and he couldn't ask at work.

"Go get Zhané, he needs a change," she said.

"Hmm?" He glanced over at Zhané, who was talking with a few people. "No, I can do it."

He took Noah, retrieved the diaper bag, and found Malik with his girlfriend to ask, "Hey, where can I change him?"

Malik seemed to hesitate. "I'll show you."

He followed the man into the house, which was clean and painted in neutrals with thoughtful accents. It was a house that belonged in a magazine. Malik brought him to the half-bath where they kept their washer and dryer.

"Thanks."

"About my sister—" he began, his voice at a normal volume but with the cadence of something being said in confidence.

"No," David said.

"Excuse me?" he asked, louder.

Noah began to fuss.

David said, "What she does, who she sees, it's not your business."

"Do you know what she does?" Malik asked, back to his quieter tone. "Do you know how she makes money?"

"Yes."

"She's not a nurse," he warned.

"I know," David said. "It doesn't matter."

"She needs a good man to set her straight, make her honest," Malik confided. "Someone should take care of her."

David didn't know what to say. He could protest or lie, either option seeming better than being trapped in this conversation while holding Noah and his poopy diaper. "I really need to change this diaper."

Malik blinked. It was not the answer he'd wanted or expected. "Please."

"Yeah, uh, fine," Malik said.

David changed the baby and returned to Zhané's side. He finally texted Ahmed back 'I'm up to hang out whenever u are' but got only 'ok' as an answer. It felt cold and he wanted desperately for the blow to have been softened by a smiley or some other emoji. The old woman was right, he needed to ask Ahmed.

He stayed by Zhané's side for the rest of the cookout, not wanting to be accosted by any other family members who wanted to know his intentions with Zhané. Around five, Zhané's grandmother came up to her, cigarette in hand, and said she was going to have this smoke and then she wanted to go home.

"Alright, Nana," Zhané said and began to make her rounds to say goodbye to the family. She did not bother to say goodbye to Daysha's family. She almost snuck out without saying goodbye to her brother, but he saw her and came over.

"Hey! You heading out?" he asked.

"Yeah. Nana's getting tired."

"We're glad you could come!" he boomed.

Noah's face scrunched up.

"See you later." She took a step back, adjusting the baby on her hip and trying to adjust the diaper bag as well.

She struggled and David took it from her without thinking about it, slinging it over his shoulder.

"Take care of yourself," Malik said gravely.

She gave him a smile that wasn't really a smile at all, but an irritated approximation. "Bye." She walked away.

David followed after, but Malik caught him by the arm, his hands large and strong, and pulled him closer. David pulled back, disoriented by the grab, panicked and nearly woozy.

Malik said, "Like I said, she needs someone who can take of her."

David knew he was staring, wide-eyed. He tightened his grip on the strap of the bag and then hurried away, past Zhané, who stepped out of his way. He found her grandmother leaning against the car, smoking and he couldn't stop there either. He needed air, space, he needed to go somewhere else.

He heard her call after him and he dropped the diaper bag by the car as he passed it. He didn't know what else to do so he walked, ready to run if he needed to.

"David!" he heard from behind him. "Jesus, David, hang on."

He should stop. He knew he should.

"Run," suggested a familiar voice.

Running was a bad idea, he shouldn't do it. It was best not to listen to voices that weren't real, he knew that by now.

He heard her shoes slapping on the road. A car honked and he looked around to see that his flight had taken him into the road.

Zhané grabbed him by the hand and pulled him onto the lawn. "Hey."

He tightened his grip on her hand; her hand felt real. Her hand was small and warm, it belonged to a friend.

"What's happened?"

He closed his eyes, then opened them, glancing at her face. "I...I *don't like* being grabbed."

She immediately tried to release his hand. "I'm sorry."

He didn't let go of her. "No. I mean. Your brother."

"He grabbed you?" she asked.

"He didn't mean anything by it. I know he didn't."

She reached out and held his hand with both of hers. "You're okay now. Come on, back to the car, alright? We'll go home."

He reached up with his free hand and wiped his eyes. He wanted to go home. He followed as she walked him back to the car, where her grandmother had climbed into the backseat to sit beside Noah's car seat. She had her hand on the baby's foot, cooing to him.

He got into the passenger seat and picked viciously at his nails until they had dropped off the old woman and returned home. They sat in the driveway for a moment, Noah burbling to himself in the backseat.

"David," came her voice, quiet and calm, "Do you need to talk?"

"It's just." He could say no more.

He knew what he wanted to tell her; he wanted to talk about the orderlies who had not been kind, the ones who had come into the job rotten or been turned rotten by years of working a shitty, unforgiving job. There had been times when he'd refused meds, refused to go or stay where they told him, things like that and they had made him do the things he'd refused to do. And there had been times when he'd been out of control, too, he wouldn't deny that, but being grabbed the way they'd grabbed him had never made him feel any safer or any more in control.

One more thing that marked him as abnormal, as no good and broken.

Zhané reached over and held his hand. "It isn't you, you know."

He glanced up at her.

"It's everyone else. When a cop shoots someone, they ask 'well, what was he doing?' and when a girl gets raped, they ask 'well what was she wearing?' but those are shitty questions. It's not their fault and it's not yours either, David, alright? It's not taking care of people if you're hurting them more than you're helping."

"They were scared, most of them, I think. The orderlies and nurses. I could have hurt someone. I know I did a couple of times. But not because I meant it."

"That's a bullshit excuse."

He looked up.

"David, I saw you when things were bad and I don't know what other kinds of people they had to deal with, what kind of precedent had been set by other patients and policies and all that shit, but you're a runner, David, not a fighter."

Noah let out a small screech that was not yet a cry, enough to let them know he was irritated with sitting in his car seat.

"I want to go in," he said.

She nodded and got out, taking up the diaper bag and the baby.

He followed her in, still trapped in his memories of Mansfield. Some of the staff had been kind and patient, they had talked to him first, before anything else. They had waited until something had happened before they touched him and they had worked hard deescalate things. Of course, not everything could be deescalated, but that was life.

Inside, he sat on the carpet and Zhané placed Noah beside him, on a crookedly crocheted blanket that must have been someone's first attempt. He reached out to touch the stitches. From where he lay on his belly, Noah wiggled around, pushing himself up and down, squirming forward to get to things. He would be crawling soon and walking after that.

Noah grabbed a ring of oversized plastic keys and shoved them into his mouth, drooling everywhere. After a few minutes, he flipped himself onto his back and found his toes. David lay down on his side next to the baby, reaching over to put a hand on his belly.

Zhané came and sat on the other side of Noah.

"Do you still draw?" he asked.

"No."

"Why not?"

"Because I'm not good enough."

"I always liked your pictures."

"You really mean that?" she asked.

"Sure," he said. She'd taken art classes as electives all through high school, giving up study halls to take extra, and he had always begged to see her projects.

"I guess...I don't know, with Nicki and Becca dead and you gone, art seemed...stupid," she said. "You know, I felt like I had to grow up and be serious."

"How'd that work out?"

"Well, I hated being a nurse."

He smiled. "Maybe you should try again. Art, not nursing."

"It's been years."

"Chicken," he accused.

She smiled. "Maybe. Maybe not. We'll see."

He took out his phone and rolled onto his stomach, opening his texts and rereading his brief chat with Ahmed earlier. He closed it a moment later. No point in dwelling. He put his phone down on the floor. "This is stupid."

"So find someone else," she suggested without even needing to ask what he meant. "Get that app. Tinder or Grindr or whatever the kids are doing these days."

He sighed. "I don't know."

"Or don't date anyone."

He sighed again.

"You should get a haircut."

He ignored her.

6/15/15

AHMED HAD gotten to work before David, as he almost always did. Johnny was nowhere to be seen, which was a relief. The older man often watched them work, something they both agreed was unnerving.

He found Ahmed in the stock room and upon seeing him, Ahmed said, "Hey, uh, it's your birthday, right?"

"Yeah."

"Facebook. Not that I checked or anything, it just tells you."

"I know."

"Happy birthday."

David smiled. "Thanks."

"How old?"

"Twenty-one."

"Plans?"

"No."

Ahmed glanced at him, a small frown on his face. "Really?"

David shrugged. Drinking didn't have much appeal, considering how badly he'd abused it in years past and how it exacerbated his hallucinations. "When I drink, I start to get convinced about the lizard people," he shared, which wasn't untrue.

"The what?"

"Lizard people." He offered no further explanation.

"Oh."

The day wore on and at one, they headed out to their cars. David had intentionally parked next to the 2007 Focus that he knew Ahmed drove. Some days they would stand beside their cars and chat for a while and today, before Ahmed moved too far towards his driver side, David said, "Hey."

"What?"

"Can I ask you something?"

"Um."

"Personal? Kind of? You can tell me to fuck off it's too nosy."

Not looking entirely happy about it, Ahmed asked, "What?"

"Um. About you not being allowed to date or, you know, be gay and all that," David began, already knowing that he had worded things badly. "I mean, I know according to the Church, I'm supposed to be celibate and all that shit cause it's a sin or whatever."

"Okay."

"But I think it's bullshit," David said.

"What's your question?"

"I mean, do you think it's bullshit too? Or, I mean, it's a sin, too, in Islam?"

"Yeah, being actively gay is haram."

"But do you believe that?"

Ahmed frowned. "Why?"

"Because I just, I know your parents don't let you date and I know your parents think you shouldn't be gay, but...is that what you think? I mean, am I totally, absolutely barking up the wrong tree here?"

Ahmed studied him for a minute. "It's a big question."

"I know."

"It's..." he paused. "David, that's a huge question."

"I'm sorry," David said, "It's...we text and stuff."

"No, I know."

Over the past few weeks, they had been texting more and more regularly. Nothing serious, definitely nothing romantic, but in a way that was friendly and could easily have been more than friendly. There were times when David had known exactly what flirty thing would have been perfect to say and he had held back from saying it; sometimes at work, they would chat and Ahmed would start to say something, then stop himself, leaving their conversation dangling as they sorted produce or shelved cans.

"It isn't that I don't like you," Ahmed offered.

David waited.

He rubbed the back of his neck and couldn't look up.

Feeling awful that he'd caused him such distress, David said, "Listen, it's not any of my business, really. Forget I asked."

"I'm sorry."

"No, I shouldn't have asked. I'll see you on Wednesday."

Ahmed nodded and headed towards his car. David got into his and drove home, but about two hours later, as he was watching Noah while Zhané headed to a job a few towns over, he got a text.

'Hey ive been thinking and I do want to talk. If u want to still'

David looked down at Noah, halfway through changing a diaper. He finished changing the baby and told Ahmed that he did want to talk.

Ahmed asked if they could meet up somewhere and suggested the reservoir. David agreed, feeling reasonably sure the police had decided to leave him alone for the time being and would not surface if he visited a former crime scene.

He texted Zhané his plan and dressed Noah in warmer clothes, as it was unseasonably cool for June. He settled the baby into the spare car seat that Zhané kept for her mother's use and strapped him safely into the back seat. He had not yet had to drive the baby anywhere alone and found it nerve-wracking.

Once at the reservoir, he sat at the agreed upon picnic table and waited for about a quarter of an hour. When Ahmed arrived, he initially gasped at the sight Noah, the same wide-eyed way that middle-aged women gasped at him, full of adoration.

"Oh, look at him," he fussed. "Is this your baby?"

"No," David said, then clarified, "He's my friend's, I'm just watching him for a little while."

"Oh."

"His name's Noah."

"He is adorable."

"Yeah. He's a good baby," David agreed.

"I love babies," Ahmed disclosed, "I mean, not just babies, kids. I think they're fantastic."

David nodded.

Ahmed came to sit at the table, on an adjacent side. He cooed at the baby for several minutes and, watching him, David got the same fuzzy feeling he did about Noah.

With his index finger firmly in Noah's grasp, Ahmed let out a long sigh. "But I guess...David, I guess that's the thing."

"What is?"

"Kids. A family. It's...it's something I want, something I've always wanted really badly." He half-smiled, as though he wished he didn't. "I know, it sounds lame and old-fashioned, but I've always just wanted to have a family."

David, knowing it was not his place but desperate to know, asked, "So are you going to marry a girl, then?"

Ahmed laughed, a small sound of defeat. "I always pretend that I can find a nice Muslim lesbian, as though that wouldn't make both of us miserable."

"That does sound miserable."

"I think about telling my parents, I mean, how bad can it go? Noor doesn't wear a hijab or anything and that didn't kill them."

Softly, David advised, "Ahmed, if you don't think it's safe, don't do it. You don't owe coming out to anyone."

"Sometimes I think that they have to know already. The way they look at me sometimes. But no one ever says anything, it's just 'someday when you're married' or 'someday when you have your own children'. Stuff like that."

David nodded. His parents said the same things.

"So you asked if I think it's bullshit."

"Yeah."

"It's got to be, right? I definitely didn't pick this and I couldn't *choose* to be straight, no matter how hard I tried. So why would Allah make his children like this if he didn't want us to actually *be* this way?"

David nodded again, knowing that Ahmed had more to say.

"But I don't know what I'm going to do. I don't know if I'm going to marry a girl or...run away. Or tell my parents. I don't know. So I can't tell you what you want to hear."

"What do I want to hear?" David asked.

"That I'll date you?" Ahmed ventured.

David gave a smile. "It'd be nice," he admitted, "But...what I really want to know is, I guess, if I should leave you alone. If I'm out of line, if I shouldn't feel this way about you."

"Even if we dated, it would probably be a secret. You'd probably never meet my parents."

David shrugged.

"I don't want to lie to them or let them down...and I don't want to give up being part of my family or my community. But I don't want to have a wife and lie to her, to never be able to love her how she should be loved. I just...I really don't know what I'm going to do, at all, I'm sorry."

"Hey," he soothed. "I'm not asking for any hard and fast answers. Just, I don't know, an idea of where we're both standing on the whole moral compass thing. I wanted to know what you believed, about all of this, cause honestly, I'm not interested in what your parents have to say."

"I'm sorry," he said again, "I don't know yet."

David wanted to touch him, to pat his arm or hold his hand. "Well, if you ever do, let me know."

His brow creased, Ahmed asked, "You're not going to wait around, are you?"

"I'm not...*not* waiting?" David offered. "It's not like I'm out cruising for hot young singles. I like you and I'm not in a hurry. I've got my own stuff to sort out."

"Like what?" Ahmed asked.

David hesitated to answer, but he had asked Ahmed something personal and Ahmed had been open enough to share. David owed him something. "I've got no career path, no school plans. No money. I'm not on great terms with my parents. I've got schizophrenia and I don't know what that's going to do to my future. I was at a center for years and I'm still learning how to live on my own." *And monsters come to steal my body parts if I don't kill things for them,* he thought.

"Oh."

"So maybe someday I'll be a real person and maybe someday you'll know what you're going to do," he said.

Ahmed gave a half-smile. "Until then, we can text, right?"

"Sure, and maybe hang out? Once in a while?"

"I don't know. Maybe."

"I'll bring Noah if we do."

"Why?"

"Because who would bring a baby on a date?" David asked and Ahmed laughed. "Do you want to hold him?"

"Can I?"

David passed the child over and Ahmed took him deftly, none of the hesitance some people had when holding a baby. "What's he? About seven months?"

"Yeah, uh, exactly," David said.

Ahmed nodded and paid David almost no attention for the

rest of the time they sat together, but he didn't mind at all, content to watch him play with the baby. At one point, he glanced at his phone and cried, "Oh! I've got to go, my mom's gonna flip. I was only supposed to be out for a little while."

David took Noah back. "I'll see you at work."

"Yeah," he said and stood, then hesitated. "I wish I had better answers for you, really."

"It's fine," he told him and meant it. "See you Wednesday."

He knew one of them would send a text between now and then. It had been a long time since they'd gone more than a day without at least one exchange, even if it was nothing more than sharing a funny picture.

Ahmed nodded and left, hurrying.

That night, as David read to Noah, his phone dinged and he glanced at it. Ahmed, saying that he was glad they'd talked and followed up a moment later with 'even if we didn't decide anything'.

David smiled and answered 'knowing we both don't know what we're doing makes me feel better tho'.

He thought about how he had told Ahmed that he was learning to live on his own, but that didn't feel entirely true. Yes, in his time since his release he had learned how to do a load of laundry and he had bought himself a vacuum, which he used about once a week, simply because he thought he should.

But he didn't cook, living on things he could microwave or eat straight from the box, and he hadn't changed over his driver's license yet. Working part-time would not be sustainable for long, not if he wanted to actually have a life someday, and he spent more time than he should have lying in bed.

Tuesday morning, he made himself get up, borrowed Zhané's computer and printer so that he could begin the process of transferring his license and car registration. He waited in infinite lines only to be sent home to get something he had forgotten.

Wednesday, when he saw Ahmed, he had to keep brushing his hair out of his eyes and realized that he did need a haircut. On Thursday, for the first time in his life, he went and got a haircut of his own volition. That, he felt was a real step towards being an adult.

Next Wednesday, Ahmed came into work a few minutes late, looking miserable and David asked, "Tired?"

"No."

"Are you getting sick?" he asked.

"It's Ramadan."

"Oh," he said and thought, trying to remember if he knew anything about Ramadan. He had seen a few things about it on the internet lately but he had ignored them, the same way he ignored Chinese New Year and Yom Kippur. "Is that the thing where you don't eat?"

Sounding irritated, Ahmed corrected, "Fasting. From sunrise to sunset."

"Oh. What time does the sun come up?"

"Like, five-twenty."

"Damn," he said. "Well, uh, let me know if you need anything."

"Thanks."

Later in the day, Johnny caught David on his phone in the back room, trying to figure out as much about the holiday as he could. He got chewed out for it and did not argue when the older man assumed he had been texting some girl or farting around on Facebook. He apologized, embarrassed that other people had been around to hear him get yelled at.

Teasing, Ahmed asked, "You couldn't hear him coming?"

Johnny wore the same sneakers every day, brightly colored and incongruous with the rest of his business casual attire. They squeaked and squelched so loud that he almost never caught anyone doing anything they shouldn't have been doing. Privately, everyone agreed that he must like the noise they made, like a child who couldn't stop squeaking their soles on a wet floor.

"I was distracted," he said with a shrug.

"By what?"

"I was reading something."

"You're being sketchy."

David sighed and admitted, "I didn't want to be nosy or anything."

Ahmed raised an eyebrow. "I haven't eaten in over twelve hours, you need to stop being vague."

"About Ramadan. I was reading about Ramadan."

"That's cute," he said. "But you could have asked, you know, the actual Muslim."

"But don't people ask you shit all the time? Doesn't it get irritating?" he asked, knowing that Zhané had gotten sick of being asked about 'black' topics by classmates, knowing that he'd walked away from conversations after a dozen questions about 'this bisexual thing'.

"Yeah, but I like you," Ahmed said. "And I don't think you'd be asking from a bad place. You know?"

David nodded.

"So what did you want to know?"

"Uh. Everything?"

Ahmed laughed and, as they packaged produce, he explained the holiday. Johnny gave Ahmed an irritated look a few times and once even pulled David aside to say, "David, if he's talking your ear off, don't worry about being polite."

"No," David said shortly. "I asked."

He didn't know if Johnny had more to say, but he turned away after that, returning to Ahmed's side, though Ahmed's good mood had soured.

Trying to be nice, to bring the warmth back to their conversation, David said, "You should be a teacher."

Ahmed snorted.

"What?"

"I *want* to be a teacher."

"Your parents?" David guessed.

"It's not that they don't want me to be a teacher..."

"But?"

"Teaching high school would be fine, teaching at a college would be even better, but elementary school? Out of the question. That's a job for white ladies."

David grinned, tickled at the idea of Ahmed surrounded by a classroom full of little minds.

"What?"

"I think you'd do great," David said.

"I think...it sounds terrible, I think I'm going to tell them I'm going for secondary education but go for elementary anyways," he admitted. "I shouldn't, I know, they've killed themselves to pay for as much as they can..."

"Sure, but come on. Imagine all those little boogers calling 'Mr. Jalali, can I go to the bathroom; Mr. Jalali, Timmy won't share the crayons with me!'," he said, smiling.

Ahmed smiled, too. "I don't know, we'll see."

David couldn't help himself from imagining a future with Ahmed in it; a cozy living room where he'd work on lesson plans and bitch about his students' nutty parents, where he'd worry about the hungry ones and try to figure out how he'd make accommodations for the SPED kids and David would...what? What would he do in this future he wanted? Watch the kids, cook dinner, keep things tidy.

He paused, overcome with a horrible realization about himself. He stared down at his own hands in horror.

"Hey," Ahmed said. "Did you find another spider?"

"No?"

"A caterpillar? It's not mushed, is it? I hate that."

David shook his head.

Ahmed came over and peered at the apples David should have been packaging but found no insect, nothing disgusting that should have made David stare the way he was. "What's wrong?"

I want to be a housewife, David thought. "Nothing," he said. "I...I realized something."

"What?"

"Nothing." *I want to be a housewife and I don't even know how to cook.*

Ahmed watched him for a second, then quietly, carefully asked, "David, is this...is something wrong? You know, uh...are you having, like...an episode?"

David glanced over at him. An episode? He had to puzzle for a second. "No, no, sorry," he assured. "The lizard people aren't coming for me yet."

Ahmed looked unsure but nodded.

They returned to work but without talking. It was funny, David thought, how people imagined his illness in episodes, as though he had moments of schizophrenia. Like a heart attack.

"It's not like that," he said, "I mean...I'm on meds, I'm stable, you know. Like, I hear things sometimes, but they're easier to ignore. Smaller, quieter. You know?"

Ahmed shook his head. "No. I don't, I'm sorry."

"It's better now," he said.

Better now, that was his mantra, even though monsters came for him (monsters that had to be real, they *had* to be, because something was wrong in the world, it could not be just him), even though he had killed a man, even though sometimes while he showered he heard his mother and it never failed to scare shit out of him. But it was better because for years he had not heard Nicki or Becca screaming for him to save them.

"It sounds scary," Ahmed admitted.

"It is sometimes." He looked over and met Ahmed's eyes.

Ahmed licked his lips nervously and David wanted to kiss him. Maybe if Ahmed knew what he wanted, if they weren't at work, he would have tried, but instead, he pushed down the feeling.

"You know, I'm learning to live, though," he said.

Ahmed nodded.

David wished he would say something else, something that would not make David feel so alien. He was glad that Ahmed hadn't asked if he was dangerous, at least.

They left work together, walking quietly as Ahmed ravaged a granola bar that surely done nothing in life to deserve such a death.

"Hey," Ahmed said, shoving the wrapper into his pocket, food still in his mouth.

David paused in front of his car. "Yeah?"

"I didn't mean to be weird about it."

"You weren't."

They stood for a moment and David wanted to hug him, to have him close. To have anyone close, because maybe that would make the ache in his chest go away. He didn't have long before he got his next call, his next visit.

How could he ever date someone, marry someone, have kids and a life if every eight weeks something bad would happen? What if they came for his children instead?

"So what did you realize?" Ahmed asked.

"I want to be a housewife."

Ahmed laughed. "If you could pass, you would be the perfect solution to all my problems. Full-on *Birdcage*, right?"

David smiled, amused by the idea for a second before he felt sad again. "See you," he said and didn't wait for the reply, getting in his car, his throat tight.

Zhané found him in the driveway, engine off and forehead against the steering wheel. She knocked on the window and he looked up.

"What are you doing?" she asked.

He took his keys from the ignition and got out of the car. "I don't know."

"Well, why don't you come do it inside the house? Come eat something, I made macaroni and cheese."

He followed her inside.

Noah had cheese sauce smeared all over his face.

"Does he like it?"

She shrugged. "He likes to play with it."

He sat at the table and ate the food she put in front of him, saying "It's good, thanks."

She nodded. "It's easy."

He stared into the bowl.

"What?"

"I want to be a housewife."

She sighed. "David, what does that mean?"

He shook his head.

"Well, you'll need a spouse who can afford you," she said practically. "Do you want more?"

"Please."

She spooned more into his bowl and then picked a piece of macaroni out of Noah's hair. "Did something happen at work? You seem out of it."

"No, just. It's going to happen soon."

She reached out and put a hand on his arm. "I know."

He sighed.

"We should have looked into more."

He shook his head. "There's nothing left to look into."

Janet Mills still had not called them back, Bill Clearwater had taken a job as a trucker and denied having been in town for either death, and James Declan was a new man, born again and all that.

"I still think that Mills woman is hiding something."

"Probably substance abuse," David suggested. "Maybe they'll go away. Maybe two is it." He knew that wasn't true. Jim Roberts would have made three. It wasn't true, but he could hope, he could pray to God with everything he had that this call wouldn't come. "You believe me, right?" he asked.

"I do."

He wanted to cry so he said, "I'm, uh. I'm gonna go to bed?"

"No Netflix?" she asked.

"I'm sorry."

She squeezed his hand. "Take care of yourself, David."

He nodded and went to his apartment, which had gained a loveseat and a small coffee table recently. He'd found the table on the side of the road and the loveseat had been bought at a nearby tag sale for thirty dollars.

He threw his clothes on the floor and crawled into bed. He clutched his blankets to his chest, wishing he had something to hold. Maybe he would ask his mother to mail Benjamin Rabbit down to him.

He reached for his phone and texted her before he grew too embarrassed. Twenty-one-year-old men did not need stuffed rabbits to sleep at night.

7/2/15

THE CALL would come tomorrow. He knew it would. He'd done the math. July third the things would call, July sixth they would come. He would not kill someone; he knew that, too. He sat on the floor of his apartment with Benjamin Rabbit on his lap; his mother, bless her, had overnighted him without a single ounce of teasing or disdain.

He wanted to call her, but it was late at night, around two in the morning. Technically the third of the month. So, the call would come today, within the next twenty hours or so. He stared at his phone because in the end, no matter how bitchy she was about him being bi, no matter that she had sent him away and probably thought he was a murderer, she was still his mother.

He pressed Benjamin Rabbit close to his face, glad for the familiar smell, the slightly matted fur, the scratched eyes that should have been shiny black but had taken two decades of abuse.

"I want to go home," he confessed to the rabbit.

He knew, as an absolute, concrete fact, if these calls, these visits did not stop that he would break, he would have to be hospitalized again because medication helped but it was not magic. He could not live his life like this.

"Please, I don't want to do this anymore," he pleaded with no one. "God, I can't."

He cried for a while, as he had cried the night before, to the point of exhaustion. Even after that, he could not sleep; he sat on the floor until his alarm went off. He set Benjamin Rabbit on his bed, but then doubled back and sat him on the edge of his sink while he showered. He didn't shave that morning and knew he looked like shit as he pulled on his clothes and pushed his glasses onto his face.

He ate two pieces of bread for breakfast, which he recognized as basically inhuman. He put the stuffed rabbit on the passenger seat of the car and would have brought him into the store if he didn't think that would be wildly unacceptable. He went to the bakery section and stole a cup of coffee. It wasn't really stealing, he didn't think, everyone did it and Johnny never said anything.

"You look horrible," Ahmed told him.

He said nothing, burning his mouth on his drink. Dully, he realized that he'd left his phone plugged in at home.

"What, did you go to a party or something?" he asked.

Was it better to be hung over or to have spent the night crying on his floor? He didn't know. "Just...rough night."

He thought Ahmed looked disappointed and he wanted to care, but more than anything he wanted to drop dead.

Around eleven o'clock, as they were breaking down boxes to be recycled (supposedly, David didn't believe that this store recycled), Ahmed let out a yelp, jumping like someone had pinched him.

David paused his contemplation of the box cutter to look over. "What?"

"I heard something," he said, touching his hearing aid cautiously. He flinched a moment later and pulled the device out of his ear, staring at it like it had betrayed him.

"What did you hear?" he asked.

"Uh." Ahmed stared at his mouth.

David realized he did not know how well Ahmed could hear unassisted.

"Would it be super weird...can I just?" he asked, reaching out for the hearing aid.

Ahmed let him take it and he put it close to his own ear, hearing faintly the crackling and voices he usually heard on his phone. Three days, must be fresh, must be human, the same as always. After a few more loops, the aid went silent and he returned it to Ahmed.

Ahmed stared down at the device like it was a bug.

"Should be fine, I think."

Ahmed looked up. "What?"

"I think it's fine," David repeated. "It's quiet."

Ahmed put his hearing aid back in, looking skeeved out. "What was that?"

David shrugged.

"You heard it too, right?" Ahmed asked.

"Yeah. It must have been interference or something," he suggested.

"I don't know, it's never happened before."

"Probably government mind control."

Ahmed didn't look amused.

"Joke."

David asked, "Can you hear in your other ear?"

"What?"

He gestured vaguely to his ear. "You only have one."

"Oh, no, I'm supposed to have two," he said. "But one got broken and my dad's insurance won't replace it for like, I don't know, another year or whatever."

"How'd you break it?"

"I didn't. Some...guy," Ahmed began, sounding like he wanted to use stronger language.

David had read that some Muslims tried not to swear during Ramadan.

Ahmed continued, "He grabbed it out of my ear and, like, stomped on it."

"What?"

"Yeah and then he got real close to me and called me a terrorist, so that was great."

"Jesus," David breathed. "That's...man, I'm sorry."

Ahmed shrugged. "Just, you know, do me a favor and don't vote for Trump."

David let out a barking laugh. "Fuck no," he said, then wondered if he shouldn't have sworn.

"Hey. Listen."

"What?"

"You really look awful," Ahmed told him.

David shrugged. "I feel awful."

"What's going on with you? Are you okay?"

David stared at him for a minute, wondering how much he

should reveal. He shrugged again. "Nothing."

He returned to breaking down boxes, wishing he'd eaten more for breakfast. He didn't dare to complain, knowing that Ahmed wouldn't be able to eat again for hours.

He tossed a box onto the pile that needed to be brought out and a horrible thought occurred to him. The things, what if, because the voices had come through Ahmed's hearing aid, they went to his house instead? What if they went after him?

He turned to Ahmed. "Monday."

"What?"

"Monday night."

"Yeah, okay, what about it?"

"Can I tell you something?" he asked.

"Sure."

"Something absolutely insane, something that's going to make you think I've lost my mind."

"Okay."

"I get these phone calls. They tell me to do things. To kill people."

Ahmed frowned.

"And if I don't do it, they take something. From me."

Ahmed reached up to touch his hearing aid. "Harvest," he whispered, "That's what I heard."

David nodded. "Harvest."

"That's..."

"But this time it wasn't a phone call," David said, "Please, be careful. If they think...God, if they come to you instead..."

"I don't, I don't think that..." Ahmed faltered.

"Just. Please."

"Are these the voices you hear?"

"No!" David cried. "No, it's different. They're not the same. You heard it, though, didn't you?"

"I did."

"Please promise that you'll just, that you'll be around someone on Monday night."

"I live at home, I have to be around someone. And it's Ramadan so people will probably be over. My grandmother and uncle at least."

David felt a little better and a whole lot crazier.

"Maybe you should go home," Ahmed suggested.

He shook his head.

"I'll tell Johnny you got sick, it's fine." He looked at his watch. "There's only an hour and a half left anyways."

David shook his head again. "It's Friday, you have to go to your thing, the Juma thing."

"Jumu'ah," Ahmed corrected reflexively.

"That, you're supposed to go now anyway."

Ahmed reached out and grabbed him by the arm, which judging by his face, he felt as weird about as David did. It was meant to be a gesture of solidarity, in all likelihood, but between two men who liked each other, who didn't know what the future held between them, it felt strange. "Go home, sleep, alright? Take a lot of Nyquil. I'll see you on Monday. I've got it covered."

"Okay."

"Okay. Good. Text me."

David nodded and left.

Zhané looked up when he came inside with Benjamin Rabbit in hand. "Oh, shit, you look like death."

"Ahmed sent me home."

"Then Ahmed officially has my seal of approval," she said.

"They called." He shuffled over to sit on her couch. "But it came in on his hearing aid."

"So?"

"So what if they think it was for him?" he asked.

"David, they've been targeting you for months, they know what they're doing. Did you have your phone on you?"

"No."

"So they used what was closest," she reasoned. "It could have been the baby monitor or the TV."

He nodded.

She made him eat and after he ate, she threatened to force feed him Nyquil when he wouldn't take it on his own. She held the pack of gel caps out to him again. "Listen, we'll be fine. I already asked my mom to take Noah for that night so I'm gonna stay with you."

"No, it's too dangerous."

"David, for fuck's sake, I'm helping you, I'm not some damsel you need to save. Will you take these, please!" She took his hand and pushed the pack into his palm.

The sharp edges poked hard into his skin.

"Can I sleep on the couch?" he asked.

"Yes."

"Will you get my phone?"

"Yes."

"Thank you." He dry-swallowed the gel caps and put his glasses on the coffee table. He cradled Benjamin Rabbit close to his chest and saw that Noah napped in the popup playpen a few feet away.

Zhané brought him his phone and set it beside his glasses.

He woke hours later, to the golden light of late evening. He felt unfocused and very thirsty. He pushed himself up, put on his glasses, and went to the kitchen to get a glass of water. He guzzled it down and then sat at the kitchen table, phone in hand and Benjamin Rabbit placed in front of him.

Ahmed had texted him, saying that he hoped he felt better.

He stared at the text. 'I just woke up' he sent.

Right away, he got an answer. 'Good'.

'do u think I'm crazy?' he asked, not wanting to know the answer. The answer he got back was simple, one word, 'no'.

Was he lying, was he being nice?

Zhané found him like that, sitting at the kitchen table, staring at his phone. He didn't know what else to do or what else to say.

"You feel better?" she asked.

"On a physical level."

She put Noah on his lap and gave his shoulder a pat. "I'll heat up something for you. You were out like a light."

"Thanks."

If he survived this, he vowed to learn to cook.

"I don't want you to stay with me," he said.

"I'm going to anyways."

"It isn't safe."

"It isn't safe for you either. They might have picked you, but that doesn't mean you deserve it. Safety in numbers. Maybe they won't even come if we're together. They left you alone while you were at that place."

"Maybe," he whispered. He gave Noah a little hug and kissed his hair, breathing in that baby smell that had made the world a better place. Was it wrong to love someone else's child this much after such a short amount of time? Not even two whole months had gone by yet.

Zhané put a plate of leftovers in front of him and took the baby while he ate.

He texted Ahmed again, asking 'are you sure?' and feeling needy, dependent on someone who he had known for less time that he'd known the baby.

Instead of texting back, Ahmed called him. David froze up, staring at his phone. He answered after a few rings. "Hey?"

"Hi, uh."

He stood up from the table and went into the living room, standing near the window. "You didn't have to call."

"I was worried," he admitted and David realized he was whispering.

"I'm okay. Now."

"About what you said," he began and David's stomach clenched. "I, uh, man, I don't know what to say but, you know, if you're crazy then we're taking the same crazy pills cause I know I heard something."

"Yeah."

"Anyways, that's...I just...you sound better."

"Thanks."

"I've got to go. I'll see you later."

"Yeah. Bye."

He tossed his phone on the coffee table and sat on the couch. Zhané came to sit beside him, handing him his rabbit.

"Want to watch something?" she asked.

"I guess." He didn't really, but he didn't want to sit silently worrying either.

That night, he slept on her couch. Saturday was a daze and Sunday morning they found that a woman in her sixties had gone missing; reporters warned that the woman may have been suffering from some form of early onset dementia and asked town residents to be on the watch, though David knew in his gut that by Tuesday she'd be dead.

MONDAY, AT work, things were tense. He didn't know what to say and it was clear that Ahmed didn't know what to say either.

"Did you get in trouble?" he asked.

"What?" Ahmed looked over at him, his brow creased.

"For missing Friday prayer," he clarified.

"No, uh, it's like...it's okay to miss it if you have a real reason, like if you're sick or the weather is really bad."

"Crazy coworker is covered under valid?"

"Providing reprieve for an unwell friend," Ahmed suggested.

"Well, thanks, either way."

Ahmed nodded.

Johnny, later in the day, pulled him aside and gave him a talk about calling out sick and who to clear it with, clearly not happy that he'd taken off on Friday. David apologized so much that sorry didn't sound like a real word anymore and Johnny seemed pleased with that.

At one they parted ways, with David pleading with Ahmed to stay with someone and Ahmed saying, "Be safe."

It was clear that Ahmed thought he was overreacting, that maybe all of this was part of his illness, but David couldn't do anything about that.

At home, he mowed the lawn in an effort to distract himself and while Zhané brought Noah to her mother's, he showered, did his laundry, and vacuumed every horizontal surface he could find.

Nothing felt better.

He thought about killing himself half a dozen times. There was no good way to commit suicide. A gun was the most effective, a gunshot to the head, he knew that. Ninety-nine percent chance of death if he used a shotgun. Slitting his wrists would probably do nothing more than get him back in the hospital, with only a six percent chance of killing him.

Maybe if he was in the hospital, they wouldn't come. Maybe Zhané was right about safety in numbers.

He didn't know.

Zhané sat at the kitchen table the whole time, quiet, still. She watched his frantic movements about the house. He wiped the kitchen counters, organized the coffee table, and emptied the dishwasher.

By sunset, he the only thing he had left to do was fold his laundry and wait. Zhané, once, suggested he try to sleep, but he couldn't. He checked the time about every five minutes and knew that if he had a gun, he would blow his brains out without a second thought.

Midnight came and went. He dozed off on the couch and woke when his phone began to ring. It answered itself and the voice came over the speaker. "Owed...harvest..."

He saw the dark shapes, darker than the moonlit room. He stood, wondering where Zhané was, if they had done something to her. One of the things grabbed his arm, wrapping him up in the same fleshy restraint as always.

Before the second one took hold of him, a light turned on in the kitchen. At first, nothing changed. The things put him face down on the coffee table, not caring that they had knocked things aside. Another light came on, this time right above him and the third thing stopped, in the middle of cutting off his shirt.

The grip they had on his arm loosened and he pulled away from them, scrambling forward over the table. He turned to see that Zhané stood to the side, her phone held up and pointed at them.

Smart, she was so smart.

The things, even without faces, seemed to be looking at her and he took the chance to crawl towards the door, bolting down the front steps.

They followed, he could smell them, the same harsh chemical smell they always brought. He made it to the street before they caught up with him again. Under a street lamp, two of them held him down again, enveloping his arms and legs as he tried to writhe out of their grip. They were stronger, they were always stronger than him.

He screamed, at first for help, but then because of the pain in his back.

Across the street, a light came on and he screamed again, vaguely aware that his voice echoed through the neighborhood. Next door, another light came on and someone opened their door, stepping out onto their porch. People moved closer to get a better look, talking to each other, calling over to him, demanding that he shut up or to know what his problem was. He could have sworn he heard someone on the phone with the police.

As more lights came on, as more people came closer, the things paused in their work. They made no sound, but he thought that he could feel the change in their mood, in the same way his skin crawled when he felt someone watching him.

A firework went off, more than likely unrelated to the scene, and after that, he felt their grip loosen. The weight of the third thing lifted from his back as it abandoned its pursuit of whatever it had wanted to take from him.

From right beside him, he heard Zhané say, "David, don't move, okay? Your back…it's uh, bleeding. A lot."

He did not move. He couldn't have if he wanted to. Stray rocks from the sidewalk dug into his chest, his face. Someone pressed something to his back, a folded towel or maybe a sweatshirt. He heard someone talking to Zhané, telling her, "I'm an EMT, don't worry. What happened?"

"I don't know," she said.

Minutes later, red and blue lights came, accompanied by more voices. By that point, the adrenaline had emptied out of his system, leaving him weak, shaky, and feeling everything. His back, low and to the right, felt like it was on fire.

On the morning of July seventh, he woke in one of the hospitals in Waterbury, where cops asked him what had happened. He said he didn't know, that he wanted to go home.

"Sir, as far as we can tell, someone tried to take your kidney," an officer told him. "Now, they didn't manage to, but you've got a pretty nasty cut on your back."

"Probably, they're pretty good kidneys," he said.

"Are you interested in pressing charges?"

He stared, almost laughed, then shook his head. The police

left, not hiding their irritation with him or with Zhané, who had simply maintained that she hadn't seen anything.

Once they had left, she showed him the video she'd taken. He threw up after watching it the first time, partly from the shakiness of the camera. After that, he watched it ten more times, unable to stop. The things were real and now he had proof. He still could not tell what they were, dark and formless things that changed their shape, stretching and molding to what they needed to do.

He went home, against the advice of everyone in the hospital; the doctor there seemed to think he'd had another psychotic break and had somehow done this to himself.

They don't like being watched, was all he could think. Zhané had been right, there was safety in numbers. The footage was crappy, but it was clear what happened in it.

Wednesday morning the police found the body of the old woman who had gone missing and that afternoon, he went to work after downing more Advil than he should have taken.

Ahmed paled at the sight of him. "I couldn't get a hold of you."

"I was busy," he said, "Sorry."

"Are you alright?"

He nodded. "Yeah, I'm fine."

"What about...those things?"

"They came."

"They didn't!"

"And then they went away."

Ahmed regarded him for a while. "You're sure you're alright?"

"Yes."

"I was worried about you, you know," he told him, a little sulky.

"I'm sorry." He held out his phone to Ahmed.

When he looked at the screen, Ahmed grinned. "Oh, he's so precious." He smiled down at a picture of Noah chewing on his own feet.

David swiped over to show a picture of the baby sleeping with his bottom in the air, and then to a video. He tapped play and said, proudly, "He's crawling now."

Ahmed cooed at the video. "Seeing pictures of him makes my day, you know?"

David nodded. He did. It had been a whim, initially, to show Ahmed a video of Noah trying to push himself onto his hands and knees, but he had been so pleased to see it that David had made a habit of it.

They heard the squeaking of Johnny's sneakers and David shoved his phone into his pocket. They returned to the work they were supposed to be doing. Once Johnny had come, surveyed them, and walked off again, they began to giggle.

Nothing had been stolen from him this time and that gave him hope.

7/20/15

THE HOPE that came with surviving the most recent visit relatively unscathed went to his head, gave him all sorts of crazy ideas. Almost as crazy as the messages Zhané had been getting from people after she'd posted the video to the internet. It hadn't gone viral, but it had garnered a lot of views from a very specific type of person.

A lot of people had written to tell them about their own experiences with demons and aliens, though none had seemed credible.

But David didn't care about that right now because the idea that, maybe, there was a solution, had made his life worth living again. At one, as he and Ahmed walked to their cars, he said, "Hey, can I ask you something crazy?"

"Sure, why not?"

"Well, it's actually a two-part thing," he said, wondering if he'd lose his nerve. "Cause there's something you should know before I ask."

Leaning against the passenger side of his car, which faced the driver's side of David's, Ahmed said, "Alright, you're making me nervous, though."

"I killed someone."

Ahmed yelped, "What!"

"The things, they come and...one time, I did what they told me to," he admitted, "But I wouldn't ever again. I think I know how to make them go away."

"Are you serious?"

"Yes."

"You killed someone? For real?"

He nodded.

"Why the hell are you telling me this?" Ahmed demanded, appropriately panicked and confused.

"Cause it's the worst thing I've ever done and I thought you should know before I ask the next thing."

Ahmed straightened up and looked around. The parking lot was mostly empty and no one was paying any attention to them. "What?"

"Do you want to get married?" he asked.

"What?"

"I said it was crazy."

He knew, rationally, that this was stupid and irresponsible, that they were just work friends, no matter how much they texted each other or caught themselves flirting. But it didn't feel that way, it felt like the right thing to ask. Around Ahmed, he felt at ease and David couldn't think of someone he'd rather bring home.

Ahmed crossed his arms. "Crazy is an understatement. David, what are you taking?"

Not thinking, David almost answered with his prescription, but he caught himself in time. "I'm not saying answer me now, think about it first."

"I don't need to think about it, David, I'm nineteen and you're twenty-one."

"So?"

"So we're too young!"

"I can wait."

"Don't be an asshole!" Ahmed said, raising his voice, then looking around to see if anyone had noticed.

"I'm not. Just...think about it. We want the same stuff, right? To have a family, to have kids. To be happy."

"My parents—"

"Won't approve. And mine won't approve. And either you're going to marry some girl, some nice Muslim girl that your parents like and you'll have kids, and both of you can be miserable. Or we can do this," David said, then added right away, "I don't mean to sound like you don't have other options if you wanted to date, I'm sure you could do a lot better than me without even trying, but...I don't know. I like you, Ahmed, a lot, like more than I should considering we've never even gone out. Seeing you makes me happy, I think about you when you're not around and, shit, I mean, I feel like you're...right. For me. It's stupid and sappy, I know."

"David."

"So say no. You won't hurt my feelings. Or think about it. Now you know the worst thing about me and you know how I feel."

Ahmed rubbed his face, then sighed. "Did you really kill someone?"

"Everything I said was true. I mean, I don't mean to sound so clinical about it, but it is what it is. I can't change it no matter how much I wish I could undo it."

"I...shit, David, I don't know."

"Think about it then."

Ahmed nodded.

"And, you know, if this is too much, if it's too weird, I'll find somewhere else to work, alright? I won't stalk you or anything."

Ahmed nodded again. "I've gotta go."

"Tell me if you don't want me to come in on Wednesday," David offered.

Ahmed nodded and left without another word.

Later that afternoon, David got a text that asking him to see if he could switch shifts for Wednesday, which he did immediately, not worried at all. Somehow, even though he had not gotten an exuberant yes, he felt that he had done the right thing.

He ended up working Tuesday morning instead of Wednesday night and didn't hear from Ahmed until he got a text at about eight-thirty Wednesday night when he would have been starting to close the store. It asked him to come to the parking lot of the local baseball field; it felt like a drug deal. Not that David knew from first-hand experience.

At nine-fourteen exactly, David arrived and parked near the t-ball field, which was guaranteed not to be in use so late at night. Six minutes later, Ahmed arrived and left a space between them when he parked.

They stood in the middle of the empty space, facing each other. Ahmed fidgeted, which was unlike him. He seemed to have lost control of his hands, which he clenched and unclenched, sometimes putting them in his pockets, other times playing with his keys.

"I need you to be honest," Ahmed said. "Promise."

"I promise."

"Are you off your meds?"

"No."

"Are trying to fuck with me?"

"No."

"Cause it's not funny."

"Ahmed, I meant everything I said," David said, unable to keep the smile out of his voice. He could not help it around him.

"So you really want to get *married?*"

"Yes."

"Where would we live?"

"I have a place. It's small. You can come see it if you want."

He shook his head.

"Ahmed, tell me no if you don't want to."

Squeezing his keys, Ahmed said, "I don't want to tell you no."

"So then say yes."

"I'm too scared."

David saw tears drip down his cheeks and he wanted to wipe them away for him. He took a step closer but didn't touch him.

"I know I keep saying I don't know what I'm going to do." Ahmed wiped his eyes with the sleeve of his shirt. "But I know I really don't want to get married to a girl. I don't want to. Every time I think about it...I'd rather be dead," he confessed in a voice that wavered, in a way that made David believe that the thought had not been a casual one. It sounded like this had been a serious contemplation and more than once. "It would be easier to be dead," he whispered, then sniffled.

"I have tissues in my car."

Letting out a teary laugh, Ahmed asked, "Would you mind?"

David got the tissues and held them out to him.

He blew his nose and wiped his eyes. "Thanks."

They leaned against David's car together for a little while, not saying anything.

"I really like you. But it'll never work."

"It *might not* work," David said, "It's not the same. There's always a chance something might not work."

He said nothing and David wondered what he was thinking. "Why does it have to be this hard?" Ahmed asked after several minutes.

"I don't know."

"What made you ask? Other than just that we like each other and we both want to have kids and all that. Where did this come from?"

"I had this moment of clarity. You showed me that stupid ghost picture about why did the ghost cross the road."

Unable to keep a smile off his face, Ahmed said, "To get to the other side."

"Yeah, that one. You wouldn't stop laughing and I just thought, you know, I could do this forever."

"Even though we've never been on a date? Or anything."

"Or anything," David confirmed.

"But you've dated other people."

"Yes."

Ahmed looked at the tissue in his hand.

"I'm not saying it will be a fairytale ending," David said, "But I think we could be happy."

"Happier than I'd be with a girl."

"Well, yes, hopefully, happier than that. Jesus. Listen, don't do it just because you don't want to marry a girl."

"No, I! That's not what I meant," Ahmed rushed to say.

David waited.

"Shit, I wish you hadn't asked me this! Do you know what it would mean for me to do this? What it would do to my parents? I don't even know if I'd dare to show my face at the mosque!"

"I'm sorry."

"But I want to say yes, despite all that."

He reached over and offered his hand to Ahmed, who stared briefly, then took his hand, gripping tightly as though he'd been praying for something to hold the whole time. "So if you want to say yes, then say it."

"Yes."

"Really!" David asked, unable to keep his voice down.

"Yes."

Giddiness bubbled up through his body, from head to toe, and he felt like he could float away. He had not felt so weightless in years. He pulled Ahmed closer and hugged him like he'd wanted to so many times. It was a stupid idea, probably childish, but it felt right.

"God, I'm so excited!" He grinned and released Ahmed so he

could look at him.

Ahmed looked different than he had a moment ago. The tightness of his shoulders, the jitteriness of his hands had dissipated. He seemed tired, almost, and David touched his face.

"Are you okay?"

Ahmed nodded. "Yeah."

"Do you want to wait a little to do it? Tell your parents first, maybe?"

"No."

"Tomorrow?"

Ahmed nodded. "Yes."

"I'll, uh, I'll get everything sorted. I'll call you when I know, okay? In the morning."

Ahmed nodded again. "That's fine. I should go home, though, you know, pack."

"Of course."

Ahmed stepped back, moved towards his car but then returned, grabbing David by the hand and kissing him, standing on his toes to press his mouth to David's. He left after that with no glance back and no words of parting.

At home, he found Zhané dozing on the couch with Noah on her lap. He went to sit beside her. "Hey, wake up."

She stirred and a moment later, opened her eyes. "What?"

"What are you doing tomorrow?"

"Nothing."

"Do you know a justice of the peace?"

"No, but you can just google it," she said and then a moment later asked, "Why?"

"I'm eloping."

"What?"

"Yeah, tomorrow."

"David, are you off your meds?" she asked, not in a cruel way, but with quiet concern.

"No." He had missed a dose once, right after they'd tried to steal his kidney and only because he'd been at the hospital when he should have taken it, but that had been weeks ago.

"Hang on, I meant to put him to bed ages ago," she said, getting up and bringing Noah to his bedroom. When she returned, she walked straight to the kitchen. "Come talk to me."

He sat next to her. "It's crazy."

She shook her head. "No."

"Aren't you going to tell me it's a bad idea? That I'm too young?"

"It's not for me to say."

He frowned. "Really?"

"When I got pregnant, everyone told me I was too young to be a mother, a good mother, that he needed a real family. My mom, until the day I brought him home, said I could—no, that I *should* put him up for adoption. As though little black boys get adopted!"

He waited.

"But he's the best thing I ever did, you know? So I was too young, who cares? I love the shit out of that kid and I *do* take care of him. So I'm not gonna tell you that you're too young or that this is a bad idea."

"Oh."

"It's your life, live it the way you want to. If you were hoping that I'd talk you out of this—"

"No! I just didn't want you to be mad."

"You told him everything?" she asked.

He nodded. "I had to."

"Well, congratulations, then." She gave his hand a pat.

"You really don't think I'm crazy?"

"I think that it's worth a shot. What's the worst thing that could happen? Divorce? People get divorced all the time. Besides, you always were a sucker for all that Disney, love-at-first-sight crap."

He grinned. "I guess I was."

"You should clean your place, though, before you let anyone in there."

"I vacuum!" he protested but knew she was right. "Fine, alright, I'll let you know what time. You will come, right?"

"Of course, I will." She reached over and took his hand again, this time giving more than a pat. She squeezed his hand and he squeezed back.

He spent the rest of the night cleaning his apartment, especially the bathroom, and then the rest of the time figuring out exactly what he'd need tomorrow. He called Ahmed around nine, asked if he still wanted to do this and then said, "At noon, alright? Meet me there?"

"Okay."

"I'll see you—"

"Wait, hang on."

"What?" David asked.

"What are you going to wear?"

He hadn't thought about that. "Jeans?" He didn't have anything nicer.

"Okay, good," he said. "Bye."

At quarter to noon, he and Zhané met up with the justice of the peace he'd spoken with that morning, an older woman named Nancy.

"Are we ready?" she asked, giving them a warm smile and waving to Noah.

"No, uh, it's not us," David clarified, though he supposed it was an easy mistake to make. "He's not here yet."

"Nervous?" she asked.

He nodded. He was and he knew he looked nervous, too. He couldn't stand still or keep his thoughts together. He needed to do something, but there was nothing to do but wait. Unlike most times he felt like this, this felt good, it felt exciting instead of terrifying.

There was the possibility that Ahmed wouldn't come, which wouldn't be the worst thing that had ever happened. David would have rather Ahmed him stand him up than do something he didn't actually want to do.

At just before noon, Ahmed arrived with two young women, one only a few years older than David and the other at least thirty. The older one wore a hijab and, judging by her belly, would be giving birth within a few months. The younger woman wore no head covering and had her hair cut into a short bob. David imagined that they both looked like Ahmed, between the younger one's nose and the older one's jawline; he hoped that they were actually related and he wasn't racist.

They both jabbered to Ahmed as they walked over and he seemed to be ignoring them. David couldn't understand what they were saying, but it didn't sound good.

"Hi," David said, looking at the women.

"These are my sisters," he said to the pavement, "And they said if they couldn't come, they would tell my parents."

"Oh."

"I'm Noor," the younger one introduced herself.

"Miriam," said the older one, her hand resting on her belly.

David glanced at Ahmed because they were both speaking to Zhané, who greeted the women in return with a baffled look on her face. Ahmed sighed, rubbed his eyes, and said, "Noor, Miriam, it's not her."

"What do you mean?" Noor asked, for a second giving a confused glanced towards Nancy.

Ahmed nodded towards David. "This is David."

Both women gasped and began speaking to him at the same time, one of them giving him a push and the other smacking his arm.

After half a minute, he stepped away from them, throwing up his hands and shouting, "*This* is why I didn't want you to come!"

"Ahmed, how long has this been going on?" Noor demanded.

"What, with him?" he asked.

"No, how long have you known you were gay?" she clarified.

He shrugged. "I don't know, forever."

"And you never told us!" Miriam scolded.

"I'm telling you now."

Noor embraced her brother. "You're an asshole, you know," she said affectionately.

"I know. Can we do this, now?" he asked.

They entered the building as a gaggle with Nancy leading the way. The entire process took no more than forty-five minutes and would have gone quicker if Noah had not needed a diaper change between getting the license and the ceremony.

The ceremony was quick, held just outside the town hall, next to a tree and a bench.

Like ripping off a Band-Aid, David thought, which felt like the wrong thing to compare his wedding to. He and Ahmed stood facing each other as the women and Noah watched. Noah made little babbling sounds every so often. David wondered if Ahmed meant this or if he was doing it just to avoid marrying a girl or because he didn't know how else to deal with being gay.

He hoped not and he didn't really think so, either, because even though his hands were a little sweaty as he held on hard to David's hands, he was smiling.

"I now pronounce you..." Nancy hesitated, but recovered with, "Legally wed."

Ahmed stared at him and he stared back, not knowing what to do with the strange elation bubbling up inside of him. He leaned in to kiss him and it felt like had been waiting a thousand years to do this. Maybe it had been crazy to do this, but sometimes, he reasoned, crazy was good.

Nancy gave them her congratulations and left.

He wrapped his arms around Ahmed and lifted him off his

feet, which made him laugh and hold on to David tighter. When he set him down, David asked, "Now what?"

"Now you tell your parents," Miriam suggested to her brother.

"I can't," Ahmed said.

"So will you let them think you've run away?" she asked.

"No, just..."

"Ahmed, it'll be all bluster," Noor said, "They'll get over it."

"I don't know."

"Come on," she reasoned, "What did they do, really, when Miriam married an atheist? Or when I wouldn't wear a hijab? Or when I went to prom? What have they done, really, about all thing things we did anyway?"

"They get pissed!"

"And then...?" Noor asked.

"Things go back to normal," Miriam said. "With time. So it took them a year to come around to Mark and maybe it will take them five years to get used to this, but it will happen."

"But it won't happen if you don't tell them," Noor said.

Ahmed glanced at David and David said, "If you think it wouldn't be safe..."

"No, no, it's not like that, my parents would never *do* anything to me."

"I'll come with you if you want," he offered.

He nodded. "Okay. But not yet."

"No?"

"Just...I don't know, give me ten minutes," he said. "Come sit with me."

David heard Zhané ask Ahmed's sisters to talk for a second as he went to sit with Ahmed. They sat on the bench together and Ahmed said nothing, just leaned against David.

"Buyer's remorse?" David asked after a few minutes.

"No. No, of course not. I...I didn't even think about not coming, you know? Does that make me desperate?" With a little laugh, he said, "See, this is what happens when you aren't allowed to date."

"If you're desperate then I am, too." He took Ahmed's hand and leaned in to kiss his temple.

After several minutes, Zhané came over. "Give me your keys."

"Why?"

"I'm taking Noor back to the house."

"Why?"

"It's a surprise."

David did not like surprises but handed over his keys; she walked away.

At about one thirty, they arrived at Ahmed's parents' house with Miriam leading the way up the steps. She glanced at one of the cars in the driveway. "Ugh."

"What?" David asked.

"It's my uncle's car," Ahmed explained. "They don't get along."

David nodded. He understood disquiet between family members. Once inside, a wave of words washed over them, a woman's voice speaking to Ahmed, at first warm and then scolding as she saw David.

A woman in her late fifties began to leave, saying, "You are supposed to tell me if you have friends over!"

David glanced at Miriam. "She needs to go get her scarf," she explained. "Because you're not family."

Ahmed grabbed her hand. "Ade, you don't have to."

She scolded him, pulling her hand back and he followed her into the kitchen. "No, Ade, he's family," he explained.

"Nonsense!" David heard her say.

"What language do you guys speak, anyway?" he asked as Ahmed and his mother went back and forth with each other in the kitchen. Ahmed didn't seem to be getting in more than a few words at a time.

"Pashto," Miriam said.

David noticed an old woman sitting on the couch.

"That's our grandmother," Miriam offered.

David waved. "Hi."

The old woman waved back and said something David didn't understand.

"She doesn't speak English," Miriam told him.

A toilet flushed upstairs and a middle-aged man came down, giving David and Miriam a sour look but saying nothing.

"That's our uncle," she said.

From the kitchen, Ahmed shouted, "Mommy, I'm gay!"

The house went quiet.

The grandmother called over to Miriam, asking a question, and Miriam answered. David assumed that she'd asked for a translation. If her grandson being gay bothered her, it didn't show.

Ahmed's mother began to wail.

Miriam rolled her eyes. "So dramatic. You stay here." She

headed to the kitchen.

The three of them argued for a while until Ahmed's mother began to repeat the same word over and over.

"I'm going, Mommy, stop yelling!" Ahmed said.

"Ade, calm down," Miriam insisted.

His cheeks red, Ahmed walked past David, jogged up the stairs, and returned with a duffle bag and backpack.

David frowned. "What?"

"Oh, she's kicking me out." The words came out with a tremble and his hands, white-knuckled, gripped the bag.

David couldn't help it, he gasped.

"No, it's...I was leaving anyway."

Ahmed's mother appeared and said to David, "And you get out too!"

"Mom!" Miriam scolded. To Ahmed, she said, "I'll call you when she's calmed down."

"Do not!" his mother said. "Get out!"

Ahmed grabbed David by the arm and pulled him out. As he left, David waved and said, "It was nice to meet you."

Ahmed pulled him along, then released him as he dug around for his keys. As he did so, David heard the door open again and turned, hoping to see Miriam, but instead found Ahmed's uncle coming down the front steps.

"Oh, no," Ahmed whispered when he noticed his uncle. He searched more frantically for his keys and told David, "Quick, get in the car."

Before they could, Ahmed's uncle grabbed Ahmed by the arm and began to shout at him in Pashto. Ahmed pulled back and said something that sounded like the Pashto equivalent of 'fuck off', but his uncle grabbed him again, this time with his hand raised and his hand curled into a fist.

David stepped forward, not thinking, and grabbed the older man by the wrist. He glanced at Ahmed, who took the opportunity to move away, keys finally in hand.

The uncle, short and paunchy, stared up at David.

"I'd like to go," David said.

The man yanked back his arm, glared at Ahmed, who had shoved his things into the back seat and gotten in the car, then spat on David, pronouncing, "Bacha baz." He stormed off after that.

Once he'd climbed into the car, David asked, "What does that mean?"

"What?" Ahmed asked.

"Bocce something."

"Oh, bacha baz. It means pedophile. Well, literally, it means you play with boys," Ahmed said, starting the car and backing out of the driveway. "Uncle Rahim is...uh. Very closed minded."

"I'm not a pedophile. I mean, you're not a child."

"No, in Afghanistan there's this thing, bacha bazi. Boy play. Like in the military and stuff, like they take little boys and, uh, you know. Listen, if you want to know more you can just google it."

"Oh. Is that what he told you, too?"

"That and that I shame my family and I should be put to death," Ahmed said casually.

"Jesus."

"He says that to Noor, too," Ahmed offered, "Says it to everyone. Said it to his wife when she divorced him."

"My Aunt Wendy," David countered, "thinks that vaccines made her son autistic."

"Every family has one."

David had to give him instructions on how to get to Zhané's house. Ahmed parked in front, on the street, because there was a third car David didn't recognize in the driveway. David helped him carry his things up the side stairs that brought them above the garage. He heard voices coming from within and started to open the door.

"No, no, don't come in yet!" Noor shouted, pushing the door closed on him.

"What?"

"Just wait, like ten more minutes."

David turned to Ahmed. "Your sister says we can't come in."

Ahmed approached and called, "Noor? What are you doing?"

"Did Uncle Rahim threaten to kill you?" she asked.

He scoffed, rolled his eyes, and sat on the stairs, his backpack between his feet. David set down the duffel bag and sat beside him.

"How many languages do you speak?" David asked.

"Fluently?"

"Sure."

"Two," he said, "But, I uh, I can get by alright in Dari."

"What's Dari?"

"The dialect of Persian in Afghanistan," he said, "And Spanish. They made me take in school. I can kind of speak a little Spanish."

"That's awesome."

He shrugged.

"So your sister doesn't wear the thing? The scarf?"

He shrugged again. "She thinks it's stupid," he said, "I wouldn't want to wear one either, probably. I mean. I don't really think it's stupid. It's complicated, though. She'll tell you about it if you ask. For, like, hours."

David reached over for his hand, brought it to his mouth and kissed it. "Hey."

"What?"

"I really like you."

"I really like you too."

"Like a ton."

Ahmed grinned, but after a second it faded.

"What?" David asked.

He shook his head. "It's...I didn't even get to see my dad or anything. If he's gonna know, I'd want to be the one who tells him. And I don't know how long this will take. You know?"

David didn't know but he nodded anyway.

"And what if they don't get over it? What if this is it, you know? The thing that's finally too much for them to deal with."

"You should call your dad."

"What?"

"If you want to be the one to tell him, you should call him."

Ahmed sighed, took out his phone and stared at it for a second. He sighed again and dialed, putting the phone to his ear and had a very short conversation.

When he'd hung up, David asked, "What he'd say?"

"That my mother's right." His face twisted, looking like he was trying not to cry, but when David scooted closer and put an arm around him, tears dribbled down his cheeks. "What if I don't see them again?"

"Hey, of course, you will. You'll see them tomorrow, won't you? At the mosque." He had meant to be comforting, but Ahmed only started to cry more. "Oh, Ahmed, hey. It's going to be alright."

Ahmed mumbled something David couldn't really hear and nestled further into his arms. After a few minutes, David pulled back. "It's really going to be fine."

He shook his head. "You don't know that."

"Your sisters seem pretty sure."

"They didn't even *talk* to Miriam for a year!"

David wiped the tears from his face. "Ahmed, it's okay."

"How do you know?"

"I just...I don't know, not for sure, but it's just...it's what I think, it's what I feel. Which I guess is nonsense but whatever."

"It is nonsense," Ahmed said and at first, David thought it was a reprimand, but a smile broke on his face.

Zhané came out on to the stairs and David turned to look at her. "Whose car is that?"

"Malik's."

"Oh."

"Come inside," she said.

They stood and entered the apartment. David grinned and said, "Oh, hey!" at the sight of the bed and dresser they'd set up. They'd added a small table and two chairs in the kitchen, making the place almost look like a real person lived there.

Zhané gave him a push. "Shouldn't spend your wedding night on a futon, you know."

He gave her a hug, one armed so he didn't smother the baby. "You're the best."

"It's just stuff from the guest room," she said. "Uh, well, Malik donated the table."

David glanced over to where Malik and Daysha stood together. "Thanks."

"It's stuff my parents wanted to get rid of anyways," Daysha said. "But we got you a real present."

"Oh, you didn't have to."

"It's just something small." She handed him a small gift bag overflowing with tissue.

He set it on the table and opened it to find a card with a gift card tucked inside it, as well as a throw blanket and a set of matching coffee mugs. "Thanks, that's really sweet," he said, looking down at the mugs which were both painted with 'Mr.' and a vintage looking floral design; they went together but were not matchy-matchy.

"Thanks a lot," Ahmed said.

"Okay, let's go." Zhané gave her brother a push towards the door that led to her part of the house. She glanced back and said, "Hey, check your side table drawer." She said it with a smile and he knew it had to be something dirty.

Noor gave her brother a hug and said something comforting to him; David wondered where he could learn Pashto, if it was even something he was capable of learning. She then caught up to Zhané and asked, "Hey, can I get a ride home?"

.

ONCE THEIR guests had left, the two men stood in the middle of the small apartment, not saying anything to each other. Ahmed looked around but didn't move.

"Go ahead, look around," David said. "Unpack."

Ahmed took a few steps further in.

David took his duffle bag and brought it over to the bed. "Come on." He peeked into the dresser and found that Zhané, or someone, had gathered up his clothes from around the room and put them in the top drawers.

Ahmed unzipped the duffle bag and then stared at it.

David sat on the bed and watched, wondering what he was staring at until he pulled out a stuffed elephant, a blush coming to his cheeks.

"I couldn't leave her," he confessed quietly.

"What's her name?"

"Mrs. Elephant."

David laughed, he couldn't help it. He took the elephant and set her next to Benjamin Rabbit, who was propped against the pillows. "Look, they'll be best friends."

Ahmed moved his things from the bag to the dresser, then placed the bag on the floor and sat on the bed.

David moved over and put his arms around him; he kissed his neck and then his shoulder. Ahmed did not move, so David pulled back. "Do you want to—"

"I'm not ready," Ahmed answered, his words coming out all at once.

"Eat lunch?" David finished. "I was too wired to eat breakfast."

Ahmed let out a breath. "Oh. Yeah. Please. Sorry."

"For what?"

"I don't know," he said, "I don't know. I'm not...I can't yet."

"Are we talking about lunch or sex?" David asked.

"I'd like to eat lunch."

"Alright, good, cause I was talking about lunch." He got off the bed and went to the kitchen, which he had used much more lately in his attempts to learn to cook. He'd even picked up some used cookbooks at one of the tag sales he'd haunted, trying to furnish his space as best he could on a budget. "What do you want to eat?"

"Uh. What do you want?"

David glanced over and saw that the tightness in his shoulders had returned. He turned away from the kitchen to lean on the half wall that separated the kitchen from the living space. He watched Ahmed for a second, then asked, "Do you want to talk?"

"No. Yes. About what?"

"You look nervous."

"I don't know."

David waited for a moment but Ahmed said nothing else, so he offered, "Okay, well, I'll just make a guess and let you know that I don't expect anything."

Ahmed snorted. "Everyone expects something."

"Oh, is that what you've learned from all the dates you didn't go on?" David asked, not able to keep his tone even like he'd meant to.

Ahmed said nothing, just crossed his arms.

"Anyway. What do you want to eat?"

"What do you have?"

"Uh." David thought. "Mostly food for garbage people. Pasta, I've got pasta. Sandwiches." He checked a cabinet. "A variety of canned soups and children's cereals." He looked through a few more cabinets and said, "I may have given you the impression that I'm a functional adult human being, but, uh..."

"No, you didn't."

David grinned. "Alright, good. As long we're clear on that. I can make pancakes."

"Pancakes?" Ahmed asked.

"Yeah. Do you like pancakes?"

"My mom wouldn't make them, I always wanted her to."

"Alright, so pancakes." He began rooting around for a mixing bowl. He found one, straightened up, and asked, "Right?"

"Yeah," Ahmed agreed, coming over to lean against the wall David had abandoned. He looked on as David cooked.

David stared down at the pancake he made, watching the bubbles, watching for the edges to firm up. He felt a little lightheaded, but he'd had an exciting day and he hadn't eaten yet.

"I can't believe you're still wasting your time like this," said his mother's voice.

He turned around, making sure she hadn't materialized. He didn't see her, so he returned his attention to the pancake.

"It's just selfish," said his father's voice.

He frowned, flipped the pancake and to Ahmed said, "Hey, come watch this."

Ahmed came over. "What do I do?"

"Just take it out in a minute." He handed over the spatula and going to the pill organizer on his bedside table. He checked the day, Thursday, and made sure that the pill from Thursday had been taken. It had. Nothing had been missed. His mother's voice he was used to; at this point, he expected to hear her. She'd been a stay-at-home mom during his early childhood and he'd always assumed that her voice would be a part of his life. But his father, his father he never heard.

"Is something wrong?" Ahmed asked.

"No." *Not yet.* He went over, took back the spatula, and scooped out the pancake. He turned off the stove and moved the pan, then said, "Go sit."

He placed one plate in front of Ahmed and the other in front of himself.

"I hope you like them."

"Smells good."

They didn't talk for a few minutes until Ahmed asked, "Are you sure there's nothing wrong?"

"Why?"

"You look all squirrely."

"Oh."

"You can tell me."

David thought. "Hmm. Alright. I heard my dad say something to me. Like, I hallucinated it. But I never hear him, ever. Not even at my worst."

"Oh."

"So, you know, I checked my pills and stuff and I *remember* taking it today, I know I did. But...uh. What if it was fake? Like if someone switched it out? But who would do that, right? Nobody. Not Zhané, that's for sure, she's got a kid that she leaves alone with me all the time."

"Oh."

"So yeah that's me right now."

Ahmed took out his phone.

"I mean she wouldn't, would she?"

"Probably not. You should finish eating, maybe you'll feel better," he suggested.

David continued to eat. He was hungry.

"I mean, really, David, how long are you going to keep up this 'bisexual' act?" his father's voice asked.

David sighed and finished his pancakes. He rinsed the dishes, loaded them into the dishwasher, and closed it. He hadn't asked if they'd been good. He'd tasted them, so he knew he'd liked them, but he hadn't asked Ahmed. He hasn't asked his husband. The reality of the situation set in. *I have a husband.*

"Did you like them?"

"Yeah, it was great," Ahmed said.

He checked the time on his phone. Just after four-thirty. He stood and looked down at it for a while, trying to figure out what was wrong. He had a feeling he couldn't shake and it wasn't the usual kind, the kind that made him double check the garbage cans to see if he'd actually heard a baby crying.

He looked around and saw Ahmed, not really paying attention to him, but looking at the elephant on his bed with his mouth turned down.

Benjamin Rabbit sat beside them.

"Oh!" The pieces clicked as he stared at the rabbit.

Ahmed looked over. "Oh?"

"Oh. I didn't tell my parents."

"Oh," Ahmed said, his tone registering the gravity.

"I should probably do that, right?" David asked, not able to keep the nervousness from his tone. That was it, that would do it. His parents wouldn't approve; he had known that going in.

He sat on the loveseat and dialed.

His mother picked up after a few rings. "David? What is it?" She sounded worried; she hadn't heard from him since he'd come to Connecticut.

"Hi, just calling."

"Oh. Really?" she asked.

"No, is Dad around?"

"No, he hasn't gotten home from work yet. He should be home around five."

"Oh."

"Why, did you need something?"

"No, um. Call me back when he gets home, okay? It's important."

"David, are you alright?"

"Yes. Just call me back."

"Alright."

He hung up and put the phone down on the arm of the loveseat.

Ahmed asked, "Do you have an outlet?"

"No, none, anywhere," he said, then pointed to the bedside table. "Behind that."

Ahmed took out his laptop and plugged it in, leaving it on the bed. He opened it up and pressed the power button, seated crisscross in front of it. "You don't mind, do you?"

"What?"

"I just wanted to write something down quick."

"No, go ahead." David watched him for a few minutes, listening to the click of the keyboard, faster than he thought anyone could type. "What are you writing?"

He shook his head. "I just, you know, I write about what happens."

"That's called a diary."

"I know," he said, not quite snapping but not happy that David had teased him.

"Did you write about me in it?"

"Yes."

"What did you write about me?"

Ahmed sighed, hesitated, and finally answered, "There's a crazy white guy at work who's ruining my life."

"Ah."

"Because when he's around I can't pretend that I'm anything but what I am. I can't pretend that I could ever marry a girl and not want to blow my brains out every night. I can't imagine..." he trailed off, his cheeks reddening.

"Can't imagine what?"

"I can't imagine ever sharing a bed with anybody but a man and right now I can't think of sharing one with anyone but him. That's what I wrote."

"Oh my god," David breathed.

"Shut up."

"No, Ahmed, that's...I don't know, it makes me feel funny. Like. Come here."

"What?"

"Come here."

Ahmed came over and David took his hand, putting it on his chest.

"Can you feel that?" he asked, "My heart is literally racing."

Ahmed licked his lips. He did it when he was nervous, David knew that by now. But good nervous, not scared nervous. "That's good, right?"

He nodded.

They looked at each other for a moment more and then, as he was about to move forward, Ahmed leaned in towards him so that, while they kissed, David had to lean against the back of the couch. Ahmed had pushed him, maybe on purpose, maybe not realizing that he still had his hand over David's heart.

His first real kiss in months and the only one he'd had in years that wasn't a secret, the gateway to another casual encounter hidden in a supply closet or locked bathroom.

He put his hand on the back of Ahmed's head and his other on his hip, pulling him closer, needing him closer. David slid his hands inside his shirt, desperate for the taste of his skin, but when he moved his hand to the button on the other man's jeans, Ahmed grabbed his hand, pulling back.

"I'm sorry, I can't," he breathed.

"I should have asked," David said.

"No, it's...I'm sorry."

He sat up and left a quick kiss on his lips. "It doesn't matter. Do you want to talk?"

"No." He shook his head and then immediately said, "Yes."

"What do you want to talk about?"

Ahmed sat back, then moved to the seat next to David, his knees pulled up to his chest, his whole body facing towards David. "I don't know."

David turned, one leg off the side of the loveseat, the other bent up and resting against the back of the couch. "So...you know where babies come from?"

"Yes. I'm not, you know, a shut-in. I know how everything's supposed to work. I've seen porn."

David tried to keep in a laugh, biting his tongue. "Sure." He couldn't help himself when he asked, "A lot of porn?"

"No. Just...enough."

"Enough?"

"Enough to know!" he said, "You know, what happens. It's not like I could ask anyone!"

"No, I know," David soothed. "When my parents gave me the talk I was convinced for like, a full two years, that girls had their parts right in front."

Ahmed snorted.

"Like a fucking coin slot," he admitted, half-laughing.

"That's stupid."

"Well, what did you think!"

"I didn't."

David shook his head. "See," he said with a gesture towards Ahmed, "That's the difference between the gay kids and the bi ones."

He snorted again. "Besides, how would they use the bathroom?"

"I didn't know girls sat to pee! I didn't have any sisters or anything."

"Dork," Ahmed pronounced.

"So you know how everything works. According to porn. Questions?"

"People don't really leave their shoes on, do they?"

David laughed, he couldn't help it. "No, no shoes required."

"Cause, like, you'd have to take them off to take off your pants and then put them back on, right?"

"Maybe if you had really baggy pants it would work." He reached out to take one of Ahmed's hands. "But seriously. Now that you know you're allowed to take your shoes off."

"I'm, I don't know..."

"Nervous?"

He nodded.

"Me too."

"Really?"

David nodded. "Sure. It's new. Different. Us, this. All of it. I was scared you wouldn't like pancakes. I didn't want canned soup to be our first meal as a married couple."

"What are we gonna do for dinner?"

"I don't know. Lucky Charms?"

"They're haram."

"Really?"

"The marshmallows. They use pork gelatin."

"Jesus. That's gotta be exhausting."

Ahmed shrugged. "You eat what you know."

"I have Cheerios. There can't be pork in those, right?"

"Cheerios are halal," he confirmed.

David's phone began to ring and he grabbed it. He answered. "Hi."

"Your father just got home."

"Okay, great, put me on speakerphone."

"How?" his mother asked.

"Uh, push the button that looks like a speaker."

"Alright, you're on," she said and he knew she'd done it right because now her voice sounded far away. "What's so important?"

"Hi, David," his father said.

"Hi. I got married," he told them, aware that Ahmed was watching him.

"What!" his mother said, "Oh, God, David."

"Mom."

"You got some girl pregnant, didn't you?" she asked.

"No."

"Now, hang on, David, this is pretty sudden," his father said, not sounding mad, but just tired like he always did. David secretly believed that his father struggled with some type of depression, though he didn't dare to bring it up.

"Uh. Yeah. It was," he admitted. "Do you want to talk to him?"

"Him!" his mother said so loud that Ahmed raised his eyebrows.

"Yeah. His name is Ahmed," he said.

"His name is what now?" his father asked.

"Ahmed. His family's from Afghanistan," he said.

"Is this some kind of green card marriage?" his mother asked. "Jesus!"

"No. He was born here," he said, "Right?" he asked Ahmed, who nodded. "Yeah, he was."

"Jesus Christ, David!"

"Mom, come on, Jesus doesn't like it when you use his full name like that," he said and he knew that, if he could see her, her left eye would be scrunched up, not twitching but ready.

Ahmed titled his head.

"Anyways, he's great. You'd love him. He wants to be a teacher and, uh, his favorite color is orange."

"Is it?" Ahmed asked.

David titled his phone away from himself. "Yeah, of course, half your shit is orange. Your phone case is orange, your laptop is orange. Your watch is orange. I'll bet your socks are orange."

Ahmed looked at his feet.

"So. Next time you have a free weekend or something, you should come down," David said to his parents.

"Have you been taking your medication?" his father asked.

"Yeah, of course. Besides, what does hearing voices have to do with getting married?" he asked.

"Well, you make questionable choices sometimes, David, let's not pretend, here," his father said.

"This isn't one of those times. So let me know if you're going to come down."

"David, does he *know* that you're sick?" his mother asked.

"Yes." Not liking the turn in the conversation, he said, "Oh, god, the stove is on fire, gotta go," and hung up.

Ahmed told him, "They are orange."

"Told you."

"That seemed like it went okay."

David shrugged. "They probably think I imagined you." He ran his thumb over Ahmed's knuckles. "You were writing! Oh, I'm sorry, I really interrupted you, didn't I?"

"It's fine."

"Go finish. I've gotta do some laundry or I won't have any work shirts tomorrow."

He had not planned on doing laundry, but someone had taken all his clothes from their pile on the chair, where he kept things that he would wear again, and put them in the laundry basket he used as a hamper.

He leaned in for one more kiss, then stood, taking his laundry, and heading into Zhané's part of the house, through the living room and to the basement, which he hated. He passed Zhané on his way and she called, "Are you doing laundry?"

"Should I not?"

"Didn't you just get married?"

"Yeah, but I still have to wear clean clothes to work tomorrow," he said.

"Whatever." She turned her attention back to the TV.

"Hey."

"Hm?"

"Thanks. For all of it."

"No problem," she said.

He returned to find Ahmed totally absorbed in his writing and didn't bother him. When his clothes were dry, he folded them, feeling strongly that folding was a waste of time.

Around nine, Ahmed started to yawn. "I couldn't sleep at all last night."

"No, me neither. Go to bed."

"No, I have to pray in like an hour," he said, "And I don't want to sleep through it."

In the time that they had been together that day, Ahmed's phone had reminded him three times to do one of his five prayers for the day. He had an app that went off automatically, which David thought was nifty.

The Catholic version, he thought, would go off just as often, but to remind him that he'd done something to feel guilty about.

"I don't have a TV yet, I've been meaning to get one."

Ahmed unplugged his laptop and came to sit beside David on the loveseat. He pulled up Netflix and asked, "Will you think I'm a loser if we watch cartoons?"

"No."

Later, after Ahmed had said his final prayer for the day, they began to settle into bed, David in boxers and a t-shirt, Ahmed in just pajama bottoms, though he had hesitated before he pulled off his undershirt.

"Do you snore?" David asked.

"No."

"I do a little." He turned back the covers and sat on the bed, waiting for Ahmed to join him.

Ahmed came to sit. "I'm going to wake up tomorrow at home, right? Cause this still doesn't feel real."

"Is that what you want?"

"No. Even if this is a dream, if I'm not here, come get me when you wake up."

"Wouldn't that make this my dream?" David asked, "Wouldn't

that just be dream-you telling dream-me what I want to hear?"

Ahmed rolled his eyes and lay down. "Maybe we're dreaming together."

David turned off the lights pulled the covers up, thankful for air conditioning, and put his arm around Ahmed. They dropped off to sleep quickly, though, at three or four in the morning, Ahmed's phone went off, so loud it scared David awake. Ahmed slept with his phone on the bed beside him so that he could feel it vibrate when it went off.

Hazily, in the darkness, David asked, "Who's fucking calling you?"

"Sorry sorry, go back to sleep. I gotta pray," he said, getting out of bed.

"You're better than me," David said. He didn't even go to church.

A few minutes later, Ahmed came back and nestled up to David for a little while until they'd both have to get up anyways for work.

When he showered, David looked down at himself. He had not seriously evaluated his body in a while. Tall, of course, all arms and legs, with more meat on his bones than he'd had in high school, when he'd been a skinny scarecrow of a kid.

The main feature these days seemed to be scars. On his arms, on his side near his liver, the one on his thigh and now a new one his back. He hadn't minded them; they were side effects, not the problem.

"Broken," accused a voice.

Some wear and tear. He'd seen that label on things, used items up for sale; things that had served their purpose and were no longer wanted.

"Used."

"Maybe that would be valid if it had anything to do with sex," he argued. But still, he had more scars than the average person. Was it too many? Would Ahmed notice? Would he mind?

He turned off the water and stepped out, drying off and heading out of the bathroom with just a towel around his waist. Ahmed sat at the table, a bowl of Cheerios in front of him. He had showered already, leaving the bathroom smelling like his soap.

"Do you want to carpool?" Ahmed asked without looking up from his cereal and his phone.

"Don't you have to leave early?"

"Miriam said she could pick me up."

"Okay." It made sense that he'd want to go to the mosque with someone familiar, especially after such a big rupture in his day-to-day life.

David turned away to dress and Ahmed asked, "What happened to your back!"

He must have looked up after David had turned away, maybe by coincidence, maybe because he'd been too shy to look up before. David glanced back as he opened his drawers. "I told you. The things."

"Oh. I forgot."

Of course, he had. They weren't real to him, not like they were to David. He wondered when it would sink in, if it would drive him away when it did. He tried not to think about it too much.

He dressed in a hurry and grabbed his keys. "Ready?"

"Are you going to eat?"

"I did," he said, which was not a lie. He had shoved several handfuls of cereal into his mouth and washed it down with milk before getting into the shower. He wondered what Ahmed would think if he had witnessed it. Probably nothing flattering.

8/2/15

"DO YOU think he knows?" Ahmed asked from the bed, where he sat in front of his laptop, but not typing anything. He had been staring at it for a while now.

"What?" David had been looking right at him but he had not heard him.

"Johnny. He's gotta know. He keeps giving me dirty looks."

"Uh, no offense, but he kind of hates you," David said.

"Yeah, well, he'd hate me more if I was gay!"

"You are gay."

"Shut *up*, David!"

"Oh, well, alright," David said, not sure what else to say. He hadn't meant to be a dick, but there he went again. "Are you hungry?"

"We could get fired," Ahmed said.

"You can't get fired for being gay or married or Muslim."

"It doesn't feel that way."

David got up from the love seat and sat beside Ahmed on their bed. "Do you want to talk?"

"No, I want Johnny to quit staring at me!"

He took Ahmed's hand. "If you don't like it, you can find another job."

He let out a harsh laugh. "Doing what?"

"I don't know, Mr. Speaks Four Languages, you tell me," he said.

"The semester's gonna start soon," Ahmed said, changing the topic. "My shifts are probably going to change."

"Okay. Are you still writing?"

"Why?"

"Cause I was gonna kiss you but if you're busy, I'll wait."

Ahmed sighed. He rubbed his eyes. He closed his laptop and put it on the bedside table. "No, I'm done."

"Jesus, pouty, I don't want to kiss you if you're going to be like this," he said, hoping that his teasing was obvious. "Maybe you should get published," he offered after a moment of Ahmed not saying anything. "I mean. You write a lot."

"You can't just *get* published."

David frowned. It would have been easy to take the bait, to start a fight. He scooted closer to Ahmed to sit next to him; the bedspread was still warm from his laptop. He put an arm around his husband and kissed his head. "Do you want to tell me what's bothering you?"

"No," he said, his voice softer now. He leaned in against David.

"Okay, I'll wait."

"Aren't you tired of waiting for me?"

"No."

"Come on, David, be honest."

"I went to the store while you were at work." Ahmed had worked the Sunday shift earlier in the day and he had come home in this mood.

"What store?"

"The one in Waterbury, the halal one. I stocked up the fridge and stuff. So we could eat like real people."

"You didn't have to."

"Uh. Well, you ate all the Cheerios and you seemed like you were sick of pasta and peanut butter sandwiches," David said.

"Thanks, I guess."

"Your welcome, I guess. Did something happen at work?"

"No."

"Is it about your parents?"

"No."

"Do you want me to leave you alone?"

Ahmed pressed his head against David's chest. "No."

David took his hand and kissed it. "It isn't just you, you know. I'm nervous, too, I meant that."

"But nervous about what? You've already...you know. You've been with people."

"I'm nervous, uh...that some of the things about me might be too much. I've got all these, these scars, you know, and I just, I don't want you to think they're ugly. And I don't want you to see me if things get bad again, if I start having a hard time."

"David, I..."

"Because I know what it looks like, you know? I know it's scary. Weird."

Ahmed pulled back to look him in the face.

"I don't want you to think that I'm too fucked up." *Broken, used up, no good.*

"I don't think that."

"No, not yet you don't." *Everyone else does.* He knew that wasn't fair to think, but it felt true.

"You don't think that about me, do you?" Ahmed asked.

"No, why would I?"

"Uh, cause I can't hear?"

"Yeah, but...it's not the same."

"Alright, what about being Muslim? We're scary, right?"

David shook his head. "Muslims aren't dangerous."

"Yeah, you say that, but what about Uncle Rahim? I'd say he's dangerous," Ahmed challenged. "What about those fucks who strap bombs to themselves? That's pretty dangerous."

"That's not *you*, though. But I am weird and scary...*I* did things that were wrong, Ahmed. It's not the same as getting lumped in with some extremists, it's the things that I've done."

Ahmed looked at him for a while, looking like he was trying to think of something to say. He was stuck, David guessed, because David had killed someone and he knew it. David had made sure he knew, about killing someone, about the things that visited.

David said, "I understand that people treat you like you're dangerous when you aren't and because of that, you want to think that people are unfairly accused. But that's not me. It's likely, it's almost statistically guaranteed that I'll have another break someday. And even if it's not a full-on, need-to-be hospitalized break, you'll still see me do things that will be...unsettling to watch."

"I don't care, David. I know you did something wrong, but...it's done, I understand why you did it, and it will get dealt with when everything gets dealt with," he explained. "As for the future, I'm not a scared little kid, alright? I'm not going to turn tail and run just cause...you know, you do whatever it is you do when you're having a hard time."

"I hope you're right."

Ahmed lay down on the bed, flopping back with an exaggerated sigh. "This sucks."

"I'm sorry."

"No, not you," he said. "I just...man, this blows."

David lay down beside him, turning on his side.

Ahmed rolled to face him.

"Do you want to tell me what specifically blows?"

"I wish I wasn't so nervous."

"Oh, that still."

"Yes."

"So you don't think I'm gross, do you?"

"No, why would I?" Ahmed asked.

"I don't know, lots of reasons. I've got all these scars, I don't wash my work shirts enough and I've slept around. I eat cereal with my hands and drink right out of the milk carton."

"The milk thing does bother me a little," Ahmed said. "But that's it." He scooched a little closer. "I don't even know if I'm really that nervous, you know, I think I'm just psyching myself out."

David didn't have anything to say.

"Cause I'd really like to, you know, do something."

"Something specific?"

"Uh. Sort of."

He put his hand on Ahmed's waist. "What?" They were lying close, almost nose-to-nose.

"I don't want to say."

"Okay." He pecked him on the lips. "Did you write anything else about me?"

He rolled away and at first, David thought he'd upset him, but he returned with his phone. He fiddled with it for a second, then asked, "You really want to know?"

"Sure."

"Today at work we were stocking the canned vegetables again. People in this town eat canned corn like they need it to live. I was doing the bottom shelves and he was doing the top ones because of course he was, he's so fucking tall. He was standing right next to me and all I could smell was Irish Spring and some kind of body spray.

I always hated that, when people smell like too much body spray, but on him, it smells amazing."

David felt his heart starting to speed up again.

"He said something, asked me if I'd heard something. I hadn't. I don't hear half the things he does, I don't know if it's because I can't hear or because he hears too much. So I looked up to answer him and he was right next to me, his legs right there. I had this thought."

He would have put money on what that thought was.

"I thought what if I grabbed him by his belt loops and unzipped his jeans and blew him. Just like that. Holding on to his legs and hearing him grunt. Would he let me? He looks at me sometimes like he's going to push me up against the wall and kiss me. He's so tall, I wonder how big he is. I wonder what it would taste like, his skin. I think he would let me," he read, his voice surprisingly even. David wouldn't have been able to read it with a straight face.

"I might have," David said.

Ahmed snorted.

"I probably would have dragged you into the back room," he said. His breathing felt shallow. He'd never had proof that he'd haunted someone else's thoughts the way they haunted his.

"What about now?"

A smartass answer came to mind, saying that there was no back room to drag him to, but instead, he only managed to say, "Yeah."

They moved in a flurry, grabbing onto each other, kissing like they need it to live. They had kissed since they'd eloped but not like this because Ahmed didn't pull back this time, he didn't tense up. Instead, he reached between David's legs, grabbing him so that David inhaled sharply and then sighed, closing his eyes.

"Get, uh, get undressed," he said, breathing hard. "Please."

David kissed him. "You too?"

"Um. Yeah. Okay."

"Don't forget to take your shoes off."

Ahmed laughed, giving him a push and then one more kiss before he tugged his shirt off. He had to stand to get his pants off and David stood, too, throwing his clothes onto the pile on the floor. The sight of their underwear strewn next to each other touched him more than it should have.

Once they'd undressed they looked at each other.

"Not that big," David said.

Ahmed snorted and putting his arms around his neck, standing on his toes to kiss him. On a whim, David picked him up and he wrapped his legs around David's waist.

"We could do it like this," Ahmed said.

"Probably," David said, "But they don't show you the beforehand stuff you're supposed to do in porn."

"What do you mean?"

"Uh. Just hygiene stuff," David said, recalling the disaster that had been his first time. He wanted Ahmed's to involve less shit and vomit. "Tomorrow, maybe, a different day. Not now."

"Okay."

He seemed disappointed so David kissed him again, then deposited him onto the bed. He leaned over him and kissed his neck, his chest, and belly. "Can I...?"

"Yeah."

His heart thrummed in his chest the whole time, while he took care of Ahmed, listening to the moans and grunts that never sounded sexy when David himself made them, but coming from Ahmed, they were the sweetest, most exciting sounds in the world. Heavy breathing mixed with words he couldn't understand and one final cry out when he came, spilling into David's mouth, hot and bitter, a taste that David had always liked, not because it was good but because it meant he had done something right.

When he straightened up, Ahmed pulled him into the bed. He licked his lips and David gave him a kiss. "If you don't want to—"

"No, I do," Ahmed said, eagerness in his voice and then wiped his mouth. "So bad I almost just drooled."

David giggled.

Ahmed leaned in over his lap and David let out a breath, butterflies in his stomach. He shouldn't have been so nervous, but he was. He didn't know how long it had been since the last time someone had done this for him, but he would have traded every time before for this. Even though there were a few stops and starts and even though at the end, when he came, Ahmed had a moment where he gagged, the whole experience had been overwhelmingly blissful.

Afterward, he felt warm, fuzzy and he took Ahmed into his arms, rubbing his back. "You okay?"

"Yeah." He coughed. "I just...I don't know what I expected."

David kissed his cheek. "So are you hungry? It's past dinner time."

"Yeah."

David prepared them something to eat while Ahmed washed up in the bathroom. They returned to bed, skin against skin for the first time. Ahmed dozed off and when his phone went off for him to pray for the last time, he didn't stir. David waffled between waking him and letting him sleep.

"Hey, your phone," he said and gave him a nudge.

Ahmed sat up, looked around, did his prayers, and returned to bed. David wasn't convinced that he hadn't sleepwalked through the process because he seemed to fall back to sleep in an instant.

THEY DROVE to work together in the morning.

"When did you two start carpooling?" asked Jen, one of the girls who worked in the bakery.

"When we got married," David answered.

She scowled at him. "Are you a dick about everything?"

He glanced at Ahmed, wondering if he also thought he was being a dick.

"We're not in middle school, alright, grow up," she said and walked away.

"People hate you," Ahmed said.

"Okay, so it's not just me, right?"

"But like, especially pretty white girls."

He looked after Jen. "You think she's pretty?"

"She is pretty, David."

He shrugged. "I guess."

"That's probably it."

"What?"

"You don't treat pretty girls like they're pretty," he said.

"Well, then why don't they hate you?"

"They'd hate me more if they thought I liked them," he said, "People assume my goal with women is to lock them up and force them to convert."

"Didn't know I paid you to chitchat," Johnny called over, his eyes fixed on Ahmed.

"Sorry," Ahmed said and walked off.

They worked separately, for the most part, that day and David suspected Ahmed wanted it that way.

Just before their shift ended, two women in suits tried to go down the aisle where David was mopping up a spill. They paused and the taller of the two looked at the shelf he stood in front of.

David said, "I'll be done in a second."

"That's fine," said the other, an East Asian woman in her late thirties.

David at first thought the Asian woman was incredibly short, but when he looked again he saw that her companion was just very tall. Almost as tall as he was, he realized. He stared at her more than he should have, taking in her broad shoulders and large hands.

"Tranny," a voice in his ear suggested.

He wrinkled his nose. He knew the voices had to pick up something in his subconscious, something nasty lurking in there because they were not their own entities.

"Bet you'd like that, like her to fuck you," came the slithering accusation. "A great big fat cock. Better than that uptight little Arab twink who won't even—"

"*Gross*," he hissed.

The tall woman raised her eyebrows. "You know what, can you just move?" she asked.

He stepped back, wheeling the mop and bucket with him.

The other woman gave him a nasty look and to her friend said, "This is why I hate cases in small towns."

"No, no," David said, but he said it too quietly.

The woman took the salsa he'd been blocking her from and walked away. Her friend gave him another dirty look.

He leaned the mop against the shelf, sidestepping the dip he hadn't finished cleaning. "Hey," he called but neither of them looked back. He followed after and said, "Hey, uh, wait."

The tall woman turned, her hand on her hip, not for attitude but to push aside her jacket and show the gun she wore.

He froze.

"I just want salsa," she said.

"No, I mean, I wasn't talking about you, I'm sorry, it was bad to say." He immediately felt like a child. Bad, nice, good, those were all kid words. He felt hot. "The voice, it said, no never mind. It's just, Jesus, I'm not like a fucking bigot or anything and I don't want this to ruin your day or whatever."

Both women stared at him and he knew it was because he had been incoherent.

"Sorry. Have a nice day. Enjoy your salsa." He turned around. He fled the aisle and left his mop and bucket behind. He would come back for it later.

"What a fucking idiot," he heard.

He bumped into Ahmed on his way to the bathroom, where he intended to hide for a few minutes to get over the embarrassment, to recover from the voices. Voices that picked at him he could stand but when they got nasty about other people he started to feel like a bad person because he knew that the thoughts had to come from somewhere. They were not real, they did not belong to some otherworldly entity that liked to whisper in his ear, which meant that they came from inside him. They were his thoughts, spit and hissed through another voice.

He splashed water on his face and want to sit down, but neither the floor nor the toilet seemed like good options.

Someone knocked on the door.

"One sec," he called.

"Hey." It was Ahmed.

"What?"

"You looked upset. I thought I should check in."

"Um."

"I mean unless you just needed to use the bathroom and I'm being weird."

"No," he said and opened the door.

"You okay?"

"Yeah. Just. I don't like it when they say bad things." There was that word. Bad. Like he was five again.

Ahmed reached out and gave his arm a squeeze.

"Sometimes what they say is so nasty."

"Sure."

"I hate it," he admitted, his words coming out a little choked. He rubbed his eyes and dislodged one of his contacts so that he had to blink furiously to get it back into place, which didn't help his mood.

One of the cashiers entered the hall where they stood and stopped at the sight of them, her face scrunched up in either bewilderment or disdain.

"Uh. Are you using the bathroom or...?" she asked.

"Sorry," David said and stepped out all the way.

She edged around them like she could catch their crazy and close the door.

"I gotta go finish mopping," he said.

Ahmed grasped his hand for a moment. "Almost time to go home."

He nodded, finished mopping and they left.

At home, they changed then went to the main part of the house, where Zhané waited for them.

"He's been in a mood today," she warned.

"He's a baby," David said.

"And babies can be in shitty moods," she said.

David reached over and picked up Noah, saying, "Maybe he just doesn't feel good. Do you feel icky, buddy?"

The baby grunted and kicked his legs, displeased.

Zhané reached over and gave the baby's leg a squeeze. "Maybe. Maybe Mommy's in a mood, too." She kissed the baby. "I'll see you soon."

She shouldered her bag and headed out.

David took the baby to the couch. "What's wrong, mister?"

Noah grunted again, squirming and rubbing his face.

"Maybe he wants to move around," Ahmed suggested.

"Maybe."

He put Noah on the floor so he could crawl if he wanted to, but once on the floor, he started to squall. David waited for a minute to see if it would pass, but Noah continued to cry so David lifted him.

"You are in a mood, aren't you?" he asked. "Cranky pants."

He looked around and found a book that was full of textured pictures, a fuzzy duck, and a scratchy beach. Noah loved this book, normally laughing when he touched the pictures.

Today he ogled at it and then looked up at David. He leaned forward and put his mouth on the book.

Ahmed reached over and poked his finger inside Noah's mouth, which David found to be a questionable choice, until he said, "He's teething." He wiped his finger on his shirt.

"Oh."

"Why are you looking at me like that?"

"You shouldn't put your finger in his mouth like that."

"I wash my hands. More than you do and you let him chew on your hands all the time," he pointed out.

David frowned but figured he was right.

Ahmed got up and David thought he was pissed until he went into the bathroom and came back with a clean washcloth. He wet it and put it in the freezer, setting a timer on his phone. He gave the baby's toes a jiggle and said something in Pashto. When the timer went off, Ahmed brought Noah the washcloth. The baby immediately shoved it into his mouth, gnawing and seeming much happier.

"Are you feeling better? Since work?" Ahmed asked.

"Yes."

He reached over and took the baby, settling him and then nestling himself against David. David flicked through the channels and found a rerun of *SVU*. With one hand, Ahmed ran his fingers up and down the inside of David's arm; his other hand had been taken hostage by Noah.

"Do you want a wedding ring?" David asked after several minutes' contemplation of his husband's hands.

"Hmm? No, not really."

"No?"

"Well, we don't have a ton of money and wedding rings are a Western thing anyways. Plus, you know, I know we're married and you know we're married. And that's what matters, right?" he said, "And I'm not supposed to wear gold."

"What?"

"It's a thing."

"Like pork?"

"Yeah," he said but sounded uncomfortable. "Well, not really. It's just for men."

"Girls can wear gold?" he asked.

"Yeah."

"Oh, well...okay."

"Do you want wedding rings?" Ahmed asked, glancing back at him.

"It doesn't matter, really," he said, but couldn't help but think of the heavy gold ring his father wore. He remembered playing with the ring when he had held his father's hand as a child.

Ahmed sat up and turned to face him. "What?"

"Do all the rules...I mean, it seems like a lot of rules. It's not any of my business, I know, but aren't they hard to keep track of?"

"Sure. But I do my best."

David wanted to ask why. He didn't understand how he could do this, abide by all the rules. "Maybe I'm just lazy."

"You're, what, some kind of Christian, right?"

"Catholic."

"Alright. Do you adhere to everything that's Catholic?"

"Uh. No. Barely."

"Does that make you less Catholic? Does it mean you believe less than someone who follows all the rules?"

"Depends who you ask."

"I'm...this is hard to say, you know, but you grow up thinking that rules are for a reason but at some point, you have to decide which rules are worth following. I'm still figuring that out because this is the first time in my life that I'm living outside my parent's sphere of influence and that's not to say that I don't think what they've taught me is important but it might be...old-fashioned. It might not be right for me."

David nodded. "Okay."

"So I have some soul searching to do."

"Keep me updated. If you want."

With a half-smile, he said, "I might."

David reached out and ran his finger along Noah's cheek, then tapped his nose. "It doesn't matter what you decide you want to do. As long as I can be a part of your life."

Ahmed opened his mouth to say something but someone knocked on the door.

"Maybe it's the stuff I ordered," David mused, going over to the window, hoping to see a package by the door, though it would have been unreasonably fast, as he'd only placed the order last night, using Zhané's Amazon account, with her permission.

"What did you order?"

"Uh, remember what I told you about sex?"

Ahmed frowned for a second. "Oh, yeah right. If I'd known there was so much prep involved, I would have decided to be straight instead."

David chuckled, peeked out the window and saw two women in suits standing outside. One knocked again. He opened the door, his heart in his throat.

When she saw him, the tall woman from the store frowned.

"Hi," he said.

"Is this the house of Zane Smith?" the smaller woman asked.

"It's pronounced jah-nay," he corrected reflexively.

She checked her notebook, tucking a lock of her dark bob behind her ear as she did so. "Is this her home?"

"She isn't in."

"I'm Special Agent Rory Frost," the Asian woman introduced herself. "We're in town investigating the recent abductions and murders," Frost said, "We were hoping to talk to Ms. Smith about them."

"I'm her, uh, her roommate. David," he said, feeling like he was going to throw up. A million scenarios ran through his head and they all ended with him dead or in prison.

Frost looked down at her notebook. "David Craft?"

"Uh. Yes." He did not like that she had his name in that little notebook.

"David, who is it?" Ahmed asked.

"Uh."

Ahmed came over, looked at the women, one in gray and one in blue, and looked at David.

"Do you know when Ms. Smith will be home?" the tall woman asked.

He shook his head. He didn't. He had no idea how long it would take her to get her nails done. He glanced down at their hands. "Soon. I think."

"We also have some questions for you," Frost said.

"Why?" he asked immediately, even though he knew why. He knew what he had done, he knew what the local cops thought.

Ahmed put his hand on David's back and that small gesture brought him closer to reality. "It's fine, David, why don't you let them in?"

He glanced over. "Uh. I guess. Sure." He stepped back from the door and looked at the other woman. "I didn't get your name."

"Ingress."

"Um. Badges? Aren't you supposed to have badges?"

They both reached into their jackets and showed their badges, though he wouldn't have been able to tell if they were real or fake. He nodded and they came inside. He gestured vaguely to the couch and took out his phone, texting Zhané that the FBI was at her house.

"Can I hold the baby?" he whispered to Ahmed. He hadn't meant to whisper.

Ahmed handed Noah over.

"Mr. Craft, why don't you come sit?" Frost asked.

He sat, feeling better with Noah's familiar weight in his arms. Ahmed sat beside him.

"Now, you grew up here right?" Frost asked.

"Yes. I did," he said and added, "I went to Vermont and my parents put me in a, uh, a behavioral center. But now I'm back."

"You seem very uncomfortable."

"Lizard people," he whispered, not sure why. He couldn't get his thoughts straight. "No, I know, you're not lizard people," he corrected. "You're not. I don't even believe in lizard people."

"Mr. Craft."

"What? You have to know. You've got records on everything, the cops must have told you too. That asshole, what's his name? Bryant? He must have told you."

The cat jumped up on the coffee table and regarded their guests, nose in the air.

"We do know that you were institutionalized following the deaths of those girls and your discovery of James Roberts," Frost said. "For a schizophrenic break."

"I take my meds," he said though no one had accused him of anything.

Ahmed touched his leg.

"I wouldn't you know the girls they were my friends. Nicki and Becca I loved them."

"Mr. Craft—"

"David," he said, "My name is *David*, I'm David."

"Maybe you should go," Ahmed said to the agents. "Come back later."

Noah dropped the washcloth and began to scream.

Ahmed took the baby. "Oh, hey, shhh, little man." He rubbed the baby's back and he settled. He picked up the washcloth and gave it back to Noah.

"Are you able to handle this?" Ingress asked Ahmed.

"Are you?" Ahmed snapped.

"I'm fine!" David said, "I just...!"

"What do you need?" his husband asked.

He shook his head and took a deep breath. He began to tap his chest, not hitting yet, and he tried to think about breathing. He saw that Ahmed had held out his hand but hadn't touched him. He took it. He didn't know how long they sat like that but eventually, it was long enough. *All things pass.* That was what his father had always said, heaving a deep sigh, speaking in that same tired voice.

He looked up to see that the agents still sat there.

"Sorry," he said. "I get worried sometimes."

"That's fine," Frost said.

He shrugged. It wasn't. "You had questions."

"We can come back a different time," she offered.

He shook his head. "No. Go ahead."

"We believe that the murders of those girls, as well as the abduction of Jim Roberts, are related to what's happening now," she said.

"And you want to know why we went to the crime scenes."

"No, actually, the statements you gave when you were arrested were very clear on why," Ingress said. "However."

He waited, aware that Ahmed's face had changed when she said 'arrested'.

"What do you know about the relationship between Ms. Smith and the local coroner?" she asked.

"Oh."

The agents glanced at each other.

"I don't know, really," he said. "You'll have to ask her."

"We don't think either of you is responsible for these deaths," Frost said, "But we do think you might know something that can help. And we want to help."

He wanted to believe her. "You really think that? That we didn't do it?"

"We understand that you've had a...strained relationship with law enforcement in the past," Frost said, "But the evidence simply isn't there, especially in these recent deaths. Your credit card records put you in another state when Mara Copeland was abducted and found."

"You checked my records."

"It's part of our job," Ingress said, brushing a lock of hair over her shoulder.

David stared at that lock of hair for a moment, transfixed by the loveliness of her auburn hair against the blue of her jacket. He glanced up at her face, saw that she'd noticed him staring. "Sorry."

He heard a car, then the engine cut and a door close. Zhané was home, it had to be her. He went over to the window, then stepped outside.

"You didn't text me back!" she said.

"Oh. Sorry."

"They're still here?"

He nodded. "They want to know about the coroner."

"Alright, well. Fuck." She went inside and he followed. She

looked at the agents and said, "I know David let you in, but this isn't his house. I'd like you to leave."

"We just had a few questions," Ingress said.

"I know. Now's not a good time. I have to go out soon," she told her, which was true. She had appointments for later in the evening.

"Ms. Smith—" Frost began.

"We know you've been getting files from the coroner about the murder victims," Ingress said.

Zhané glanced at her, eyebrow raised. "Am I under arrest?"

"No, you aren't," she said, "But it's urgent that we find out as much as we can before it happens again."

"Why don't you leave a number or something? I'll give you a call," Zhané said.

Ingress produced a business card and handed it over. "Please, it's very important."

"Yeah, thanks."

The two women left, though they didn't seem happy about it.

Zhané came over and took Noah from Ahmed. "What's with the washcloth?"

"He's teething," Ahmed said.

A moment later, David echoed, "He's teething."

"Oh, right," she said, "They do that, don't they? Feeling better?"

Noah rubbed his face and grunted.

"Miriam would give Layla some Tylenol," Ahmed suggested. "But I didn't want to, you know, dose your baby without your say-so."

"Appreciate it," she said. "Maybe we'll give it a try. What do you think, mister?" She looked at David. "Hey."

He looked up. "What?"

"You okay?"

"What, yeah, why?"

"Uh, cause you're just...kind of staring," she said.

"What time are you going out?"

"Eight."

"Sleep. Before you go. I'm gonna get some sleep."

She nodded. "Sure, alright."

He stood and left; he knew Ahmed had followed him. When they were alone, back in their apartment and David had lain down on the bed, on top of the covers, Ahmed sat beside him.

"Do you want to talk or anything?" he asked.

"About my inability to cope with stress?"

"I guess."

"No."

"Are...hmm. David, do you think you should be seeing someone? A professional?" Ahmed asked.

"I should be. I don't want to."

"Is that healthy?"

"I'll go if I need to."

Right now, he could handle it, he was holding it together and he did not want to go back, he didn't want to see a therapist. Maybe if he went to a real therapist, not some two-bit idiot, it wouldn't so bad, but he couldn't make himself take that leap yet.

Ahmed made a sound but said nothing.

"I promise," he said.

"I trust you."

It felt like an unreal confession. "I'm sorry."

"What?"

"I'm sorry I got you into this. I should have been more upfront about what this would be like."

"I think you were appropriately upfront," Ahmed said. "I mean, not when you proposed, but beforehand, while we were working and stuff."

"You think?"

"Yes."

David turned a little so he could look up at him. A silly thought struck him and he started to smile.

"What?"

"I proposed." He hadn't thought of that way before; proposals were supposed to be thought out and romantic.

Ahmed reached over and ran his fingers through David's hair, which sent a pleasant chill through his body. He wondered what conclusions Ahmed would come to about his religion and about the traditions his parents expected him to keep. Both of his sisters, in some way, had diverged from that path already.

"I'm glad you did," Ahmed said.

David took his hand and kissed his fingers. "Come snuggle me."

Ahmed lay down and David put his arms around him, holding on to his hand.

"Little spoon," David teased.

"The shame."

David pressed his lips to the back of his head. He didn't mean to fall asleep yet, but he drifted off anyways.

Ahmed woke him up just after seven, saying, "I made some dinner."

He pushed himself up, feeling sweaty and disoriented. "You did what?"

"I heated up some leftovers, I didn't really make anything," he said. "Come on, we've got to go over in a little while."

He got out of bed, his eyes sticky and pained. He went to the bathroom and switched out his contacts for glasses, then went to their little table. "Thanks."

"No problem."

He stared down at his plate; rice, chicken, and green beans. He took up his fork and began to eat, his eyes fixed on the plate until he set down his fork and looked up. He stared at Ahmed until he looked up from his phone to take a drink and noticed David's gaze.

"What?" Ahmed asked.

"I love you."

Ahmed coughed and set down his drink. He wiped his mouth with the back of his wrist. "Wow." He coughed again. "They're just leftovers."

David laughed and Ahmed laughed, too.

"No, sorry," Ahmed said when he'd finished laughing. "I love you too."

"Alright, good, I'm glad," he said.

They ate and cleaned up, then headed back to Zhané's part of the house. She showed them a little bottle of children's Tylenol and set it on the kitchen counter, saying, "Gave him some and he's out cold. Poor guy must have been exhausted. Anyways, if he wakes up he can have another dose around ten."

"Yeah."

"Hey, no more secret FBI visitors," she said.

David half-smiled. "Are you going to call them?"

She shrugged. "I need to think."

"If you're keeping secrets, you might end up in more trouble," Ahmed said.

"Like I said, I need to think."

Around midnight, as he lay with his head on David's lap, Ahmed got a text which made him sit up.

"What?" David asked, turning his eyes from a *Red Dragon*

rerun.

"Miriam's having her baby!" He stood up for a second, then looked around, seeming to realize that he had nowhere to go and sat back down. He gave David a push and then grabbed him by the hand.

In the morning, they went to the mall in order to buy a gift to bring to the hospital and in addition to the real gift, David insisted on buying a onesie that said 'I love My Uncle' and tacking on an s in permanent marker. At one point, he lost track of Ahmed and started to worry after about half an hour.

He took out his phone and texted him. He responded a moment later saying he was on his way back. Once they reunited, they returned to David's car and as he sat in the driver's seat, Ahmed said, "Hey. Wait."

"What?"

"Close your eyes."

"Um."

"Put out your hand."

David obeyed, putting out his hand palm up. Ahmed placed something in it, something warm and solid, but more than that he couldn't tell.

"Open your eyes."

He opened to find a plain gold band sitting in his palm.

With a grin, he said, "Go on, put it on."

When David didn't, only looking, Ahmed reached over and took it back, sliding it onto his finger.

"Wrong hand," David said.

Ahmed rolled his eyes. "Then fix it!"

He adjusted the ring, putting it on his left hand. "How'd you know the size?"

"Zhané knew. She's got a great memory."

"Thanks."

"Hey, come on, I could tell you wanted one."

"Yeah but, you know, you don't just get one wedding ring," he said, feeling spoiled and petty.

"David, I'm not stupid." He took a box out of his pocket and showing it to David, who took it and peeked inside.

"I thought you weren't supposed to wear gold."

"I'm not supposed to suck your dick either." A little grin grew on his lips.

"Ahmed..."

"Don't give me that, David," he said.

"Don't do it just for me."

"I'm not. I mean. I am, sort of, but...you know, I'm not gonna miss prayer to make you happy, or skip Ramadan or eat ham to make you happy because those things shouldn't have to do with our relationship. But I want you to have this and I want people to know we're married."

David looked at the box he still held.

"Cause I mean it, I love you."

David took out the ring and slid it onto Ahmed's finger, who leaned in to give him a kiss.

"Besides, I'm already wearing shorts that go above my knees, so I'm fucked."

David gave him another kiss and wondered what biblical rules he ignored on a day-to-day basis; he wondered how many stipulations there were to being a good Catholic and what percentage of them he had broken without even knowing they existed.

"You don't follow your rules, either." Ahmed pulled back and settled into his seat. "You don't even go to church."

"So?"

"So I don't tell you how to be Catholic," Ahmed said, "And I *went* to Catholic school. So don't get weird about what I do."

"I will get weird about everything forever," he warned.

Ahmed gave his leg a pat. "I know you will. Let's go."

They passed Ahmed's parents leaving with Noor as they entered. His sister stopped to give him a hug and gush about the baby, a little boy named after his father. Ahmed's parents stood two yards away, arms crossed.

David waved and they didn't wave back.

"They're pretending you died," Noor confided to her brother.

Ahmed sighed and glanced at his parents, who looked away. They had been staring at him beforehand and he called over to them, his voice kind and little pleading. They ignored him more clearly, turning their backs to him.

"Baba," he said, "Ade."

Though Ahmed could not, David saw the looks on his parents' faces. They did not look any happier than he did; turned away from him, they could pretend to be stony, disapproving but David got the sense they wanted to turn around.

"Would you rather have me be dead?" Ahmed asked his

parents, "Because that's almost what you got."

David hated to hear him talk like that. His own suicidal ideations seemed normal to him, a symptom of illness and his visitors, but hearing such things from Ahmed made his skin crawl and his stomach churn.

His parents walked out after that and David thought he saw his father's face twist, almost in tears.

Noor scoffed at them. "Ridiculous. They'll get over it," she promised her brother, "They got over me. Now it's 'Noor, when are you getting married? Noor, you do such much *dating*, will you ever find a husband?', and oh, don't forget, 'Noor, how do I make that Netflix go away?'"

She gave her brother another hug and waved goodbye to David.

Ahmed didn't want to talk about his parents and brushed off David's attempts at comfort. His mood improved marginally when he visited Miriam and the baby, though they only stayed for a little while, not wanting to intrude too much.

"Let me know if you need anything," Ahmed offered as they made their way out. "Really. Babysitting, help around the house, whatever."

"That's what I got married for," Miriam said with a smile.

As they left the hospital, David put his arm around Ahmed's shoulder. "I think it will be okay."

Ahmed stepped out of his embrace and spoke only in short answers for the rest of the day. David didn't hold it against him; he couldn't. That night in bed, as Ahmed lay rolled over all the way to one side and David lay on his back, hands folded on his stomach, he said, "You know we're not supposed to go to bed angry."

"What?" Ahmed asked.

David forgot sometimes that Ahmed couldn't hear almost anything without his hearing aid and would try to speak to him when he didn't have it in.

He began to speak but Ahmed said, "Hang on." David heard him fumbling in the dark and finally he asked, "What?"

"You shouldn't go to bed angry."

"You made me put this back in to say that?"

"Yes."

"I'm not angry."

"You seem sort of a little angry."

"Then I guess I'm going to bed angry!" he snapped.

"Can I give you a kiss?"

"No."

"What about a big squeeze?"

"No," he said, took out his hearing aid again and dropped it down onto the bedside table with finality.

David didn't try to talk to him again and continued to stare up at the ceiling, his eyes adjusted to the dark somewhat. A voice suggested that Ahmed was going to leave him and he brushed it aside; he felt vindicated when Ahmed rolled over and put his forehead against David's arm.

"I'm not mad at you," he murmured.

David moved onto his side, one arm beneath Ahmed's head. He could feel his breath on his chest, warm and moist, the smell of toothpaste lingering.

"I know you don't have it any easier."

He didn't know if he'd be able to hear if he said anything back, so he kissed the top of his head and put his other arm around him, holding him close.

8/17/15

MONDAY MORNING hadn't started well. Nothing, in particular, had happened, but neither of them had slept well the night before and they had been grumpy with each other so far, with Ahmed snapping that they were going to be late and David shooting back that late and not fifteen minutes early were different.

They arrived on time at the IGA, in the door by the time their shift started. Jen in the bakery gave him a nasty look, which she had most days since interpreting his statement of marriage as a tasteless joke. He hated that look and he had hoped their wedding bands would make her stop, but it hadn't. He didn't think she'd noticed; he decided to do something she would notice.

He took his husband by the hand. Ahmed paused, giving him an odd look and when David leaned in to kiss him, he raised his eyebrows but allowed it to happen.

"So anyway, Brian forgot to take out the garbage last night," Ahmed said. "I know cause he texted me to let me know, which is not as helpful as actually taking out the garbage."

"Did I interrupt you?" he asked. He hadn't been paying attention, instead dwelling on Jen and her sour look.

"Kind of."

"Sorry."

"So...can you take out the garbage?"

He nodded and went. He took the two black bags that had been left behind, went out back and pushed open the dumpster. He started to swing the bags up but saw a white garbage bag sitting on the bottom. It should have been empty; the garbage truck came on Sunday nights to empty it.

He stared down at the bag for a while, then set down the garbage beside the dumpster and said to Ahmed, "Hey, there's something in the dumpster. Will you come look at it?"

"Uh, I guess." He followed David back outside.

Ahmed peered into the dumpster. "Oh. It's probably an animal. People dump them instead of paying to get them cremated."

"Oh."

Ahmed pointed. "I think it's a dog, look, you can see the fur."

David looked again and saw a tuft of golden fur sticking out of the drawstring top. "I guess...do we call the cops?"

"Yeah."

Once he had phoned in the issue, David returned to work until the town's lone animal control officer came and he showed her the dumpster. With little hesitation, she climbed, snapped on a pair of gloves and lifted the bag.

She frowned immediately.

"What?"

"Doesn't feel like a dog," she said and set the bag back down. She tore it open, then gasped.

David stared. Within the bag was not a dog or cat, but a little girl no more than three. The tuft of fur that had poked through was a lock of her hair, sun-bleached and matted with dirt. He could not stop staring and was overcome with a need to touch the body, to look at the dirt under her nails and run his fingers along the finger marks on her neck.

"Jesus," the woman breathed. "God, Jesus." She climbed out of the dumpster and headed over to her car, calling back, "Don't touch anything!"

He nodded, his eyes fixed on the girl and her hair. She should have been in pigtails but one had gotten pulled out.

Her little pink shorts were filthy, her orange tank top ripped. She had no shoes.

He should have felt revolted. He should have felt horror that her life had been so short and had ended so brutally, and he did, but it was a distant horror in the back of his mind. The thoughts that consumed him were of the need to touch her, to feel her dead skin and wash the dirt out of her hair.

He wondered, not for the first time, if this fascination was necrophilia, but felt no sexual compulsion towards the body.

"Sir, you gotta move back," the animal control officer called.

He stepped back, realizing that he had put his hands on the dumpster and leaned in closer. Left alone for a minute more, he might have climbed in.

"Come over here," she said.

He went; she told him he needed to wait. The FBI agents would be over soon; they'd want to talk to him, she figured. Johnny came out and she advised him to close the store for the day.

"Why?" he asked, "Over a dead dog? Was it rabid or something?"

"It's not a dog. The FBI will be here soon," she said.

"The FBI! Jesus, it's not that serial killer, is it?" Johnny demanded.

"Sir, you really ought to close the store, this is going to be a crime scene and we don't need a lot of rubberneckers."

Johnny walked away, muttering to himself. The other workers came up and Ahmed came over to stand beside David.

"It was a body?" Ahmed asked quietly.

David nodded.

"Are you okay?"

He nodded again, unable to shake the image of that little girl in a ripped garbage bag, at the bottom of a sticky dumpster.

"You can head home," the officer told Ahmed.

"He's my ride," David said. "Please don't make him leave."

Ahmed took him by the hand. "It's really better if we wait together."

She didn't protest but didn't seem convinced.

The regular police came a few minutes later, followed by Agents Ingress and Frost in their own car, shiny and black.

Ahmed tapped David on the belly with the back of his hand when they arrived. "Hey, are you gonna be okay talking to them?"

He nodded. "Sure. I think so. Fucking lizard people."

"David, what does that mean?" he asked.

"Lizard people," he said again. "They're lizard people."

"What? Like Sleestaks?"

"Just...you know. Lizard people. You don't trust them," he said. He lacked the ability to articulate what lizard people really were to him. It was not hidden monsters in the government, but people who were fundamentally not to be trusted based on who they were and what they did. "You watch *Land of the Lost?*"

"Sometimes, yeah."

"Are you a nerd?"

"Are you not?"

"I think I'm better classed as a loser. Or a creep."

"You're not a creep," Ahmed assured.

David didn't argue.

Frost and Ingress came over to them, not looking impressed that they had run into each other again.

"I feel like I shouldn't be surprised," Ingress said.

David gave an apologetic smile. "I'd love to have fewer corpses in my life," he said, but it wasn't true. He didn't want that child to be dead, but he could not deny the pull he felt towards her. "What's gonna happen to her?"

"The medical examiner's gonna have a look," Frost said. "Tell us what happened."

He related the brief tale for her, dwelling on the words 'medical examiner'. He would google it later. Maybe it was something he could be.

When he finished, Frost said, "Alright, David, we'll be in touch if we need you."

He nodded.

"Your friend never got back to us," Ingress accused.

"I'm not in charge of her," David reminded. "You don't think this is related to the other deaths, do you?"

"Hm?"

"The timeline is all wrong," he said. "It shouldn't be until the end of August."

Ingress frowned, crossing her arms. "You're pretty up on this."

"Fifty-six days."

"David," Ahmed hissed.

He glanced over. He'd said too much. "It's easy to track."

"Killers change," Ingress said and it almost felt like a challenge.

He shook his head and wanted to argue. Yes, a killer could change, devolve and break their patterns but not these ones. They had a schedule to follow and it wasn't set by them, it was set by the things and David hadn't gotten a call from them. So far, his calls had lined up with the deaths and he didn't think it was a coincidence.

"Is there something you wanted to tell us?" Frost asked.

He shook his head again, the words on his lips. He wanted to tell everything, to beg for help, but they wouldn't believe him. The FBI dealt with terrorists and bombers, with serial killers and school shootings, not with impossible things.

"Can I go home?" he asked.

"We'll let you know if we have more questions," Frost said and handed over her card. "Call if you think of anything."

He nodded and slipped it into his wallet. He handed his keys to Ahmed, too distracted by the girl, by the skewed timeline, to be a safe driver.

At home, he googled how to become a medical examiner and immediately dropped the idea when he saw that he'd need to become a doctor. The name should have been a giveaway. After that, he lounged, not knowing what else to do.

Ahmed went out on his own to attend to Friday Prayer and David lay on the bed, looking up at the ceiling, running his finger over the scar on his side, over his liver.

The things had not broken their pattern, they never did.

He scribbled down what had happened in the notebook and texted Zhané to let her know what had happened. She texted him back with a picture of a little girl and asked 'is this her?'.

He had to stare at the picture for a minute, he had to imagine her with her face bruised and bloated, with dirt in her hair. Finally, he answered 'yes why'. Instead of texting back, she walked through the door to his apartment.

"I thought you were out," he said.

She shrugged. "Just dropping Noah off with Mom. That girl just got reported missing, like, today, around ten. From, uh, Meriden. Amber alert and everything."

"Really?"

She nodded and came to sit on the bed, next to his legs. "Was it your friends?"

He shook his head. "I don't think so. We'll see."

She gave his shin a pat. "So hey."

"Hm?"

"You got that package you ordered," she said.

"I did." He pushed himself up so he could look at her while they talked, leaning against the headboard.

"So you guys seal the deal or what?"

He laughed. "Working up to it," he said. "It, you know,

actually really nice to have, you know, real lube and stuff though cause at Mansfield we did not and, uh, soap does *not* make good lube and the shower doesn't always cut it for cleaning things out."

"Jesus."

"But if you can steal, like, some vegetable oil from the kitchen, that's alright," he mused.

"Oil breaks down condoms," she pointed out, slightly worried.

He shrugged. "If you use them."

"David!"

"What?"

"Oh my god, did you get yourself tested?" she demanded, real concern in her voice.

With another shrug, he sure, "Sure."

"Really?"

"Yes, really."

She asked, "How's he dealing with everything?"

"What, like in general?"

"No, tell me the exact progress you've made with putting stuff in his butt," she said, rolling her eyes.

"No, he's...I think he's doing okay. His sisters keep in touch a lot, they're really sure his parents will come around to things. It's good that he has them."

"And what about you?"

"Hm?"

"Who do you have?"

"You?"

"Your mom and dad haven't said anything about coming down?"

"No."

"Have you tried to talk to them again?"

He shook his head. Once was enough; he had told them what he'd needed to tell them and what they decided to do with that information was up to them. "Pointless, I figure."

"I'm not working tonight. Do you guys want to hang out or something? Get something to eat, watch a movie?"

"I'm down, I'll ask him when he gets home."

Ahmed, when he returned, agreed to the plan. The night was cozy and having a real body, warm and human, in his arms made David forget the idea he'd had about necrophilia. Maybe the pull he felt towards the dead was normal; after all, lots of people had jobs that involved dead people. Maybe he simply needed to channel his interest into something appropriate.

In bed that night, he poked Ahmed in the back.

"What?" he asked, rolling over and sitting up.

David opened his mouth.

"Wait, hang on."

David waited while he turned on the light and put his hearing aid back in.

"What?"

"Do you think I could be a doctor?"

"Do you want to be a doctor?" Ahmed asked, his nose wrinkled. "No offense, but I don't see you having a great bedside manner."

"Not like a regular doctor, a, uh, a medical examiner. But you need to be a doctor to do it."

"Oh. Yeah, sure."

"Really?"

"Yeah, that might be, uh, actually perfect for you."

"You think so?"

"Sure. I mean. It *is* a long time to go to school so you might, uh, struggle with that. It would be a lot of stress."

"Yeah. I don't know anything about going to college."

The prospect seemed immense, considering that he was already twenty-one and had no degree to start with, not even an associates. He had done his last year of high school at Mansfield and he wasn't even sure that counted for anything. It would be easier to continue in this slipshod life, but he knew it was not sustainable, not if he wanted to have children and give them a good home, not if he wanted to someday have his own place to live.

"I'll help you look into it," Ahmed offered.

He nodded.

"Besides, you're young."

He furrowed his brow. He did not feel young, he felt old and out of touch, a lifetime away from who he had been, away from the future that should have been his.

Ahmed kissed him. "I'm going to sleep now unless you want to talk more?"

He shook his head. "No," he said but knew he sounded upset. His voice had cracked.

"Maybe you can ask your parents?"

"Maybe."

Ahmed took out his hearing aid and turned off the light; he

stayed sitting up, arranging David on his lap and running his fingers through David's hair. He warned, "Don't say anything, I can't hear you. I think you can do it. I think you can do whatever you want, David, and I think you're a lot more than you think you are."

David wrapped his arms around Ahmed's waist and they lay like that for a while, his head on his husband's lap. He wanted to cry because he'd found something he wanted and it seemed so far out of his reach. How could he make it through school with things coming for him? He needed to find a way to get rid of them and since their last visit, they'd come up with no ideas. They hadn't talked about it. Life got in the way.

"I love you."

"I told you I couldn't hear you."

He reached over for his phone and texted him.

Ahmed felt the buzz and saw the light, so he turned his head to look. "Oh, I love you too." He scooted down into the covers, elbowing David by accident and saying, "Oops, sorry," and then nestling against him. He gave David one last tight squeeze and said, "I'm going to sleep."

David didn't sleep much that night, consumed by his new-found worries, and by the time Ahmed's alarm went off for his earliest prayer, he had only started to doze. Ahmed crawled out of bed then came back. By the time his second alarm went off, David had given up on sleep and gotten out of bed, borrowing the laptop and trying to find out as much as he could about what he hoped to do.

Ahmed found him like that and after his prayers, stood in front of the loveseat, arms crossed. "You're supposed to be sleeping."

He looked up.

"Are you still worried about that college thing?"

He nodded.

"It's too late to try for this semester anyway. I mean, you could, but it'd be a crazy rush. We'll look into it, alright?"

He nodded again.

"Are you coming back to bed?"

He yawned and his husband held out a hand to him. He took it and returned to bed, his eyes aching from using the computer in the dark. He put his ear to Ahmed's chest when they had laid back down and ran his fingers up and down his torso.

"Ugh, quit it, that tickles," Ahmed said, giving his hand a

push.

He yawned again and drifted off after that, though he still didn't sleep well, this time because he dreamt of the little girl. He woke late in the morning with the realization that, disturbing as it was, the tenderness he felt towards corpses was not unlike the way he felt when he saw a stray animal. He wanted to help.

"Oh, morning, sleepy," Ahmed greeted him.

He rolled onto his stomach, resting his head on his arms, turning to look at Ahmed. "Hi."

"Feel better?"

"Kind of."

His husband came over and ran his hand along his back, scratching a little with his nails. David rolled onto his side, looking up at him. "You really think I could do it?"

"I really do."

"It's a lot of money. A lot of time."

"You'll probably be done before you're even old," he said, "And I'll have my degree in a couple of years. Teacher pay isn't great, but we'll be able to keep our heads above water."

"What if I have a breakdown?"

Ahmed shrugged. "We'll deal with it when it happens. It's not great advice but it's all I've got."

"No, it's good, I'm just scared."

He gave David's shoulder a squeeze. "We'll be okay."

"Hey, you know what?"

"What?"

"Not everyone does anal."

Ahmed frowned, taken aback by the change in subject. "What?"

He pushed himself up onto his elbow. "Some guys aren't into it. So like, don't feel like we have to."

"Um."

"I don't know, we only really talked about it that one time and I went ahead and got all supplied without even asking if you wanted to."

"Do you want to?"

"That's not what I'm saying," David said. "It's not about what I want to do, it's about if you *don't* want to do it."

Ahmed looked at his hands, then back at David. "I'd like to try. At least once." He didn't sound enthusiastic or even cautiously interested.

"Alright." David didn't care for that answer, or more precisely, he didn't like the way Ahmed had said it.

"And maybe," Ahmed began.

David prompted, "Maybe what?"

"Uh, I could try topping, too?"

David shrugged one shoulder, having no qualms with the proposal. "Yeah, sure."

His eyebrows shot up. "Just like that?"

"Yeah, whatever, I don't mind."

"Really?"

"What? Don't look so surprised."

"No, I guess I thought you wouldn't want to."

David's mouth turned down a little. "Why?"

"I don't know, cause you're not gay?"

"So?"

"Well, I don't know, it seems like you wouldn't want to."

David couldn't help but laugh. "Being bi isn't like that. It's not like I'm half gay but not the half that bottoms. Or...it's not that I'll fuck dudes if they're enough like women."

"Oh."

He sat up and gave him a kiss. "Yeah."

"I didn't know."

"Now you do. I guess it's on me a little cause I assumed you didn't want to top."

"Why?"

"Cause why would you be so nervous about that?" he asked. "I figured if you were nervous it had to be because you were nervous about, uh, getting penetrated."

At the word 'penetrated', Ahmed gave a small shudder and murmured, "Ugh."

David sat up straighter. "Hey."

"Hm?"

"Do you *want* to bottom?"

He shrugged.

"Ahmed, come on, be honest."

"I don't," he admitted. "David, I'm sorry, I really don't. Maybe someday, but not anytime soon."

"Why didn't you say anything!" David cried, feeling atrocious that he'd had no idea.

"Cause I want to have sex and I didn't want to disappoint you," Ahmed confessed, "And I thought I'd be able to, uh, get used to it or something."

"Jesus Christ," he said, putting his arms around his husband. "Don't think like that. Fuck, Ahmed, that's awful."

Ahmed's breathing hitched.

David kissed the side of his head, his throat tight. He couldn't believe that Ahmed would have forced himself to do that and he felt even worse that he'd been so oblivious to his level of discomfort. "I'm sorry. Jesus, I'm so sorry."

"No, it's...you didn't do anything."

He hugged him tighter. He had made himself do things he didn't want to do, he had let people do things do things to him just to gain their attention or approval so he knew the sick way the regret and the feeling of being used would have sat in Ahmed's belly. "I will never ever be disappointed over something like this."

Ahmed gave a nod.

"And I will never expect you do something you don't want and I will *always* stop if you ask me to."

He nodded again.

"Hey, look at me."

Ahmed looked at him, his eyes red-rimmed.

"I promise. Do you believe me?"

"Yes."

David gave him another hug and Ahmed hugged him back, so tight David worried for his ribs. After a minute, he had to admit, "I need to pee."

Ahmed laughed and released David. He continued to laugh, flopping back on their bed and laughing himself breathless. It was laughter born of nerves, but it was better than tears.

David used the bathroom, then got into the shower. After David had had enough time to clean himself and reevaluate what his sex life might be like, Ahmed knocked and called, "Hey, can I come in?"

"Sure."

Ahmed stepped into the bathroom. "I didn't catch what you said but I assumed you said okay."

"I did," David confirmed.

"I'm sorry I'm so dumb," his husband's voice came through the shower curtain, muddled by the sound of the water.

"You're not dumb."

"I feel stupid.

"Makes two of us," David said, deciding not to share the

thought that he also felt a little like a rapist. Consent was the presence of a yes, it was not the lack of a no. Nothing had happened, really, but he felt terrible that something could have.

Once clean, he stepped out and Ahmed handed him a towel. While he shaved, Ahmed sat on the toilet seat and watched. When he had rinsed his razor for the last time and wiped his face, his husband stood and kissed pressed his lips to his upper arm. With that, David felt better.

IN THE days that followed finding the girl's body, David learned that she had been on the verge of her third birthday and that her name had been Braylee, which was unfortunate, but not her fault. Her parents had reported her missing but, as best as he could follow from the news report, hadn't known she was gone until hours after her body had been found. They had assumed her safe with a relative.

"Would you ever just assume you knew where Noah is?" he asked Zhané over breakfast.

"You still worked up about that?" she asked.

"Yes!"

"David, you saw the same interview I did. They're clearly on something. A lot of something," she said.

He took out his phone.

"Do you know what day they're coming?"

"The twenty-eighth."

Ahmed glanced over, finally turning his attention away from the pancakes that David had made for everyone, even Noah, that morning. He said nothing but David felt him looking.

"What?"

"Uh." He looked at Zhané. "Have you, um, seen the things that David sees?"

Her mouth turned down. "You didn't show him?" she asked David.

"Hm?"

"You didn't show the man you asked to marry you that video?" she asked, her words slow and clear.

"Uh." He had, in all honesty, not thought about the video in weeks. Immediately following the last attack, he had not wanted to think about the next one; he had also been filled with hope and nonsense ideas about proposing and such a dour video hadn't felt romantic. "No. Forgot, I guess."

"Forgot?" she asked, her eyebrows raised.

"Yeah."

She tapped her nails on the table, her irritation with him plain, then took her phone and set it in front of Ahmed. She played the video, staring down David while his husband watched the attack.

It made his guts churn to hear his own screams again and he reached up with one hand to cover the ear closest to the source.

Ahmed watched it again, then once more. After that, he stood up and walked out, saying, "Don't, I need air," when David moved.

David stayed seated.

"I can't believe you," Zhané pronounced.

"I told him everything."

"Telling and seeing aren't the same."

"It's not my fault if he didn't believe me," he countered.

"David, *you have schizophrenia*. He could not have known that this wasn't a hallucination."

"He's seen the scars."

"And the ones on your arms?" she asked.

"You're not being fair."

"I'm not...!"

He stood, walking away, and heading out the front door. He sat on the stairs that lead up to their apartment. He heard Ahmed behind him, pacing and arguing on his phone in Pashto.

Finally, Ahmed hung up with a frustrated shout and came back around to the front of the house, passing David as he did so.

He did a double take, then came to stand in front of David, arms crossed.

"I have to go pick up my grandmother."

"What?" David frowned.

"She has an eye doctor appointment and everyone else is at work. So now they'll talk to me," he spat. "So you need to move your car."

"Oh. Right."

He headed upstairs, Ahmed on his heels. He moved his car and Ahmed left without another word.

David waited for him to come back. Just shy of a month was not so bad as far as idiotic elopements went. He would be alone again the next time the things came. He had hoped to weather it with friends, that maybe three would have been too much of a crowd for his visitors.

He lay on the bed with Benjamin Rabbit cuddled close. He hadn't cried yet but felt like he might soon.

Ahmed returned after an hour and a half, looking worn out. He tossed his keys on the kitchen table, followed by his wallet.

David watched.

His husband turned and glanced at him, heaving a sigh. He asked, "What?"

"I'm sorry, Ahmed. I should have shown you but I really didn't think of it."

He shook his head.

David sat up and set Benjamin Rabbit on the bedside table.

Ahmed crossed the room and embraced David with little warning. "I'm sorry these things happen to you, David, it isn't right."

It was not what he expected. "You aren't mad?"

"I'm in an awful fucking mood, but I'm not mad at you," he said, "Why would I be?"

"Because I didn't show you proof? Because you thought I was just crazy instead of...I don't know, haunted and crazy?"

Ahmed pulled back and sat on the bed. "I never thought that. I mean. I did for a little bit but...I heard that voice in my hearing aid, David."

"You needed air."

"Yeah, cause that was horrible to watch! Those things hurt you, I *saw them* cut into you. If I could never hear that sound again it would be too soon!" He reached out to take David's hand.

David sniffled and Ahmed leaned in close, slid his hand behind David's head and kissed him hard, in a way that felt frightened, protective. The kiss left them both out of breath; Ahmed did not release him but kept their foreheads pressed close until he kissed him again.

He pushed David back, settling on top of him, putting lips to David's throat and jaw. He pulled his shirt off and pushed David's up, moving down to kiss his stomach and along his waistline, just above where his boxers showed above his pants. "David."

"What?" he asked.

Ahmed leaned in close again and kissed his neck. "Can we...?"

"Absolutely."

Ahmed paused momentarily, for the first time faltering. "You're, uh...good? Ready? You know, whatever?"

David couldn't help but laugh. "I would have said no if I wasn't."

"Oh."

"I actually would have been like, oh let me go clean up and we can revisit this later," he admitted. "But no, I'm good, come on. You were kissing me like...all, um, gee, I don't want to say manly like to imply that you aren't usual—"

Ahmed cut off his ramblings with a kiss, doing his best to pull David's shirt off and mostly succeeding.

Once undressed, they moved in a rush, rummaging in the side table for lube and then once they had it, kissing fiercely until Ahmed pulled back and asked, "Now what?"

David grinned, opened the bottle and asked, "Well, do you want to have to look at my face or the back of my head?"

"I'm pretty fond of your face."

"Great. Besides, you can always close your eyes." He squirted lube onto his hand and applied it to Ahmed, who let out his breath all at once, swallowing hard. "Take it slow, alright."

He nodded.

"Unless I start saying something like 'god, faster, please, harder' in which case, do that."

Ahmed shook his head. "You're *weird*."

"How would you know? You've never been with anyone, maybe this is normal sex banter," he teased and kissed him to soften the joke.

Ahmed moved inside of him carefully, probably out of nerves as much as consideration. David consciously made himself relax, taking slow breaths. At no point did he plead for Ahmed to go harder or faster; it had been a while since he'd done this and though they had started off fevered and hasty, the slower pace worked for both of them. Going slow gave them time to savor things, to check in with each other and make sure things were right. Not perfect, but right.

Hard and fast could be saved for another time.

Ahmed had his hand beside David's head, leaned in so he

could kiss him from time to time when he wasn't too busy sighing or groaning. Sometimes he would whisper something breathy and incomprehensible until he pressed harder and closer, moving in deeper for a few thrusts and then crying out, gripping the pillowcase.

He stayed still for a moment, catching his breath. He brushed a lazy kiss across David's mouth.

"Hey," David said.

"Hm?"

"Uh. Do you think you could finish me?" he asked, not sure how else to say it.

Letting out a breath through his nose that was almost a laugh and giving a small smile, he said, "Yeah, sorry."

When he pulled out, David let out a moan he hadn't meant to, the feeling making him shiver. Ahmed scooted down and took David into his mouth, finishing him and then pulling back with the same mildly displeased look on his face he always had.

"You can spit."

"And what, keep it in my mouth all the way to the sink?" Ahmed demanded. "So much worse."

David chuckled. He took Ahmed by the arm and pulled him closer. He kissed his hair and then his shoulder. He felt that he should say something but didn't have anything to say. Ahmed didn't have anything to say either, lying nestled against David and running his fingers over David's arm.

"Anyone ever tell you that you're pretty fucking cute?" David asked.

"Not in those words exactly and not the way you mean it."

After a few minutes, David asked, "So what are you mad about?"

"Oh. Ugh. Family stuff."

"Well, they're talking to you again."

"Sure, I go pick her up and drop her off. And I mean, she's fine, she's so old I don't think she gives a shit about anything except keeping her glaucoma in check."

"That's kind of mean."

"Well, I mean, she cares about us, of course, but like...she doesn't care what we do. You know? She's just...too tired."

He nodded.

"But when I drop her off, she says goodbye. Whatever. Like I said, she's fine. She asks me to bring this dish back to my parents, said she'd meant to but forgot. Not a big deal, I take it, go drop it off and what do I get from my mother? Not a fucking word. She won't even look at me."

"Oh."

"So I called her out on it, told her that if she's going to pretend I'm dead, then the next time I'm not helping anyone out."

"That's fair."

"You'd think that! But apparently, I'm a bad and ungrateful son and all that shit."

"I'm sorry."

"Whatever, I guess at least she spoke to me," Ahmed huffed.

David took his hand and kissed his knuckles.

"You don't think I'm manly?" he asked after a minute.

"That wasn't the right word. Actually, the first word I thought of was fierce but I didn't know if that was too camp."

"Oh."

"You're adequately masculine for my taste, though, why?"

"I was just thinking about it." He traced along David's collarbones, then down his sternum. "We will find a way to get rid of those things. I'm gonna think about it. We should have been planning this whole time..."

"I was busy."

"Doing what?" Ahmed asked, his nose wrinkled.

He could only think that he loved the way he wrinkled his nose like that. "Getting married, finding corpses, deciding a career path."

"Oh right." He said nothing for a while, his finger still moving along David's chest. "Adequately masculine?"

"That's what I said."

"You like girls, though."

David frowned. "What does that have to do with anything?"

"Do you think I'm girly?"

"Does it matter?"

"No, just...I don't know. Do you?"

"The thought honestly never occurred to me," David said.

"Oh." Under his breath, he repeated, "Adequately masculine."

"It's just...you're so tiny."

"I am not!"

David made a face.

"I'm five ten! That's average!"

"And what, like a hundred and forty pounds soaking wet?" he said. He rolled over to face him and wrapped an arm around him, pulling him close. He kissed his forehead. "Besides, why do you want to be manly anyway? Gender is a construct."

He sighed.

"Isn't it more important to be brave and caring and sweet?" David asked. "Cause that's what you are. Not some vague word that means, what? That you're tough? Strong? Manly is bullshit, girly is bullshit. We're just people."

"I don't know, you're right, it's just...a thing. A hang-up."

"We all have them." He kissed him again, this time on the mouth. "I have to mow the lawn."

"I'll do it."

"Really?" he said.

"Yeah, sure, you did it last time."

David, at no point in his life, had ever had someone offer to share his chores. He gave Ahmed a squeeze. "Thanks."

"No problem, I have to shower anyway." Ahmed gave him a kiss, got out of bed, and stretched. He pulled on his clothes and headed outside.

Several minutes later, David heard the lawnmower start. He nestled into the covers, feeling wonderfully spoiled as he lay in the air conditioning.

Zhané let herself in, Noah in her arms. "You're making him mow the lawn?"

He looked towards her, not caring that parts of him were not covered by the blankets. "He offered."

She raised an eyebrow.

"He's not mad at me and he believed me anyway," he said, feeling entitled to be a little snotty.

She looked at him again. "So, how was it?"

"Nice."

"Hmm." She shook her head.

"What?"

"I can't believe he married you."

"No, me neither," he said, then started to frown. "That's kind of mean, though."

She came over to the bed and tapped his feet. "Move, let me sit."

He moved, tucking himself under the covers better.

She sat and set Noah down. The baby immediately crawled over to David, cuddling up to him. "Jeez, he really likes you."

"Cause he's my little buddy," David said, giving Noah's head an affectionate pat.

"So what are we going to go?"

"About what?"

"Uh, the horrible monsters that are coming to harvest your body parts."

"Oh."

"Yeah. Oh."

"I don't know," he admitted. "Do what we did last time?"

"You want to go to the hospital again?"

"No, but," he said not wanting to tell her that going to the hospital was better than waking up in his sheets soaked with his own blood trying to figure out what had happened. After they'd taken part of his liver, he'd dragged himself to an urgent care clinic, begging to know what had happened. They'd called an ambulance for him after determining the fate of his liver and he had snuck out the back door after hearing his diagnosis, fearing that his story was a one-way ticket back to Mansfield.

He wondered if Frost and Ingress could be any help. He had convinced Zhané and Ahmed that the things were real, maybe he could do the same to the FBI agents. They might have been lizard people, but they seemed like they could turn out to be a reasonable lizard people.

He didn't voice this to Zhané. She still hadn't contacted them about her relationship with the coroner and when they'd stopped by again, she'd told them to leave, to come back with a warrant.

Frost had looked disheartened and Ingress had looked irritated, like she'd wanted to argue. She had waved to him, though, when he had waved to her and he hoped that the damage that his comment in the chip aisle had done was repaired.

"Hey, space cadet," she said.

He looked over at her. "Hm?"

"Were you listening?"

He thought about lying. "No. I wasn't. Sorry."

She sighed. "Alright, well come find me when you're ready to actually do something about this."

"I'm sorry."

She picked up Noah and he felt that he should have cleaned up and dressed, then gone after her, but he didn't. He nuzzled into the pillow and fell asleep with Benjamin Rabbit in his arms, lulled by the sound of the lawn mower, recalling weekend mornings as a child.

He woke up when Ahmed came back inside. "Hey, come here," he said.

Ahmed approached.

David took him by the hand and sat up, giving him a kiss. He smelled of cut grass and gasoline and sweat. He smelled a lot like sweat. "I want you to meet my parents."

"Okay."

"A lot. I want them to meet you and love you as much as I do."

Ahmed kissed him, his hand under David's chin, pulling him closer. David felt trembling and breathless.

When Ahmed released him, he said, "God, you really smell."

His husband frowned.

"Like, you fucking stink. Jesus." He reached up to kiss him again, his skin flushing. "I think my eyes are watering."

Ahmed walked away, straight to the bathroom.

David threw back the covers and followed him. He watched Ahmed undress and grabbed him by the hand, kissing him again when he went to set his hearing aid on the counter.

"I thought I smelled."

"You do, it's fucking *horrible*." It was a smell that he seemed to crave though, wanting another kiss, wanting to have that smell on his own skin.

Ahmed turned on the shower and got in without waiting for the temperature to adjust, which David found absolutely horrifying.

"Do you always just get in like that?" he asked.

"What?"

"God, that's manly as fuck," he said.

David climbed in once he saw tendrils of steam coming from the shower. Ahmed frowned, his eyes closed as he washed his hair. "Did you just get in?"

"Yes."

"What?"

David touched him and he recoiled a little.

"You didn't want to ask, I guess."

"You can't hear me anyways."

"What?"

David laughed and kissed him again, regretting it a little because he tasted like shampoo. He rinsed his mouth.

Ahmed rinsed his hair and opened his eyes. "What's gotten into you?"

"Why do you ask me things when you know you can't hear

me?"

"Because I can read lips, shithead," he said, his eyes trained on David's mouth.

"What! That's the coolest!" David said, once again impressed with all the things Ahmed could do. "Why are you so cool?"

He shrugged.

David reached behind him and grabbed the pouf, squeezing shower gel onto it.

"That's not my soap," Ahmed said.

He ignored him, taking him by the arm and moving him so he wasn't directly in the stream of the water. He scrubbed him down, banishing the stink of sweat and fumes and replacing it with the smell of Irish Spring.

Once he was clean and rinsed, David put his lips to his neck and Ahmed leaned in against him, one arm around his waist, another around his neck.

"Oh, hey, David!" he said, giving him a small push. "Hang on, cut it out."

David pulled back. "What?"

"I got an idea!"

"Uh. What kind of idea?" he asked, but Ahmed had already climbed out of the shower, leaving David to stand there.

David turned off the water and followed him out. "Hey."

Ahmed turned around, toweling off his hair.

"What kind of idea?"

"I need to see that video again."

"Uh. Okay."

Ahmed nodded and finished drying off, putting his hearing aid back in and then walking out of the bathroom.

David wasn't sure what had happened, but Ahmed seemed invigorated by whatever he'd thought of. He headed out and pulled on the clothes he'd shed earlier that day, to find Ahmed already in a pair of sweats, heading into the main part of the house as he pulled on his shirt.

When he caught up with him, he had Zhané's phone in his hand and David could hear his own screams again.

"They don't like being watched," Ahmed said.

"No. We sort of figured that," David said.

"So we have to be somewhere public."

"They come at night," David reminded.

"What's open at night?" Ahmed asked.

"A bar," said Zhané.

"A club," David answered at the same time.

Ahmed's mouth turned down at the corners. "I wouldn't be able to go with you. I'm not twenty-one."

"You don't have to."

"But I *want* to be with you, David, you shouldn't have to do this alone. Two people clearly aren't enough to get them to go."

"Hold up," Zhané said. "I know a place. I think. I'll have to make a call."

"Where?" Ahmed asked.

"My cousin Amari bartends at this place in the city. I mean, we can take the train down, right? Shit, we can even drive. I'll ask my mom to watch Noah. I'll see if he can get you in. Let me call him."

He handed back her phone and she walked off to make the call in private.

"You don't have to come," David offered again.

"And I'm not going to leave you alone for this," he insisted. "We should get a better camera. Better proof."

"For what?" David asked. Posting the last video had garnered the attention of conspiracy theorists and cryptozoologists, but no one who had offered any answers or solutions.

"Because. When crazy things happen, you document it. Think about, David, there could be someone else dealing with this."

"Sure, right in town."

Ahmed tilted his head. "What?"

"Oh, right," he breathed and looked around the kitchen. "Wait."

He retreated to their bedroom and returned with the notebook and coroner reports, holding them out to Ahmed. "This is everything we've figured out."

He leafed through them. "Is this what the FBI wants to know about?"

David nodded.

"How...?"

"I really don't know."

"That little girl, do you think...?" he asked.

He shook his head. "No. She wasn't missing anything. Not that I could see, anyways. She was...uh, whole. No blood, just bruises." *And dirt.* "And the timeline is off. She's too early."

Ahmed sat at the table, looking through the notebook more seriously this time. "You're right." After he had spent a while reading through the notebook, he looked up and asked, "David? This list."

"Hm?" David looked over, pausing the game of peek-a-boo he played with the baby. He had long since given up on regaining Ahmed's attention with that notebook in front of him. Noah grabbed his hands and leaned forward to wipe drool all over his fingers.

"These body parts."

"Yeah?"

"They don't match up with what's missing from the dead people," he said.

"I know."

"This is what they've taken from you?"

"Sure."

"David! Your *liver*," he cried.

"Not all of it."

"For fuck's sake, how can you be so calm?" His breathing had gone uneven and his cheeks had flushed the same way as when Johnny called him out for something he let slide with others, or when a customer asked if there was someone else who could help them.

"What am I supposed to do? Shout? Break things?" he asked. "I did that already."

Ahmed frowned, flipped through the notebook again, riffling through the coroner's report.

David turned his attention back to Noah until Ahmed pushed the notebook and the report on to the floor; he glanced over to see that he had tears trailing down his face.

Zhané came back. The smile slipped from her face when she looked at the things strewn on the floor. "What happened?" she asked, her voice soft and concerned.

"It isn't fair," Ahmed whispered hoarsely.

David reached out for his hand and he grabbed on. Watching him cry, David wondered how many times he'd been alone, with no one to hold his hand, while he'd cried for himself. Surely he must have, in his bed at night, his future full of dread and impossible dreams. He gave his back a rub. "Things will be okay."

Ahmed swallowed.

"Amari says he'll get you in," Zhané told them, coming to sit at the table. She gave Ahmed's arm a squeeze. "This might be it, you know."

"What if it isn't? Will they ever stop?"

"It's a lot, I know." She offered him a napkin and he took it, wiping his face.

He shook his head. "It's not fair. Things shouldn't *be* like this."

David wondered if this would be too much for him. "You don't have to come."

"David, for shit's sake," he whispered, "I'm going with you."

"Okay." He tightened his grip on Ahmed's hand for a moment, overwhelmed that in such a short time he'd found two people who were willing to help him, despite a significant risk to themselves.

8/29/15

THIS TIME the call had come in on David's phone while they'd been eating dinner with Zhané and the baby. No one had been in a good mood since. Ahmed sat on the floor with Noah, Zhané had the cat on her lap and David sat at the end of the sofa, staring down at his phone. He'd texted his parents earlier that day, saying he'd really like them to come down. He had gotten no response so far.

When his phone began to ring, he immediately felt sick and his hand trembled when he lifted it to his ear. He knew who it would be, just his mother, but he couldn't shake the feeling that this was bad.

"Hello?"

"Hi, David. We got your text."

"Oh."

Neither of them said anything for an uncomfortable, unusually long moment.

David swallowed. "I'd really like you to come down."

Ahmed and Zhané had both glanced at him and then away, trying not to be nosy. He stood and stepped outside.

"Mom?" he asked since she hadn't answered.

"Why do you want us to visit? Is there something you need?"

"Yeah. I need you to come meet my husband."

"Oh, that," she said.

"Mom!"

"David, I have to say, we thought this would blow over."

"It hasn't."

"It's a long drive down just to meet some guy."

He sighed. "He isn't just some guy."

"How long have you even known him? You haven't even been out of state that long."

"What does it matter how long I've known him?" he asked.

"You've never really been one for commitment," she said, dismissive.

He wished she hadn't called, that he hadn't even asked her to come down. "That's not even true."

"We'll see if we have a free weekend, I suppose."

"Mom, this really matters to me."

"I'm sure."

He bit his lip. His throat felt tight and he blinked a few times, not sure who he was trying to hide his tears from. "It's not because he's a boy, is it?"

"Oh, don't be dramatic."

"Mom, I mean it. Is it because he's a boy?"

She sighed and he knew that she, far away in Vermont, had rolled her eyes. "I can't say I'm thrilled."

He waited.

"Honestly, David, what that man did to you—"

"Who? Louis?"

"You can't let that overshadow your life."

"What?"

"Jesus, David, do you want me to say it? You were *raped*, that doesn't mean that you have to play along. You weren't asking for it."

He didn't know what to say. Louis had been older and yes, it had been bad judgment for him to be involved with a minor and a patient, but he had never forced or cajoled or even persuaded David into bed with him.

"It wasn't like that."

"And all the acting out you did afterward? You can't tell me *he* didn't have something to do with that."

"Oh, holy shit." He had not expected this conversation to take such a turn. "Louis didn't rape me."

"You were seventeen!"

"Yeah and that was questionable on his part, but it was consensual," he said. "And besides."

"Besides what?"

"I'd been with other guys before Louis," he told her, thinking of Paul LaRosa. "I'm bi, Mom. I always have been and I always will be, okay? And Ahmed...he's wonderful. And I want you to meet him."

"I wish you would be more reasonable."

"And I wish you would come meet my husband." He hung up. It had been childish to hang up, but it had made him feel better. He shoved his phone deep into his pocket and went back inside.

"What's that look for?" Ahmed asked.

"My mom thinks I'm only bi because I got sexually assaulted."

Ahmed's eyes went wide and his mouth opened. "Oh, I—"

"No, no, I didn't, I wasn't. She just thinks that."

Ahmed put his hand on his chest and let out a breath.

"That's fucked up," Zhané said. "I mean, on so many levels."

He nodded and went to sit on the floor beside Ahmed and Noah. Noah crawled over to him, reaching out his arms to be picked up. David scooped him up and settled him in his lap, giving his head a kiss and breathing in.

He tossed his phone on the coffee table. "It doesn't matter what she thinks."

Ahmed gave his thigh a comforting pat.

"But I know if she'd come meet you, she'd change her mind, I know she would," he said.

Noah leaned forward and David let him go. He crawled back to Ahmed, grabbing a toy and shoving it in his mouth, one of his little hands on Ahmed's knee.

"David, I'm sorry," Ahmed said.

"I just...I don't understand! It shouldn't be this big of a deal."

"Tell me about it." He barely smiled.

David glanced up at him. He hated the look on his face, the melancholy acceptance that they were alone. He leaned over to grab his phone and went back outside, this time calling his father.

"Hey there, David," his father said when he answered.

"Hi, Dad."

"I heard your mother on the phone with you."

"Yeah."

"Didn't sound too happy."

"No."

"Did you want something?" his father asked.

"I want you to come to Connecticut and I want you to bring Mom."

His father let out a long breath.

"Dad, come on, she's thought up this turned-gay-by-rape nonsense," David said, "And I know she wouldn't think that if she met Ahmed."

"Where did you say he's from?"

"He's from here. His family is from Afghanistan."

"Hmm."

"*Please.* His parents won't even talk to him."

"No?"

"No, and...it hurts, Dad. It feels fucking awful."

"Now, David."

"Don't! This isn't just some passing thing, alright? Or are you two never going to see me again?"

His father sighed.

"Because I'm not going to pretend, okay?"

"It's an awfully long drive, David."

"And I'm your son!"

Silence hung heavy between them.

"Please," he begged. "I want you to meet my husband. Please."

"I'll see what we can do."

"It means a lot to me."

"Seems that way," his father said, "Anyways. I've got to go, time for dinner."

"I love you." He felt like he was reminding his father that families said that.

"You, too, son."

He hung up and wished it wasn't so difficult. "Fucking Republicans," he whispered to himself.

He went back inside again and sat back on the floor. He kissed Ahmed and rubbed Noah's back. He looked at Zhané and asked, "What kind of bar does your cousin work at?"

She shrugged. "I'm not sure."

He lay down on his side and Noah crawled over, using him as a prop to help himself stand. He yawned and the baby grabbed on to him, scratching him. He wondered if it was normal to be this tired all the time.

He ended up dozing off after a few minutes and thought, after a while, that he heard Ahmed asked, "Should we wake him?"

"No, he's fine," Zhané said.

David nestled his face further into his arm, his bones feeling heavy. He thought to himself several times that he should get up, but wasn't able to, his eyes shut and refusing to open. He dreamed on and off that Ahmed had given him a shake or that he'd walked over to the couch, but when he woke with a start an hour or so later, he found himself still on the floor.

He heard Figaro land with a thump and recalled that the cat had come to lie on his chest; there was a patch of fur on his shirt to show that he had not imagined it. She must have jumped off.

He pushed himself up and Zhané greeted him from the couch. "Hey there, sleepy."

"Hm?"

"Your husband went out. Something about his grandmother? I don't know."

"She must have another appointment," he said, rubbing his eyes. They felt gummy and he needed a drink.

He shuffled into the kitchen and gulped a glass of water with such vigor that Zhané looked over at him, distaste on her face. "Sorry."

"There's food in the fridge," she told him.

"You ate without me?"

"You wouldn't wake up. We tried."

"Oh." He took a plastic wrapped plate from the fridge and put it into the microwave, jamming the minute button several times. While he waited for his food to heat, he leaned forward at the waist, folding his arms on the counter and resting his head on his arms. He groaned.

"You okay?"

"No."

"The usual level of not okay or should I be worried?"

"Slightly elevated but no risk of escalation."

The microwave beeped; he took his plate out, taking it over to the table as fast as he could, then clenching his hand once he'd set it down. He grabbed a fork and sat, staring down at his food for a minute, contemplating the peas. By the time he'd finished eating and put the plate in the dishwasher, Ahmed had returned.

"Hey," David greeted him.

He glanced over. "Oh. Hey."

"What's up? Where'd you go?"

Ahmed came to sit beside him and said nothing for so long

David started to worry. Finally, he sighed and said, "My grandma called me to come over to fix something with her DVD player."

David could not imagine the woman he'd seen, quiet to the point of seeming stoic, having a DVD player or ever using it.

"Anyways, she'd told my parents to come over for dinner."

"Gee."

"The good news is she gave my parents shit about telling people I was dead."

"Bad news?"

"She says she has to meet you and your family before she can decide if she approves," Ahmed reported.

"Approves?" It seemed unlikely that any adult in their lives would ever approve.

Ahmed snorted. "Yeah, turns out her and her best friend were having an affair for like...ten years until their husbands figured it out."

"Damn."

"Yeah."

"Well, fuck, Ahmed."

"I know, right? Anyways, so my parents are dealing with that and I think now my dad blames my mom for me being gay on account of *her* mom being gay. So I might have destroyed their marriage. Which is exactly what I set out to do. Mission accomplished."

"Jesus."

Ahmed twisted the ring on his finger and David wondered if the fiddling was a sign of regret or an attempt at comforting himself.

"She can meet me anytime she wants," he offered.

"Thanks."

"My parents I can't make any promises for."

Ahmed nodded.

"That's, um, I mean that's kind of good, right? That she might like me?"

"No, it's definitely better." His phone dinged and he fished it out of his pocket.

"Hm?"

"Just Noor," Ahmed assured.

They sat together, neither saying anything until Ahmed got up. "I'm, uh...I kind of need to process. Alone."

"Sure." David knew that he would find him bent over his keyboard later. "Let me know if you need anything."

Ahmed nodded and gave David a pat on the back as he walked past him to get to their apartment.

8/31/15

WHEN THEY all went over to her mother's house in Zhané's car to drop off Noah, Amanda did not seem thrilled to see them. She frowned at David and glanced over Ahmed dismissively.

"Whatever it is you're doing, make sure you come home to that baby," Amanda warned as Zhané handed over Noah to her father.

Zhané's eyes widened as she tried not to say anything back and she dropped the diaper bag by the couch.

"Ought to know better," Amanda muttered.

David grimaced.

"Know better than to what? Go out for a night?" Zhané demanded.

"I thought you went out *every* night," her mother said.

"I don't have time for this," Zhané said. "I'll see you in tomorrow."

David knew that wasn't true. They were running a little ahead of schedule, but he didn't think that was what she meant. He followed her out, Ahmed on his heels, and said, "Uh."

She glanced back at him.

"Do you want me to drive?" he offered.

"No."

He climbed into the passenger seat and Ahmed climbed into

the back, taking care not to sit on the little camcorder they'd gotten. Small enough to hold in one hand, it, they hoped, would provide more concrete images of the things. It seemed important to be able to see them well because when unknown monsters demanded that you kill for them, it was probably best to find out as much as you could.

Zhané had spent all of yesterday playing with it and David had faith she would get the footage she wanted.

More than he wanted to know what they were, he wanted the things to go away.

He slid the seat back to give himself more legroom and then glanced back at Ahmed. "Excited?"

"No."

"Mad?" he asked because the answer had been short and terse.

"I'm *worried*. This could go wrong."

"Oh, right. I know. But still. Maybe it will be fun. Uh, you know, before they come."

"I'm not gonna drink."

"No, me neither." Drunk did not seem the best way to greet the things. "But maybe there will be a band or something."

"Maybe." He didn't sound like he thought anything could make this better.

David couldn't blame him. He'd never dealt with this before and he was right, something could go wrong. Even last time, when things had gone better than usual, David had ended up in the hospital.

"Love you," he said.

"You too," Ahmed said.

Zhané snorted.

"What?" David asked, turning back to face her.

"You two are gross."

"Jealous."

"Not even!"

He knew there was truth to her statement. She had never been one for mushy stuff, for lovey-dovey nonsense. He didn't blame her; life would be easier without schmaltz and worrying if things were romantic enough. Some people were simply drawn to it, unable to help their love for storybook endings as others were unable to help a love for candy. The love-life version of a sweet tooth.

"Do you ever think about dating?" he asked.

She glanced over.

"Not that it's my business."

"It isn't," she agreed but without any bite in her tone. "I used to, uh, you know, wonder if Noah would do better with a fucking male role model and all that patriarchal shit. Or if he would do better with two parents instead of one cause someday he might be mad at me and still need someone to talk to."

"But?"

"But now he's got you." She glanced over at him, her eyes shiny and dark as they darted back to the road after just a second.

"He does," he confirmed.

"For a while, I figure."

"Yeah, forever." He found himself unable to contemplate ever leaving Noah behind, no matter what turn his life took.

She smiled, looking relieved. "I don't really think about dating that much, to be honest. I've got friends, I've got Noah. I'm alright."

He nodded, admiring that she could live her life without becoming infatuated with the first cute stock boy she saw. Not that he regretted the turn his infatuation had taken.

They arrived in the city around eight, found a parking garage near the bar where her cousin worked and walked over to meet up with him. They found him leaning against the wall near the bar's side door; he glanced them over and straightened up.

Zhané hugged her cousin and when he pulled back, he asked, "How's Aunt Mandy?"

Zhané let out a bark of a laugh, not like her at all.

"Still giving you a hard time?" Amari asked.

"I don't know, does your mom still give you a hard time about Blake?"

David wondered, only mildly curious, who Blake could be. He glanced at Zhané, the question in his eyes. It was possible her cousin was gay, especially when he glanced around the bar where he worked, all low lighting and dark wood with a vintage feel, it gave off an atmosphere of being either hip or queer. Amari had the same look to him: tight, deep red jeans cuffed over brown boots with a flannel shirt to match, his mass of dreads pulled back into a ponytail.

"White girlfriend," Zhané informed him.

He nodded. He remembered that part of their relationship, the odd clash of cultures, of long-standing tension between privilege and oppression. The accusation that David sought the thrill of conquering the exotic, that Zhané thought she was too good for black boys.

Amari showed them around the bar, pointing out the bathrooms and urging that Ahmed not cause trouble, lest he cost Amari his job. He set them up in a booth off in the corner and returned to his job.

They sat quietly together, all of them on their phones, no one sure what to say. The camcorder sat on the table just in front of Zhané.

David could only pray that they were right, that the things would flee another public scene. He leaned back into the leather seat of the booth, running his fingers over the sharp plastic edge of the menu. He dug the pad of his thumb onto the corner of the menu. He knew he could not push hard enough to draw blood, but the nerves that bubbled in his stomach made him wish he could.

It had been an unexpected shock to realize that, living in close quarters, the outlet of self-harm was no longer available to him as it had been. The night before, full of anxiety and terror, he had searched furtively for a razorblade, unable to remember where he had left it the last time.

Ahmed had asked, "What are you looking for?" and the question had sent a wave of odd numbness and fear through him. Ahmed could not know. He had seen the scars on David's arms, even the new pink ones from the last time David had needed something bright and sharp to cut through the haze, and he had not asked about them, but his eyes lingered there sometimes when he thought David wouldn't notice.

"Nothing," David had answered.

Ahmed had asked if he'd needed to talk and he had said no. He had found his razor and hidden it in his pocket, nervous as he had never been before. This was a not a fear of getting caught, of losing privileges, it was the feeling that hurting himself would hurt Ahmed, that his husband would not be able to understand the cause. He worried Ahmed would take it personally.

He'd locked himself in the bathroom and had flushed the bloody tissue down the toilet when the wounds had scabbed. He'd even stuck a bandage over the four new lines as some kind of disguise.

Ahmed had noticed the bandaged, asked what happened and David had lied. "Just a bug bite," he'd said, his ears ringing, "Couldn't stop scratching it."

Ahmed had accepted the lie and even now, as David picked

idly as the lint-fuzzed edge of the bandage, he wondered if Ahmed suspected.

He hated that he had lied. He had been able to confess to murder, but not to this.

His husband reached out and wrapped his hand, thin and brown, around David's. He pulled David away from repeatedly running his fingers over the bandage, the rough fabric impossible to leave alone. He looked up to meet David's eyes, his chin raised up, making him look confident.

"Hm?" David asked.

"You don't have to tell me," he said softly. "But don't feel like you can't."

He blinked.

"You're a bad liar, David."

He let out half a laugh, more of a breath. "Thanks."

Ahmed leaned in and rested his head against David's shoulder, wrapping his arms around David's arm and squeezing it for just a moment. He pressed his lip to the bare skin beneath the hem of David's short sleeve.

"You have a lot of eyelashes," David said.

Ahmed looked up, a wary half-smile on his face.

It had been all David could think to say, struck by the long, curled lashes so dark they acted almost as eyeliner.

"Dork," Ahmed accused, now smiling all the way.

"Gross." Zhané glanced up from her phone to say it. She had no malice in her tone, but a type of affection.

People had begun to trickle in around them, filling up the booths and tables with their bodies and the air with their voices. A waiter stopped at their table, dropping off a menu and taking their orders.

Two sodas, for the men, and for Zhané an expensive mixed drink made mostly of liquor. "And a glass of water," she added when she'd handed over ID.

"Uh, also..." David squinted at the menu, wondering if he needed a stronger prescription for his glasses. "Can we get some mozzarella sticks?"

"Sure thing," the waiter had said, handing back Zhané's ID and heading off.

"It's one drink," Zhané said defensively, though neither of them had said anything.

"Okay."

"And I'm done nursing." It sounded like a big announcement, a declaration almost.

"Okay."

"He's totally on solids now," she said.

"I know," David said.

"Also what kind of bullshit is breastfeeding for *years?*" she demanded, "I'm fucking exhausted."

Ahmed laughed.

She raised an eyebrow.

"You sound like Miriam," he explained.

"How is Mark Jr?" she asked.

"Good," Ahmed replied, "Really good."

"We can do playdates when they're older."

He grinned at the idea. "Miriam would love that."

Around eleven, the bar seemed full. At midnight, David didn't think it would be legal to let any more people in, but by just after one, the number seemed to have stabilized.

In order to make up for taking up a table but not drinking, they ordered a few more plates of appetizers.

At about one thirty, a new band came on, more upbeat and playing original songs instead of covers.

Ahmed watched people dance, his eyes trained on the space cleared of tables and chairs. A few dozen people swayed there, in couples or groups, a few dancing alone. David glanced over towards where he gazed.

Before Ahmed could say ask anything, David told him, "Zhané's a better dancer than I am."

"Unless you've got it memorized," Zhané said.

"Well, if you can get them to play Single Ladies or some show tunes, I'll dance."

Ahmed frowned, as he did sometimes when he wasn't in the loop. It wasn't jealousy, just confusion.

"David's really good at dancing, as long as you give him three weeks to learn the steps. And I mean *flawless*, it's uncanny," Zhané said, leaning over David to speak to Ahmed over the sound of the club. "But he's hopeless on his own."

"And I can do 'Goodbye Horses'," David volunteered.

"What?" Ahmed asked.

"The 'would you fuck me' song from *Silence of the Lambs*," he said.

"Oh." Ahmed regarded David with an odd look in his eyes and

unfamiliar set about his mouth.

In his ear, Zhané suggested, "Do the thing with your hand," and then drew back.

David considered her suggestion. He flexed his hand, out of nerves and in preparation for the gesture.

Ahmed watched curiously as David brought one hand up to touch his mouth, his fingers crooked artfully and barely touching his bottom lip to tug it down just a little. It was an essentially feminine gesture, reminiscent of Bowie or a magazine ad, and would have found completion if he'd had his eyes painted or his nails manicured.

His eyes, pale blue since the day he'd been born, would have really popped, drawn the gaze, with a little bit of liner and eyeshadow. He'd never wanted to draw attention to his eyes, though, because people had often told him that his eyes were cold, that they felt like he could see through them.

Ahmed licked his lips.

David pulled his hand away from his mouth, feeling a little silly. Confidence was really what he lacked to pull off the look. "I have to use the bathroom."

Ahmed scooted out of the booth so he could leave and asked, hesitant, "Should I come with you?"

David laughed. He bent down to kiss him, amused at the idea but not intrigued by it. He had fucked in bathrooms before, bent over sinks, jammed up against the particle board in a stall. It would not be like that with Ahmed, it could never be. He loved him too much to have the smell of urinal cakes and strangers' feces intrude on their time together.

"No, I've just got to pee." He kissed Ahmed again. "Be right back."

In the bathroom, he selected a urinal an appropriate distance away from the man already in there. He left before David did and once alone, David felt uncomfortable. The drip of the sink and tick of the pipes reminded him why he was here, what their goal was.

He zipped his fly and considered not washing his hands, wanting to be back among the people as soon as possible. It seemed impossible that another man had not come in yet.

He skipped the sink and headed right for the door, catching a whiff of the acrid chemical scent before he saw them.

Three of them, oozing out from a stall, down from the ceiling. He'd never seen them arrive like this before, in full lighting. They straightened themselves into the semblance of men and surged forward.

He heard the muffled sound of voices from his pocket and he backed up, not wanting to take his eyes off the things. When he pulled the door, he found it locked.

The things came to him, pressing him up against the wall. They were faceless, only two dents where eyes should have been and a crease for a mouth. He heard someone approaching, a few voices.

Salvation, except that when they tugged, the door didn't open.

The thing directly in front of him put a hand over his face, smothering him with one hand with the others held his limbs tight to the wall.

With one of those odd, shapeshifting hands, a thing held open his eyes and he realized with gut-wrenching horror, that eyes were not needed to live.

He could not scream. He needed to but he could not, he could not even breath.

Someone banged on the door and he thrashed, his lungs burning and his vision fuzzing.

Without warning, he heard a click and the door fell open. He tumbled out of the grip of the things, hard onto his back.

One of the men, one of the bartenders, gathered outside demanded, "Hey, what are you—fuck!"

David scrambled to his feet and fled; he glanced back to see the things on his heels, slithering forward after him. He burst onto the dance floor, interrupting everything. They parted around him and he saw, out of the corner of his eye, Zhané with the camcorder. Smart, prepared, she was always prepared.

Someone, maybe Amari, turned the lights on and everyone drew further back from David as the things swarmed him again. The bar went silent as they pressed him to the floor, covering his body with their antiseptic-scented flesh, with their heavy limbs that felt like the lead cape at the dentist's office.

Absurdly, he thought of his childhood, of cavities and remembered that he hadn't been to a dentist in years.

As the thing held open his eyelid and lowered a scoop close to his face, someone screamed. Loud, high. A woman. A few more joined her, with people swearing, demanding to know what was happening.

A glass hit one of the creatures with a whump and then clattered against the floor. It had not hurt the thing but had gotten its attention.

A clamor rose in the crowd and someone screamed "Gun!" The shot came, deafening, sending the club into pandemonium. A spatter of goo spurted out of the thing's body.

The things drew back, leaving him on the floor, lying like he'd been discarded.

He stared up at the ceiling, drips of thin gray snot on his face, down his clothes. He didn't see where they went to or even how they left. He didn't move; he felt that if he moved he would begin to scream and never stop. His breath was caught in his throat and a hard feeling of panic sat in his chest.

Someone came to kneel beside him, but it was not someone he knew. They grabbed him roughly, trying to help, he knew this person was trying to right him. A drunk onlooker with no idea what they were doing.

They pulled him so he was sitting upright and he jerked back. His ears rang from the gunshot and his whole body trembled with adrenaline.

The onlooker put hands on him again, trying to soothe him with touch but it didn't work. They called him buddy, told him he was fine, their words slurred and their breath stinking of beer. He pushed the onlooker away, pushed them so hard they fell.

He clambered to his feet but found a crowd gathered around him, pressing in now that the things were gone. They demanded to know what had happened, if he was okay, what those things were, if they were gone. He tried to back up but there was nowhere to go.

He screamed, covering his ears and crouching. He squeezed his eyes shut. He wanted to rip his ears off to make it quiet. Dug his fingernails into his scalp.

"Move," someone insisted. A good voice, a friend.

Zhané had pushed her way through the crowd, followed close by Ahmed. He, ridiculously, knew them by smell rather than sight. The smell of her lotion and perfume, the smell of his soap.

"David," she said, near him but not touching. He could hear her breathing.

"No," he said. It was all he could say but it was not what he meant. He meant *help*, but there was nothing left that could be done. The things were gone, he had not been maimed, probably nothing more than bruised. But the feeling in his throat and chest would not go away, he could not think.

"David, can you look at me?" Ahmed asked from in front of

him.

He dared to open his eyes, fearing the gaze of the crowd but found that Ahmed had knelt in front of him. His hands hovered near David's shoulders, protective but scared. He didn't know what to do. No one ever knew what to do, they were scared of him and they should have been. He could hurt people. He had tried to hurt people, lashing out when he could not think, when his thoughts had been too many, too loud, too real.

"Can you get him to the backroom?" someone asked.

"I don't know," Zhané said.

"Trap," a voice suggested in his ear. "They'll send you back."

"No," he said.

"David, please, it will be quieter," Ahmed said, mistaking what he had said for refusal.

"The police will come and no one will have seen. Only you," the voice reminded him. "*You're* the crazy one."

"No," he insisted.

"Please," Ahmed urged, his voice gentle, "You're okay, you're with me. We can go somewhere quiet."

He clamped his hands over his ears more firmly and squeezed his eyes shut, but nodded. He leaned into Ahmed's hand and when he did that, Ahmed took ahold of him, gripping his arm and helping him stand. David did not know how he could be so strong.

They walked to the backroom, a hybrid office and lounge, with a computer and fridge, a coffee table and a couch.

Ahmed steered him to the couch and then stepped back.

David looked up at him, at the stiff line of his body, the tightness in his jaw. Either he had not seen the things and believed David to be crazy or he had and he wanted nothing more to do with this.

A voice whispered to him and he began to tap his chest, hard raps that made his bones ache.

"Can I sit with you?" Ahmed asked.

He nodded, unable to stop his hand from hitting against his sternum, knowing it was weird, freakish. He knew he'd started to ramble but couldn't keep track of the words that dribbled out of his mouth.

A hoarse sound escaped Ahmed, a sneeze or something and David glanced over, caught off guard.

"Bless you," he whispered without thinking.

Ahmed stared at him. "What?"

"Did you sneeze?"

"No."

They stared at each other for a moment and David felt heaviness settle into his limbs, the panic lingering but pushed aside by a weird mixture of confusion and exhaustion. He feared what would have happened if Ahmed had not made that sound, whatever it had been.

"Are you okay?" Ahmed asked after a long, uncomfortable silence.

"I want to lay down."

Ahmed stood but David caught his arm.

"Stay."

Ahmed nodded, sitting back down.

David lay down, curling up against the arm of the couch with his neck at an awkward angle with Ahmed seated beside him.

Zhané had said nothing and when he looked at her, he saw it was because she had her eyes fixed on the camcorder. He could see the video reflected in her eyes as she watched it.

Ahmed put a hand on his back, his skin warm even through David's shirt.

David closed his eyes.

AMARI ENTERED the back room. "Cops are on their way."
Zhané looked up and took a few steps towards her cousin.
"What the fuck was that?" Amari asked.
"We don't know," she said.
No one spoke.
"He's underage," Amari reminded, glancing at Ahmed.
"Backdoor?" she asked.
"Yeah."
"David, come on," she said.
Ahmed stood, taking David's hand and leading him along.
Amari let them out the back door of the kitchen and David shambled with the other two, not sure where they were going even when they entered the lobby of apartment building, cold air washing over him.

He tried to pull away from Ahmed. The air should not have been so cold. Waiting for him somewhere in the building had to be a doctor, an alien, a lizard person.

"David, we're almost there." Ahmed kept a hold of his hand.

He took his hand back. "Crawling all over."

"You're okay. Will you hold my hand?"

"No. I...it's. No."

"We're almost there."

"Can't. It's...the place isn't good." He took a step back. This wasn't a good place to be and he should go. He didn't know where he was, he wanted to go *home.*

"You can trust me."

That much felt true.

"Give me your hand, David." Ahmed offered his hand.

David took it.

He did not understand what they were doing there, not when they took the elevator up to the fifth floor and not when Zhané let herself into an apartment with a set of keys he'd never seen before.

The lights were already turned on and sitting on the couch was a white woman a few years David's senior. She had a book in her lap and a pencil against her mouth. She looked over at the door, her pale brown eyebrows knitted for a just a second, until she said, "You must be Amari's cousin."

Zhané nodded.

"I'm Blake," the woman said, getting up and coming over to them. "He said you'd be staying."

"Yeah."

"You guys alright, you look, uh...frazzled," she said and David knew she was looking at him.

He wondered if he looked the way he felt: like he'd been drugged. He took a step back towards the door but Ahmed didn't let go of him.

"Just tired," Ahmed said, reaching out to give David's arm a rub.

"Sure, of course," Blake said. "Bathroom's over there, I'll get the living room set up."

David went to the bathroom, lead in his feet. He realized he didn't have a case for his contacts and threw them away, glad that he had at least remembered to take them out. He didn't know how he was going to see tomorrow, but he didn't care. He hadn't packed well for the trip. When he turned to leave the bathroom, he found Zhané outside holding his glasses and a toothbrush.

"Can't help it, I'm a mom," she said.

He smiled, almost, and took the items she offered, pushing his glasses on to his face and cleaning his teeth.

Upon his return to the living room, he found the couch pulled out and made up with worn, pale pink sheets and a gaudy yellow bedspread. Ahmed lay on his stomach, his eyes on his phone. He glanced up when David entered.

"Zhané said she'd take the floor but I told her she could share the bed if she wanted," he said. "I felt bad."

David nodded. He went to sit on the foot of the pullout.

"You feel okay?"

"I'm tired."

Ahmed sat up and kissed his cheek. "I thought I was gonna lose you for a second there."

David shook his head. "I just needed to get it together. Just needed time."

"No, not that," he said. "I thought...watching them hold you down, I thought they would kill you."

"They don't kill."

Ahmed squeezed him. "I was still scared. I can't believe someone had a gun! All I did was throw a soda at it!" He sounded disappointed in himself.

David wanted to soothe him, to let him know that there had been nothing for him to do, but the thoughts swirled vaguely in his mind while his tongue sat heavy on his mouth. Instead, he leaned in and put his forehead against the top of Ahmed's head. "I'm tired."

"Go to sleep," he said and David felt like he had been given permission.

He handed Ahmed his glasses and crawled up the bed. He was too tall for it, but couldn't make himself care that his feet overhung the end. He pushed his face into the pillow and barely noticed when Zhané walked past.

She began to arrange things on the floor, reaching over to take a pillow and a blanket from the pullout.

He touched her hand. "Bed."

She looked up.

"Don't sleep on the floor, come in the bed."

"I guess," she said.

She settled in beside him, on her back, her hands resting on her stomach.

He woke in the morning to find his pillow wet beneath his cheek. He sat up, looked around the unfamiliar apartment and rubbed the crust from his eyes.

To his left, Zhané said, "I thought you'd be out longer."

He yawned into the crook of his arm. "Where's Ahmed?"

"Good morning, Zhané," she prompted.

"Sorry, morning."

"He's in the shower."

He nodded.

"Doing okay?"

"Better when we're home, I think."

From the kitchen behind them, he heard Amari say, "You've got some serious problems, man."

David twisted to look at the other man.

"What the fuck were those?"

"I don't know."

"I'd be in the looney bin if it was me," Amari said and it was an attempt at camaraderie, David knew, but he didn't know how to react.

"Been there," he said, "Done that."

Amari, looking hip even in his jammies, frowned a little and glanced at Zhané. Out of the corner of his eye, David saw her shake her head. He didn't mind that she'd done so, not feeling any of the irritation he did when his parents tried to steer away from the topic. She'd done it for him, not to avoid her own embarrassment.

David yawned again and lay back down. "Did you shower yet?" he asked her.

"No."

"Can you go next?"

"Still sleepy?"

He buried his face in the pillow and grunted.

"You snore," she said.

"Yeah, but he can't hear," he said.

She let out a half-laugh. "You can't sleep too long, okay? We have to go home soon."

"Food?"

"We can grab something."

From the kitchen, he heard Blake say, "No, don't. Stay, we'll make something for you."

"You don't have to," Zhané said.

"No, please, I'd love to talk a little. I'll make you my specialty."

David said nothing, not caring what they ate or who made it, until he had to push himself up and look into the kitchen. "Is it halal?" he asked.

"What?"

"What you're making. Is it halal?"

"Are you Muslim?" she asked, her brows knitted again.

"Ahmed is," he said, not sure how there could be any doubt.

"Who?"

He gestured toward the bathroom. "Ahmed."

She put her hands to her mouth, then, in an exaggerated

whisper, said, "I thought his name was Thomas! I assumed he was, like, Hispanic or something! Is French toast halal?"

"It should be," David said once he'd considered the ingredients.

Ahmed confirmed when he came out of the bathroom, dressed and toweling off his hair. Zhané passed him as he came over to the couch and David said, once they'd cleared up the matter of French toast, "I didn't pack a change of clothes."

"I know you didn't." Ahmed sat beside him, his legs crisscross and his feet bare. "Do you feel better?"

"You know when you have a bad dream and you wake up and it still feels real?"

Ahmed nodded.

"It feels like that."

"I'm sorry this happens to you."

He shook his head. "Nothing happened this time."

"David, something happened," he said, pointing to David's elbow where a deep purple bruise bloomed.

"I bruise easy." The statement functioned as a brushoff, as well as a statement of truth; his fair Irish skin was prone to sunburns and bruising.

Ahmed raised his eyebrows, waiting for David to admit the truth.

"It's *better*," David insisted, "I have all the same parts as I did yesterday."

"You should tell those FBI people."

"They'll think I'm crazy."

"Isn't that why we recorded it?"

David sighed.

"I know it's scary..."

"You know?" David asked, not sure why he'd asked so nastily. Maybe because the things came after him, maybe because he'd spent so long dealing with it alone. Maybe because he knew his word was unreliable by default.

"Yeah, I know. You think if you tell your teacher that Scott Mendelson pinched your nipple so hard it bruised she'll think you're lying cause he's the best student in the class, you think that if you let anyone know that Maggie Jacobs calls you names they'll think you're a little crybaby or—"

"I get it," David interrupted, not liking the way he could rattle those things off like it had been yesterday. He reached out to take his hand. "I'm sorry. I am scared." He brought Ahmed's hand to his mouth and kissed his knuckles.

Ahmed smiled. "Where'd you learn to do that thing with your hand?"

He shrugged. "Makeup ads and those modeling shows on Bravo."

"Really?"

"I watched a lot of reruns in high school."

"Oh."

David sat up a little straighter and did another one, this time with his palm turned away from his face and his fingertips near his eyes. Ahmed stared at him again and David broke the pose, smiling and giggling, butterflies in his stomach.

"Quit staring," he said, wishing he hadn't done anything.

"No, just...uh."

David waited.

Ahmed's eyes glanced towards the kitchen, where Blake and Amari were chatting as they cooked. "Don't take this the wrong way."

"I'll do my best."

"It's just that you normally don't try. I mean, you've got that whole casual, doesn't-give-a-fuck look."

David didn't consider it a look so much as the only way he knew how to live his life.

"I've never seen you try to, uh...look pretty."

His eyebrows shot up. "Pretty?"

"Not like that."

"No?"

Ahmed sighed and raked a hand through his hair. "To see you...sit up straight and look confident. It's different."

"Bad?"

"No!" Ahmed said, waving his hand as if he could waft away the idea. "No, it's just. It makes me wonder what you'd be able to do."

"If I tried?"

"David, come on, I didn't mean it like that. I meant...I'm excited! To see where you'll go."

"Oh. Uh. No one's ever said that."

"I can tell."

David half-smiled.

"Plus it's kind of sexy."

He laughed, he couldn't help it, and put his arms around Ahmed, pulling him close and pressing his face into his neck. "You're my favorite."

Laughter floated out from the kitchen, accompanied by the smell of vanilla and cinnamon. He felt comfortable and warm for a minute until he pulled back and hissed, "It's got alcohol in it!"

"What?"

"Vanilla extract, it's made with alcohol," he whispered. "In the French toast."

"Oh."

"You can't have it."

"Uh."

"I made you pancakes!" he said, giving him a push. "God, I'm such an idiot."

Ahmed shook his head. "You're sweet. Don't worry about it."

"I'll get you something to eat, I promise."

"David, I'm not gonna be rude and it's only a little bit, not a drink."

"Are you sure?"

He gave David's hand a pat. "Remember when I told you not to get weird about things?"

"Sorry."

"I'm gonna follow you around during Lent slapping hamburgers out of your hand," he warned.

Zhané finished in the shower before breakfast was ready and David took his turn in the shower. He returned to find the four of them eating, passing Zhané's phone around. Pictures of Noah, he knew.

They looked so content and cozy he almost didn't want to intrude. Ahmed turned around and gestured for him to come over. He put out his hand and David took it. "Were you just going to creep over there?"

"It's what I do," he said, wishing he'd said anything but 'creep'.

Ahmed snorted. "You say the weirdest shit."

"Yeah, that too." He'd tried to keep his tone light but worried he sounded pouty.

Ahmed's mouth twisted a little, but he said nothing. Not until later, anyway. As they drove home, he leaned forward onto the center console.

"Hey."

David glanced over and asked, "What?"

"I didn't mean to hurt your feelings or anything," he said, then clarified, "When I said you were creeping."

"No, everyone does it," he said. "I *am* a creep."

"And you're perfect like that," Zhané said, a little defensive. "I like you creepy. I like you weird."

He half-smiled.

"You wouldn't be you otherwise," Ahmed said with a real smile, one that reached to his eyes. He gave David's forearm a squeeze.

9/2/15

DAVID HADN'T wanted to go work and Ahmed had encouraged him to call in sick on Tuesday night, but he'd dragged himself out of bed anyway. He'd been able to sleep in late, at least, but didn't know if he'd make it to nine.

He began the day with the conviction that everyone in the store was staring at him and told himself that he was just being paranoid. No one was looking at him and if they were it was because they couldn't find the gluten-free bread they wanted.

Ahmed came to find him as he emptied out the mop bucket. A little kid had gotten sick in aisle four and David had offered to clean it up, seeing as Ahmed had gone green around the gills at the sight.

"Don't tell me he puked again," David said, looking up. Ahmed looked just as ill as he had eying the vomit.

He shook his head. "Those FBI agents are here. They, uh, David, they're looking for you. They want you to come with them."

"Oh." He set down the bucket and wiped off his hands. "Does Johnny know?"

"He's pissed."

He nodded. Another woman had been murdered in Milwater while they'd been in New York: Lily Pacheco, 39 and single. Also last seen at City Pizza. It might have meant something or it might have meant nothing. Everyone in Milwater ordered pizza there, it was a thousand times better than Rosa's Pizzeria.

Ahmed grabbed his arm.

"It'll be okay. I didn't do anything."

"I know, but sometimes even if you don't do anything, you can still end up in trouble."

"Yeah, it's called a scapegoat. Been there," he said. He wondered if Ahmed would come to visit him in jail. He decided that if Ahmed asked, he'd get a divorce without a fight. He hoped it wouldn't come to that, but he wouldn't blame him. No one would want a serial killer for a husband.

"You should tell them about those things."

"Maybe," he said, with no intention to do so.

"One-way ticket back," a low voice suggested. "He wants you gone."

He headed towards the front of the store where Ingress and Frost waited for him.

"Hello, David," Frost greeted him pleasantly.

"Hi."

"There's something we'd really like to talk to you about."

He nodded.

"You aren't under arrest, but we do think you have information that will help us," Frost said. "Can you come with us?"

He glanced at Ahmed, who had followed him to the front. "Uh. Sure."

Ahmed squeezed his hand.

Frost and Ingress walked out and he followed them. Ingress glanced back and said, "The ring is new."

He looked down at his hand. "Yeah."

"You don't think you two are a little young?"

"Probably. And I'm probably too crazy to keep it together and he could definitely do a lot better than me," he said, too fast and oversharing.

She looked at him again, raising her eyebrows a little. "Sore spot. Got it."

"My parents won't come visit."

"That's too bad," she said and opened the door to their car's backseat for him.

He slid in and they headed towards the police station.

"Ugly fucking man hands," the voice began, "You can't slap fake nails on a fag and pretend—"

"Shh," he hissed.

Both women ignored him.

"The Oriental one—"

He grunted and pressed his fingers against his chest. He counted backward from a hundred.

After a few minutes, he leaned forward a little and, to Ingress, said, "I really am sorry about what I said."

She turned around. "Don't worry about it. I always come into towns like this with a bad attitude, anyways. I knew what I was expecting and I thought I'd found it."

"Milwater isn't so bad, really."

"He says about the town that thinks he's a murderer," she said.

"Julie!" Frost scolded.

"Do they?" David asked.

"Just half. Bryant and his buddies," Ingress told him.

"I don't know what I ever did to piss him off."

Frost shrugged. "There's always one. He thinks you and Ms. Smith are some kind of...murder couple. That she's the brains, you're the brawn."

David snorted.

"It's not unheard of."

"No, but we'd have to be a couple," he said. He thought of the flimsy excuses he'd given Bryant for sneaking around crime scenes.

"He's convinced you're her 'baby daddy'," Ingress confided.

David let out a bark of a laugh. "And what does he think I'm doing with Ahmed?"

"That's what I said."

"Something about playing both sides of the field," Frost scoffed with an eye roll.

David leaned back into the backseat and wondered what they could want to talk to him about. The mood between them was light; he didn't feel as he had the last time he'd been escorted to the police station.

Frost pulled into a parking spot right near the front and stepped out. Ingress followed and David clambered out from the back, wondering how Ingress, tall as she was, had managed to exit the car with grace instead of looking like a giraffe.

"What?" Ingress asked.

He shook his head, then admitted, "I don't know how you take so much leg and make it work for you. I always feel like...a baby moose."

"You have to practice," she said.

He nodded and followed as the women walked into the police station. When they entered, he felt dozens of eyes on him. He wouldn't ever leave this place except to be brought to a real prison, tried, and convicted with nothing more than hearsay and a bribe. It could happen, it had happened and it would happen. Zhané could throw him under the bus, make something up to save herself, or she could leave Noah to be raised by his grandparents or maybe his uncle until she got out of jail.

They brought him to a conference room, not to the sparse interrogation room he had expected. Frost gestured to a seat and he took it. She sat to his right and Ingress brought over a laptop and set it in front of him.

"Maybe you can shine some light on this for us," she said, clicking play on the video she'd pulled up.

He recognized what it was right away, there was no way he'd forget the bar. He hadn't watched the video yet, but he'd known that Zhané had posted it the same way she'd posted the last one.

He clicked pause, his fingers shaking. He couldn't watch, not when he had lived it so recently.

"Now, maybe we're mistaken, but that's you, isn't it?" Frost asked.

"Yes."

"David, do you know what those are?"

He shook his head. "No, they just...they come. Every eight weeks. They tell me to kill people." His voice shook as badly as his hands and he hoped he wouldn't cry. "And I think they're doing it to someone else."

"Because?"

"Because the people who've died, they line up with when the things come," he said, "And it isn't me. It isn't."

Prison would be worse than being hospitalized; maybe he could plead insanity. But then again, Dahmer had been declared sane.

"No, of course not," Frost said, "There's no way."

"We didn't ask you here because we think you're responsible for this," Ingress said. "We think you can help us get these...things."

"Do you know what they are?" he asked.

After a pause, Ingress admitted, "No. But we've consulted with some, ah, experts in the field of strange and unusual things."

He frowned.

She placed a business card on the table. The color of bone,

with small, neat letters, the card informed him that The Sunshine and Specter Paranormal Detective Agency could be found in Greenwich Village. He flipped it over to find neat handwriting that said, "We're here to help. Call us anytime, Mr. Craft" with two signatures beneath it.

"Misters Sunshine and Specter have offered to help us end this business."

"End it?"

"They believe they have a way to capture these, uh, beings," Frost said.

He stared down at the card in his hands. "You believe them?"

"Yes. They've helped us before."

He looked up at them, studying their faces. "With what?"

They glanced at each other. "Two years ago, we crossed paths. We were investigating an arsonist and they were trying to find a salamander."

"The lizard?"

"They're amphibians," Ingress said.

He frowned, half at being corrected, but half because he knew that salamanders were amphibians and wasn't sure why he'd said lizard.

"But no," she said, "A type of fire elemental."

"They do good work," Frost assured.

"So we should call them," he said. "Right?"

"I believe it would be a good idea," Frost said, "But it also poses a risk to yourself."

"But they'll come anyway," he said.

"Now...the other issue we might run into," Ingress said, "Is that your visitors might not come. You've thwarted their attempts twice now, right?"

"Yes," he said. "How...?"

"We've seen the other video as well."

"Oh."

"Our plan is to, with your help, find their other target, put you both in the same place."

"Do you think you can do that?"

Ingress said, "We hope so."

He picked at his nails and asked, "What do you need my help for?"

"They might talk to you more readily. And you'll know if what they're saying rings true more than we will."

He nodded.

Ingress looked at the clock on the wall. "So, do you want to get lunch? Hammer this plan out some more? We know you've been poking around with Ms. Smith, maybe you've learned something we haven't."

"I should go back to work," he said, not because he wanted to go, but because he felt bad about leaving Ahmed to finish the shift alone.

"We can swing by and pick up Mr. Jalali as well," Ingress offered.

"Tomorrow. Tomorrow would be better."

"That's fine," Frost said.

By the time they returned him to Greene's, he had only been gone for about an hour. Johnny told him to make sure his timesheet reflected the time he'd missed and he promised that he would.

He found Ahmed putting out bags of cheese in the dairy section. He put a hand on his shoulder and Ahmed jumped.

"Shit!" he swore, turning to face him. "Oh. David, you scared me."

"Sorry, I didn't mean to."

Ahmed wrapped him up in a hug, pressing his forehead against David's chest.

"Everything's fine," David assured.

He tightened his grip then stepped back. "Want to help me with this?"

David grinned.

The rest of their work night progressed as normal, though their ride home was quieter than usual. Once inside, Ahmed let out a huge breath.

David glanced over. "What?"

He shook his head.

David pulled his work shirt over his head and tossed it onto the chair where he kept his clothes that could be worn again.

Ahmed threw his clothes on the floor beside the hamper and judging by his sigh, he hadn't meant to miss.

David picked it up for him. "What?"

"I don't know."

He hadn't told him everything he'd talked about with agents. He thought it would have sounded better, more sensible coming from them tomorrow. All he'd said was that they'd both be meeting up with the women the next day.

"Are you hungry?" David asked.

He shrugged.

"This was stupid, David, it's never going to work out," his mother told him.

David shook his head, ignoring her. "I want to go to Vermont."

"What?"

"For Christmas."

"I don't do Christmas."

"I know you don't, doofus," he said.

Ahmed shook his head. "No, I mean...I don't think I can do it. It seems horrifying."

David couldn't help it, he snorted. "Are you serious?"

"Absolutely. I've never heard anything good about it and I don't have any interest in that kind of shit show."

"Is this some Catholic school shit?"

Ahmed frowned. "Maybe. Maybe if you had to spend twelve years learning about the most *bullshit holiday ever* and then getting told you're the cause of a fucking war on it...!"

"But you'll get presents."

"For fuck's sake!" Ahmed gave him a little push.

"I'm not trying to convert you."

"What? No, that's..." He sighed. "That's not what I'm saying."

"I want to see my mom and dad," David confessed. "I think if I show up for Christmas they'll have to let me stay. And I don't think they'll ever come to see me."

Ahmed put his hands over his face for a moment, then pulled them away.

"I'll trade, I'll do Ramadan, that's way worse."

"Ramadan's not..." He paused, sighed and said, "You don't have to do that. We can go to see your parents."

"For Christmas?"

"Yes, for Christmas," he confirmed. "I'm not getting you a present, though."

David shrugged. "That's fine." After a moment, he asked, "How many kids do you want?"

"Four," he said immediately.

"Oh."

"Too many?"

"No, you just sounded like you've thought about it a lot."

"I have."

David waited for a beat, then said, "Four is a lot, though."

"It depends on how we're doing, I guess. Money and all that."

David wondered if 'and all that' included his mental health. It had to. He also wondered if this constant worrying would ever go away, if he would ever stop thinking that Ahmed could do better.

"So why do they want to have lunch with us?" Ahmed asked.

He shrugged. "It will make more sense if they explain it. I'm bad at stuff like that."

"Fine, keep your secrets," he said, his tone light. "Can you take care of your dishes from breakfast? They're starting to smell...uh, milky."

David obliged. He had been trying to be more human, less of a slob, lately but he didn't always manage.

"Disgusting," his mother said.

"Four always seemed like the right number to me," Ahmed said.

David glanced over. "We're not even ready for one yet, we'll talk about it when we get to it."

Ahmed said nothing but ran his hand along David's back.

He set the dishes in the drain rack and wiped his hands on his pants. "Are you hungry?"

"Not really."

"You want to come snuggle?"

"Yeah."

In bed, Ahmed nestled against him. "Do you think they'll be able to help?"

"I hope so. They're not so bad for lizard people."

After a few minutes of quiet, Ahmed asked, "What kind of kids do you want?"

"Human ones."

"You're such a dick."

"I mean, even if they weren't humans, I'd probably love them anyway. I'd be okay with a Dracula baby. Probably. Or, uh, a star child."

"A what?"

"You know, a star child. Part alien."

"What if it was a lizard person?" Ahmed asked, his tone light and teasing.

David answered instinctively, saying "Kids can't be lizard people." He said it too quickly, too harshly and the teasing smile on Ahmed's lips faltered.

"Your crazy is showing," someone warned, their voice low and rough.

He ignored it, or tried, putting his arm around Ahmed's waist and moving closer to him. He nuzzled close to his throat. "Would you like me better if I didn't have schizophrenia?"

"Would you like me better if I could hear?"

David sighed, the irritated breath slipping out.

"How many times do you want me to say it?"

"Until I believe it," he confessed, feeling needy and weak.

Ahmed turned and kissed him. "Then I'll keep saying it. I love you the way you are."

"I love you, too."

Ahmed kissed him again, pressing closer; the pressure of his mouth, the roaming of his hands caused David to grow warm, his skin flushing. Ahmed grabbed on to him, his fingertips digging into his back. From the heat of their first few kisses, David thought that things would move quickly, but Ahmed did not rush.

He took his time, brushing his fingers or lips against all the most sensitive parts of David's skin until David breathed, "Will you...I want you in me."

Ahmed nodded, rolling away and coming back with lube he'd retrieved from the bedside table. Even as he eased himself in, he seemed to be taking his time until David couldn't stand it. He pulled him in deeper, arching his back and sighing; he moved his hips, hardly feeling like himself as he writhed beneath his husband, desperate for more, for release.

This was not the sex he was used to, quick and full of thoughts of other things; instead, he thought only of Ahmed and of what they were doing, wanting this to last forever but begging to come.

"Please," was all he could say.

Ahmed ran his hand along David's length, his thumb brushing against the tip, causing David to cry out. At that, Ahmed lost a little of his composure, grunting. From then, they were both undone, a slightly messy melding of mouths and other body parts, until they were spent.

Ahmed pressed his forehead against David's, his chest heaving. David wrapped his arms around him, keeping him close long after both of them had gone soft. It had been so long since he'd wanted to hold someone like this. Too many of his brief affairs had ended with disquiet in his belly and the inability to look his partner in the eyes.

He tightened his embrace so that the entirety of their torsos touched and Ahmed made a noise of displeasure. "What?" David asked.

"You smooshed me into your cum," Ahmed said.

"Oh, gee, sorry." David rolled his eyes.

"It was all cold!" he said but made no attempt to move away. He adjusted himself a little so that he could lay more comfortably and remained quiet for several minutes.

"What are you thinking about?" David asked.

"What my life would have been like two hundred years ago."

"Like if you lived in seventeenth-century Afghanistan?"

"Well, first of all, the seventeenth century was not two hundred years ago."

David rolled his eyes. "You know what I meant."

"I guess...I don't know. I just wonder about things."

"The lube wouldn't have been as good."

Ahmed snorted.

"It was all olive oil and shit like that."

Ahmed pulled back, rolling away onto his back. He rested his hands on his stomach, but pulled them back, making another face.

David snagged his boxers from where they had been discarded and handed them over. Ahmed wiped himself up.

"You would be beautiful, I bet," David reflected.

"Hm?"

"Out in the sun all the time, dressed in one of those long linen things. A tunic? A white one."

Ahmed didn't look impressed. He sat up, his legs crisscross, and his elbows resting on his thighs. "And what would you look like?"

"An Irish Catholic peasant," he suggested.

"Probably unwashed," Ahmed added.

"Probably." He thought for a minute. "I think that was a late Middle Ages thing, though, I think Europe used to have bathhouses where all the hookers used to hang out. I'm pretty sure I read about it."

Eventually, Ahmed needed to wash up before he could pray, and after that hunger compelled them to eat. They settled into bed, cuddled beneath the blankets to ward off the chill of the AC.

THURSDAY MORNING, around eleven, David received a text that said, 'Be over in about an hour' from a number he didn't recognize. He stared down at his phone for a second, mind whirring.

Ahmed glanced over, slipped the phone out of his hand, typed something then handed it back.

"What did you do?"

"I asked who it was."

The thought had not occurred to David; he had been too caught up wondering if his monstrous visitors had learned how to text.

A moment later, he got a response that said 'sorry, this is Agent Ingress. Pulled your number from your file. Hope you don't mind'.

"Who was it?"

"Ingress."

Ahmed took his phone again and texted something back. This time he didn't return it, instead slipping it into his front pocket.

"What are you doing?"

"Nothing."

"Why'd you take my phone?"

"I didn't."

David frowned. "You did."

He had taken it and now he had lied. David pressed his fingernails into the newest cuts on his arm, made earlier that morning, three deep lines that would leave raised scars, he knew.

Ahmed glanced up, a single eyebrow raised at the snap in David's tone. His face softened after a second. "Is this a thing for you?"

His first instinct was to lie, his ears ringing, but he made himself say "People always say they didn't do things. Even when I know they did."

"People?"

"My parents," he clarified. "My parents pretend things didn't happen, that they weren't looking through my stuff, that they weren't going to leave me in that place forever..."

"Do you want your phone back?"

David sighed. "No. Whatever. I don't care."

"Hey, I was just fooling around." He fished David's phone from his pocket and held it out to him. "I'm sorry."

He took it and returned it to his own pocket, his stomach uneasy. He thought about going to the bathroom, digging out the razorblade from where he'd hidden it beneath a spare box of tissues.

Ahmed looked at his feet, his jaw clenched.

His phone dinged and he looked at it, then had to go back and read the silly message Ahmed had sent to understand what Ingress meant. He sighed, went over to his husband, and put his arms around him. Ahmed leaned into his embrace, a little of his tenseness sliding away.

"It's not a big deal," David said.

Ahmed tightened his arms around David's waist, his cheek against his chest. He remained like that for a minute, pulling away eventually to go sit on the loveseat, scrolling through his own phone.

David sat beside him, his legs tucked close.

"Look how big he's getting," Ahmed said, turning his phone to show David a picture of their nephew.

"I can't believe how much hair he's got."

"I know! It's like a mane."

David moved in a little closer and Ahmed leaned against him; together they wasted time until the agents announced their arrival by honking.

As soon as they entered the car, Ahmed leaned forward from the backseat. "So what's going on, anyway? This one is being sketchy."

Ingress, in the passenger seat, as usual, turned around. "We're going to meet some people who should be able to help with these...uh, interlopers."

"Really?" Ahmed asked, his brow wrinkled.

"It's my sincerest hope."

"Are you guys the X-Files?" Ahmed asked.

David snorted and Ahmed gave him a dirty look.

"There's no such thing as the X-Files," Frost said.

"But you do see your share of strange and unusual things in this line of work," Ingress admitted.

"Besides," Frost continued, "Mulder and Scully weren't *the* X-Files, they were the investigators *of* the X-Files."

"I think there's a very strong case against that statement, especially given the nature of Scully's abduction—" David began.

"Please don't start," Ahmed said.

"Sorry."

The car went silent and Frost cleared her throat.

"Most of our cases are pretty pedestrian," Ingress said.

After half a minute, David asked, "Where are we going, anyway?"

"That diner."

"Tommy's?"

"No, the other one," Frost said.

"That place is gross," he said.

"It's not, really," Frost said.

"Full of truckers, I think is what David meant," Ahmed said.

In his ear, a voice suggested that a few large, greasy truckers could teach Ahmed a lesson or two about when to keep his mouth shut.

"Truckers mind their own business. No townies eavesdropping," Ingress said.

David had never actually set foot in Suzy's diner, so he couldn't back up his stance that it was gross. He also reflected that he shouldn't be throwing stones about what was gross and what wasn't, considering that he currently wore jeans that hadn't been washed in well over a month. Maybe it was just snobbery that kept locals from going into the place.

Once inside, the place didn't seem as scuzzy as people made it sound. The table wasn't even sticky. A waitress seated them at a big booth when they stated that they were waiting for two more and handed over the menus.

Ingress checked her phone for the time.

"The men in black," David said suddenly, sitting up straighter. The thought had come to him out of nowhere, in between deciding if he wanted pancakes or a cheeseburger.

"What?" Frost asked.

"You're not the X-Files, you're the men in black," David said, "Well, uh, you're not men and you're not in black."

"And we're not here to threaten you into silence, either," Ingress said. "We're just FBI agents."

She sat up straighter, looking towards the door, then waved someone over.

Two men approached the table, similar in height and build. About the same height as Ahmed but with more bodily substance. One had golden-blond curls and a healthy tan, as well as orangey-yellow eyes like a cat. He was well built, broad-shouldered and moved with an athlete's grace. The other, narrower through the chest with lanky limbs, had hair so pale David couldn't decide if it was blond or white; his veins stood out plainly through his pale skin and his eyes were dark, darker than any eyes David had ever seen before.

Pancakes, he decided, as they shuffled around in the booth to make room for the men.

"Mr. Craft," said the orange-eyed one.

"Hi, uh, just David," he said.

"I'm Sunshine," he said, "This is my partner, Mr. Specter. We operate out of New York to help people in unusual circumstances."

"Yeah, I got the business card. This is, uh, this is Ahmed," David said, gesturing to his partner.

"Nice to meet you," Sunshine greeted him. "Are you similarly troubled?"

"No, just married to him," Ahmed said.

Sunshine's mouth tipped up a little and Specter titled his head slightly, though neither of them made a comment.

"So you know what we're dealing with?" David asked. "These things."

Sunshine looked up from the menu. Specter did not, his fingers running down the list of breakfast items as though he were studying a ledger.

"Well, I can't say we exactly know what they are in the way that we know what, say, a cat is. But I can tell you that they are interdimensional beings," Sunshine said, "Which is not my particular area of expertise. Mr. Specter should be able to tell you more."

David turned his eyes to Specter, waiting, but he didn't look up from the menu.

Sunshine cleared his throat.

Specter glanced up. "You've got harvesters."

"Figured that one out," David said tersely.

This time when he looked up, Specter met David's eyes. "They generally like to slide under the radar. No killing. Targeting people that are, hmm, societally vulnerable as their interpreters. As far as we can tell, they will not kill, maybe not even when acting in self-defense."

"Interpreters?" Ahmed asked.

"Those to whom they relay their messages," Sunshine explained, "We find that not everyone is able to understand them."

"There's actually more people who can understand them than can't," Specter informed them, "We find that, ah, the people who benefit from society the most cannot understand their messages."

"So...white guys?" Ahmed asked.

"In this country, yes. In Ghana, not so much," Specter said, "Well, that's just a hypothetical, we actually don't have any reports of these sorts of things in Africa...but that might be a shortcoming on our end. Anyway, it seems like the sick, the marginalized and so on are most often the ones asked to act on behalf of these beings."

David tightened his hands into fists a few times. Ahmed reached out to give him a pat on the leg.

Specter had returned his eyes to the menu and didn't speak again until the waitress came to take their order.

Ahmed's jaw had gone tight again, his shoulders stiff. "So then what's the plan?"

Sunshine frowned. "The last visit just happened, did it not?"

"Yes."

"And we do have two months to get our plans in order?"

"Eight weeks," David muttered, not as a correction but just because he needed to say it.

"I'm sorry if we've come across as less than concerned with your problem," Sunshine said, "We intend to help you to the best of our ability but—"

"But we just sat in bridge traffic for an hour and a half," Specter said. "And a four-car pile-up on the parkway."

"Uh," Ahmed said.

"He's cranky when he's hungry," Sunshine said.

"You'd be hungry too," Specter grumbled.

Sunshine smiled beatifically at the other man's mood and David was overcome with the strange notion that he was in the presence of something Godly. It was not a delusion he'd ever experienced before and it took him aback.

Sunshine noticed him staring and turned his eyes to meet David's. "My partner has some dietary needs that can be difficult to meet."

"Cursed," Specter whispered.

"What do you mean?" David asked, knowing he was being nosy and not just because Ahmed had frowned.

Sunshine hesitated to answer but Specter asked, "What do you know about fairies?"

David frowned. "Nothing," he said, but then his lips curled back into a goofy smile.

Specter rolled his eyes. "If you eat food in the Otherworld...nothing that doesn't come from there will ever taste right again, nothing will ever fill your stomach, slake your thirst."

"Oh."

Sunshine gave the other man a small pat on the arm, barely even making contact. "I've heard rumblings there's a new king. Or, well, that the old king is back in the Otherworld. Perhaps we could petition him."

If Specter had heard, nothing on his face registered that he had. He was quiet until their food came, at which point he began to eat ravenously. David worried that he would eat the fork and knife too if he wasn't careful.

Once his plate was empty and, seeming more at ease, Specter leaned back in the booth and said, "About these things."

David waited, feeling his heart jump up into his throat.

"The application of any one standard magic would be, I believe, useless," Specter said.

"Wait, magic?" David asked.

Specter ignored him. "I think our best approach would be to use a combination of arcane and demonic magics. Of course, such things aren't traditionally combined, but I think it will be effective. Fairy magic would work wonders, but I don't feel up to dealing with such, hmm, mischief right now." He looked at his hands. "Or ever again," he muttered.

"Magic," David repeated.

"Yes, Mr. Craft, magic," Sunshine said.

"Demonic?" Ahmed asked.

"As long as there are no objections," Specter said, "Otherwise I can make myself scarce."

David looked over at the FBI agents; Frost was on her phone, checking emails, and Ingress was finishing her fries. He returned his eyes to Specter. "Are you...?"

"Son of the Dark Prince himself," Specter announced with a tired flourish, "Only one born in the last couple hundred years. He must have really liked my mother."

"Uh."

"So is it a problem?" Specter asked, "Catholic as you are."

"How...?"

"God, I can smell it."

"Oh." David glanced at Ahmed, who looked intrigued more than concerned. To Specter, he said, "If you can help I don't care if you're the Devil himself."

With a wry smile, Specter warned, "Don't let Dad hear you say that. He'll show up and steal the show."

A horrible feeling in his gut made David think that was true.

"The other interpreter," Ingress mumbled around a mouthful of fries.

"Right," Sunshine agreed. "It does seem imperative to find the other who suffers as Mr. Craft does. Otherwise, we risk letting these things slip through our fingers."

"Uh, I don't know how. We've been trying."

"I need your phone," Sunshine said.

David took his phone from his pocket and, before he handed it over, asked, "Why?"

"In our office, we have a psychic. It is my belief that she should be able to use your phone to tap into the energy they use to contact you," Sunshine said.

"One second." David flipped through the settings in his phone to set up away messages in case anyone tried to contact him. He included Ahmed's cell in the message and asked, "Is it okay if tell people to get to me through you?"

"No, whatever, that's fine," Ahmed said.

Once David handed over his phone, Ahmed rested his hand on David's back and leaned in to touch his forehead to David's arm. It was a gesture of relief and it seemed, for a second, that Ahmed might cry. Instead, he gripped David's shirt and pressed a kiss to his arm, then straightened up.

Ahmed's phone buzzed and he looked down, frowning. He ran his hand through his hair, leaving his normally neat hair mussed. "I have class tomorrow."

David glanced over. "What?"

"Yeah, I meant to tell you."

"Uh. When?"

"I've got two in the morning before I go to prayer."

David nodded. It didn't occur to him until after they had paid the check that it meant they wouldn't be working together.

"Mr. Craft...David, our agency will be in touch," Sunshine promised as they walked out together.

"Yeah."

"It was wonderful meeting you." He offered his hand for David to shake and he took it. Sunshine's hand was not any warmer than that of a normal person, but David felt some of the radiance he had felt when Sunshine had smiled.

When Sunshine drew his hand back, Specter offered his as well. After handshakes and farewells, Sunshine and Specter headed to their car, an older model town car. As they walked, their hands brushed against each other and, to David's surprise, Specter flinched away.

He looked over to see if the others had noticed, but they were talking in a close triangle. David went over to join them and found that they discussed the book the agents had tossed into the back seat.

"Ready to go home?" Ingress asked when she noticed that David had approached.

He nodded.

At home, he nestled into the loveseat with Benjamin Rabbit and looked at Ahmed, who didn't notice until he had taken his shoes off and tossed his keys and wallet onto the table.

"What?"

David shrugged.

"Is it about classes?"

He nodded. It was about a lot of things but it was mostly, right then, about Ahmed's classes.

Ahmed came to sit beside him and handed over his phone. "That's my new work schedule. We don't have any shifts together. My schedule ended up being all Monday-Wednesday-Friday classes. And this online class on Tuesdays which seems like it's gonna be fucking awful."

"I didn't think we'd work together forever," David said. It was childish to be disappointed, he knew. He handed the phone back.

"You'll, um...David, you'll be home alone a lot. I mean, there are days when I work and I go right to class after."

"You don't have to worry about me."

Ahmed blushed and looked down at his hands. "I'm sorry."

"I, uh. I appreciate it though. I know it's because you care."

Ahmed nodded.

"I'll find something to do with the time. I'll hang out with Noah. Zhané's home during the day usually. Finally read some books." David took his hand. "It isn't normal to spend all our time together anyway."

Rolling his eyes, Ahmed said, "Fuck normal."

David laughed. "I should, uh, probably get more hours or something. Or work a second job?"

"If you want to."

David wrapped his arm around Ahmed and pulled him closer. "You smell nice."

"Thanks."

"Do you think you can print out your schedules for me? I know I'll end up forgetting," he said, "And I don't want to get worried if you're not texting me back or anything."

"Sure, of course."

Neither of them spoke for a while until Ahmed offered to get his laptop and put on something to watch. David agreed but dozed off halfway through the first episode.

9/17/15

AHMED HAD already left for work; he'd been reassigned to morning shifts on Thursdays, as well as the closing shift on Tuesdays and Fridays. David had meant to get out of bed a few hours after Ahmed had left, but it hadn't happened. He had moved between fitful dreams and hazy wakefulness.

Around eleven, he slunk out of bed and pulled Ahmed's laptop onto the loveseat with him. He checked his emails and saw that his mother had gotten back to him, though she had ignored his proposal to Skype with him and Ahmed. He didn't press the issue, though, considering that he planned on crashing Christmas.

He glanced at the word processor icon on the desktop and knew that if he clicked on it, he'd be able to read everything Ahmed had written. He'd have access to the journal he kept, as well as the stories he had written. The idea tempted him; Ahmed had never offered to let him read anything and he'd never had the courage to ask.

Instead, he spent the better part of an hour watching videos on YouTube, then ate when his head began to ache. By the time that Ahmed came home, he had showered and tidied up around the house.

"How was work?" he asked as he took the dishes from the

drainboard.

Ahmed shrugged. "Work."

He placed a coffee mug in the cabinet and turned to lean against the counter. Ahmed headed in his direction and David knew he must have been headed towards the fridge until he wasn't. He walked past the fridge and slid his arms around David, resting his head on his chest.

"What?"

"I love you."

"You too."

David put an arm around him and kissed his hair.

"They're mailing your phone back."

"Hm?"

"Those men. The detectives. They called and said they got what they needed from it."

"Oh."

"And I guess we'll see if they're nuts or not."

David snorted. "They didn't seem nuts."

"No, not really," he said, "I just can't believe that now all these things are real. Demons and...interdimensional poachers or whatever."

David checked his impulse to apologize. He tightened his arm. "Maybe by Halloween this will be done."

"I've never done Halloween."

"Ever?!" David asked, straightening up.

"It's not a thing for us."

"Aw, come on, it's fun," he said. He'd been a Halloween enthusiast as a kid, always doing a group costume with the girls. Even in Mansfield, he'd made a point to give out candy, though the costumes had been lackluster.

"I don't know, maybe," he said.

Zhané knocked and then let herself into the apartment a moment later. She closed the door and set Noah down on the floor. He sat for a moment then began to move around. He headed towards the bed, knowing that was where David kept his stuffed rabbit.

A large part of him knew he should let the baby have the toy, but another part screamed at the thought. He needed the rabbit still in a very real way.

"I'm ordering Chinese," she said.

"Mmm," David said, a thinking sound. He glanced down at

Ahmed. "What do you think?"

"I don't know," Ahmed said. "We need to cook that chicken that we thawed."

"Stay for chicken," David suggested to Zhané.

"What kind?" she asked.

"I don't know," he said.

"We should try that recipe," Ahmed said, still leaning against David. "The one for chicken parm? Your mom's?"

"I'll stay for that," Zhané said.

David fought the urge to pick up his husband. Without warning, Ahmed peeled away and went into the kitchen, leaving David feeling cold; he went to the fridge and took out chicken and eggs, then asked, "Can you pull it up on my computer?"

David went and found the email he'd gotten from his mom. She'd willingly sent the recipe but had ignored all mention of Ahmed.

Zhané didn't help cook but instead watched the two of them move around each other, David reading instructions and peering over Ahmed's shoulder as he worked. He was less squeamish about touching raw meat than David was.

"Are you out on Facebook?" Zhané asked.

David glanced over and realized she wasn't talking to him. He nudged Ahmed who said, "Uh, yeah, I guess so."

"Good, I changed your profile picture."

"You what?"

"It's a really cute picture," she said, "Cheekbones for days."

Ahmed pursed his lips then said, "Let me see."

She turned his phone toward him. "Noor already liked it."

David looked at the screen and saw why she'd asked if he was out. In the photo, he had one hand on Ahmed's waist as he leaned in close, their faces closer than just friends. "It's a good picture," he said. "I think you need to flip that."

Ahmed glanced into the frying pan and flipped the last piece of chicken. Noodles had already been strained and waited in the colander.

David's mother whispered in his ear, accusing him of all sorts of things, disappointed in the types of people he'd taken up with. He did not like it when the voices used slurs, but he didn't know how to stop it.

While they ate, David couldn't help but watch Noah squish up bits of chicken and noodles in his fist and then shove the whole fist into his mouth.

"Quit staring at him like that," Zhané said.

"Like what?"

"Like he's gross."

"He *is* gross, his whole face is covered in goo."

She reached over and wiped a smear off the baby's cheek. "It's not his whole face."

"What do you think he'll be like?"

"I don't know."

"I think he'll be like you," he said.

"I hope not, I was fresh."

He let out a small laugh, not quite a chuckle. "There are worse things than fresh."

"Not the way my mother tells it," Zhané told him.

Under the table, Ahmed nudged him with his foot. He glanced over, eyebrows raised. "What?" he asked when Ahmed looked back at him without a clue.

"What?"

"You kicked me."

"Oh, I thought it was the table leg. Sorry."

He nodded and used his fork to cut off a piece of chicken. It didn't taste the way he remembered it. Maybe because the sauce wasn't homemade, maybe because he'd spent too many years living on powdered eggs and microwaved Hot Pockets. Maybe it just didn't taste the same because his mother hadn't made it.

After dinner, they all watched TV together, with Noah nestled against Ahmed's chest and Zhané feet tucked under Ahmed's thighs. David wasn't surprised that the two of them got along; Ahmed said that Zhané reminded him of Miriam and Ahmed was nothing at all like Malik.

"What do you want to do for Thanksgiving?" he asked.

They both turned to look at him.

"Probably go to my parents," Zhané said.

"Oh."

She gave him a hard look for a second then said, "I'll tell them you're coming."

"No, you don't have to."

"Come on, like you have other plans."

He shrugged.

"Fine, stay home and feel sad for yourself," she said, "Ahmed will come."

"I will?"

"Sure, you don't want to stay home with David being a big sad sack."

David sighed.

Zhané poked him in the side. "Come to my parents' house. Daysha's super interested in how you two are doing."

"Really?"

"I don't think she knows any other gay people," she said. "Her family is...just so goddamn religious. I'm pretty sure her little sister's in the closet. Super deep."

"Aw. Poor baby."

"So come to Thanksgiving."

He shrugged and said, "Sure," but thought *As long as I'm not dead.*

She gave his leg a pat as though she could tell what he was thinking.

David nodded off around ten and Ahmed had to wake him so they could go to bed. Once in bed, he couldn't get back to sleep and lay awake, his hands folded on his stomach as he looked up at the ceiling, consumed by the idea that the shadows were moving and that the creaks and whispers he heard were monsters.

It made him think of being a little boy again, awake long after his parents had gone to bed and filled up with the reality of boogeymen and monsters under the bed. It was a fear that paralyzed; if he moved, if he had anyone more than his face sticking out of his blanket, the monsters would pounce, ready to consume him.

He woke in the morning with a stiff back and neck, his body still held in the same position as the night before.

"You sleep like a Dracula," Ahmed said.

David looked over at him. He was lying on his stomach looking at his phone, his hearing aid already in. "Maybe I am a Dracula."

"Maybe. Vampires are usually pretty gay."

"Bisexual."

"Yeah, you're right." Ahmed set down his phone. "I always thought that was a weird trope, though, the 'so old I'll try anything', like I don't think I'd ever get to that point."

"I think it's more like most straight people are in denial of being kind of queer, not most gay people are in denial about being bi?"

"Maybe."

"What do you write about?"

"Nothing."

David made a face. "Okay, sure."

But he didn't press the issue. He rolled onto his side and kissed Ahmed's shoulder. "I had a bad dream."

"About what?"

"It wasn't really bad. Weird, I guess. You were...you and Zhané and Noah, you were all..."

"All what?" Ahmed prompted.

"You didn't believe me anymore. You wanted me to turn myself in."

"Oh, some latent insecurities there."

"If by latent you mean all-consuming, then yes." He headbutted Ahmed's shoulder. "It would be so easy for all of this to be in my head. Even you."

"Me?"

He nodded.

"If you were going to imagine yourself a pretend husband, you really think *I'm* what you would make?"

"Yes."

"I can see the logic behind it, I guess, damaged, unappealing to general society, but functional. Goes with your brand of barely holding it together without being outlandish."

David tried to think of something to say, to tell Ahmed that he was anything but unappealing but he couldn't think past the rapping on the side door, the scratching on the glass windows. "Did you...uh..."

"I didn't hear anything."

David nodded, glad that he hadn't started to doubt Ahmed yet. Lots of people hadn't heard what he heard, but he'd always assumed they were lying. "I went through this time where, um, where I thought that I could make people sick by thinking bad things about them. There was this nurse I *hated* and she, uh, she had...in her brain...?"

"A tumor?" Ahmed supplied.

"Yeah. And I thought I did it to her, that all my bad thoughts had gotten into her brain, that I'd put them there."

"What happened to her?"

"She died."

Ahmed looked at him.

"So when I killed that guy, I sort of thought, well, I already killed Melissa."

David didn't know what reaction he'd expected, but it hadn't been the smile that broke across Ahmed's face.

"I used to pray for Allah to make me a girl."

He couldn't help the shock on his face. "Ahmed…" He scrambled for something supportive to say but the confession had taken him off guard.

"I didn't want to be a girl, but I thought that only girls could like boys, you know, and I wanted to fall in love with a boy so badly. It wasn't until, uh, I think it must have been third grade, Scott Mendelson called Brittany Thomas a fat lesbo. I asked my mother what it meant and it was all downhill from there."

"I wouldn't care if you were a girl," David told him, his mouth finally catching up to what he'd wanted to say.

"You should get in the shower."

David had forgotten that it was Friday. "What time is it?"

"Alarm would have gone off a minute ago."

He buried his face in his pillow and groaned. He felt Ahmed kiss his head. He turned to look at him. "Come with me?"

"Of course."

They showered together, ate breakfast together, a companionable quiet between them. He kissed Ahmed goodbye, more than a little disappointed that he wouldn't see him until after Ahmed had worked the closing shift.

"Have fun in class."

"I try."

"Love you."

"Love you lots." Ahmed kissed him goodbye and smoothed the sleeve of David's shirt, which had rolled up on itself.

At work, David asked for more hours. Johnny told him, "I'll keep you in mind if we need anything."

When he got home, the mail had come and he found a package from New York in it. He ripped it open as he walked and his phone came tumbling out, landing on the driveway. He scooped it up and found it undamaged, but without any charge.

He brought it inside and plugged it in, then found a note from the detectives, requesting that he call them at his convenience.

While he waited for his phone to charge, he picked the marshmallows out of a bowl of Lucky Charms, then reluctantly ate the cereal part.

He looked at Ahmed's laptop.

"He's probably writing about you."

David rolled his eyes. "Of course, he's writing about me, we're married."

"He knows what a mistake he made. He's going to leave."

He checked to see if his phone had charged yet, but found that it had not. He went to the bathroom and took his razorblade from where he'd hidden it. He moved it often, afraid that Ahmed would find it and confiscate it.

Things had been good. They had been quiet, mostly quiet, for some time. They had not gotten very bad yet, but they could. They almost certainly would.

For a while, he inventoried the lines on his arms, the old white scars, the new pink ones, the scabs that had not yet healed.

He picked at the scabs. Sometimes that hurt enough. One of the scabs took a long time to pick away and left the cut beneath stinging and bleeding a new.

He hid his razor again and went to check his phone. He found it sufficiently charged and dialed the number the detectives had given him.

A woman answered the phone and forwarded his call when he stated his business. Specter answered, "Mr. Craft?"

"David."

"Right. Sorry. I've checked in with our friends at the FBI already, but I imagined you might want to know this as well. We believe that the same things that come for you are also visiting a woman named, let me check..."

David knew that he would say Janet Mills.

"Here it is. Laura Richards."

"What?" he asked, not because he'd misheard, but because he knew Laura. She had been in Becca's grade.

Specter repeated the name.

"And you...uh, you said these things come for...you know, people with problems?"

"Generally, that is my experience. Why?"

He couldn't believe that Laura Richards had anything wrong with her. "Nothing, uh. Just. You know, she was, uh, I think she was valedictorian."

"Intelligence is not unique to those with sound minds."

"I guess not. Should, I, uh, should I talk to her?"

"No, I wouldn't advise it. Sunshine and I will come down in October."

"Oh."

"We don't want to give her a reason to leave the area."

"Right."

"We'll be in touch, David. Thank you for lending us your phone."

"No problem."

When Specter hung up, David immediately turned on Ahmed's laptop and creeped on Laura's Facebook. She appeared to have her life together. She had lots of pictures, looking successful and well-groomed in all of them. She smiled and it reached all the way to her eyes; he couldn't imagine that smile on the face of a serial killer, even one who was coerced by interdimensional monsters.

She'd gone to a good college, gotten her degree, and moved back home after graduating. She worked somewhere in town or nearby, he assumed.

He wondered if he should tell the others, not knowing if Zhané would heed Specter's advice to leave Laura alone for now.

Ahmed found him still on the computer when he came home from work. He looked absolutely beat and David couldn't blame him. Two classes, prayer, then a shift at work. He'd been awake for more than half the day.

He watched Ahmed set aside his keys and wallet. "Fuck."

"What?"

"I was going to make dinner."

"Oh. Don't worry about it."

A voice that felt very close to him suggested that he was a lazy piece of shit, that Ahmed would leave him to find some burka-wearing wife who could at least make a decent meal.

"He's *gay*," David reminded.

Ahmed glanced over. "Hmm?"

"Nothing."

David went over to the fridge and pulled out leftovers from yesterday. He put them in the microwave and Ahmed wrapped his arms around David, resting his head against his chest. "You're not working tomorrow, are you?"

"No."

Ahmed tightened his arms. "Good."

They ate leftovers and watched Netflix; Ahmed fell asleep almost as soon as he lay down in bed, leaving David alone.

It wasn't fair to think of it that way. People needed to sleep. It wasn't Ahmed's fault.

But it didn't stop David from lying awake for hours, too afraid to move, and wishing that Ahmed hadn't fallen asleep so quickly.

He woke in the morning to find a post-it note on Ahmed's pillow, letting David know that they'd run out of a few things, that he would be back soon.

Soon took a long time and David started to worry; he worried more when Ahmed didn't text him back.

Worrying was always a weak spot, a place where all sorts of bad thoughts could worm through his defenses.

This brought him to the bathroom, fishing his razorblade out from where he'd stashed it.

He was being stupid, clingy, childish, he knew, but knowing it didn't make him feel any better. It made him feel worse. He should have known better.

The first cut hurt but didn't bleed much. The second one bled a lot and by the time he'd made the third one, he heard the apartment door open.

"David?"

He didn't know what to do. He threw his razor under the sink and grabbed a bunch of tissues, pressing them against his arm and closing the bathroom door.

He heard the fridge open and close, then he heard footsteps approach the bathroom. He squeezed his eyes shut when Ahmed knocked on the door.

"David, uh...are you okay?"

"Fine."

"There's...um. There's blood on the door."

He didn't know what to say. The tissues on his arm had soaked through. He grabbed more and pressed them on top of the saturated ones.

"Can I come in?"

"No."

"Will you talk to me, then? So...so I know you're okay?"

"I'm fine."

"You're going to bleed to death one of these days," his mother told him.

"Better that way," someone else mused.

Ahmed said, "Listen, David, just, you know, if you're *using* the bathroom, let me know, but I'm, just, I'm worried."

He tried to think of a lie. "I was about to shower."

"Can I shower with you?"

"No." He added more tissues, then finally gave up and pressed a hand towel against his forearm. He sat on the floor across from the sink.

He didn't hear Ahmed walk away.

A few very long minutes passed. David started to get nervous about the amount of blood that had stained the pale blue hand towel.

"David?"

"What?"

"I just...I don't think you should be alone in there. I don't want to upset you or anything but I'm worried. Please."

"Uh. It's free."

"What?"

"The door. It's...open."

Ahmed entered the bathroom. He sat in front of the sink, facing David, his jaw clenched. He reached towards David but pulled his hand back before he made contact. "Do you need anything?"

He shook his head.

"I...can I sit next to you?"

He nodded.

Ahmed scooted over next to him; when he put a hand on David's leg, his hand shook.

"I."

"What?" Ahmed was instantly attentive.

"The bleeding. It's...more than..." David took a deep breath. He didn't think this would be something that would scab over, that he could throw a Band-Aid on.

"Can...can I look?"

David didn't remove the hand towel but he moved his arm more plainly into view.

Ahmed swallowed. "Maybe we should go to the hospital."

Fear shot through him and he recoiled from the idea. "No."

"That's a lot of blood. You might need stitches."

"No, I won't, I won't do it. It won't be good."

"Okay."

"I *won't*."

Ahmed placed a hand on his shoulder. "David, alright, shhh. Okay."

He shook his head. "Don't."

Ahmed moved away from him, but not to leave, just to position himself in front of David again. He put both hands on either side of David's face. "I'm not gonna make you, okay, I won't make you do anything. Do you believe me?"

He didn't but he nodded anyway.

"I'm gonna take out my phone but it's not cause I'm calling anyone. I'm gonna look up what to do."

He watched, wary, as Ahmed took out his phone. He didn't dial or put it to his ear, so David felt a little better.

Ahmed put his phone down, then handed him another hand towel, folded in half then in half again. "Put this on top, then lift your arm up. Press hard."

David pressed the cloth over the old one and lifted his arm.

"When it stops bleeding we have to clean it."

He nodded.

After about ten minutes, the bleeding stopped. While they waited, Ahmed went through the cabinets to see if they had gauze and medical tape. He found them in David's toiletry bag but didn't ask why he had them.

Ahmed washed his hands, then helped him peel away the bloodied cloth and tissues. He tossed them all into the garbage, then turned on the sink. "Can you stand up?"

David tried, bracing himself against the tub.

"Don't, hang on." Ahmed turned off the sink, then turned on the water in the tub.

Gingerly, they washed the wound, patted dry the skin around it. Ahmed taped a folded piece of gauze over the cut, which gaped unpleasantly, but he didn't suggest going to the hospital again.

Cautiously, Ahmed asked, "Can we ask Zhané? She was a nurse, wasn't she?"

David shrugged.

"Maybe later, then." Ahmed gripped David's hands. "Do you want to stay in the bathroom?"

His voice came out hoarse, quiet. "No."

Ahmed walked with him back to the living room, sat with him on the love seat, holding his hand the entire time.

They sat, uncomfortable and quiet.

"Do."

David looked over.

"Do you want to talk?"

He shook his head.

"Can I tell you something?"

He nodded.

"I think you need to see someone."

"I wasn't trying to kill myself."

Ahmed took a breath. "No, but...but you've been having conversations a lot lately. With people I can't hear. Since we got back from the city. You've been...out of it a lot. More than usual. You're hurting yourself."

"I'm fine."

"I don't think you are. I think you need help."

"No, I'll go if I need to."

"See?" his mother sneered. "He's trying to get rid of you."

"Stop!"

Ahmed flinched. "I...I'm worried. Really worried. We both are."

"Both."

"Zhané, too, we've sort of been talking. We don't want anything to go too far."

"You'll put me away."

"Yes."

Ahmed shook his head. "No! That's not what I'm saying, I don't *want* you to go anywhere, but I'm scared that if things get out of hand, I won't have a say in it. People are shitty, David, and I don't want them to hurt you."

He didn't think his parents had ever worried that he'd be the one getting hurt, or if they had, they'd never told David as much.

Ahmed took him by the hand. "Mark's a social worker. He'll know someone good. Someone we can work with."

David couldn't look at him.

"It's all this shit with those things, I know it is, but...until they're gone, we need to talk to someone."

"About the monsters that come and demand that I kill people?"

"You don't have to talk about that. I'll go with you if you want."

He shook his head. "I don't...I don't want to."

"Can you think about it, at least?"

He shook his head but didn't mean it in a negative way. He didn't know what he was going to do.

Ahmed ran his fingers over David's fingers, one by one, like he was checking to make sure they were still there. "There's nothing I can really do to stop those things, David, but taking care of your mental health is something I can have a part in. Even if we just go to get some ideas about...about other ways for you to cope."

He shook his head again.

"I love you."

David knew what he wanted to say, what he should have said.

"And I'm really happy we're together. I'm glad I'm with you. I don't want to lose that."

"I told you things would get bad again."

"Why do you think I'm talking to you about this?"

"Cause I'm being a freak."

"No! That's not it at all. I'm worried that you're going to get hurt, David, I'm *fucking* terrified. It's not because...you know, it's not because you're acting weird, I don't care about that, you *always* act weird. I'm worried that this bullshit with the things is...is pushing you to a point I don't want you to get to. A point—"

"Where I'm dangerous."

"Where it will be too much for you. Where I'll come home and calling the hospital won't be a choice, it'll be because I need them to save your life."

David shook his head. "No, I don't do...I don't do that. I don't."

"Do you believe me? That this isn't about losing some free time or things being inconvenient or getting rid of you. It's about keeping you with me. Cause I think, I mean, I *know* I'm happy and I think you are too. I want you to stay happy."

David rubbed his face.

"Am I wrong? Are you happy?" He sounded so unsure.

He hated that, that he'd made Ahmed think he wasn't happy, that this hadn't been the best month and half of his life. He nodded, then put his arms around Ahmed. "I am."

"Alright, good, let's keep it that way."

"They're so *mean*."

"They're wrong, then."

He pulled his husband closer. "You're so small."

"I'll get fat someday, just like my granddad. A big belly and little skinny legs."

David snorted, not ready to laugh yet. "I'm gonna go gray by the time I'm forty."

"Heart disease."

"Diabetes," David countered.

"I love you."

"I love you, too, a lot."

"What do you want for breakfast?"

David shook his head. "You don't have to make me anything."

"Eggs? Yes? Good." Ahmed stood up and when David moved to follow, he waved a hand at him. "No, stay there, I'll make breakfast."

Before he went to the kitchen, Ahmed handed David his stuffed rabbit. He brought him back a plate of eggs and turkey bacon, making David wish he hadn't let himself be goaded into the bathroom, into dragging the razor against his skin. He didn't want to make anyone else worry about him.

After they'd showered, and when they felt that it wasn't too early for her to be awake, they went into the house and found Zhané in the kitchen.

She looked up from spooning mush into Noah's face. "What?"

"Can you take a look at something?" Ahmed asked.

David had gone over to kiss the top of Noah's head.

"If you think it's infected, it probably is," she told him.

"No, not...David, come here." Ahmed gestured for him to approach.

David pushed up the sleeve of his hoodie to reveal the gauze pad. "He thinks I need stitches."

"Well, if you think you need stitches, you probably do. Medicine is sort of like that. It's better to be safe than sorry."

"I don't want to go to a hospital."

She sighed. "Alright, fine, let me see."

He sat next to her.

She handed the jar of baby food to Ahmed, washed her hands, and peeled the gauze off his arm.

She peered at the gaping cut. "Christ, David."

His stomach flipped. *Don't be mad.* "Sorry."

"Alright, stay here."

She went upstairs and returned with a first aid kit under her arm. He went over to the sink when she gestured for him. He winced and couldn't look as she cleaned the wound again and applied several strangely shaped bandages that he'd seen before but never used.

"These are butterfly closures. They're good for stuff like this...if you're going to keep it up."

"I, uh, it wasn't supposed to go that deep."

She glanced at Ahmed, who contentedly spooned puree into the baby's mouth.

"He told me you talked."

"And?" she asked.

"I don't know."

"Come on, I told you all that shit about how I want you to be around for Noah. You can't do that if you're not taking care of yourself."

"I know."

She taped another piece of gauze over the cut, then washed her hands. Without looking at him, she said, "I want you to be around for me, too. You're pretty much my best friend."

"I'm sorry."

"Don't be sorry, David, I'm not mad at you." She gave his upper arm a squeeze. "Did you eat yet?"

"Yes."

"I was gonna take Noah to story time at the library in a little bit. Do you want to come?"

"People will think—"

"I don't care what people think. Come with."

"Okay."

Noah gurgled and Ahmed spooned more banana mush into his mouth. "Remind me I have a book to bring back before we go."

"Anything good?"

"No, I couldn't even finish it. Noor said it was good but I don't know. It wasn't my deal, I guess."

9/21/15

A SENSE of deep unease and nausea sat in David's stomach from the moment he woke up all through work. Ahmed had, with his half-hearted permission, asked his brother-in-law for the number of a good psychiatrist who was taking patients and accepted David's insurance.

The woman had been more than accommodating and had offered to meet with them Monday afternoon.

Ahmed had promised to stay with him.

They met back at the house after they'd gone to work and class. David changed out of his work clothes but spent several minutes staring into the laundry hamper.

"You alright?"

He nodded.

Ahmed rubbed his back. "Well, why don't you put your shirt on instead of looking at the hamper like it owes you money?"

He pulled on his shirt. "Do I smell?"

"Like deodorant and body spray."

He nodded. That was an acceptable smell.

"Are you ready?"

"No."

Ahmed pressed his lips to David's mouth, quick and sweet.

"Everything will be fine."

David didn't think that it would be, but he got into the car anyway. Halfway there, he forgot where they were going and when Ahmed parked, he looked around.

"Where are we?"

"What, sorry?" Ahmed asked, adjusting his hearing aid.

"Where?"

"Uh, two thirty-four Bank Street."

David nodded, though the answer didn't help him. As they walked inside, he asked, "Why?"

"To see a therapist?"

"Oh. Right."

Ahmed took his hand and they found their way to a small office on the second floor. Ahmed knocked timidly on the half-open door.

A woman appeared from one side of the room. "You can come on in."

They stepped inside, Ahmed first, with David only entering because Ahmed hadn't let go of his hand.

She offered her hand to both of them. Ahmed shook without hesitation but she didn't seem phased when David kept his hands to himself.

"Nice to meet you, I'm Doctor García, or you can just call me Paloma, it doesn't matter."

David doubted very much that he'd ever address her by name.

"Ahmed," his husband said, pronouncing his name as only a native speaker could; David knew he still hadn't gotten it right, that he butchered his husband's name each time he said it. Ahmed insisted that he didn't, but David had ears, he could tell that he said it wrong. "We spoke on the phone."

"So you must be David?" Her eyes turned towards him.

"Yes."

"Come on in, have a seat." She gestured to a loveseat the color of unbleached linen. It had pale purple pillows and looked cozy, like it should have been near a window and someone should have been snuggled in with a blanket, sipping a hot beverage.

David sat when Ahmed brought him over.

"Tell me a little about why you're here."

David said nothing.

Ahmed looked at him, expectant.

He shrugged.

"Well. We're. David has schizophrenia. Mark, uh, Mark said that you've worked with other people who've got it, too."

"I have. Is this a professional diagnosis?"

"Yes," Ahmed answered but it sounded unsure.

"And you've received treatment for this before?"

Ahmed looked at David again. "Uh. Yes."

David should have said something, but he didn't want to. He didn't want to be here; it had been Ahmed's idea to come, not his.

"Can you tell me what sort?"

"Well. David, uh, he was..." Ahmed struggled for the right word. Everyone always did.

David wanted to watch him struggle but thought of all the times when Ahmed had provided him with the right word, easy and willing. "I was residential at a behavioral health center for a few years. My parents' idea. Not mine. I saw a doctor, I have a prescription. I take it."

"Was it your idea to come here today?"

"No." He pressed his fingers against the bone in his chest. "It's not about the voices. It's about. Uh. How I deal with them."

"Okay. Can you tell me a little more?"

"It's. It's stress. I know it is. And I just. I need to do *something*."

A slight quirk in García's mouth told him he had not communicated his point.

"I hurt myself. Sometimes. Normally. It's." He looked at Ahmed. "It helps. But it's not what I should do. Someday I might...you know, accidents happen. And that wouldn't be good."

Ahmed squeezed his hand.

"So I. I don't know. I need another way."

"Alright, well—"

"That's it. I don't want to talk about anything."

García tilted her head slightly. "I'm here to help you with whatever you need, David, so if there's something you're not ready to talk about, we'll leave it alone."

He shrugged.

"But I do need to know some things, otherwise I'm just grasping at straws."

"I guess."

"So, you mentioned you were stressed. Is there something specific going on?"

Ahmed took a deep breath.

"My mother," David answered. If he had to be here, he might

as well be honest. "Both my parents, really. And his."

Ahmed's mouth hung open a little bit.

"There's other stuff going on, I mean, it's not just that. But. I mean, these other things..." David searched for what he wanted to say.

The things that came were awful; they hurt him, scared him shitless. Even now, knowing that they would come again, recalling the feel of their flesh, the chemical scent that lingered once they were gone, his heart started to quicken.

"But the things, they're a problem that, uh...that I can try to fix. That people are trying to help me with."

"The things?"

He shook his head. "The things I don't want to talk about. But I can't do anything to fix what's going on with my parents."

"Can you be more specific about what's going with your parents?"

He hesitated and began to parse out his family problems in bits and pieces. García probed with a few questions, asking for clarification or more detail, but eventually, David spilled his guts. He said more than he had meant to, especially when he had walked in so staunchly against talking to this woman, and he knew at times his stream of consciousness rambling had to be incomprehensible to the others, but they let him talk. While he spoke, he pressed his fingers into the bruise that had formed on his chest from the repeated rapping. It ached enough to bring him the clarity he needed to stay on topic about his parents and only mention lizard people a few times.

"I don't want to talk about anything," a voice mocked.

He tried to ignore it.

"Crying about your mother—"

"Stop it," he snapped.

Ahmed gave his leg a pat.

"Are you hearing someone right now?" García asked.

"No, I always yell at the air." He had meant to sound like a dick that time because it was a stupid question. He wormed his fingers between Ahmed's, twining their hands together. "So. Anyway. Suggestions, I guess."

García studied him for a minute, looked down at her notepad. "Have you ever kept a journal?"

"Uh. Not really."

"I'd like you to start if you don't mind. About how you're

feeling. When you're hearing voices. What they're saying."

His doubt must have shown plainly on his face.

"I recommend it to almost everyone. A lot of my other clients find it helpful."

He could not imagine taking the urge to hurt himself and channeling it into words, into pen and paper.

"And have you got any hobbies?"

He almost laughed. "No."

"If you could find something like that, some kind of pastime, that would be good, too. Things like this help with managing stress. Making time for ourselves is important."

He glanced at Ahmed's watch, glad to see that their time had almost run out. He didn't want to journal or find a hobby.

He listened to García wrap up with one ear, running one finger over Ahmed's wrist, over and over again until Ahmed pulled his arm out of David's grasp and rubbed where David had been touching.

"Sorry," David said.

Ahmed shook his head. "You're fine, it just, uh, started to tickle a little. When do you want to come back?"

He glanced around. García had her planner open. "I don't."

Ahmed clucked his tongue.

David groaned. "Ugh. I don't know. Mondays are good. Or Thursdays."

"Does Thursday at eleven work for you?" García asked.

His first instinct was to say no. "I guess. Sure."

"Great, I'll see you then." She handed him a business card with his appointment time jotted on the back.

David took it and, to Ahmed, said, "That's bone. And the lettering is something called Silian Rail."

"Could you not?"

"Not what?" he asked, following Ahmed out of the small office and down the stairs.

"Not quote a homicidal maniac in a therapist's office."

"Feed me a stray cat."

"David, it's *not funny*."

"Why are you mad at me?"

Ahmed didn't answer. He got in the car. He said nothing more until he'd started to drive. "Are you taking this seriously?"

Of course, he wasn't. He couldn't. He'd done this same thing, done these sessions, too many times to care what one doctor or therapist or counselor had to say. "I went, didn't I? I said I'd go back. I'll get myself nice and normal for you, don't worry."

"David! You could have *died.*"

He grimaced. That seemed like a hell of an overstatement. "I wouldn't have died."

"And don't give me that shit like I'm trying to make you do this for me."

In the mood to pick a fight, knowing he was being unfair, he accused, "You're not doing it for me. *I'm* not the one who has a problem with how I cope."

Ahmed braked hard at a red light. "That's fucking bullshit."

"Fuck you." He had no other defense. He had never been good at fights, just at starting them. He never had his thoughts organized enough to make an argument, but his sense of persecution was always ready to take offense.

"Yeah, fuck me. If what you're doing is so fucking great then why are you always *lying* about it?"

David said nothing, his face hot, his guts twisting.

"If it's not a problem then why are you always hiding in the bathroom?"

"Light's green."

The car jerked forward as Ahmed hit the gas. "Next time you can just fucking bleed to death, how about that? If everything is so fine!"

"Don't."

"So you can be dead and that will be *fine.* I'll go crawling back to my parents and my mother can tell me—"

"Ahmed."

"What!"

He tried to gather his thoughts. "It isn't."

"What isn't?" His question had more bite, none of his usual calm and quiet patience.

"It isn't fine." He wanted to reach across and take Ahmed's hand, but it didn't feel right, not after he'd started this on purpose. "I don't want to talk about it, I didn't want you to know. I didn't want you to see me like that."

Ahmed sighed.

"It's embarrassing."

"You don't—"

"No, it is. There's...there's a lot of negative perceptions about, you know, about mental illness, about being a burden, being a drain. About infirmity and weakness. How, uh, self-harm is for attention-starved teenage girls."

Ahmed glanced over, then looked right back at the road. "I, uh."

"And I know I've internalized a lot of it. It's why. It's why I want to say I'm fine, even when I'm not. It's why I don't *want* you to worry about me. It's easier." He rubbed his nose. "It's easier to pretend that you're being selfish than it is to admit that I need more help than you should have to give me."

Quiet filled the car and David wished it wouldn't. He wished Ahmed would say something, he wished the hard lump in his throat would go away.

"If I was sick, would you want me to tell you?" Ahmed asked.

"What?"

"If I had cancer or something, would you want me to tell you? Or would you rather have me keep it a secret?"

"I don't have cancer."

"But it *is* an illness. So, would you want to know or not?"

"Of course, I would want to know."

"And would you want to help me?"

He sighed. "Yes."

"So, I want to help you. And however much help you need is the right amount of help. It's not *too much*, you're not *too sick*. Okay?"

David shrugged.

Ahmed reached over and took his hand. He took his eyes off the road for a moment. "Cause I know we're new to this whole marriage thing, but, I kind of thought that was what it was about. Being helpful to each other."

David had never heard it phrased like that. Marriage had always seemed love-swept and romantic, not a thing of practicality.

"The world is a lot for one person."

He brought his husband's hand to his mouth and kissed his knuckles, not sure what to say.

Ahmed cleared his throat. "I guess, uh, I should also probably not get all...douchey about stuff. If I'm going to be helpful."

"I started it."

"And I knew you were trying to. I fed right into it."

He kissed Ahmed's hand again. "I don't know how to keep a journal."

"How about step one we buy you a notebook. Step two...uh, we throw away that razorblade."

"Um."

"Cause it's kind of been sitting under the sink and I don't think that's sanitary. Plus, maybe, if it's not there it won't be such a temptation."

"Maybe."

Ahmed took his hand back so he could make a turn and David stared out the window. The world was a lot for one person. He understood what Ahmed provided for him and wondered what he provided for Ahmed.

"Am I helpful to you?"

"Immensely," Ahmed answered without hesitation.

"Are you sure?"

"Of course."

It felt like fishing for a compliment but he asked anyway. "How?"

"You accept me. You don't try to change me, but you do try to get me to be who I am without any agenda of your own."

"Maybe a little bit of an agenda."

Ahmed grinned. "And you're funny. I smile more when I'm with you. I feel...I feel good with you. It feels right. And that is helpful. In the realest possible way."

That night, after they had gone to Target and bought a notebook for David and after he had retrieved the razorblade and thrown it in the garbage, David sat on the floor in front of the coffee table and stared at the first blank page.

Ahmed looked up from his laptop. He had been seated on the couch, typing away for nearly half an hour, with little pauses every so often. "Doing okay?"

"I need, uh." He made a scribbling gesture.

Ahmed plucked a pen out of his backpack and tossed it over.

"I don't know what to write."

"Write that. Write anything."

He shrugged. He put the pen to paper and wrote *This is stupid.* He wrote it again. *This is stupid. My mom keeps telling me I'm going to die alone. Not my real mom. The one in my head. But I'd bet a million dollars it's what my real one thinks.*

I wish I hadn't thrown my razor away. It's easier.

It's easier to hurt.

Isn't that fucked?

He wrote down everything he could think of, sporadic and

rambling. He didn't know if it made him feel better, but it distracted him. He assumed that was the point.

He filled up one page, then another.

Ahmed set down his laptop and leaned over to kiss him, pressing his lips to his temple. "I have class in the morning. I'm gonna go to bed."

David closed the notebook, slipped the pen into the spiral binding.

"You don't have to come."

"Well, maybe I want to." He turned around, running his hands up Ahmed's thighs to rest them on his waist.

Ahmed put his hands over David's, sliding his thumbs under so they pressed against David's palms. "I'm going to sleep."

"Okay."

David didn't mind the warning. He hadn't followed Ahmed to bed with the intention of fucking. His fingers ached from holding his pen too tightly, his eyes had started to sting from staring at the pages.

He left his glasses on his bedside table and heard a slight clatter that let him know Ahmed had taken out his hearing aid.

Someday they'd have to get his other one replaced. He didn't know if Ahmed's parents had kept him on their health insurance or not. It seemed important to know.

Instead of asking, he nestled into bed and put an arm around Ahmed's waist. He snuggled close, pressed a kiss to the back of Ahmed's neck.

"Sleep," Ahmed reminded.

"I know."

Minutes slipped by, quiet and dark; Ahmed relaxed, his breathing even, his body going slack as he leaned more into David's embrace. He fell asleep before David did. He almost always did, especially now that the semester had started. Work, class, Noah when Zhané went out to work. Babysitting Noah had never been Ahmed's responsibility, but he had stepped in to help. He had all that and David. David who still needed to be sorted out. David who had monsters, real and imagined.

IN THE morning, Ahmed had to pull himself out of bed to sit in front of his laptop and do some sort of online class meeting. It seemed terrible and David tried to be quiet, but once he'd knocked over the pile of dishes in the sink and shouted at one of the nastier voices that came to call, he made himself scarce.

He sat out on the stairs, not sure what to do. He fiddled with his keys, trying to think of somewhere to go.

He took out his phone and called Noor.

She answered, her worry immediately clear. "David? Is everything okay?"

"Yeah, everything's fine. I, uh, I had a question and it kind of felt too long to text."

"Uh. Alright. Go ahead."

"It's just...about your parents and stuff. Do you think...uh, do you think it would be worth it to, you know, talk to them about this? I know you and Miriam think they'll come around but I know he's...you know. He's upset."

"Well, I don't know. I mean. I know our grandmother wants to meet you. There's some stuff going on with our family right now, I'm sure Ahmed told you, but I can call her if you want."

"Would you?"

"Sure."

"Maybe...maybe some weekend we can get together or something," he proposed cautiously.

"I'll see what I can do. I'll keep you updated."

"Thanks."

"You know what, I bet Miriam can pull this off, everyone's so excited about the baby and all. If she asks them to come over...I'll talk to her and our grandma, okay?"

"Thanks."

"How are you two doing?"

"Good. I think."

"You think?"

"I feel bad. He's got classes and work all the time."

"Yeah, he's a busy bee that one."

"Yeah. Anyway. Thanks."

"I'll let you know. Talk to you later."

"Bye."

When he'd hung up, David wiped the ear smudge off his phone's screen and returned it to his pocket. Ahmed's family might have reacted more emotionally, but their family appeared tight-knit to David's eyes. Ahmed seemed to have a close relationship with his parents, something David had never quite had. They had reacted the way they had because they cared, even if their care was misguided.

He chided himself for that line of thinking, for equating homophobia with culture, bigotry with caring. He'd done it because he wanted any reaction from his parents, even a shitty one. He wanted them to give a fuck.

Early in life, he and his mother had been together all the time, but she'd gone back to work when he'd started kindergarten. After that, with his father at work all the time and his mother at work all the time, there hadn't been a lot of those little moments that made a family, the movie nights and Sunday breakfasts. They'd gone on summer vacations, sure, and they'd had some things that were nicer than most people might have had, but he'd been babysat by various relatives and teenagers with no siblings or pets to keep him company.

He sent a text to both his parents, an 'I miss you' and a little heart emoji, and waited for their response.

In Mansfield, he'd sneered at their infrequent visits, knowing they'd stayed away because he'd turned into something they hadn't recognized. But he'd also wished they'd come more often.

When five minutes went by without a response, he went back inside. Zhané wasn't home, either, she'd taken Noah to a doctor's appointment. Her mother suspected he had an ear infection and she had gone just to be sure.

He checked to see if Figaro had food and water, cleaned the litterbox, and then vacuumed up the litter that had escaped the box.

With all that done, he returned to the apartment, finding Ahmed still on his laptop, his eyes fixed on the screen and his fingers moving furiously.

David hesitated in the doorway, wondering if he would be a disruption.

"The lecture part is over, it's just the discussion board now."

He moved further into the apartment and Ahmed gestured for him to come over to the loveseat. David joined him, glanced at the screen, but his eyes slid over the words without recognizing any meaning.

"Can I ask you something?"

"Mhm."

"You, uh, I know I said you should publish some of your stories and you thought it was stupid."

Ahmed glanced up. "I didn't. It's hard, though. And no one will want to publish what I write anyway."

"Why not?"

"Short stories, mostly. Genre fiction. And it's gay as fuck."

David didn't know what genre fiction was or why short stories would be an impediment to publishing it. "I don't know, I'm sure it's good though."

Ahmed snorted. "You've never read it."

"I would. If you wanted me to."

He looked up, his eyebrows raised somewhat, but he looked back to his laptop a moment later. "I've got to finish this."

David sat and waited for him to finish, picking at the edge of the large bandage that still covered his most recent cuts.

Finally, Ahmed ceased his typing and put his laptop on the coffee table. He turned on the couch to face David, one leg still on the floor, the other pulled close to his chest. "I've never let anyone read anything."

"You don't have to."

"Plus, if want to be a teacher, I don't think it's a good idea to have a bunch of gay shit published."

"You can use a pen name."

"I guess." His finger traced over a seam on the couch cushion.

David put his hand over Ahmed's, linking their fingers. "I love you."

"You, too, David."

"I think...what if I did school part-time, at first. Maybe one or two classes."

"That's a good idea."

"You have to close tonight, right?"

"Yeah."

"You should eat before you go."

Ahmed and David both checked the time. He had a little more than an hour before he had to leave.

"I'll make you something. What do you want?"

"Can I have a kiss?"

"Yeah, but what do you want to *eat?*" David asked.

He leaned in for a kiss, which turned into a second and then a third kiss, as Ahmed slid his arm around David's neck.

"I don't want to go."

Then stay home. "You kind of have to."

"I miss you while I'm gone."

"I miss you, too." *Don't leave.*

David recalled the ache that came with separation during his previous relationships; with Louis and Zhané, he'd wished to have them back once they'd parted ways, and even with Paul LaRosa, douche that he was, David had wanted something more. But this ache was different. It was more of a hollow feeling, less fevered.

Ahmed kissed his throat, ran his hands along David's sides.

David pulled away, sliding onto the floor, kneeling in front of the loveseat. He rested his hands on Ahmed's hips, hooking his thumbs into the waistband of his pants. He hadn't changed out of his pajamas yet, hadn't done more than brush his teeth.

He needed to shower, he needed to eat. David shouldn't have been letting him waste his time.

Ahmed scooted forward a little, his knees pushed apart as David pressed closer; he was, for some reason, almost proud to see that Ahmed was hard. He pulled down his pants and Ahmed lifted his hips to help.

It didn't feel like wasting time. It felt right and important to do this, to give him something nice to go with his busy schedule.

He made his husband moan and sigh, he made his breath catch in his throat and his hand scrabble for something to grip. He made him come, too, and looked up to see Ahmed all but melted into the couch, relaxed, blissful.

He leaned in to kiss him. Ahmed ran his fingers through David's hair, languid, tender. David wanted to bring him to bed, to cuddle and wait until he could go again, and then he wanted Ahmed inside of him.

Of course, time didn't permit for that. Maybe tonight, when he came home, if he wasn't too tired from closing.

"You want me to...?" Ahmed asked, his thoughts clearly not fully gathered.

"No. What do you want to eat?"

"Uh." He pulled his pants up. He slid his arms around David's neck again and embraced him. "Would you mind making pancakes?"

"Sure. Go shower."

Over pancakes, they traded a few words, but mostly they ate in companionable quiet; when Ahmed came home that night, David had remembered to cook dinner.

10/1/15

DR. GARCÍA greeted him with the same calm and open smile she had last time. Ahmed had not accompanied him to this session. It shouldn't have been necessary, they weren't going to couple's counseling.

"Hi, David, how are you doing?"

"Fine. You?"

"I'm good, thanks for asking."

David sat stiffly on the couch.

"So. Anything you want to talk about?"

He shrugged. "It's not you."

"Hm?"

"This whole therapy thing. I'm not good at it. I'm...you know, I'd be an asshole if I wasn't trying all my options though."

"When you say you're not good at it...?"

"Talking. Admitting things."

She glanced at her notes. "You were open with me last time."

"Cause it's easy to say what other people do. To say that mom and dad don't...don't, you know, give a shit. The hard part is, uh."

"Is what?"

"Is the stuff that happens..." He tapped his chest, then shrugged. "Anyway."

"How have things been since last week?"

He told her, grudgingly, how he'd felt, what he'd done. His feelings on journaling. How he missed the sting of the razor, how it had cleared his head, cut through his most overwhelming feelings.

She told him it was normal. He didn't think many people had said that about him in a while.

He did his hour and agreed to come back next week.

He got home around the same time as Ahmed. They had a long uninterrupted stretch of afternoon together, plenty of time to have sex and nestle together afterward. David listened to what had happened at work and Ahmed asked what he'd talked about with Dr. García.

"If you want to tell me."

"Nothing interesting."

Ahmed's fingers played along the length of David's forearm, almost tickling. He didn't seem to notice the myriad scars, or if he did, he checked his reaction well enough.

They lay together in bed, the sheets and covers turned aside, their legs hooked together.

David pulled the covers up and rolled onto his side. He put an arm around Ahmed. "Is it bad that I want to take a nap?"

"No."

"Do you want to take a nap?"

"No. But you can go ahead."

David didn't mean to, but he dozed off anyway. He woke to find Ahmed still cuddled up against him, his phone in his hand. He had his calendar open.

David tightened his grip and kissed the back of his husband's neck.

"Good nap?" Ahmed asked.

He yawned.

"Miriam is having a thing this weekend. Saturday."

"What kind of thing?" David asked even though he knew the answer.

Ahmed rolled over to face him, propping himself up on one elbow. "The thing you and Noor talked about."

David couldn't help but raise his eyebrows. He had assumed Noor wouldn't speak to her brother about what he'd told her, but then again, David had never had any siblings. He didn't know what type of information sharing transpired between them.

"Are you mad?" David asked.

"No."

"But...?" he prompted, recognizing the uncertainty in Ahmed's eyes.

"But ambushing my parents at a family party might not do us any favors."

"Do you think..." The question didn't feel right and Ahmed always been adamant that his parents wouldn't do him any physical harm. "Do you want to go?"

"I want to see my family. I just...I don't want them to hate me for it."

"I don't want your parents to hate me either."

"Yeah, well, you kind of blew that when you converted their only son into a filthy sodomite."

He was teasing, David knew, but it still stung.

David wiggled his fingers between Ahmed's, needing something to hold, something real and warm.

"But maybe I'm wrong. They like Mark now."

"How come?" David asked.

"Hmm?"

"Why do they like him?" he asked, wondering if he could unravel Mark's path to acceptance and mimic it.

Ahmed seemed to guess at his meaning. "He got Miriam pregnant."

"Oh." That path, then, was out.

"First grandchild and all that. They had to deal with him if they wanted to see the baby, so I guess they adjusted."

He ran his fingers over Ahmed's nails, occupied with only that for a few moments. "I'm sorry."

"That you can't get pregnant? You're forgiven."

David cracked a smile. "Maybe if we keep trying..." he suggested, running a hand along Ahmed's side, letting his fingers rest on the small of his back.

Ahmed grinned and leaned in for a kiss. "I'll try as many times as you want."

They kissed a few times, but David couldn't forget about Miriam's invitation for Saturday. "So are we gonna go?"

"Uh." Ahmed pulled back.

"On Saturday," he clarified.

"I think so."

"I can stay home if...if you know, if you want to go on your own." Maybe Ahmed's parents could simply ignore their marriage the way David's had; it wasn't ideal, but at least then Ahmed would get to see his family with minimal conflict.

"No, I want you to come with me. You're my husband, whether they like it or not."

"Is that how the vows went?"

"Verbatim, I think."

He wrapped his arms around the other man, glad for the feel of smooth skin, warm and brown, against his arms. "I love you."

"You, too."

"Lots?" David asked.

"Yes."

"Bunches?"

"Like a fucking vineyard," was Ahmed's reply.

David laughed and hugged him tight again. His parents would like Ahmed, he knew they would if only they gave him a chance. He could only hope Ahmed's parents would like him, too. They would find out Saturday.

Zhané came into their apartment later that afternoon, Noah on her hip. By that time they had migrated to the love seat. She approached and Noah began to lean out of her arms towards Ahmed.

He reached out automatically to take the child. "What's up?"

"Wondering if you two studs were interested in taking in a show tonight?"

"I don't know, doll, I hear you've been going around with other fellows after I gave you my pin," Ahmed told her.

"You know I wouldn't do that. You're my guy, don't ya believe me?"

Ahmed grinned. "What did you want to see?"

"Uh, my mom's church group—"

Ahmed and David groaned together.

"I know! But I don't want to go alone."

"Don't go," David advised.

"You *know* that's not an option."

David sighed. He reached out to wiggle Noah's hand. "Is it gospel?"

"Spirituals."

"You don't think, uh...well. You know, you don't think we'll be out of place?"

She rolled her eyes. "Come on, what's the worst thing that can happen?"

"Uh...I'll have to feel my feelings?" he suggested. "And maybe deal with some of my unresolved issues with organized religion."

"Yeah, so, come with me. We're leaving at five-thirty."

David looked at Ahmed, who shrugged. "Maybe you should deal with your unresolved issues."

"Are you gonna come?"

"Sure. I made it through Catholic school. This might even be kind of fun."

"Fun for you. None of those songs are about getting free from their Muslim owners," he pointed out.

"So hard to be white," Ahmed mocked.

At the same time, Zhané whined, "Oh no, it might be *awkward*."

With that, David found himself outnumbered. He pulled Noah out of Ahmed's arms. "Fine, but I want to hold Noah."

"Alright," Zhané agreed without a fight. She came over and perched on the arm of the loveseat. She ran her fingers through David's hair. "You need a haircut."

"I just went."

"Uh, I'm pretty sure that was before Ramadan," Ahmed noted. "Definitely before we got married."

David blew a raspberry.

"Ahmed, tell him he needs a haircut," Zhané prompted.

"No. I like it."

Zhané wrinkled her nose and David tried not to take personal offense. "Why?" she demanded.

"Gives me something to hold on to."

She let out a surprised, delighted burst of laughter.

A pleased rush of embarrassment sent blood to David's face. He squirmed a little and leaned over to place a kiss on Ahmed's cheek.

"Ew," Zhané teased.

Noah burbled, then pulled on David's glasses, making them crooked and leaving a smear across one lens.

Ahmed took Noah back while David cleaned his glasses, but Noah screeched, "No!" and reached for the glasses again.

"Hey, cut it out, little man," Ahmed warned.

'No' was not the only word that Noah had conquered, but it was his favorite. He reached for David again and this time no words came out, only a string of nonsense.

"They're my glasses."

Noah babbled some more and reached over again.

"Yes, come here." As soon as David had taken him back, Noah reached again for his glasses. David stopped him. "No."

Noah frowned at him and tried once more.

David took a hold of the baby's hands and moved them away. "No," he repeated, keeping his tone stern.

Noah screeched.

"Well, because they're mine. I need them to see."

Noah didn't try to reach for the glasses again, but he did writhe his way out of David's arms and onto the floor.

"He's gonna be just like you," David warned.

"I hope so, he better not be like his father."

A question almost pushed its way out, but David stopped in time. David knew nothing about Noah's father. No one did.

She glanced at him, seeming to realize what she'd said. Finally, she sighed. "You can ask."

He shrugged, shaking his head. It wasn't his business. "I don't really want to know." He added a moment later, "Unless you want to tell me."

"Not really."

After a beat, Ahmed chimed, "I mean, I kind of want to know..." He said it with a crooked grin that indicated he didn't really want to know, that he was teasing.

She grinned, too.

They all watched Noah bustle around the room, pulling himself up, then falling onto his bottom.

"You ever think about writing a kid's book?" Zhané asked.

"No," Ahmed replied.

"You should."

"Why?"

She shrugged and David thought she wouldn't elaborate, but she told Ahmed, "Cause I want to illustrate one but I'm a shitty writer."

A grin lit up Ahmed's face. "Zhané, that would be super cool!"

"You think?"

"Yes, I will definitely help you write it."

She smiled, but barely. She was not used to unbridled enthusiasm when it came to creative pursuits. David supported her, but he couldn't always work up the right level of energy; her parents, he knew, thought art was okay for a hobby, but not any way to try to pay the bills.

They always reminded her, "You have that baby to take care of."

"You definitely should," David urged.

She shrugged again. "Maybe. I don't know."

"Do it." He gave her a nudge.

Ahmed pushed David. "Move, switch with her."

David moved, going to the floor to sit with Noah.

Ahmed reached for his laptop, turning off Netflix and pulling up a blank document. "Tell me what you were thinking."

"Oh...I don't know, I..." She shook her head. "I just, I want Noah to have something where he can see boys like himself being, you know, sweet and kind and...not destined to do time, deal drugs, that shit."

David scooped Noah into his arms. "He won't—"

"A black boy, son of a young, unwed mother who's also a sex worker? You know what everyone's gonna think when they look at him. You know what his teachers are gonna say when he acts up, who they're gonna blame."

David sighed and gave the little boy a hug, kissing his hair. "They'll be wrong. He will be excellent, no matter what he does."

She smiled.

To Noah, he mused, "You could be a...prince or a knight. Or...a spaceship captain. Or what about a wizard? You'd be a very cute wizard."

"I thought he was going to be excellent, not living in a fantasy world," Ahmed said.

"What kind of little boy dreams about making a decent living in middle management?" David scoffed. He raised Noah up into the air and the baby giggled. "Look at you fly, rocket man. Noah goes to the moon."

He heard a flurry of keystrokes and looked over at Ahmed, wondering if he'd taken a shine to the idea. A bit of pride stirred at that thought, but immediately he knew he was being egotistical.

He lowered Noah and kissed him.

Not a moment later, the little boy wriggled out of his arms and crawled across the floor towards the kitchen. He pulled himself up using one of the kitchen chairs.

David fished his phone out of his pocket and checked his phone while keeping an eye on the baby.

Ahmed continued to type, occasionally nudging Zhané and turning the screen towards her. She would approve of what he showed her, or shake her head, saying, "I don't know."

"Can I see?" David asked.

"No," Ahmed told him, then amended, "Not yet."

David nodded and turned his eyes back to his phone.

They passed time like that until five-thirty came and Zhané hustled them into her car.

David walked into the church carrying Noah like a twenty-pound talisman but he hadn't anticipated the baby being such a center of attention. Malik and Daysha wanted to see him, and he had expected that, but so did a dozen other people.

He ignored the people and focused on the sounds of musicians tuning their instruments, the plucks and honks floating back from the front of the room.

"Dad, do you know Ahmed?"

"No, I don't think we've met," her father said.

David noticed him give Ahmed a hard, probing look, the same one David himself had gotten when her father had thought they were seeing each other.

"This is my dad, Nate. This is, uh," she began.

"Someone you're seeing?" Nate guessed.

"David's husband."

Several heads swiveled towards David, then back to Ahmed. He had allowed Daysha to hold the baby and without Noah's comfortable weight, he felt exposed.

He pressed his fingers against the cuts on his arm and wanted to start picking at the scabs, start the wounds bleeding again. No more than a few seconds passed before Ahmed took his hand, pulling his fingers away from the cut.

"Hmm," was the only response Nate gave.

Malik boomed a bit of baby gibberish at Noah, which made the child start to fuss. Zhané reached to take him, but Daysha calmed him.

David didn't think that it had done anything to make Zhané any fonder of the other woman.

Zhané crossed her arms. "Nana didn't want to come?"

"She's on some kind of date, I guess," Malik informed the entire church.

Zhané grinned. "Good for her."

A smallish man with deep brown skin and salt-and-pepper hair made his way up to the front of the church and raised his hands. "Alright, now, folks, let's get settled in."

The crowd hushed and everyone found a seat.

David reclaimed Noah from Daysha and sat between her and Ahmed.

The people from Amanda's church group filed up onto the risers that had been set up for the occasion. The musicians started the music, a jazz standard even David could recognize, and then the people on the risers began to sing.

Noah cooed and gurgled the entire time.

David sat and observed the wonderland of curls and fluff that grew from Noah's head. He smelled the milky baby smell and half-listened to the spirituals.

He should have cared. He should have been moved, or at the very least, impressed. Perhaps faith was something he had to cultivate, something that required more than childhood memories of church and the secret fear that he would go to Hell when he died.

People whooped and cheered after each song, calling out praise for the singers and musicians. He clapped using Noah's hands, which made the baby laugh.

The performance lasted about an hour and afterward, everyone filed into the church basement. David followed and as they descended, the scent of warm bread and what he thought was macaroni and cheese greeted him.

Ahmed's eyes skimmed over the food laid out on the plastic banquet tables and David knew he was inventorying what, if anything, he could eat.

The smell David had guessed to be mac and cheese turned out to be scalloped potatoes with bits of pink ham. The chicken and mushrooms, sitting pretty in a creamy yellowish sauce, smelled of white wine.

By the time they had reached the end of the buffet, David had green beans, a roll and a bit of salad. He glanced back to see that Ahmed had piled a little of everything onto his own plate; David frowned but didn't say anything.

When they sat, Ahmed pushed the plate he'd made towards David and pulled the sparse plate of bread and veggies in front of himself.

"Hey."

"Hey, *you* don't have any dietary restrictions."

"I'm allergic to shellfish."

Ahmed stabbed a green bean. "Eat."

David stared at his food, secretly relieved but also feeling guilty. He sliced off a bit of chicken, finding it perfectly cooked, the sauce rich. He couldn't shake the idea that he should have turned away this food.

Zhané's family found them once they'd made their way through the line. Amanda had a proud glow about her and David made sure to mention that they'd sounded really good.

"Didn't expect to see you," she replied.

"Yeah, well, I guess I'm...you know...a." He tried to find the right word. "A bad penny."

Amanda didn't appear to know what to say.

He turned his eyes to his plate and cut his food into tiny pieces.

When Zhané went back up for seconds, her mother followed her. Amanda took Noah out of her arms, settling the baby onto her hip. The three of them, for a moment, looked like something out of some wholesome family show.

"I don't know why you let him hang around."

David did not know if that was what Amanda had said or something he had imagined.

Zhané's voice floated back to him. "He's not *hanging around*, he's my friend."

"Mmm, is *that* what they call it. And what about that other guy?"

"What's it matter, anyway? Why do you care so much?"

Ahmed rested a hand on David's leg. "You're staring."

David dropped his eyes.

"He could be dangerous," Amanda said. "You don't know what he could do, Zhané."

Malik gave David a brotherly pat on the back. "Mom will come around. She's just stubborn. Both of them," he announced.

"David *isn't* dangerous," Zhané snapped.

David nodded. He shoved a forkful of potato into his mouth to avoid saying anything. He followed up with more green beans that he could have reasonably expected to chew.

Nate confided to his son, "Can't blame her for worrying. Zhané, she doesn't always make the best choices. Someone's got to look out for her."

"What bad choices do I make?" Zhané asked, her voice loud enough to cut through the room.

The people around them turned to look, going quiet, their

forks frozen halfway to their mouths.

Quiet, her father warned, "Don't be like this."

"If you can say it to Malik then you can say it to me, Daddy, what bad choices am I making?"

Neither of her parents said anything, but they stared her down, their mouths set and their eyes flinty. Their need to save face outweighed their need to control their daughter's defiance. Better to have her be mouthy than to let the whole church known she did sex work.

Zhané reached for Noah but Amanda stepped back.

"Give me back my baby," Zhané warned.

Amanda hesitated but returned the child to his mother. "One of these days, you're gonna need to do right by him."

"Or maybe I won't raise him to be ashamed." She turned and walked out after that.

David glanced at Ahmed, not sure what to do. Ahmed had already shouldered the diaper bag. Together they stood and followed her out.

The pastor caught them on their way out. "Where's the fire?"

She flipped him off.

Ahmed audibly gasped, then put a hand to his mouth, mortified at her gesture and his reaction.

"Well. Alright, Zhané, you come back anytime. I'm sure I'll hear about it from your mother on Sunday."

She stopped to snarl, "And you can tell her to go fuck herself."

"I probably won't."

By this time, tears had spilled down her cheeks. She walked out of the church with the other two on her heels. She buckled Noah into his car seat with shaking hands, then slammed the door shut.

"Zhané," David said.

"I never did anything to anyone, I don't know what her problem is."

He put an arm around her shoulder and pulled her into a hug. He wanted to tell her that it didn't matter what her parents thought, but knew it would be a lie. He wanted to tell her that her parents loved her anyway, but being loved *anyway*, being loved *despite* didn't take the sting out of knowing she was a disappointment. "It sucks."

She returned his hug, her arms snaked around his waist and her cheek pressed against his chest.

"You're a great mom."

She tightened her grip on him and he was brought back to

junior year when she'd been told, *no*, under no circumstances would she be going to school to study something like art.

"You want me to drive?"

She nodded.

Instead of taking her home, he drove to the grocery store and bought several pints of Ben and Jerry's, one for each of them. They all took refuge on the couch and he handed over the ice cream.

Phish Food for Zhané, Americone Dream for himself. He handed a pint of Vanilla Caramel Fudge for Ahmed.

"It's kosher," he said. "I figure it would be...acceptable?"

"Thank you."

They watched TV for hours, binging at least a dozen episodes of *Criminal Minds*.

10/3/15

DAVID STARED at the pile of fresh, warm laundry on their bed. He had pulled on his best pair of jeans, no rips or worn spots, dark wash, but had faltered when trying to find a shirt. He owned, he realized, no nice clothes, nothing more than t-shirts and jeans and clothes for lounging around in.

"Pick literally any shirt," Ahmed told him.

Twenty days until he got the next phone call. Or maybe it would come in on the radio or Ahmed's hearing aid.

Twenty days and I'll blow my fucking brains out if this doesn't stop.

"You should go without me." He wondered if the detectives from New York would be able to get rid of these things.

"The worst thing that will happen is that they'll turn around and leave."

"What about your uncle?"

"Rahim? Miriam doesn't let him around her kids."

He wondered why but didn't ask.

Ahmed pulled a t-shirt from the pile and pressed it into his hands. "Before we're late."

David pulled the shirt over his head and swapped out his glasses for contacts. He double checked himself in the mirror and his usual messy self. It would not do anything to impress his in-laws.

He finger-combed his hair a little but wasn't able to make any difference.

Ahmed came over to lean against the bathroom doorframe. "Hey."

"What?"

"You have pretty eyes."

"What?"

Ahmed grinned and took him by the hand. "Come on."

"Aren't you nervous?"

"Terrified. I think it's...like it's gone full circle, I'm so stressed that I'm calm."

David nodded. He knew the feeling, though, for him, it was more 'dead on the inside' than 'calm.'

On the ride over, David couldn't stop playing with the door lock, flicking it between locked and unlocked about a thousand times.

"Is, hmm. Is anxiety part of schizophrenia?" Ahmed took his eyes off the road for a second.

"There's a degree of comorbidity, but it can also be a side effect of anti-psychotic I'm taking. But hey, wouldn't you feel anxious if the ability to correctly perceive reality eluded your brain?"

Ahmed grimaced.

"But this one didn't make me fat *or* give me, like, *constant* diarrhea like the first one. I don't drool on it, either, so I'd say I'm satisfied."

"That's, well. That's good."

"Yeah. All very unsexy things to do."

Ahmed shrugged, probably since it wouldn't have been polite to agree that his previous medication's side effects were unattractive.

"I mean...I did gain weight but not...shit, on the first one, I think it was like eighty pounds, which is a lot, even at six-four. On, uh, on this one, it was like fifteen, maybe twenty...I don't know. Not that bad at all."

"You look great."

David snorted. He didn't know if *great* applied to him. Average, as far as looks went, and borderline freakishly tall.

"Shut up and take the compliment, David."

"Uh. Related but sort of unrelated."

Ahmed looked over.

"I. The, uh, my therapist and all that. She says exercise or whatever is. You know, it's good for you."

"It is."

"I used to play soccer."

"I'm aware."

"Zhané says there's a softball team that plays around here in the summer."

"Probably. It is, uh, October, you know."

"I know. I don't know. Maybe we could do something together though. Some kind of physical activity. Or something."

"I'm not saying no, I'm saying come back to me with more details."

David nodded.

"We can get jacked and look like the gay couples they have on TV."

"You know Muslims don't get to be on TV unless they need a terrorist."

Ahmed laughed.

"And they don't let bisexual people have relationships, we're just people who sleep around and don't like labels. And usually, we're women."

"Alright, fine, super-hot TV couple is out. How about mildly attractive indie film couple?"

"As long as we don't have to move to France."

"And neither of us die at the end."

"And neither of us die at the end," David agreed and it felt like a prayer. He reached over to take Ahmed's hand. Despite the uncomfortable certainty that he'd eventually kill himself, it wasn't what he wanted.

Ahmed had to take his hand back a few minutes later to pull into Miriam's driveway.

Inside, Noor and Miriam greeted both of them with hugs and kisses on the cheek. Mark Sr shook David's hand and Layla, a girl of three, told David that his shoes were muddy and that he had to take them off.

David looked down at his shoes.

"Layla, baby, they're not muddy, they're brown," Mark Sr told the child.

"From the mud!" she insisted.

"We are a 'shoes off' family," Miriam mentioned.

David took his shoes off and wished he'd paid attention to whether or not his socks matched. He resolved to get his life together but knew he'd probably never follow through with it.

Mark Sr gestured for them to come into the living room and offered them drinks. They accepted and, while they waited, looked at Mark Jr, asleep in his little bouncy chair.

Layla leaned over the baby, planted a kiss on his head, and said to her uncles, "You gotta be quiet."

David nodded.

She pointed to the teddy bear next to David on the loveseat. "That's mine."

He handed it over to her; she took the bear and wandered away, pulling herself onto the couch to sit next to Noor.

"How's everything been?" Noor asked.

David glanced at Ahmed. He didn't know much Ahmed had told her about anything.

"Fine," Ahmed answered with a shrug. "Busy."

"Good busy or too busy?"

"Uh, busy enough."

She turned her eyes towards David. "What about you?"

"Uh. Working. You know. You?"

She nodded and took a sip of iced tea. "Also working. You know, trying to be a human adult."

"What do you do for work?"

"Uh, you know, your typical barista-slash-web designer."

"Oh."

"It's actually going really well. I might even be able to drop the side job soon enough. So, you know, one step closer to success as defined by this whole..." She waved a hand in a vague gesture. "Bourgeois standard we apply to ourselves."

David nodded. "You got colors."

"What?"

He made a gesture that he hoped indicated that he meant the pastel purple ends of her hair.

She touched the tips of her hair. "Oh. Yeah."

"It's pretty."

"Thanks."

They all turned towards the foyer when they heard the door open. Miriam began to speak in Pashto and warm voices filled up the house. Ahmed's mother cooed with delight when Layla toddled over.

Ahmed's father stepped into the living room and stared at them, his face frozen with his mouth half open. He'd clearly been about to say something. His hand dropped down to his side, dangling by his skinny, khaki-clad leg.

Ahmed stood. "Baba."

The warmth disappeared from the voices right away. Ahmed's mother came into the living room, looked at her son, and then turned on her heel, marching back towards the door.

Noor sighed, rolling her eyes and going over to the door. "Mommy, don't be like this."

Ahmed's grandmother walked past her son-in-law and came to sit in an armchair in the living room.

David waved to her and she waved back at him. She said something he didn't understand and he glanced at Ahmed, who translated, "She wants to know if your parents are coming."

"Oh." He looked at the old woman and shook his head. "No."

She asked something else.

Noor and her mother had started to argue. His father continued to stand there.

"Safia!" Ahmed's grandmother called.

The other two went quiet.

She said something else and everyone in the house came to sit in the living room, Ahmed's parents looking displeased. Noor had her arms crossed and Miriam had Layla in her arms, the little girl looking on the verge of tears.

"See, you're going to make Layla cry," Noor spat at her mother.

"Noor, don't," Ahmed said, almost begged.

Their grandmother beckoned Noor to come stand beside her. "She wants to know why your parents won't come."

"Um. Cause they...uh. I guess because they think this is a phase."

Noor translated for him.

Ahmed's parents sat stiffly on the couch across from their son, beside Miriam.

"She wants to know what you do for work," Noor translated.

"You don't have to answer that," Ahmed told him.

"And what you went to school for," Noor added.

"You don't have to answer that either."

David debated what to say. "I work at the grocery store. I haven't gone to school to study anything yet."

At that, Ahmed's mother whispered something to herself and all her children gave her a dirty look.

"Ade, you don't have to be mean," Miriam scolded.

Noor and her grandmother argued back and forth for a minute

and finally, Noor asked, "She wants to know why you didn't go to school."

He licked his lips.

"David, you don't have to—"

"I stayed at an inpatient behavioral health facility for several years."

Noor hesitated. "I don't know how to say that..."

Miriam suggested a phrase and Ahmed suggested something else. Whatever it was, it seemed to get the point across to their grandmother.

"Why?" Ahmed's father asked.

It was the first thing David had ever heard the man say and he didn't really feel sure that he'd been talking to him.

But there was no other reason he would have asked in English.

David did his best to explain how he'd ended up in Mansfield using coherent sentences; it was harder to keep his thoughts together when he was nervous.

Noor translated to her grandmother as he spoke and when he finished, they all sat quietly. Mark Sr cleared his throat and Layla announced that she was bored.

Miriam gave the girl to her father. "Go ahead."

"You sure?"

She nodded.

Mark Sr took the toddler and brought her to the kitchen.

David pressed his fingers against the bones in his chest. Ahmed shifted in his seat.

Noor told him, "Anaa says you should go to school for something good because teachers don't make any money."

He couldn't help but grin. "I want to be a medical examiner."

"Really?" Noor asked. "That would be cool, you could be on *Forensic Files* someday."

"I'll have to get a doctorate and all that, and I think...uh, I have to do a...uh."

"A residency," Ahmed said for him.

"So it's a lot. But maybe I'll be able to do it."

Ahmed took his hand. It was the first time they'd touched since his parents had arrived and David thought he could feel everyone's eyes focused on where their skin met.

Ahmed's mother fixed her eyes on her son and told him something in Pashto; David caught the word *haram*. Forbidden. Then she got up.

Her husband didn't stand right away, but when he did they both made their way towards the door.

"She says it's a sin, no matter what you do for work," Ahmed informed him.

"I..." David stood and went over to his parents, cutting them off before they could get to the door. "Can I just...can I tell you one thing?"

They both stared up at him. He knew Ahmed's mother wouldn't touch him to get by and he doubted his father would either, though for different reasons.

"I know I'm the opposite of what you wanted for him, in every way possible. But, uh...you know, if you can ignore that for a second...I just. You two mean a lot to him and I know he means a lot to you, too."

His father said, "Please move."

"So I know...uh. I know it's a big shock." He hadn't quite been able to say what he wanted to yet. "No matter, uh, no matter how disappointed you feel, you should...you should stay. Cause. Uh. Lots of things are haram, you know, even Lucky Charms."

"We would like to leave," his father said.

David nodded. He'd done the best he could at saying what he'd wanted, so he stepped aside.

When he returned to the couch, Ahmed had his face in his hands. For a second, David thought he was crying, until, his voice muffled, he said, "Even Lucky Charms."

David sat beside him. "I tried."

"I was convinced," Noor said. She said something to her grandmother. "Anaa thinks so too."

Ahmed leaned against him. "I told you they would leave."

"We could have blocked the exits."

"Fire hazard."

David slung an arm around his husband's shoulders. "We can keep ambushing them."

"It worked with Mark," Miriam told him.

The baby in his bouncy chair woke and started to gurgle.

Miriam scooped him up, gave his diaper a sniff, and then told them, "Come on, anyway, let's eat something. I'm starving."

In the kitchen, she handed the baby over to his father, then with Noor's help, bustled around, filling up the kitchen table with enough food for an army. David didn't know what any of the dishes were, but the smell was enough to make him hungry.

When the time came to eat, he copied what Ahmed did, hoping that he didn't look like savage in front of the rest of them. Noor and especially Miriam and Mark were real adults, older than both of them, with careers and families.

"These, uh...the little dumpling things..."

"Mantu," Ahmed provided.

"They're really good."

"Thanks," Miriam said.

"It's all really good."

"Thanks."

He shoveled some more food into his mouth. Layla helpfully pointed out that he had food on his shirt. He tried to dab it up and only smeared it.

"It'll come out in the wash," Ahmed assured him.

David nodded.

"So, uh, you don't have to tell me anything, but is everything working out with Dr. García?" Mark Sr asked.

"It's fine." David knew he'd been short. "Uh. She's fine. She seems to know what she's doing. I'm uh, I just. With the lizard people and all, you know. It's hard to...to get used to...the way other people are on the outside."

"He means people in positions of power with the potential to abuse that power," Ahmed explained, "Not actual people who are lizards."

"Is that what I mean?" David asked, not to be snarky, but having always lacked the ability express what lizard people were.

"As far as I can tell."

"I should get it printed up on business cards."

Mark Sr told him, "I'm glad it's working out with Paloma."

David nodded.

"And how's this whirlwind marriage doing?" Miriam asked.

A smile bloomed on Ahmed's face. "Good."

His sister smiled, too, but said, "Mm. I still think you two are too young. Don't get me wrong, I'm not trying to be negative."

"You're probably right," Ahmed told her.

"We'll probably get divorced. Statistically," David agreed.

Miriam scowled. "I didn't say that."

"But it's what you thought," Noor pointed out.

"Oh! Don't pretend you didn't say the same thing," Miriam scolded.

"How about both of you stop?" Ahmed suggested. "Cause

either it will work out or it won't."

Mark Sr chimed in, "Besides, we all know gay love is the purest love, so they've got that going for them."

Everyone fluent in English turned to look at him, except for Miriam, who continued to urge her daughter to eat.

"Bisexual," David whispered, having lost his voice to shock.

"Nice." Mark nodded his approval. "Same here."

"Nobody tells me anything," Noor pouted.

"Oh, I'm sorry, sister-in-law, I didn't know my sexual history interested you," Mark returned, a good-natured smirk on his face.

She rolled her eyes and Ahmed started to shake his head.

"What?" Miriam asked.

"Nothing," he told her.

David understood, though. An openly queer brother-in-law would have been nice to have.

Mark seemed to understand, too, because he told Ahmed, "If I'd known..."

Ahmed shrugged. "Ah, Ade and Baba never wanted you around anyway, it wouldn't have made any difference."

They stayed for coffee and a slice of chocolate cake, then lingered around the table until Ahmed's grandmother said something to her grandson.

He nodded and replied to her, then said to David, "She wants me to take her home. I can, uh, if you don't want to go...?"

"No, I think I'm ready to go."

They thanked their hosts, exchanged hugs goodbye, and brought his grandmother home. She sat in the front seat and talked the whole time. Occasionally Ahmed would say something back to her, but she seemed to be telling him a story.

Ahmed didn't translate any of what she said. He almost seemed to forget that David was in the car.

I'm not real, David thought but pushed the thought aside. *I'm a ghost.*

Ahmed walked his grandmother inside and came back with tears dribbling down his cheeks. He wiped his face with his sleeve before he got in the car.

If this was a movie, David would wipe away his tears for him, but he just asked, "Happy tears, sad tears?"

Ahmed shook his head. "I don't know. Both." He sniffled and wiped his face again. "Fucking Mark, though, can you believe that?"

"I have to say, I thought I was hearing things for a second

there. It was nice when everyone else looked at him, too."

At that, his husband laughed.

When they got back home, they settled into bed, even though it was really too early to go to sleep. Ahmed pulled his laptop onto his stomach and David scooted closer to him.

"We should really get a TV or something."

"Why, you don't like cuddling with me?" Ahmed asked. "Am I that close to being your ex-husband already?"

David pressed his forehead against his shoulder. "Statistically it's pretty likely. It's called a starter marriage."

"Yeah, well, Afghans don't do starter marriages."

"So when you don't love me anymore...?"

"We'll grow old together and hate each other in bitter silence."

"Promise?"

"Promise." Ahmed offered his pinky and David shook it, but he also pressed his lips to his husband's, giving a long kiss, a kiss that said 'forever and ever', a kiss that really meant 'till death do us part'.

10/18/15

ALL ACROSS the pages of his journal David had scribbled the same words over and over. *Five days five days they're coming five days...*

Writing things down had helped, sort of, for a while. He hadn't hurt himself since the time he'd cut too deep, at least, he hadn't done anything more than pick scabs and rap his knuckles against his chest.

Five days

Five days

They're coming again

But now, with only five days until those things would call, eight days until they would be here, ready to snip open his skin and pull out his organs.

He scribbled one big, angry slash across the page, then threw the notebook across his room.

That angry slash should have been across his skin. It should have bled, but instead, it just crinkled the paper.

Ahmed had gone out.

The doorbell rang.

Zhané would get it.

Except a minute later it rang again. Then once more.

David gathered himself as best he could, distracted from

wondering how sharp the knives in their kitchen were, walking as quiet as he could across to the main part of the house. He peered out the window and saw two men standing on the stoop, one pale, the other golden.

He pulled open the door.

"Mr. Craft," the golden one said.

"Why...why, what...what do you want?"

"We spoke yesterday," Specter reminded, his dark eyes, as black as Zhané's, fixed on David's face.

Sunshine nodded. "Regarding—"

"The things, the things, I know, you're...uh. Gonna..." One hand hovered over his ear, not because he had heard anything, but because he knew he would and didn't want to.

Sunshine looked at Specter and David knew the thoughts that had to be going through their heads.

He was crazy. He was absolutely fucking nutso, there were no monsters, only him.

Specter gave Sunshine a nudge with his elbow. Sunshine offered his hand, palm up, to David.

"Will you take my hand?" asked the golden man, flawless and peaceful.

"Why?"

"I can help you calm down."

Specter gave an encouraging nod.

David took Sunshine's hand and that odd, warm glow made itself known. This man was something good, something pure, and a sense of well-being spread over David, calming the panic that had been lodged in him for days.

Sunshine smiled at him, gave his hand a reassuring squeeze, then released him. "Are you home alone?"

He nodded. Ahmed had gone to bring his grandmother to the store, a quick errand. "You don't need to get up, I'll be back soon," he'd said.

And Zhané had gone to the animal shelter to take some of the dogs for a walk.

"I'm alright now," David told the two men.

Sunshine smiled. "Wonderful. Would you like to get dressed? We are supposed to be meeting Agents Frost and Ingress at the police station."

"I forgot."

Specter's mouth quirked up at the corner. "We can tell. Go on, take a shower, we'll wait."

David stepped back and gestured for them to come in. "Ten minutes, tops."

The two men nodded.

He hurried off to shower and halfway through washing his hair, realized he might have been wrong to let them in, to leave them unattended in Zhané's part of the house.

Sunshine seemed so implicitly trustworthy that David hadn't thought twice.

He came back from his shower to find them sitting on the couch, the cat perched between them. They'd been laughing together, not raucous laughter, but the easy, mellow kind that came with long friendship.

He raked his fingers through his damp hair and cleared his throat.

"Ready?" Sunshine asked.

"What are you?" He pushed his glasses up.

Sunshine raised an expectant eyebrow.

"If he's a demon..." David nodded towards Specter.

"An angel," Sunshine admitted.

David's mouth hung open; he must have looked like an idiot because Specter grinned.

The pale man reached over and gave Sunshine's curls an affectionate ruffle. "Handy to have around, don't you think?"

"Are you two..." David began but stopped because it wasn't his business.

Specter reached over and took Sunshine's hand. At first, David thought it was an affirmation of their relationship status, but after a little less than half a minute, the demon's face contorted and he released Sunshine's hand.

He held up his palm to show angry red marks, like burns, across his pale skin. "Can't very well leap into bed together, can we?"

Sunshine smirked. "You say that like I have any interest in leaping into bed with you."

Specter stood and headed towards the door. The other two men followed behind him as he teased, "You tell yourself that, I know how hard the truth is for you."

Sunshine scowled.

"Is...I mean, is it cause you're opposites?"

Specter shook his head. "No. It's a protective ward against we unholy and despicable things."

"You can't undo it?"

"It can only be undone in Heaven," Sunshine informed him, "And if I were to return to Heaven...well, let's say I wouldn't be making it back down here anytime soon."

David nodded as though it made perfect sense. He slid into the backseat of their car, unable to think of any reason that a person would not want to return to Heaven. He tried desperately to think of one on the drive to the police station until finally, he had to lean forward and ask, "Why wouldn't you want to go back?"

Sunshine glanced back at him in the rearview mirror. "I failed the task I was given."

"Oh." David frowned. He thought some more. "They, uh...they don't want to track you down?"

"As far as the archangels know, I am...hmm, a hostage, shall we say? Or maybe a prisoner. I was sent as an assassin, after all, it must seem fair recompense for my target to keep me bound. So no, there are fifty-nine others like me, I am not so missed that they've made any effort to bring me home."

Specter cleared his throat.

"And God?"

"He knows all, of course." Sunshine's hand slid along the wheel as he made the turn into the police station. "It is all a matter of whether or not He is interested. In a rogue soldier who solves mysteries for you mortal things, I'm sure He has little interest."

The idea didn't sit right with David. That God could be real and just as absent. "M-maybe...maybe He just...maybe He likes you where you are."

"Perhaps." Sunshine parked, cut the engine, but none of them got out.

Specter reached for the door, but David asked, "About..."

"Hmm?" Sunshine glanced back when David didn't continue his question.

"About...you know. Hell. Sins."

"Which sin are you worried about, David?"

David shrugged. He knew he should not have been ashamed, not in twenty-fifteen, not when so many people had been so brave and bold to make space for him in the world. An answer telling him that he was sinful would not have made him change his ways, but it would dissolve what remained of his faith.

"You will be judged, if you believe," the angel assured him.

David shrugged again. "About, uh, you know, about being with guys." He ran his hand through his hair.

"All of us were made by Him, every angel was *designed* in every aspect, and right now in Manhattan, there is an angel hoping to marry his boyfriend of maybe...fifty, sixty years and that is not some Earthly corruption, it is how he was made by our Father, to be a man and love men. Does that answer your question?"

He nodded and wanted to cry. "I think so."

Sunshine smiled and Specter smirked, then opened his door. "I believe our friends at the FBI are waiting for us, Sunshine, let's not keep them waiting."

Frost and Ingress were waiting, sitting in a bare-bones conference room with a laptop and their coffees. They both looked up when an officer brought the trio of men into the room.

Frost paused with her coffee halfway to her mouth. "We were starting to think you wouldn't show."

"I forgot," David admitted.

"You're here now," Ingress told him, "That's what matters. Have a seat. We've been doing some digging about Laura Richards."

David rubbed his nose and tried to think, but after an embarrassingly long stretch of silence, he had to ask, "Who?"

"Laura Richards," she repeated.

He shook his head.

"Our psychic traced the connection from your phone—" Specter began.

David nodded. "Right, yeah. Sorry. What about her?"

"We've been doing some digging," Ingress continued.

"Yeah, I Facebook stalked her, too."

"She lives over in those condos on Oak Ridge Road, has a live-in boyfriend. Works for a real estate company in town, does well for herself. No record of crime, violent or otherwise. No family history of mental illness," Frost read from the laptop. "Cute, too, if you're into blondes."

David bobbed his head, though blondes had never really been a selling point for him. "Grade above me in school."

"And the same year as one of your deceased friends," Ingress said.

"Becca."

"Rebecca Livingston," Ingress said at the same time.

"She hated that. Just Becca," David informed them, even though Becca surely had no preferences after being buried for four years.

More than four years now, he realized. He wondered if Nicki and Becca would have been glad to see him married, if they would have loved Noah and Ahmed as much as he did. If any of them would have stayed friends throughout college or if they would have drifted apart. He would never know. Their parents would never know what the world would have held for these girls.

"Becca, sorry," Ingress said. "We want to go out and talk to Laura. If she's anything like you, she's worked out when they call, when they're coming."

He nodded.

It did not occur to him until they had all piled into one car and driven over to the condo complex that they expected him to be the one to do the talking.

"You ever realize how condo is one letter away from condom?" he asked as they walked up the long sidewalk to the condo, manicured green grass and picture-perfect trees flanking them on either side.

"Never really thought about it," Frost told him.

"Rather frequently," Specter said.

"If you say the whole thing, condominium, it's got the m," Ingress noted.

The statement made David feel at home, so he ventured, "Imagine if they were houses made of condoms."

The other four snorted and Ingress was so amused by the idea that she pressed a hand to her mouth to hide her grin.

"Get it together," Frost warned.

By the time she had to rap on Laura's door, Ingress had pulled her face into her usual smooth, calm mask.

Sunshine and Specter hung back, still on the sidewalk, and David hesitated halfway up the stairs, a few steps behind the landing where the agents stood.

A man little older than David opened the door. It took a few moments, but David eventually recognized him as Paul LaRosa's older brother. If Laura Richards had stooped to dating a LaRosa, maybe her life was not as together as her Facebook made it seem.

The agents introduced themselves and the older LaRosa told them that Laura had gone to work.

"She works weekends?" Frost asked.

The man nodded. He had started to peer past the agents, towards David. He squinted, then called past the women, "Hey, do I know you?"

The agents turned to look at David, both of them with raised eyebrows.

David put his foot up on the step, raked his hands through his hair. He didn't know if it was his place to speak or not. "Uh, I grew up around here."

"You used to, uh...were you friends with Paulie?"

Friends seemed an overstatement and David couldn't check his grimace soon enough. "Played soccer together."

The older man nodded. "Thought so. You used to come over sometimes, right?"

David bobbed his head in agreement, wishing he could remember the brother's name. He dug his teeth into his cheek, checking the impulse to admit that he'd gone over to blow Paul, his breath almost always tainted with alcohol, never in any shape to be driving.

The memories of Paul's bedroom, with its twin bed and a pile of laundry by the closet, of the taste of his skin and the smell of him after soccer practice, sent a strange, almost painful jolt through David.

He'd wanted to be special to someone so badly, special to anyone, even a douche like Paul LaRosa.

He'd wondered so often what would have happened if he hadn't been taken away to Vermont, but he'd never imagined what would have happened if he'd stayed in Milwater. They seemed to be two opposite things, the potential of what he could have done and the reality of what would have happened.

How long would he have kept drinking? How many secret hookups would he have endured with Paul? How bad would the voices have gotten and how long would it have taken him to be driven to suicide?

"Mr. Craft is helping us with our investigation," Ingress said.

David didn't know how much, if any, of the conversation he had missed.

"About all those murders?" the older man asked.

"Yes."

He bobbed his head. "What, uh, what did you want to talk to Laura about?"

"We think there might be a connection with some empty properties up for sale," Ingress told him.

David wondered if they'd found evidence he didn't know

about inside one of the houses. "Over by City Pizza, there are some houses up for sale."

He knew because he'd driven by one with Ahmed one day and had joked, "Do you think three bedrooms will cut it or will all the kids need to have their own room?"

"Shit, you really think that has something to do with it?" the man asked, his voice cracking halfway through the question.

David didn't know what he would do if he found out Ahmed had been hanging around places that might have been a killer's hunting ground.

Frost handed over her card. "Can you give this to Laura? We'll be back; hopefully, we can catch her at a better time...but have her give us a call if she thinks of anything."

Tom! That was the older brother's name, David finally remembered. And he hadn't gone to the public high school, either, he'd gone somewhere in Waterbury. Maybe a technical school or one of the magnet schools.

"Sure, I'll tell her." Tom stared down at the card, then slid it into the pocket of his jeans.

The agents made their farewell, heading back down the steps. Once the door closed, Ingress told him, "She's not at work, we already called the realty office."

David wondered if that indicated guilt.

"So...either he's covering up for her or she's not telling him something," Ingress noted.

"Maybe he's stupid," David suggested.

Both women glanced at him.

He shrugged. "His brother isn't real bright."

"Either way, it seems fishy, especially with what we've got from these two." Ingress nodded her head toward Sunshine and Specter. "Let's swing by the realty office."

David stuck around for the ride, but they found nothing of use. Laura hadn't been in that day and she didn't have anything lined up.

Before they could declare it a total wash, the woman they'd been talking to suggested, "Maybe she took a spa day, though. She does that sometimes, doesn't tell Tom about it cause he gives her hard time about spending a lot on 'girly shit', he calls it. Like it's any better to spend money on scratch cards..."

"How often does she do these spa days?"

The woman shrugged. "I don't know, maybe...every other

month."

At that, the agents exchanged looks, thanked the woman for her time, and left, but not before getting the name of the spa Laura liked to visit.

As they walked out of the realty office, David's phone began to ring, sending a wave a panic through him. He almost only received text messages and when he saw that Ahmed was calling, his fingers shook when he answered the call.

"What?" he asked.

"Where are you!" his husband demanded.

"I, uh...I went out with the...the..." He looked at the agents, at the detectives, knowing who they were but missing the right word. "Not...to see about Laura Richards?"

"Who the fuck is Laura Richards! Where are you? Are you alright?"

"I'm fine."

"You scared me, David...I...your journal was all scribbled in...I thought something bad might have happened."

"You read it?"

"I found it on the other side of the bed."

David recalled that he had thrown it. "Oh. I...no, I'm...with the FBI!" He grinned, glad he was able to remember the right word.

"Alright, well...I'll see you when you get home."

"Yeah."

"I love you."

"You, too."

When he hung up, the other four looked away as though they had not been watching him or listening in.

Frost drove them towards the spa and David sat stiffly between the two detectives, trying not to let himself sprawl too much, no matter how much his limbs wanted to move, or how badly he wanted to press closer to Sunshine.

On the previous ride, Sunshine and Specter had sat next to each other and Specter had exited the car with a couple of burns. After that, David had offered to serve as a buffer.

The drive to the spa would take them two towns over. When David wriggled to fish his phone out of his pocket, he noticed Specter peering at the screen as he typed out an apology for making Ahmed worry.

"Cute," Specter told him, "The two of you."

David shrugged. "We'll probably get divorced."

The demon frowned. He shook his head. "Why would you say that?"

"We're too young, I guess, and I'm too crazy. Better to face facts, I guess..." David felt guilty for having said anything, but he couldn't help it. He knew what people thought, he knew the likelihood of failure. He always figured it was better for him to say it than have someone else point it out.

Specter shook his head again. "If you love each other, you'll find a way to make it work."

David didn't know what to say so he shrugged again. "I hope so."

He looked back down at his phone when it buzzed. Ahmed told him he was forgiven.

After a few minutes of nothing but the radio making noise, David asked, "So you know, uh...you know how to catch these things?"

"We have an idea," Specter told him.

David nodded.

"And if we can't catch them, we will do what we can to get rid of the things," Sunshine told him.

"Oh."

"They aren't invulnerable."

David nodded. He recalled the spurt of thin goo that had spattered his face, the thin, snot-like drip they had found on the broken window. "I need them to be gone."

"I can only imagine," Sunshine said, his voice so full of care and sympathy that David needed to dispel his pity.

"I...I listened, once," he admitted.

"I hope I didn't just hear that," Ingress warned, turning around in her seat.

David's stomach dropped and a chill spread through him. He'd forgotten for a moment that the women, although they were not quite lizard people, still worked as agents of the law. He stared up at Ingress, knowing he must have looked terrified because her face softened.

"I didn't hear it. I'm just warning you that if I do hear something, I can't ignore it."

He nodded.

She reached back and gave his knee a reassuring pat. "I didn't mean to scare you."

He bobbed his head again, feeling far away from his body, like he might slip out of it and never find his way back.

He tried, for the remainder of the ride, to keep himself calm, though when they all climbed out of the car in front of the spa, David felt himself almost gasping for breath. The agents walked ahead of them and Specter slung a friendly arm around his shoulder.

"I can give you the name of several very good lawyers if you think you might need them."

"Uh..."

"Not that I think our friends at the FBI would do anything to you if they can avoid it. They are...incredibly kind, despite being employed by the government."

The weight of Specter's arm soothed him, as did the scent he gave off. "You smell like flowers."

"Violets," Specter confirmed, then pointed his chin towards the women and released David. "I believe Agent Frost needs you."

David headed towards Frost, who had been staring at him.

"We'll go in and see if we can find her...the location I guess isn't ideal, but she's going to be here all day and I personally don't feel like waiting around. We'll tell her what we know, tell her that you have the same problems. Hopefully, it will get her to open up."

"Or?"

"Or we'll take her into custody and hold her until we have those things taken care of."

"Isn't that, uh...I mean. Can you just do that?"

"Sure, we're the FBI." She shrugged and pushed open the door to the spa.

David stepped inside, almost overwhelmed by the smells and set on edge by the gentle trickling from the water feature that took up the entire wall. The place was serene and it made him feel that something very bad would happen.

He couldn't settle on a single suspicion, so he cycled through the thoughts that popped up, entertaining each of them for a minute or two.

The young woman at the desk and spoke with the agents in a voice so sweet and musical that David wanted to close his eyes and curl up next to her desk.

Specter went over to look at the water feature and Sunshine sat, picking up a magazine and flicking through the pages. David realized he was standing in the middle of the room without doing anything, so he went over to stare at the menu. He had never been to a spa before, though his mother had gone on spa days sometimes.

She hadn't seemed any happier when she'd come back, though, so he questioned the benefits of mud masks and seaweed wraps.

Eventually, the agents called for him and he followed them back to an empty room. The girl at the front desk left them there and promised to return.

Frost looked at the bottles of oils and lotions gathered on the counter. He poked the massage table and wondered if it would be sturdy.

"You guys aren't gonna murder me, right?" David felt compelled to ask.

"No," the women said.

He nodded, not quite believing them. He texted Ahmed that if he went missing he was alone with the FBI right now.

'ok but they don't want to murder you' Ahmed messaged back.

'I know but I just want you to know that if I die its cause they murdered me.'

'where are you even??'

'some spa'

The door opened and a woman wrapped in a big, fluffy white robe entered, her hair piled on top of her head in a messy bun. Bone-thin legs protruded from the bottom of the robe. She did not look like the happy, successful girl he'd stalked on social media.

"Ms. Richards?" Frost asked.

She nodded, her eyes big as saucers.

"We recognize that this might not be an excellent time to speak with you, but we felt that the matter was serious enough to come interrupt your spa day."

"A-about what?"

"About the murders that have been happening around town."

She gripped the neck of her robe, her fingers digging hard into the plush fabric. "I...I don't know anything about those."

"We're here to help," Ingress told her.

David looked down when his phone buzzed but looked back up when Frost cleared her throat.

"David, would you mind?"

"Uh, yeah, sorry. I, uh...the things. They come to me, too."

She shook her head. "What things?"

"You know, the uh...they're sort of these amorphous fleshy things, they smell like a hospital..."

"I don't know what you're talking about."

David fidgeted. "Anyway, I guess they can talk to people like, uh, me, people with...mental health issues."

She shook her head again, more emphatically this time. "I don't *have* mental health issues, that's..." She stopped herself.

David wanted to point out that eating disorders counted as mental health issues, and based on the blue of her fingernails and the hollows of her cheeks, he would have put money on her having some kind of ED.

"That's who?" Frost asked.

"You really...I don't know why you think I've got anything to do with this," Laura said, moving towards the door.

"We've traced some calls to your cell phone."

Her face pulled tight. "Mine?"

Ingress pulled a notebook from her pocket and rattled off, "Three two nine nine?"

She shook her head. "That's Tommy's number."

They all exchanged a look. "Your boyfriend?" Frost asked.

She nodded. "He's on my plan, I get a discount through work."

Frost asked, "How long have you two been dating?"

"Well...we were kind of long distance for a while...uh, but when we moved in together in the fall."

"Kind of long distance?" David asked, the phase striking him as odd.

Laura nodded. "Tommy used to drive trucks cross-country but now he just does local routes...that's why we decided to move in together..."

Ingress and Frost looked at each other; Ingress asked, "Ms. Richards, are you sure there isn't anything you want to tell us?"

Laura looked at the floor. "Could I...do you think I could get dressed first?"

"I think maybe we ought to do this at the station, anyway," Ingress said. "Will you meet us there?"

Laura nodded. "Yeah, I..." Her voice wavered and tears dribbled down her cheeks. She wiped them with the back of her hand. "I kind of thought something was going on with Tommy..."

She left the room and the agents conferred among themselves.

"Does that mean I can go home now?" David asked.

"Yes, I'm sure Sunshine and Specter can take you home when we get back to the station," Frost said.

David nodded. If they wanted him to talk to Tom, they would

let him know.

When the detectives dropped him off, he took the stairs two at a time to get to the apartment. Ahmed embraced him as soon as he came in, then pulled back and asked, "So, who the fuck is Laura Richards?"

David explained what he'd neglected to mention before, but Ahmed didn't seem upset that David had kept anything from him.

Instead, he said, "Hang on, wait, Tom LaRosa?"

He nodded.

"*Tom?* Are you sure? Not one of the other brothers?"

He shook his head. "No. Why? Did you know him?"

"Yeah, he was a senior when I was a freshman."

"Really?" He hadn't figured Tom for the Catholic school type.

"Yeah, he thought he was real hot shit cause he had some kind of...sports scholarship or something. He..." Ahmed trailed off, then shook his head.

"What?"

"He used to corner me in the bathroom, make me eat soap and..."

David waited, giving him a gentle nudge.

"And one time he made me..." Ahmed swallowed. "He made me strip down and took my clothes and hid them in the bushes outside."

David imagined the small, skinny kid Ahmed must have been at fourteen. "What happened?"

"I hid for the rest of the day and snuck out to get them once everyone had gone home."

"You didn't tell anyone?"

"Tell them that I got naked for another boy? Even if he did threaten to beat the shit out of me, that wasn't something I wanted my parents to know."

David slid an arm around his husband and pulled him close, kissing his hair. "And here I was feeling bad that the things were after him."

Ahmed wrapped his arms around David's waist and pressed hard against him. "I don't want to talk about it anyway."

David held him for a while, unable to shake the memories of what he'd done with Paul LaRosa, his mind chasing those and other memories, recollections of what he'd done with Louis, of the orderlies, male and female, that he'd slept with.

"Do you think we would have gotten together sooner if we'd

gone to school together?" David asked.

"Uh, weren't you dating Zhané in high school?"

"She told you?"

"*You* told me."

David didn't remember that.

"Do you ever wish you'd stayed with her?" Ahmed asked.

"I don't know. It's...I'm glad she's in my life again, it doesn't matter if we're dating." A thought occurred to David and he said, "But, uh...you know, we're only friends now. I don't...you know, you shouldn't worry about it or anything."

"Worry about what? The two of you getting together?" Ahmed asked the question as though the idea were impossible.

"I don't know. I wouldn't, though, I'm not...I'm not that kind of guy."

"I hope not since it was your idea to get married in the first place."

"It's just...you know, bi people kind of, we've got a reputation..." David shrugged.

Ahmed laughed and said, "Oh, I've heard about your reputation, mister, going around with all kinds of dames."

David half-smiled.

"Even going around with *guys*," Ahmed teased, but when he saw that David had failed to be amused, he stood on his toes and pressed a kiss to his mouth. "I trust you, David, and I don't care that you've been with other people. No matter how many."

David peeled away to rifle through the fridge. Once he'd found something to eat, he settled in at the kitchen table. "How's your grandmother?"

"Good. She was...incredibly concerned when I said that neither of us really knew how to cook. Like she thinks I'm gonna starve cause I never learned how to make a hundred types of rice." Ahmed nodded towards a pile of loose-leaf paper on the kitchen table. "That's why it took me so long to get home, she handwrote like...fifteen recipes."

David picked up the papers and saw that he couldn't read them, so he returned them to where they had been.

"I had to make her stop, I'm sure next time I go over she's gonna have twenty more...Are you alright?" Ahmed stopped, giving David a hard look. "You look like you're gonna be sick."

He shook his head. "No, I'm fine, just thinking."

"Oh, well, stop, you're making me worry."

"Sorry."

Later in the day, Specter called and informed David that Laura firmly believed that Tom LaRosa had something to do with the murders.

"She says he gets phone calls sometimes, ones that get him worked up. That he'll stay out all night sometimes."

"So...you want me to talk to him or something?"

Specter hesitated. "Uh, no, we don't think so."

"Really?"

"We're thinking that, hmm...that Tom might be more of an active participant than you are. The young lady really did have some concerning things to say about her boyfriend."

"Oh."

"So we don't want to give him a reason to, you know, flee the area or anything. Our FBI friends are thinking that we'll just take him into custody and hold him until the things come."

David glanced at Ahmed. "And what about me?"

"We'll be in touch."

"Hey, uh...is he. Do you guys think he had anything to do with the murders in twenty-eleven?" David asked, his stomach threatening to revolt.

"We're really not sure, David, but we will let you know."

"Thank you."

"We'll be in touch."

"Bye."

Ahmed came over and kissed the top of his head. "We're almost there, it'll be over soon."

David nodded. He'd lost his appetite.

Ahmed rubbed his back.

"I'm sorry."

Ahmed frowned. "Why?"

"You should be with someone better."

Ahmed sighed and David knew he'd annoyed him. It had to be exhausting to act as a crutch all the time, to always be propping up someone else's self-worth.

It had to be exhausting to provide help and support to someone who couldn't even ask for it.

"You'll believe me someday," Ahmed told him, "Someday when you don't have monsters trying to tear you apart, I bet. Until then, I'll keep reminding you."

"Thank you."

Ahmed put an arm around and pulled him into a quick hug. "Finish eating." Then he added, "Even if you're not hungry anymore," before David could protest.

10/25/15

FROST AND Ingress had brought Tom LaRosa to the police station for questioning on the twenty-third of October. They'd done so with a warrant they'd gotten based on the things Laura had told them.

On the night of the twenty-fifth, the detectives came to pick up David. They would bring him to the location where they'd chosen to trap the creatures and meet up with the agents.

Ahmed stood when David stood and David shook his head. "No, you...you've got to stay here."

"I'm coming with you," he insisted.

"No."

"It really is better if you stay here," Specter agreed.

"He's my husband."

"And we will keep him safe for you," Sunshine promised.

"Ahmed, come on." Zhané put a hand on her friend's shoulder. "I need you to keep me from going crazy waiting around."

Ahmed swallowed.

"I need...I need you to be here," David told him.

Not looking happy at all, Ahmed had said, "Fine. But you better come back."

He nodded. "I will."

So far his visitors had only ever taken pieces, but he didn't know if this would escalate things.

Hopefully, Specter's magic would work and the things would be captured or dead.

Their drive to meet up with Ingress and Frost was silent, punctuated ever so often by one of the detectives saying something encouraging or asking if he was alright.

They arrived at the abandoned gas station where the body of Kevin Duran had been found, the same one where he and Zhané had gone to make out sometimes. Half a mile away from the baseball field where Ahmed had agreed to marry him.

He stepped out of the car with the feeling that he wouldn't be going home.

On the other side of the parking lot, the agents let Tom out of the backseat of the car. His hands had been cuffed.

"You know what they're going to do to me—"

"I don't know, did you already tell us fifteen times?" Frost snapped.

"It's not your ass on the line!"

Specter crouched before the door to the gas station, seemed to whisper to the lock, then pushed open the door.

Inside he set about lighting candles and David could see that things had been rearranged. All the shelves had been pushed up against the wall, leaving a large open space in the middle.

On the floor, someone, he suspected Specter, had painted a variety of symbols David had never seen before in a great winding circle that looked more like a maze than anything else. In the center of the maze sat two folding chairs.

"And...that will stop them?"

Sunshine shook his head, his golden curls bouncing. "Not on its own, no, at least, we don't think so. It should keep them in one place though. It will give Specter the chance to incapacitate them...or slow them as much as he can."

"And then?"

Sunshine pointed towards one of three contraptions resting on what had once been the checkout counter. It looked like a larger version one of those expandable plastic fidget toys that he'd played with in elementary school, the ones that started out condensed and spiky but could be pulled to make a latticed orb.

"It's like, uh, you know the cartoon with the little lighting weasel," Specter told him.

"He means Pokémon," Sunshine explained. "And Pikachu is a mouse."

Specter rolled his eyes.

"So can I ask what the fuck is going on?" Tom demanded.

"You're bait," Ingress told him. "And then you're gonna be a convict."

"I—"

"And maybe if you cooperate, you won't get the death sentence," Frost cut him off. "And *maybe* if you can keep your mouth shut for the next couple of hours, we won't let those things cut into you before we grab them."

Specter put his hand on David's elbow and urged him towards the center of the room but didn't step inside himself. He gestured for him to have a seat in the chair. "We did bring snacks...though I don't imagine you're hungry."

"No." David settled into the folding chair.

Tom sat beside him when Frost nodded for him to go.

"Does anyone mind if I eat?" Specter asked.

No one said anything for a few seconds until finally, Ingress declared, "No, go ahead."

He ripped open a bag of chips, the crinkle of the foil resoundingly loud.

Frost and Ingress began to set up a camera in one corner of the room, training the lens on the two men in the center.

And after that, they waited. At first, all of them jumped at the smallest sound, let out nervous bouts of laughter, or yelped when a roach skittered through their field of vision.

Around midnight, they began to relax.

Specter produced a book of crossword puzzles and after fifteen minutes of tackling it on his own, he asked, "Five letter word for spirit or style."

"Moxie," Frost suggested.

"Ends in o."

"Gusto," Tom said after a while.

Specter's pencil scratched across the paper. "Uh, what about, ten letters, starts with o. Muddled."

"Obscure?" Tom asked.

"Ten letters."

"Obscured," Tom tried.

"*Ten* letters," Frost said.

"Obfuscated." David counted the letters on his fingers. "Yeah.

Obfuscated."

Specter filled in the word. "Very nice. What about...got a g in the middle, six letters. Group or crowd."

"Why did you bring that if you were going to ask for help on every word?" Sunshine asked.

"I'm not asking for help," Specter snapped.

An hour passed like this, but around one a.m., Tom's phone beeped and David leaped up out of his chair, away from the other man.

"Stay in the center, please, David," Sunshine said.

David nodded.

Tom pulled his phone out of his pocket. "It's just a friend."

"Who's texting you in the middle of the night?" Ingress asked.

"What's it matter to you what time I get texts?"

"Julie, leave it," Frost warned. "We have to maintain until those things get here."

Ingress crossed her arms.

"What time do they usually come?" Frost asked.

"Around now," David told her.

"Do you think..." She glanced at the detectives. "Do you think there are too many of us?"

"I did wonder about that," Specter admitted. "If the two of you wanted to wait in the car for a while...we could take shifts."

The women exchanged looks. "We could."

Specter walked over to the door and opened it for them. "And you'll be sure to come running if you hear a ruckus."

"We'll come switch in an hour," Frost said.

David wished they wouldn't go, but understood the necessity.

The four men set in relative silence after the women left. Specter had put aside the crossword puzzle for now and had taken up another bag of snacks.

"You some kind of albino?" Tom asked.

"No," Specter answered. "Demon."

"A what?"

"A demon."

Tom snorted. "And are you a fairy?" he asked Sunshine.

The angel declined to answer.

To David, Tom asked, "So, what's your damage?"

"Sorry, what?"

"You're all squirrely, hitting yourself so hard I feel like *I'm* gonna get a bruise just watching."

"Just nervous."

"Alright, sure." Tom rolled his eyes.

David looked around the room, fidgeted for a while, then asked the question that had been on his mind for days. "Did you kill Becca and Nicki?"

"Who?"

"They were in high school. Before Jim Roberts."

Tom turned to face him, looking over dead. "I really thought they were gonna pin all this on you...Local nutjob's a better target than a star athlete."

"You killed them," David accused.

Tom shook his head. "No," he said but he looked away when he said it. "Didn't kill anyone."

David smelled them before he saw them, just a hint of chemical acridness wafting through the air.

He turned around, searching all the dark corners of the room, scanning the ceiling. They would be here soon.

He opened his mouth to tell the detectives, but before he could get a word out, Tom clubbed him in the back of the head with both hands clenched together.

David stumbled, his ears ringing and a wave of nausea passing through him. Before he could recover, Tom wrapped an arm around his throat.

"Sorry, but I'm not—" the other man began.

Tom screamed when David sunk his teeth into the meat of his arm, biting down so hard he tasted blood. The other man released him, but just for a minute before he was grabbing at him again.

Specter shouted something, some word that was either in another or language or that David was too dizzy to understand.

Tom collapsed to the floor, gripping his stomach.

"David—!" Sunshine warned.

A flat tentacle oozed around David's waist, tightening, and pulling him back. The things had come, he could hear their usual crackle over someone's phone.

A second tentacle snaked around his leg and they started to pull him down to the ground, enveloping him with their flesh.

Would it really cost him an eye this time, would they take his other kidney or a length of intestine?

No one came to help but he could hear Specter chanting.

After what felt like forever but must have only been seconds, the grip the things had on him loosened.

David pushed at their flesh which was pliant but weirdly firm, feeling like he was drowning in silly putty.

The two things that held him continued their movements in slow motion, with a third one dripping down from the ceiling, something sharp and silver glinting.

Specter threw one of the strange orbs and it stuck into the flesh of one of the things like a bur. Slowly, glacially, the thing's flesh began to ooze inside the orb.

David finally disentangled himself, stepping away from the things.

"Stay in the circle!" Sunshine warned.

Specter lobbed the second orb and it did what the first had done, but when he threw the last one, something went wrong.

Instead of sticking to and absorbing the thing, the orb bounced off.

After first David thought it had just been a bad throw, but he realized that the third thing had picked up one of the folding chairs and used it as a shield.

"The spell isn't holding," Sunshine said.

"Thanks, I can actually see that!" Specter snapped.

"What do I do?" David asked.

"Stay in the circle," they both shouted.

David looked at the third thing, which had started to reach towards him. "I really don't feel comfortable doing that..."

He scooted out of its reach, but it followed, slow but persistent.

"If you leave the circle, you might break the wards," Sunshine warned, "We need them to hold for as long as possible."

"I've got to go around, get the other orb," Specter told him, edging around the maze, careful not to enter it.

"Uhhh..." David watched as the third thing turned its slow attentions towards him and reached for the other folding chair.

By now, the other two things were in their orbs, contained and sitting motionless on the floor.

"Uh, I think...I think it's going after you!"

Specter hurried around the edge faster. David didn't know what would happen if he stepped inside the maze, but with the way he avoided it, it wouldn't be good.

Like an elastic band snapping, the last thing's tentacle regained its full speed, darting forward, and grabbing the chair. It hurled the chair towards Specter, knocking him to the ground.

Specter sprawled and landed with a grunt, one of his hands

flopping inside the circle.

The thing pounced, not able to leave the maze but dragging the demon inside with him.

Specter screamed at that, his body going stiff and his back arching as though he'd touched an electric fence.

David grabbed ahold of Specter's leg, trying to pull him out of the thing's grip. To his surprise, the thing released Specter, letting the other man's full weight fall on top of David, leaving them both huddled on the ground.

"Get him out of the circle," Sunshine said.

"I thought I needed...to stay in the circle." David tried to sit up.

"Get him out!" Sunshine barked.

David wrapped an arm around Specter's body and tried to drag him out; the thing wrapped around his leg, yanking him back.

He kicked at it, but it had no more effect than stomping on a piece of padded flooring. He twisted and wriggled but couldn't get free.

"David!" Sunshine insisted.

With all that he had left, David heaved Specter's body to the very edge of the maze, enough that one leg landed outside of it.

In a heartbeat, Sunshine hurried over and pulled the other man all the way out, leaving him to rest against one of the shelves.

David thought that Sunshine would scoop up the remaining orb, but instead, he stepped right up to the line that marked the edge of the maze. He took something from his belt and tossed it next to David.

David snatched up the penknife but didn't think it would help much against the thick sheet of gray flesh that had started to wind around his legs, squeezing them together so hard it made his bones ache.

"Break one of the symbols."

"Which one?"

"Any one!"

David fumbled to open the knife and stabbed randomly at the circle, dragging the knife through the paint and scraping up some of it.

The thing hardly seemed to care, instead pulling him in closer, squeezing him tighter. He didn't know what the thing would do without its companions, if it would break its tendency not take a life on its own.

He would, by the end of this, at least have some bruised ribs because its flesh had enveloped him up to the chest now, was pressing all the air out of him.

He wheezed, "Broke it!" and saw Sunshine take a hesitant step inside.

Once he saw that the circle had no ill effects, the angel sprinted over to David and plunged his hand into the thing's flesh, not just bouncing off put sending up a spurt of thin, gray goo, filling up the air with a smell that made David's eyes water.

Sunshine did this over and over again, his hand moving, a golden flash so quick that it took David a full thirty seconds to realize that he had a blade in his hand, a short, glimmering dagger made of some greenish-silver metal.

The thing, after a minute, loosened its grip, and after two, it collapsed, nothing more than a quivering puddle on the ground, oozing and leaking.

Sunshine continued to attack, though, his blade slicing in and out until there was no way the thing could have ever pulled itself together, nothing more than a few quivering piles of jelly studded here and there with what might have been bits of human teeth.

David, on his knees, watched, turning his head to the side and vomiting at one point, his ears still ringing, his whole body screaming.

Sunshine put away his dagger and helped David to his feet, bringing him over to sit beside Specter.

The angel reached over and gave the demon a brusque shake. Specter gasped as though he'd been startled.

"Are you—" Sunshine began but Specter grabbed him by the front of the shirt and yanked him close.

Specter pressed his mouth to Sunshine's and kissed him, hard and long, until suddenly he jerked back with a sharp, quivering cry, a sound of pain and dissatisfaction, one that hurt even David's heart to hear.

A bright red burn slashed across Specter's mouth, livid, leaving his lips blistered and the lower one dribbling blood.

"Felix..." Sunshine stared at the other man, his voice tender, hardly more than a whisper. He reached out as though he would wipe the blood from Specter's face but pulled back before their skin made contact.

His breathing ragged, Specter told him, "It had to happen at some point."

The angel licked his lips, then swallowed.

David pushed himself more upright, wishing he could gather himself enough to leave, but his head spun.

Specter moved in again, but Sunshine put a hand on his shoulder and gently pushed him back, shaking his head.

Specter sighed, then wiped his mouth on his sleeve. He gave the angel a rough shove and struggled to his feet. He limped out the door and they could hear him call over to the FBI agents waiting in the car.

"Hey! I thought we agreed you *would come in* if there was a ruckus!"

Sunshine looked at David. "Are you alright?"

"I think I need to throw up again."

Sunshine nodded.

"What about you?"

"I was made to be a soldier."

David shook his head, sending searing pain through his skull. "No, about...about him."

Sunshine opened his mouth, then shook his head. An unattractive sob ripped from his throat, almost like a wet-sounding cough. He cleared his throat. "You watch from Heaven and you think humans are so dramatic, talking about things like a broken heart, as though a feeling could be enough to do you harm. But then, when you have a heart and it really does hurt..."

"There's got to be something..."

"Of course there is, there's always something that can be done, the real question is whether or not I'm willing to pay the price. But to return to Heaven would be to leave him behind."

"They wouldn't let you come back?"

"To return to the demon I was sent to kill, to return to the *thing* that has kept me bound to this realm for decades, to come back because I missed the anti-Christ? No, they would think I'd lost my mind."

"I. Uh."

"Are you two coming or what!" Specter called from the door. "Grab those things, why don't you, and make yourself useful."

Sunshine helped David to his feet and while they packed up the car, David emptied his stomach again. Specter tossed the last orb on the dead thing, just for good measure, then they loaded them all into their trunk.

The agents gathered up their recording equipment and offered to take David to the hospital.

"I'm pretty sure you've got a concussion," Frost said when he refused.

"I just want to go home." He looked at Tom, who still hadn't woken.

The agents didn't seem pleased.

"Zhané's a nurse."

"I thought she was a prostitute," Sunshine murmured, glancing down at Tom, who they had deposited against the side of the agent's car. "What did you do to him?"

"He'll be fine in a few days," Specter promised. "Come on, David, we'll drive you back."

Ingress put a hand on David's shoulder. "We'll be back to check in on you tomorrow, alright?"

He nodded and he thought for a second she was going to hug him. He wouldn't have objected, and she took half a step closer, but then pulled back and kicked Tom's foot. "At least he's shut up now."

The ride home was quiet, uncomfortable, and Sunshine reached for the radio dial, but Specter slapped his hand away. "For fuck's sake, I don't want to listen to that goddamn conspiracy theory show!"

Sunshine drew his hand back without a word.

For a solid five minutes, no one spoke.

Finally, Sunshine sighed. "Felix..."

"Don't."

"What about your father?"

"Out of the question," Specter pronounced.

David sent up a prayer of thanks when the ride ended.

The detectives promised to keep in touch, that they would share whatever they discovered from their study of the things.

He promised to call them if anything weird happened.

"But it should be done," Specter said with a nod towards the trunk of the car.

"I guess we'll know in eight weeks."

Specter gave him a pat on the back, Sunshine clapped him on the shoulder, and he made the slow climb up the steps to his apartment. He felt hollow, far away from his body.

He found Zhané and Ahmed waiting for him, waiting together, with Noah asleep in the playpen. He'd already called to let them know he was alive.

"I need a shower," he announced.

Ahmed threw his arms around him and kissed him anyway.

David couldn't summon the right response, needing all his wherewithal to remain on his feet.

He wondered, distantly, when the anxiety attack would come, when some delusion would set in or a crowd of voices would fill up his ears.

He took a bath, with Zhané sitting Indian-style on the toilet seat cover and with Ahmed trailing his hands through the water, making sure he got all of the goo out of his hair. He noted all the new bruises on his body but was glad to come out of it without another scar. He told them what had happened, or tried, breaking down crying halfway through and never managing to finish the story.

He collapsed into bed, too tired to care that surely tomorrow would be a bad day, a terrible day, for him, that for days, things in his mind would not be settled in quite the right way. For now, though, he had Zhané asleep on the loveseat and Ahmed holding on to him so hard it made his ribs hurt, bruised as they were, and he could hear Noah's soft snores drifting up from the playpen.

12/18/2015

AHMED TOOK his last final of the semester and after that, they packed up the car for the long drive to Vermont.

David still hadn't told his parents he and Ahmed were coming, convinced that if they knew they would move just to avoid them. He hadn't told them about the things, either, and he definitely hadn't told them about the seventy-two hours that he'd spent in an involuntary hold following a neighbor's call to the police.

The emotional aftermath of getting rid of the things hadn't been pretty and sometimes it had involved screaming, on his part, never by Zhané or Ahmed.

But things had settled since then. Mark had stepped in to help them navigate the system and Dr. García, to her credit, had been upset with how the police had handled things and had vouched for his ability to live independently, convinced the other doctors that he was not a danger to himself or others.

"It really could have been handled better. The police don't have much training in this as they should."

"It was...it was a lot of screaming," David had admitted sheepishly, more embarrassed than angry.

Ahmed, on the other hand, had been livid. He'd even filed a complaint against the officer in question, which David thought was a little much, but Zhané had supported him doing so.

"The cops didn't help," Zhané had said, "We would have had it handled."

David shrugged, so used to being told that he could have hurt someone, hurt himself, that he didn't know what to do with the outrage of the other two.

They had both said, "You aren't dangerous," at the same time.

He had shrugged again, though he had been a little amused that the two of them knew him well enough to know what he was thinking.

Maybe they could read minds and had been holding out on him this whole time.

Ahmed had wrapped an arm around him and rested his head on David's shoulder. "You were mostly just being loud."

"So loud," Zhané had teased.

He had cracked a smile at that.

David tossed his duffle bag into the back seat and pushed the door shut. "Maybe they won't be there..."

"I don't think anyone would sell their house just to avoid seeing you," Ahmed assured him.

"You think that, but you don't know my parents."

Ahmed shook his head, gave David a kiss, and climbed into the driver's seat. "Driving five and a half fucking hours to see them, they better let us in," he grumbled.

"Maybe you'll like Christmas."

"Yeah, cause a week with my conservative, white in-laws sounds like a great way to get into the holiday spirit."

David reached over, pressed a kiss to his cheek, then rested a hand on Ahmed's thigh as he backed out of the driveway, still grumbling about the things that could and probably would be problematic during their visit.

"If they're really shitty, we won't stay," David promised. "We'll go skiing or ice fishing or something."

"Do you...David, do you know how to ski?"

"No, but, I mean, how hard can it be?"

Ahmed shook his head, a smile spreading across his face.

No phone calls came, not during the drive, not during a mostly silent dinner with David's parents, and not while they stayed awake late into the night having the quietest sex they could manage, giggling and shushing each other.

ABOUT THE AUTHOR

Dan is a writer and educator who has lived in or around Wolcott, Connecticut for their entire life. They received their BSED from CCSU in 2013 and has written their Master's thesis on representation of women in same-sex relationships in contemporary Spanish literature and cinema.

What Everyone Deserves
2017 Rainbow Awards **Honorable Mention**
"Although the story deal with some real 1950's issues – discrimination, homophobia, interracial couples and hate crimes – it did it in a way that perfectly suited the characters and the story." - Divine Magazine

In this 1950s period drama, Junius is a New York City fertility demon with a crush. Ever since falling from heaven he's been alone. Except for the mothers and children he watches over.

James Kelly Rosenburg, a black soldier with snowflakes in his hair, walks right into his life with a big problem. James Kelly, turned vampire during the war, is new to New York and its prohibition against vampire killing in city limits.

Junius offers to teach him to overcome his bloodthirsty instincts and live a proper Manhattan life. Their growing friendship leaves them both conflicted as they explore a city both welcoming and alienated by their kind.

That Doesn't Belong Here
"I liked the ... atmosphere that he created, alongside the paranormal creatures that roam the street. I liked that he wrote characters I could emotionally care for. If Ackerman writes another LGBT fiction, I will give it a try for sure."- Ami, **The Blogger Girls**

That Doesn't Belong Here begins when Levi and his friend Emily discover an impossible creature in an abandoned pick up. The thing is wounded, frightened and the two friends cannot leave him to the mercy of rubberneckers and tourists. This novel explores what it means to be a person, as the creature, Kato, begins to display not mere intelligence or friendliness but what can only be explained as humanity. The question of who we are allowed to love arises for Levi and Kato, as they are not just crossing the boundaries of gender or sexuality, but of species.